the Lure of Old Tunes

the Lure of Old Tunes

They made music together
...but success changed the tune

Shikha Biswas Vohra

BLUEJAY

Bluejay Books Pvt. Ltd.
A-8/76, Ist Floor
Sector 16, Rohini
Delhi 110 085
info@bluejaybooksindia.com

First published in 2013 by
Bluejay Books Pvt. Ltd.

Typeset by EGP

Printed and bound in India

Dedicated to SANJEEV KUMAR
one of the finest actors cinema has produced,
my friend and guide

Acknowledgements

REENA MOHAN, Editor and Film-maker, for loaning me her precious books on the subject of cinema.

Ms MINOTI CHATTERJEE, Principal, Kamala Nehru College and Newsreader, for guidance on Bengali theatre.

Shri JAIRAJ, actor, for his delineation of silent cinema.

Ms SHOBHANA SAMARTH, actor, for her depiction of the era of the thirties.

Ms MEENA BHAGAT for interesting details of her film and theatre family, which went into the characterization of the book's personalities.

Ms PRIYA PAKANATI and SAMARJIT ACHARJEE for editing and related comments.

Ms PAROMITA VOHRA, writer and well-known film-maker, for her advice and staunch criticism which inspired many changes.

Ms TUHINA VOHRA GUPTA and SAMIR RAUT for helping with the cover design.

Mr TEJPAL SINGH CHADHA for setting up the Facebook page.

Author Mr KAMLESH TRIPATHI for printing and publishing processes.

Ms TANUJA, well-known actor, for goading me to edit, edit, edit.

HARIHAR JHARIWALA for his inspiration and guidance.

My son-in-law MILAN GUPTA for keeping me grounded.

Please note: Songs mentioned do not have a chronological reference. They have been chosen from the relative era to fit the situation.

AUTHOR'S NOTE

Doing a series on Early cinema for a magazine during my freelance journalistic career, I had the opportunity of interviewing veteran actors like Jairaj, Lalita Pawar, Shobhana Samarth, producer-director B R Chopra, and singer Talat Mahmood. In order to prepare the interview questionnaire, it was mandatory for me to do some research on their times and careers. It was during this preparation, that I became aware of this fascinating period of trial, experiment and adventure. Whatever they told me was like a gateway into another dimension, an era that completely bewitched me. I thought how little was chronicled about these times, and was inspired to write a book about this magical journey. Instead of a documentation, I preferred to embark on a fictional tale, which would present me with the opportunity for some imaginative forays. Totally passionate about the songs of that period, I thought of weaving them like paisleys into the narration. And that was the genesis of The Lure of Old Tunes.

But what of the story? Having been brought up in a film family, I realised I did not have to look far. There was a story right in my backyard. However, before it can be misconstrued as autobiographical, or even biographical, let me clarify the point that although the storyline was borrowed from life, situations and happenings are absolutely fictional. If some characters are recognisable, they may have generated from people I know or heard about, but have been highly magnified with negative or positive shades for literary purposes only, to heighten shades of drama, and not meant to be deliberately derogatory. There is no intention to hurt anyone's sentiments. A story needs heroes as well as villains, and thus have some characters emerged. Some well-known names have been mentioned for verisimilitude, or to anchor the story in a time period or setting. I have attempted to intersperse some little-known facts about early cinema, which even I, despite having lived in that environment, was not aware of. Cinematic metaphors and prototypical screen characters have been used to make it into an allegoric tale of the development of Hindi cinema, which will be more noticeable in the sequel, SOLO.

The book is nothing more or less than a tribute to my love for cinema of the golden era, and my passion for the music connected to it.

Prelude

MAGIC LANTERN

She sits every day at her usual place at the window, still as an ancient portrait, her once-magnificent eyes gazing at nothing. Quietude has spread into her life like a wave upon the shore. Dignity embellishes her fading eyes; pride distils itself along the lines of her face framed by silent silver hair.

Beyond the diamond-shaped railings of her window, is the busyness of Pali Hill, residential realm of Bombay's tinsel town. Inside the parameters of the flaky walls, however, time has been stoppered by a semi-colon. Rusty awards adorn age-old sideboards. Sepia frames of muhurats and premieres cluster the walls. A full-face close-up, the type film stars keep autographed for their fans, sits in ochre tints on her dressing table. Years of dust have settled tenaciously on her crystal powder bowl and perfume bottles, testimonials to the splendour of another time.

The rubber plant that she, Nandini, had planted fifteen years ago along the compound wall, has stretched into a tree. It yawns towards the azure sky, bottle-green leaves outlined against gouty branches. She observes suddenly that a tree of some wild heritage has sprung up beside it. After many days a thought churns her consciousness. If people could be more like trees, she ponders, one could shed one's memories in winter, and rejuvenate in spring, fresh with new leaf-thoughts. Ready to flower, distribute pleasure, and lend a magnificent shade.

The thought processes more thoughts, and memories move inside her like broken glass. She shuts her eyes against them. But her lids close upon fragrant colours, and in the dark auditorium of her mind, scenes begin to shift and glide and mingle. Like slides they move, melting in the layered colours of her mind. Phased-out scenes flash with unexpected clarity. Rising out of the deep sea of years gone by, they deposit at her feet the seashells of forgotten moments. Scenes interplay, sometimes sharp, sometimes unfocussed, like the unpreserved print of an old feature film. Things buried beneath her deep silences begin to stumble and surface.

The centripetal forces of old age turn you inwards towards the past. Through a telescopic scan you review it; with love, self-disgust, and more often than not, with regret. Often things come upon you suddenly, filling your insides with a warm and silken nostalgia.

How much are we really responsible for our deeds through the process of scheme, thought or conscience? Does history really repeat itself in a planned program? How affected are actions by heredity and environment, by the influence of planets and their positions, by the railway network of palm lines, by hormones and genes or chemical substances in the cranium? Is Destiny but a brilliant garland of cause and effect? Or an entertaining computer game being played by some Energetic Whizkid in another time zone?

Perhaps a jigger of each truth subscribes. But sometimes one contrapuntal change of tune can play an awesome part. One gentle shake of the kaleidoscope, and voila, the pattern of your life has changed.

Hey tree, why are your arms so mangled, wonders the old woman.

'Why don't you ask my goddamned roots?' it whispers.

FLASHBACK

Bengal. The very word preludes a sweetness, of tongue as well as of tooth. Yet the sweetness of its *mishti*, its syrupy chamcham and its dry, rubbery sandesh, is spiked by the sharpness of its main condiment; *mustard*, whose acrid flavour fillips his senses with its pungent tang. No Bengali can ever be accused of being phlegmatic. From fish to philosophy, he feels strongly, and speaks loudly, about his subject. In teahouses and corner-stores, and in green-shuttered government offices, in neat banana groves and by multi-purpose fishponds, the Bengali Babu debates furiously and crusades fervently.

By contrast, the women go about their household chores with daintiness and grace. Dressed in starched Tangails and Shantipuris, keys dangling from the ends of their pallus, they devote themselves to the artistry of alpona, to preparing macher-jhol and distilling sweetmeats. They fill their unostentatious abodes with their mellifluent voices. Their copious charm lies in their kohl-lined eyes and their abundant tresses, aromatic with coconut scents. Having elevated paan-chewing to an art, the Didi-moni is as fragrant and crisp as the betel she chews and strews in well-partitioned paan boxes.

Mishti and mustard. The Bengalis, indeed, are galvanised by a strong bond of culture and tradition, of which they are justifiably proud.

Such fierce passions of kinship stirred the Bengalis to protest when, aligned to the British principle of divide and rule, their state was splintered into East and West Bengal. The sight of laden steamers flowing down the Hooghly towards the sea and England, carrying huge profits for the East India Company, had long aroused an ache in the stomachs of a famine-stricken people. The inspiration of Mohandas Karamchand Gandhi now fanned the flames of patriotic revolt amongst the Bengali youth. Bands of krantikaris roamed around the countryside with blood and revenge in their eyes. Everywhere there was insurrection, non-co-operation, desperation and fear. The smell of death was in everyone's nostrils. It rose up from the blood-soaked streets, suffocating the lungs of the people.

MYTHOLOGY AND ADVENTURE

In a district grown like a wart onto the East Bengal town of Barisal, a short, dusky Brahmin lad made his way furtively towards the swamps that lay beyond the edge of the town. He walked with short, swift strides, dark eyes full of purpose. Twilight strode ahead of him, merging his shadow with the gloom. From time to time, he flicked his long, curly hair from his nape to shake off the heat. The intense humidity made trails of sweat pour down his back, taping his kurta to his skin. He hummed softly, ruffling the traces of a young moustache. For what he lacked in stature, the goddess Saraswati had amply compensated with a voice full of passion and power. And his mother had trained him and his sister, Paromita, in most forms of music, and together they enthralled the surrounding villagers with kirtans and jatras. They had been taught never, ever, to regard their music with frivolity, but to mingle it with the fragrance of humility, like an agarbatti in a temple.

But music at this moment was furthest from his mind, though subconsciously on his lips, the fragment of reflex. Patriotism droned like the sa-pa-pa-pa of a tanpura. He thought of his childhood friends Dhiren Mazumdar, Runu Bose, and Nazrul-ur-Rehman, a co-ordinated quartet famous in the township for its amity. Together they had grown, sprouted and sprung in the same field, despite differences in caste, religion and temperament. He thought right now they should be busy studying for their matriculation exams, barely three months away. Especially if they intended to execute their young dreams of sitting for law or administrative exams and fighting for self-rule within the parameters of British bureaucracy. But, as educated, sensitive beings, could they be indifferent to the Dandi March or the revolt of the indigo growers? Should they turn a deaf ear to the spirit of Mangal Pandey that called through the historical mists, or ignore the voice of their motherland beckoning for deliverance?

Aniruddh's ice-fire eyes flashed for a second.

His preoccupation and the late evening haze unfocussed his vision, as he strode through untidy fields. Only when he discerned ahead the gloaming silhouettes of the bamboo grove, the venue of their secret meeting, did a sharp clarity like newly pointed pencils, intensify his pupils. There was no sign of his friends. Good. It was prudent to be cautious. If they were caught, ah, horrific to contemplate—the British, as the literary-minded Runu said, did not regard acts of sedition with 'the quality of mercy'.

Flies scattered around him as he entered the grove. The shadowy leaves of bamboo closed around him darkly. Inside its cluster, a hand shot out in the stillness to grip his forearm.

"Ki re Ani? Whatever happened to you, hain? We were worried," said Runu's shadowy form. Four yards ahead, Dhiren and Nazrul emerged into the darkening evening with a swish of bamboo leaves.

"I had to fetch a brew for Shubir's cough from the hakim's cottage. And you all know Ma. She's not going to sing an epithalamium to all this. She's always watching me, a hundred questions in her eyes."

"Let's leave these family matters." said a restless Dhiren. "Have you heard the latest? Last week the daughter of a Baul singer in the neighboring village was raped by an English sergeant and left naked on the riverbanks. How long are we going to permit such indecencies?" A fire blazed in his combustible eyes.

Nazrul, older by a year and many degrees calmer, made a clucking noise. "Relax, Dhiren," he said. "I understand these Englishmen walk with their British boots all over our country. Like you, my blood boils, too. But as you know, our exams are not far away, and our participation in the struggle must be more passive until we are free of scholastic pressures."

"But Nazrul-Da, We have to stoke our fires, or they will die."

In the ensuing silence of their thoughts, the discordant croaking of the frogs from the swamps beyond sounded like radio static. Suddenly, the dispersed lines of Aniruddh's face sharpened.

"Dhiren, what did you say about the neighbouring village?"

"A girl was raped…'

"No, no, whose daughter?"

"Ani, you are hopeless. Grave matters are at hand and all you're concerned about is bloody ancestry! The Baul.."

"The Baul singer! Yes! Suppose we form a troupe of wandering minstrels, carrying messages and recruiting people, and stirring everyone's patriotic sentiments through national songs?"

Runu, who considered his best friend to be the most talented and intelligent person he had ever known, looked at him with awe. "What an excellent idea! Now why in the world do these things not occur to me, re?"

"That is because your head is always jammed in a book," retorted Dhiren. "Where is the time for you to *think,* hain?"

"At least I will learn something, unlike you. You will always remain a Bhondunath."

Dhiren chuckled, and slapped him affectionately on the forearm. Nazrul's grave voice summoned their attention.

"Let us be serious, comrades. Indeed, that is a good idea, Ani. You can write and compose your own songs. And we can borrow from Rabindra Sangeet to suit our purpose. Maybe Kazi Nazrul Islam, too."

For some years, the songs and poems of a bearded bard named Rabindranath Tagore had fired the imagination of the nation. Pride in Tagore, son of their particular patch of soil, now clustered them more closely under their cultural umbrella.

"And Masterda Shurjo Sen, and Mukundo Das. 'Chilo dhaan, gola bhora, shet indure korlo shaara,'" quoted Ani.

'"We could really make this work, you know." Face brightening with restless energy, Dhiren began to roll up his sleeves, as if he were imminently about to bash up an Englishman.

"So, it's agreed then," corroborated Nazrul. "We'll meet here again after four days on the pretext of studying together, same time."

It was a convenient meeting-place, unfrequented because of snakes and rumours of crocodiles in the swamps near the main waterways from where the steamers plied. The four placed their hands together, palm over palm, in joint resolution. The tops of the bamboo trees looked down, silent witnesses.

"Jai Hind!" they recited in chorus. Then, one after another, strengthened with resolve, they stepped out of their miniature world of adventure. Faces grim, the simple-minded but earnest quartet made its way back to the mundane world, to the business of books and families.

Close by, the ruined contours of an old temple sighed in the silence of its age-old neglect.

From that day onwards, they were even more closely bound by their common purpose. Besides traversing the countryside with their ektaras, they forayed into the army bivouacs to harass the white soldiers. Encouraged by their success, they ventured a daring raid on the small armoury, on the lines of Surya Sen's activities in Chittagong, managing to steal three revolvers and some shot before the alarm was raised.

"At least we're 'half-a-league onwards' quoted Runu. "Now there's not to reason why, there's but to do and die."

'Bidhir bidhan katbe tumhi, aimon shaktimaan.'

'Banglaar maati, banglaar jol,
banglaar bayu, banglaar phol,
Punno ho, punno ho, hey bhagowan.'

The widow Konkona was suspicious about her son Aniruddh's activities. She had observed the cloud of restiveness that hovered on his horizon. She was mortified to consider that her son might be involved in the freedom struggle. The corpses dangling from the trees sent a frisson of terror down her spine whenever she paused to contemplate their putrefying images. But Ani's assurance that he was only spreading the good word of the Vedas tranquilized her slightly. In any case, another recent development pre-occupied her these days. She had noticed that her daughter Paro had taken to sitting most of her spare time in the company of Pranoy Biswas, a young musician. She would spend hours listening to his haunting flute, singing along with him in her rich soprano, songs of wild splendour in the woods, of daisies blooming in crevices. Pranoy's remarkable flute, an unusually long and thick bamboo reed, was heard in the quiet dawn, mellifluous and magnificent. At night, people trudging home would stop and listen, touched by the magic of his notes. Below his broad forehead, his dark eyes, full of wizard's spells, were brooding in their concentration. But this soft-spoken, introverted boy was also a very *married* boy, with a very *pregnant* wife. Konkona wondered if Debashree was aware of the musical bonding between her husband and Paro. Konkona, with her reputation for piety, wondered how to deal with this Meera-Krishna drama tactfully without damaging the sensibilities of the shy and sensitive Paro.

Radha rani de daro na bansuri mori

A small contingent of white military men came riding out of the sunrise, their horses snorting and shoveling dust. They shattered the morning tranquility by rudely invading homes, marshalling young men out and shoving them indignantly into carts. There, under vague suspicions of treason, they were dumped into barrack cellars. The four friends were among the suspected miscreants. The matriculation exams being a few days away, there was a tumult of protest by people who had gone to great lengths, borrowed and mortgaged heavily to educate their sons. The onus to interpolate finally fell on the Zamindar of the district, a seasoned British ass-kisser. Normally, this feudal lord would not have condescended to divert precious time from pigeon rearing and cock fighting to appeal on behalf of a bratpack of self-styled freedom fighters. But those incarcerated were able-bodied men, and the rice-fields required transplanting.

The British Resident was appeased only to the extent of permitting a single condition. Let the boys write their papers in jail. As the zamindar pronounced with literal severity from his imposing balcony, Beggars can't be choosers.

Thus between thrashes and lashes, Aniruddh and his friends appeared for their matriculation exams. Circumstances, however, did not allow Aniruddh to learn of his results till almost three years later.

Many days later, the Resident decided to release the prisoners on insufficient evidence, proclaiming it an act of true British kindness. Actually, it was logistically expensive to feed them. Besides, they made an infernal din singing fiery songs of patriotism and shouting slogans of 'door hato.' Loosely translated as Get Lost, Go fly a kite. It was not only a strain on their vocal chords, but also uncommonly rude!

Konkona was relieved to see her son returned to her without much damage. Contrarily however, the boys wrapped the blanket of patriotism more tightly around the raw wounds of their lashes, and became all the more determined to fight for liberation. But the atmosphere around the four was electric with danger, and they knew that every step they took had to be trod with utmost care.

The theft in the armoury had confirmed the presence of local insurrectionists, and the British were now vigilant for any natives in the possession of firearms. Anyone caught with a weapon was hung like a puppet from the nearest tree without benefit of trial. The friends thought it wise, therefore, to hide the stolen pistols away in some place where they would not be linked with the foursome. On Aniruddh fell the onus of formulating a plan to dispense with the fire-arms. He checked the weapons inside the musical instruments where they had been concealed earlier. Thankfully Ma had not found them, for even had she searched, she would never have thought of looking inside the harmonium. All four were in agreement that the firearms would be safer stashed away in the ruined temple near the swamp, where, if discovered, they could be connected to anyone at all.

So one night, a week later, wrapping the pistols in a thick red cloth, he stole out of the house as his family slept, and proceeded cautiously towards the mire.

The moon had deserted him. Only the starlight cast a subtle glow, by which Aniruddh navigated his way. It was still and oppressive, the pre-monsoon humidity strangulating. Mosquitoes hummed in weird strains. The dark veil of night was sequined with fireflies. Eerie nocturnal sounds invaded his senses...the moo of a yet-awake cow, the flapping wings of a bat, the cacophonic conversation of crickets. The staccato croaking of the frogs made him realise the marsh was near.

As he approached the ruin, his musical disposition made him conscious of a sound that was somewhat disharmonious with the surroundings. He stopped and listened. It sounded like the snort of a horse. What would someone be doing so dangerously close to the swamps this time of night *on a horse*? Not many people came this way, unless, like him, they were familiar with these parts. There it was again, quite unmistakable. The unhurried clip-clop of a horse, approaching along the rough and stony path.

Aniruddh's pause had delayed him, and he had no time to dive into the tall bulrushes lining the road when the horseman turned the path and was upon him. He was suddenly arrested in the circular halo of a small lantern.

"Is that you, Bulbuli?" said a distinctly British voice in Hindi. The man, in the uniform of an English captain, spotted the dark figure with the long curly hair that he had mistaken for a woman, and his jaw unhinged in surprise.

Aniruddh was trapped, caught firmly in the spotlight. His nostrils dilated in fear. Even if he tried to make a run for it, the Englishman was taller and stronger, and would most definitely be swifter of foot. The parcel in his hands trembled, and the light from the lantern reflected incriminatingly on the pistols coming loose from their cover. The Britisher was momentarily distracted. Aniruddh pounced upon that second of surprise, granted to him like Durgama's blessing, to pick upon the only option that occurred to his panic-stricken mind. He fumbled for a revolver before the soldier had a chance to reach for his holster, cocked it, and pulled the trigger of the .38 straight in the direction of the officer's chest.

One shot, then another, and another.

The sound of the bullets pierced the heart of the night, then blunted into the thick undergrowth with an eerie, whistling echo. The Englishman slumped, slithering off his steed in slow motion. With one foot still dangling from a stirrup, he hit the ground with an enormous thud.

Aniruddh stared in frigid shock at the figure of the fallen horseman, at the arms askew, at the open, inverted eyes. There he was, dangling upside down, and he was dead by Aniruddh's hand. His shocked senses couldn't adjust to what he had done, an act contrary to all the refined clauses of his upbringing.

His body began quivering like a beggar in winter, his teeth throbbed like an engine just cranked. He crossed his arms on his chest, gripping each shoulder with his hands. Gradually, with a controlled deceleration, the shock started to evaporate. His body steadied, and the realisation that he had struck not just a Dhiren-jab in the air, but a solid blow in the face of his enemy, made the scent of bloody triumph head up his nose with its mustard-y tang. He felt, for a fraction of a second, slightly euphoric.

But a minute later, the terrifying import of his action struck him like a fist. Fear of the consequences, the moral and legal repercussions, attacked his mind like a swarm of locusts. The buzzing in his brain attained a crescendo. Then, as if propelled by some poltergeist's force, he began to run.

Without direction, he ran, and ran, and ran.

"Karim!" yelled Lt. McArthur to his orderly. "Go make my bed and remove that blessed mosquito netting. And see that my shoes are polished till you can see your bloody black face in them. Understand?"

"Ji, Sahib," replied the darker man, looking with abject humility at a dry speck of grass on the verandah. "And have you seen Captain Andrews Sahib anywhere?"

"No, Sahib."

Damn. An AO announcing a surprise inspection had been put up on the board at the barracks of the small army contingent at Barisal. Going into Kevin's room to apprise him of it, he had been puzzled to find the bed not slept in. The mosquito net remained draped as still as a shroud over the bed. That was unusual. The raunchy devil occasionally spent half the night with his dusky, doe-eyed Bengali girl in the old temple ruins near the swamps bordering the other side of town. But he was always back in the early hours of the morning, looking smug and satiated. This unknown woman, probably full of hot-blooded Bengali mystique, seemed to lure him each night with the songs of her native body. As for himself, he preferred his fragrant English roses, daughters and nieces of other military personnel or wives of the railway officials at Dacca.

He returned his attention to Capt. Kevin Andrews. No amount of hot, native cunts however, would result in his being AWOL. So where on earth was the bugger?

When Capt. Andrews' absence was conspicuous at the inspection parade later, a frown of apprehension darkened his handsome Highland features. God, he hoped like hell the blasted fellow hadn't been sucked into the quagmire. There was nothing to do now but go out for him. He began to organise a search party.

They came upon the horse, grazing comfortably on some dry grass near the ruins. Dangling from the stirrup, like an upside-down trapeze artist, was a very dead Kevin Andrews, shot, at close range, in three different places.

By early evening, as fast as a cholera epidemic, the news was all over town.

It palpitated through the streets, shivered inside mud-baked walls, sent people scurrying and whispering and trembling with concepts of the grotesque forms British vindication would surely take.

In the military camp, outrage swept over the barracks like a mistral. The senior officers did, of course, consider the possibility of his having been killed by a fellow Englishman, especially when the post-mortem stated that a bullet from a .38 Webley and Scott had killed him. It could have been some gruesome crime of passion, luring Andrews out to the swamps and pumping all those bullets into him. But there had been no signs of another horse, nothing to indicate that he had had company. With Angus clamping his mouth upon Kevin's not so palatable secret, it became extremely convenient to blame the killing on a fighting-for-liberty native. Liberty? Give it to them, and they would roll it up in a paan and chew it, the bloody black bastards!

They publicised their rage by riding a storm all over town, their horses harrumphing down the narrow lanes, scuttling playing children and scattering the few roadside hawkers out in search of a desperate sale. They pulled people from homes, slamming them into the barracks for questioning. But most people showed them empty faces, expressionless with ignorance or determination.

So the next day, they changed tactics by announcing a reward for any kind of information, bait for the poor and the avaricious.

Fear sat heavily on the chest of the people. Aniruddh and his friends stayed within their respective houses, hiding deep inside darkened rooms. Ani's stricken eyes were unusually restless and he refused to sing in the temple, blaming his mood on his recent imprisonment. He stared sightlessly at empty spaces, unable to take in the incredible reality of his actions and its colossal, public aftermath.

He sat silently, and waited.

Fazlu Rehman, the local water-carrier, who moonlighted as gravedigger, sat on the front porch of his shack. The strong antiseptic smell of recently layered cow-dung had still not left the floor and walls. Such rural customs, like drawing water from wells, were still prevalent in this rustic, outlying part of Barisal town. He pulled raspishly at his hookah, the smoke making his eyes rheumy. His mind was sorting out his observations of the past week. From the room within, the sounds of pots and pans were signs of the preparation of the evening meal. His daughter, Bulbuli, the subject of his ruminations, was making her presence felt. But it was her absences that were causing him concern. Once or twice he had noticed her entering the house at a time just before dawn. When questioned, she claimed to have gone to the common well before the regular daybreak rush of women. Her sari tucked around her waist, bare shoulder jutting like an outcrop of rock, she had seemed in an indescribable mood, nervous yet defiant. To continue the metaphor, however, her explanation didn't hold much water. Three nights ago, he had peeped into her room from the window, and found her missing from her charpoy at a time when no woman would venture alone near the well. Alarmed, he had gone out in search of her. Bulbuli he had not found. But dashing into him from the direction of the swamps had rushed a shadowy form. He couldn't be too sure, as his cataract fogged his vision, but the figure panting like a mast elephant had seemed very like Aniruddh, the widow Konkona's son.

He coughed and spluttered, then yelled for his son to come from the inner room and sit beside him.

"Listen son, I must tell you something," he whispered, voice lowered in conspiracy. "But you must keep it very quiet, for it is a matter of family honour."

His son nodded.

"You know that our Taslima, our Bulbuli, is betrothed to Anwar Hussein, the mosque keeper's son. But of late I have noticed things about her. She is like a woman unfolding, a flower in bloom."

"But that is quite natural, Abu-baba; she is shortly to be married."

"Oh, but then she hardly meets Anwar often enough, and that too with her purdah, for him to put a song on her lips. Do you know that often she is missing from her room in the early hours? Says she goes to the well to avoid the morning rush. But once, at dawn, I saw her coming out of the clump of bamboo trees near the old temple ruins. Tauba tauba, now what would a good Muslim girl be doing near a kaafir's place of prayer?" He pulled deeply at the hookah. "The night the angrez was killed, she was missing again. I went in search of her, but someone came dashing out of the bamboo grove at a furious speed and knocked me down. To me it looked like that-boy-who-sings, Aniruddh Ganguly. Now it is not dignified for me to question Bulbuli, this motherless child, about such delicate matters. Perhaps I am afraid of what secrets may lie in her answers. Khuda khair kare, so many mouths, so many tales."

He moved his head from side to side. "If there is some scandal, then who will marry her? She will sit on my chest for the rest of her life. Do you think it is possible this Aniruddh is… ?"

"Bulbuli and Aniruddh? Aashchoryo! It cannot be. Surely there must be some other explanation."

"Who can tell with these idol-worshipping boys? His mother so pious but Aniruddh, just out of school, scarcely begun to shave."

"I can tell you Abu-baba, this is a highly unlikely story, there is no truth in this."

"How do you know? You were in jail last month."

"Agreed. But so was Aniruddh."

"Then there is another explanation. It is possible that he may be linked to the murder of the Angrez that night. I must report it to the British authorities immediately. They are offering good money for this information. It will come in useful for Taslima's nikaah."

"Abu-baba, I don't think…"

"Your job is not to *think*, it is to *find out*. And do it tactfully, understand? We can't afford to risk Bulbuli"s reputation. A woman's reputation is like a glass bangle. And think of the reward." His eyes glazed with rapacity, a covetousness even his cataract could not cloud.

Nazrul's breath resonated with anxiety. He knew why Ani had gone towards the swamps that night. But none of them had been in communication with each other or with the underground because of the following upheaval. However, if there were a vestige of truth in what his father suspected, it would mean a total collapse of their carefully structured operation, their hopes and dreams, and most definitely the end of Aniruddh. Aniruddh, who would surely swing on some bare branch and become fodder for the vultures. Nazrul knew his father would never be persuaded to refrain from going to the authorities. To him, the identity of his rulers made not the slightest difference. Let it be the Indian National Congress, or the Muslim League, or some king sitting on a distant island thousands of miles away, what did it matter?

"Er..I'll see what I can do, Abu-baba."

"You had better. He's *your* close friend. And, if you find him guilty, then do what you have to, to avenge the dishonour to your house."

He said, "I'll do the needful", in a tone as earnest as if he would throw the body of the culprit to the alligators in the swamps at once, and left straightaway for Ani's house. Old Fazlu nodded approvingly, and pulled at his hookah with a satisfied sigh.

Fortunately Ani's mother was at her evening puja, counting beads with a concentrated frown, when he stepped into Aniruddh's modest cottage. He was shocked to see Ani, his face the colour of ashes. It confirmed Nazrul's worst fears.

The straw-roofed patio was empty. There the two friends huddled in conference, so that the sound of their words floated outwards into the air. Ani sat tensely, legs curled up like a foetus. Aghast, Nazrul exclaimed "Ya Allah, Ani, you didn't……"

Ani shushed any further talk by clutching tightly at Nazrul's arm.

"I had no choice. What in heaven's name could I do, Nazrul? He would have shot me for a rebel. A split second's difference, my friend, and you would have been chanting prayers at my pyre."

Wisely, he refrained from disclosing anything about Bulbuli's association with the Englishman.

"That's all very well, Ani, and I for one am not grieving about the Englishman's death. But we have another problem."

Nazrul related to him the discussion that had transpired between him and his father. "If they catch you, they will torture you, then either hang you publicly or put you in front of a firing squad. There's only one thing to do, Ani. You must make a run for it. I'll tell the old man it was true about you and Taslima, and that you ran away because I threatened to kill you. It will at least disconnect you from the murder."

"But I can't do this to an innocent girl for my own safety, nor should you even think of maligning your sister this way."

"But she will deny everything anyway. Besides, Taslima's ignominy is a small price to pay for your life. We still have to find out the reason for *her* nocturnal outings. Who knows? Who knows what's really happening? "

Aniruddh shifted uncomfortably from one leg to the other.

"But where will I go? What about Ma and Paro, and Subir? I can't just leave them like that. And the very idea of Bulbuli and me might *kill* my mother".

Nazrul collected himself, thinking more clearly as the initial shock began to dissipate.

"You *have* to. I'm being practical." Aniruddh accepted Nazrul's level-headedness; he was always able to think more rationally than the other more emotional three. "Don't worry, we are like your brothers. We'll take care of them. Perhaps once everything has blown over, we can explain to Ma. She's made of strong stuff. But, right now, it's just safer for her not to know anything. Better a disreputable son than a dead one. You must disappear, preferably in the melee of a large city like Calcutta."

"Calcutta? Oh no, I couldn't possibly, Nazrul. I know nobody there. How will I manage alone, without money, without…no, I'm scared. Oh Maa, ki haube?"

"I can understand how fear must block your mind. So let me think for you. Imagine the consequences if you stay here. My father will swear on the Holy Quran it was you he saw, just to gain the reward. All the British need is a scapegoat. They'll make a public example of you. It's best this way. Just gather a few clothes. As for money, the three of us will give you what we can. I know your mother keeps some coins in the grain bin. Once you get into the city, contact my maternal uncle. He's also part of the movement. He'll hide you somewhere safe, arrange a job for you. As you're educated, that shouldn't be a problem. Once things have cooled down, we'll send your family on to you. So you must leave immediately to gain a head start. Keep off the main roads, hitch rides on bullock-carts, cross rivers in a crowd. But don't take the bus, or the steamers. They're sure to check the public transports. You do understand, Ani, that you can't come back here. Because of Taslima my kinsmen won't spare you."

Ani nodded silently, thinking of Nazrul's well-built relatives, Rehman Ali the butcher and Mohsin Khan who worked in the jute-field, men who possessed evil-looking hatchets. Words flew from him, scattered by the winds of fear and anxiety. He would have to leave the security of his family and hide in corners like a fugitive.

Yet, he knew with a certainty begotten by common sense, that there was no alternative. Destiny had scratched its pencil on the scroll of his life. As Runu would have quoted, the moving finger had written.

"Yes, perhaps, this is the best way. There is no time to consult our underground for any alternate action. Perhaps soon we will gain independence, the British will leave, perhaps…But I will remember you always, my friend, and the things we have shared. I will pray that sometime, somewhere, our paths will cross again. The world is a small place."

In a bizarre repetition, someone would speak these very words to his daughter one day. But not for him now to contemplate the perplexities of Fate, as he let go of Nazrul's arm to search for a pen and paper so Nazrul could write out the letter of introduction to his uncle. Nazrul rubbed his arm where Aniruddh had gripped it, where the redness was spreading as if someone had inserted a dye into his skin.

He began to write.

From her religious corner, Konkona glanced at them with approval, watching them engrossed as if in some academic matter, maybe filling out applications for an institute in Dacca.

Late at night, his friends came stealthily to the back of Ani's house to say good-bye. All of them, though confounded with shock, were proud of their comrade and his astounding achievement. They embraced him with a feeling of glory, and without fuss, let him go.

"We won't tell Ma," said Runu, 'after all, ignorance is bliss. May Durgama grant you shakti."

With the coins he salvaged from the grain tin, that convenient safe deposit of the times, and the money his friends managed to pool together, Aniruddh had a sum of seventeen rupees, ten annas and two pice. If he was not wasteful, he could manage to survive on this amount comfortably for two to three months. He collected his meagre belongings and left stealthily at dead of night. There was no time for good-byes with his family. In a few days, he would celebrate his seventeenth birthday in a place full of strangers.

Ye raatein, ye mausam, ye hansna hansana,
mujhe bhool jaana, inhe na bhoolana.

NEW SCREENPLAY

After two days of walking, a tired Aniruddh decided it was safe to board a bus. But halfway the bus had been stopped, and he cursed himself for ignoring Nazrul's warning, as three constables came aboard, the late afternoon sun glinting off their dangerous-looking rifles. He had felt a fearful vibration in his jaw, as if his heart had jumped out of his ribcage and was beating in his teeth. The jaggery-maker in the neighbouring seat, who had been travelling all the way from Backerganj, clutched his henna-stained beard for support, whilst Aniruddh looked outwards at his lost freedom. But they had only dragged aboard a wounded revolutionary shot in the shoulder. Then the bus had taken off for Cholna.

It was only later, when he was crossing the river Padma in a boat filled with several people that he had relaxed, becalmed by the tuneful sweetness of the boatman's *bhaatiyali*. Music was indeed, the panacea for the body and the soul.

He now considered it safe to continue the rest of his journey from Khulna by train.

Alighting at Howrah Station, he traversed the magnificent cantilevered Howrah Bridge back to the city side. Below him, the barges on the wide Hooghly looked like dark paper boats bobbing on the water. On the other side, he was met by the clamour of the warehouses at Fairlie Place, pink buildings dusted black by the soot of the steamers, and a bewildering crowd of men that was constantly rushing. Everything looked alien, as if he had climbed out of his life and entered an entirely new dimension.

The first thing that struck Aniruddh on entering the city of Calcutta was the volume and variety of noise. Contrary to the rural sounds of the grunting of buffaloes, the metallic rhythm of the blacksmith's bellow, the tubercular coughing of Pujari Moshai, cowbells at dawn, Pranoy's flute at dusk, and the chatter of women at the well, here there was a cacaphonious medley. Making an almighty din in the centre of the road was a long red tapeworm clanging on rails. On enquiry, he was informed it was a tram. The obstreperous cries of the street hawkers overlapped the shouts of rickshaw pullers. These, in turn, telescoped into the spaced chant of the palki bearers carrying ladies of decadent noble families to the bazaar. Klaxon horns of motorcars sounded alongside the clip-clop of the tongas, a 'teen taal' on macadam.

He gazed in awe at the looming structures; tall, imposing buildings crossed by an overbearingly British signature. The domed features of a sprawling, white building in the middle of a huge maidan suggested it might be the residence of a king. Red buildings like new wounds rose upward amidst white ones with green shutters.

He strolled towards the interior of the city along a wide, open road. The afternoon was hot and humid, and he rested in the dusty doorway of a building, nibbling from a paper cone of peanuts and Bengal gram that he had bought for half a pice. After a while he walked on, asking passersby for directions. Some looked at him dubiously as he asked, some laughed. Ani wondered whether their laughter meant they recognised him for the country bumpkin that he was.

By early evening he arrived at his destination. He peered down the narrow street that angled off the main road. Narrow buildings nudged each other, hemmed by decorative grills. Except for a man selling gajras of scented jasmine and a paan wallah preparing paans at a stall, it was curiously deserted. No neighbours chatting, or vendors calling or street hawkers with bamboo baskets and sweetmeat sellers with cloth-wrapped trays. He could hear the faint tinkling of anklets.

Somewhere down the road, the doleful notes of a *sarangi* cried, and, as he strolled along, a stray voice sang in a nasal timbre to a tabla beat soft as the fluttering of pigeon wings. Ah! It was a musical-minded locality, where he could adapt just fine. Perhaps there might be a music school here, where he could find employment, for he was a master of the *raags* and *raaginis.* After many days, optimism elevated his spirits.

A beaded curtain veiled the entrance to No. 26. He was just figuring out how to draw the inmates' attention, when a tough-looking man materialised from nowhere. The 'pehalwan' stared at the scrawny lad with undisguised curiosity. It was too early for customers, even the enthusiastic or the uninitiated, and this one was no idle son of the rich, either. He looked as if he couldn't pay for a paan, leave alone an evening of pleasure.

"What do you want, boy?" he asked in a gruff voice.

"Bhai," said Aniruddh, with his customary small-town politeness, "can you tell me if one Rehman Miya lives here? I come from his hometown, and have news for him."

"Who is it, Hiralal?" asked a sharp, matriarchal voice spiralling down the stairway.

"Nobody of consequence, Badibi," Hiralal answered up the stairwell. "Just a waif inquiring about Rehmanbhai. Says he's from his village."

"Well, don't let him in till I say so, village-shillage notwithstanding. One can't be too careful in these times."

A minute later, the same voice called "Hey you, you there!"

Aniruddh looked upwards and saw an elderly face appear in a jharoka, like a painting in an antique frame. It was heavily coloured, the rouged cheeks in stark contrast with the dark, beady eyes lined with thick kohl. She rested her chin on her hand, and gold lights flashed off the bangles at her wrist. In the twilight, the diamond stud at her nostril winked like a flirt.

"Who are you, lad, and what is your work with Rehman Miya?"

Obviously a lady from a big house, thought Aniruddh. Respects were due, at least for her age. With hands folded, he bowed politely.

"Pranaam, Badi-Ma. I bear tidings from his sister's house in Barisal. Please, Maa-go, I have walked a great distance. Do not turn me away."

Attaribai regarded him with a strange, almost amused, expression. She stopped abruptly the spasmodic mastication of her betel leaf, pursed her lips and spat a little orange pellet squarely in his direction. Why, he was just a harmless little country boy, she mused. She leaned further out of the jharoka and instructed Hiralal to let the boy enter. Aniruddh followed him up a flight of narrow stairs to the first floor and into a large room, where a man in his late forties, with the build of a boxer, glared at him in suspicion. Attaribai's chief bouncer towered before Ani's frightened face. The weary runaway, though intimidated by his pirate looks, thought his piercing scrutiny was not so unkindly.

In a voice strong and resonant, he said, "I am Rehman. So, you bear messages from my hometown. What news do you bring?"

Aniruddh's fears seemed to alleviate slightly at the thought that this ferocious man was from his native place, and that was a bond stronger than a blood tie.

"They wish to know if you are coming for Taslima's marriage," said Aniruddh timorously for the benefit of Hiralal, who was staring at him with blatant curiosity. "This letter will explain all, Mamujaan," he continued, handing over Nazrul's all-important epistle.

Rehman scanned the note, whilst Ani inspected the ornate mirrors lining the wall. His gaze fell lovingly on a pair of tablas reposing in a corner. Spotless white sheets covered thick mattresses. From the carved ceiling dangled a spectacular chandelier. Like a musical interlude, the sound of peppered laughter drifted in from another room, followed by a sharp retort like a 'sam.'

Rehman's head jerked up, bird-like. The letter explained everything, including the English officer's killing. So, the boy was a part of the movement. So much experience at such a tender age!

Rehman Miya's steely exterior hid a palpably tender heart. His own contribution to the freedom struggle was to lure local British administrators and officers from Fort William to Attaribai's kotha with the prospect of a titillating Oriental experience and plop their diplomacy into a glass of whisky like an ice-cube, where it melted and moistened their tongues. Their lust, complacence and arrogance often unloaded confidential details to the nautch girls. It was the oldest ploy in the espionage business, and one that surprisingly, always worked.

What remained to be seen was how this boy could help them. Anyway, the primary thing was to shelter him, and what better place than a 'kotha' for concealment, where one's antecedents were not so carefully looked into, where being anonymous was a way of life, and where an ambrosiac forgetfulness was what most people came for. Failed businessmen, harrassed husbands, noble nawabs, decadent zamindars; so many sought temporary amnesia here from the arsenic of the world; here, where senses could be wrapped in a woman's dupatta. But convincing Attaribai was not going to be the proverbial piece of sandesh. She had an eye as sharp and focussed as that of the legendary Arjun, and the butter of her heart would have to be melted before it could be spread on the toast of her attitude.

He was just contemplating how to appeal to that particular part of his employer's anatomy, when the situation resolved itself quite dramatically. Before his perplexed eyes, Aniruddh suddenly shrank in a faint, slumping to the floor like a collapsed spring. The commotion following his graceful thud as he fell to the ground brought the lady striding out of her quarters in agitation.

"What exactly is happening here, Rehman?" she demanded, her eyebrows executing a Kathak toda.

"The poor boy's collapsed," explained Rehman, seizing the chance with the alacrity of an opportunist. "Perhaps he had better stay the night. He looks hungry and exhausted. He told me he's walked all the way from Barisal. He's only a poor, lonely boy who's come to the city in search of work, Badibi."

"So? Am I supposed to harbour all the hungry strugglers who come to the city looking for employment? This is a place of business, Miya, not a charitable institution. Send him to some remand home or yatimkhana, whatever. But get rid of him."

She turned to go, then halted abruptly, "Well, perhaps he may stay, on one condition" After all, the boy had called her Maa. "Ustaadji is a little indisposed, so if he can play the tabla, he may take his place tonight. Otherwise let him sleep on the terrace and dispose of him in the morning." And, with a regal flash of her sequinned dupatta, she sashayed out of the room, the edges of her gharara gliding over the parquet floor.

Rehman thumped his forehead loudly. How could Attaribai expect any person who came in from the street to be a tabla exponent or a sarangi maestro? He prayed like hell that this boy could at least drum some kind of a rough beat on the instrument. After all, Nazrul had made mention of a troupe of singing minstrels in his letter.

Rehman picked up the rose water dispenser near the entrance, and sprinkled it generously on Aniruddh's face. The cold, sweet liquid hit Ani's eyelids. The two men propped him against a wall.

"Can you play the tabla?" questioned Rehman anxiously as Aniruddh came to. Aniruddh smiled a weak and exhausted smile.

To Rehman's incredible relief, he confessed that beating a mean 'kaherwah' was for him the 'play of his left hand'.

Tomorrow,they would think. Right now, it was time for the 'mujra' to begin.

The English doctor in the nearby missionary hospital diaganosed Ustaadji with pneumonia. Which meant Aniruddh had a job for a month at least.

Aniruddh soon settled down in the place, blending into the routine with the considerable ease of youth. In the afternoons he practised with the dancing girls, and at nights accompanied them during the mujra. The girls pampered the young boy and Attaribai, gradually emolliated, began to regard him with a certain modicum of tolerance. Mala, the frisky Nepalese damsel with the slanting eyes and the full lips, flirted with him outrageously. Ani was not yet familiar with the artifice of cosmetics or the practised coquetry of the female language. Having been brought up with an antipodal attitude towards women, he found completely distasteful the familiarity with which the men visiting the kotha treated the girls. He realised that something about this establishment was not what his mother would have approved of, but as Rehman Miya explained in his practical and prudent way, where else could he go? So he acquired expeditiously the first norm of city life; to live-and-let-live. In this new environment, unlike back home, your business was not everyone else's. Moreover, nobody had the time to be judgemental.

He soon learnt to recognise whores, pickpockets, and pimps, and to subtract from them their seediness. For they were all in the common endeavour to eke out an existence, to keep heads covered and stomachs full.

Once Aniruddh had accepted the nature of the place, he also realised the underlying human values of its inmates. They were as tough as English tweed, but as soft as Dhaka mulmul.

Saara aalam dhoka hai, ye jaana hai

Aniruddh attributed Rehman Miya's unapproachability to a lack of musicality, which was surprising when he was surrounded by so much music. Ani remembered Runu, who most certainly would have piped up with the quotation of 'Water, water everywhere, but not a drop to drink.' So Ani's responses automatically flowed towards Shabbirbhai, the sarangi player. Shabbir, a lanky widower in his fifties, had thin strands of hair straddling his balding pate, and a pockmarked face eloquent with experience. The connection they began to share in just a few days vibrated in their music. It was an understanding that can only exist in the harmony of two musicians who have learnt to play in a mutually enhancing partnership, where one's experienced art complements the other's natural talent. In the spare hours of the morning, when most of the inmates were still in the process of rousing, they would stroll down to the café in the corner standing at the junction of the street and the main road, and share tea and thoughts.

These mornings were an education for Ani, who was hungry for more than the buttered slices. Shabbir had so much musical knowledge to impart, salve to Ani's bruised mind and loneliness. It was Shabbir who introduced him to the ghazal, a form of poetry with which Ani was instantaneously enamoured. He made Shabbir interpret the Urdu words, explain their nuances. The balance in the lines, the poetry in its nature, the cadences in its metre, all appealed to his sense of rhythm. It was Shabbir who corrected his pronunciation, for he had the Bengali habit of pronouncing a "V" or a "W" as "B". So his Wah! Wah! ended up like "Bah! Bah!' a contradiction of expression. It was Shabbir who taught him fascinating words, honeyed, soft and sweet as his own mother tongue. It was old and modest Shabbir, who, lifting him by the hand, opened a parachute and made him fly over the spaces of an entirely unexplored world of language and romance.

Three weeks later, Aniruddh was apprehensive about his future, and expressed his fears to his friend.

"What will I do, Shabbirbhai, once Ustadji is recovered, and I am not needed here anymore? I have to find a place to stay, as well as a job."

"Who wants a job, Babu?" interrupted the tea boy who was serving them. He had got quite accustomed these past weeks to this strange combination of old artist and raw protégé. "There's a job here for a dish-washer, if someone's interested."

"Dish-washing? Me, a Brahmin, wash someone else's *jhoota*? Nahin bhai, not for me. Besides, washing dishes is women's work."

The waiter laughed, an erratic, broken laugh. "Arre, Khokhababu, you must be new in the city. Otherwise you would know that no such division exists. The food you eat here is cooked by a man. And you know why the washer boy left? He got a chance to work in the theatre, in a woman's role, playing a character in the Mahabharat. It even pays not to have a moustache and a voice that sounds as if your balls were cut off."

"But why can't a woman play the role? And what kind of theatre do you have here? Is it like a jatra, or nautanki or what?"

"Arre, acting is not considered very respectable for women of your high caste. Although some from the lower classes, a few Muslims, and some Christians, do act. So, men dress up like women and perform on the stage or even in a 'phillum'."

"Phillum? What are these strange names you take,bhai?" queried Ani, relieved that he had a moustache of sorts, and stroking it with some re-assurance.

"Have you not seen those big buildings with colourful posters and life-like hoardings of people in costume? These are theatres showing phillums. Phillums are stories told with running pictures on a screen. Very good entertainment for people like us, who cannot read and write. One ticket costs four annas. And if you are prepared to spend eight, you can have seats reserved. In these stories, there are some women who act, but many characters are played by men dressed in women's clothes."

"Men dressed like women? You mean, like those.."

"It reminds me of my hometown in Samastipur," interrupted the boy, not registering Ani's insinuation. "My little brother played Seeta in the Ramleela when he was twelve. All gora-chitta and sweet he looked, even though he was squint-eyed. Then a few years later, they asked him to play Draupadi in the Krishnaleela. During the Vastraharan, a gust of wind blew his sari up. Nice hairy, hairy legs he showed. If the Kauravs had had a glimpse under his petticoat, there would have been no Mahabharat, what!" And he broke into his fractured laugh.

Aniruddh stared at him, fascinated by the entire exposition. He was suddenly recalling a travelling tent back in Barisal, where he had been told they were showing some moving pictures. Curious, they had wanted to go too, and Runu had found out that if one was willing to sit behind the screen and watch the pictures in reverse, one could do so at half the price of the ticket. But many people had eschewed it as some kind of evil, a form of black magic, and his mother had forbidden him to go.

"Shabbirbhai, next timc Badibi pays us, we shall go and see this phillum that is being talked about."

"Yes, only fighting-fighting, no talking. Sometimes there is an American phillum that the Parsi-boss Madan brings. They are very popular. Showing chooma-chooma and all," said the waiter, making smacking sounds to elucidate.

"But tell me, bhai, how did an ordinary dish-washer get a chance like this?"

"It is all because of Satyajit-babu. When his theatre was undergoing repair he used to rehearse close by on the main road, you know the theatre with the elephants at the entrance? He still comes here when he has the time, to drink his favourite chai. Smart and all in his pum-pum. In his theatre, women do their own roles. But he has managed a part for Pahari in some other theatre called the Corinthian, famous for its ballet. Very kind bhadralok, our Satyajitbabu." He polished a plate and laid it with a clatter on the next table.

Shabbir, slurping his tea, was quick to advise Aniruddh to fill the vacancy. "You can start in the morning, when you are free. In a week's time, Ustaadji will be back, then you can work full time. They will probably give you free food."

The bearer nodded. "And a place to sleep, if you are prepared to work late at night. Pahari used to sleep in the cafe once it closed." He flicked his cloth over his shoulder, raised an eyebrow, and looked enquiringly at Aniruddh. "Interested?"

"Bas, what else do you want. And you will be close to us, you can come over whenever you like."

It was particularly the last condition that made Aniruddh apply. Once out of Attaribai's establishment he would be completely alone in a strange city all over again. Somehow, that thought seemed to frighten him, like a child afraid of the dark is frightened of his own shadow.

For the next four months Aniruddh steadfastly washed dishes, mopped tables, stirred gravies, and made himself useful as general dogsbody. He edged the mundane fabric of his tasks with the delicate frill of his music, humming and singing to keep his soul looking away from dejection He found lyrics in the recipe of a dish, a beat in the features of a daily customer, a song in the cook's bad mood. In the post-lunch hours he would entertain his colleagues with his compositions. The touch of his East Bengal accent lent a certain flavour to their catchiness. Soon, he was filling in requests from customers, who tapped the tables for the beat. The owner grudgingly raised Ani's salary by a couple of rupees, as people began coming in with noticeable regularity.

On his first day off, Aniruddh and Shabbir went to see this 'phillum' that the bearer Bihari had spoken so knowledgeably of. It was a tale of adventure, a 'stunt' film, running at the Globe. Related in a series of shifting frames, it moved along jerkily, without sound but with plenty of horses galloping and chivalrous heroes helping damsels in distress. There was an orchestra sitting in the pits, playing music at places to highlight certain effects.

After the first ten minutes, Aniruddh felt something move inside him. It seemed like a light, a warm and wondrous illumination that ignited like a sparkler and graduated after the first half-hour, into an uninterrupted fountainburst. He moved onto the edge of his chair, slapping his thighs in time with the horses' trotting, his imagination rolling along with their gallop, his mind free of all thoughts other than the action that was happening on that fluttering screen.

It was love at first sight. It was as if some kind but unknown person had tapped him from behind on his shoulder, and he had turned and found his hand clasped in an eternal handshake. There was a connection between him and that rectangular white sheet up front, a suspension that estranged him from himself, made him into that hero up there performing all those marvellous feats, sent his creative juices churning.

Shabbirbhai, too, came out of the theatre with a rapt expression, a wiped-clean, glowing expression. For two whole days they could talk of nothing else but their spellbinding experience. Though it felt somewhat subtracted without sound. You missed some action trying to catch up with the sub-titles.

"Look at the endless possibilties it offers. One can convert one's thoughts into moving images on a screen, tell a tale in a manner more fascinating than a story book with static photos or illustrations!" remarked Anirudh.

Shabbir looked at Aniruddh with paternal approval. He was amazed at the responses of a boy barely seventeen. Here was a volcano of talent, waiting for the right climatic conditions to erupt. He played the tabla, sang with a voice powerful enough to invoke tears, and had already tuned Mir and Ghalib. What would he be like at twenty-seven, he wondered?

Business that day was slow. Chabi Babu, the chief cook and Aniruddh were alone in the kitchen, actually relieved at the sight of the empty tables outside.

"Always you are singing for the public in the front. Today for me please sing something special. One kirtan, hein?" requested Chabi Babu.

Aniruddh needed no secondary insistence. The artist within him required an audience, even if it were a sole person in a smoky kitchen. Ani shut his eyes, fancying himself back in the village temple, joss sticks aromatic in his senses. Chabi Babu, ready and rapt, jumped on to the platform of the choolah. Ani began to sing, his voice resounding clear and pure in the small backroom kitchen. The notes floated and quivered as they ascended, but never lost their 'sur'. When the song ended, he opened his eyes gently, almost reluctantly, like a patient whose eyes have just been unbandaged.

In the frame of his vision, stood a stranger, powerful and tall. He was dressed in an immaculate white dhoti, a kurta starched to perfection, and a shawl slung like a casual thought over his shoulder. A man with brooding eyes, clear-cut features, and a sharp nose. Arms folded across his large chest, he was regarding Ani with a concentrated expression.

"I'm sorry," he said with extreme politeness. "I shouldn't be here. But there was nobody to attend, so I ventured into the kitchen."

The cook hastily rubbed his eyes with his gamcha, and brought his professional self to attention. Aniruddh stood as if some hypnotist had commanded him to be very still. The tall man cleared his throat like he would expectorate his embarrassment.

The cook said, "I will send the boy with your special chai, Sarkar."

"And don't forget your exceptional padwal sandesh." His shawl swung into the outer room.

" You sing with much dedication, young man. You actually brought tears to the eyes of the cook. Where did you learn to sing like this?" asked the stranger, as Ani brought him his tea.

Ani answered in a tone cultured enough to match his. "Back home, Moshai, in the village. PujariBabu taught us."

"Pujari Babu. So. Do you know any more like this one?"

Enthusiasm lit up Ani's face like a bulb. "Oh yes, Moshai. I know many. We used to go from place to place singing…." His voice trailed off, for he was suddenly conscious of revealing too much.

"You mean like the Baul singers? Tell me, would you like to sing on the stage? You will be paid, of course," he added quickly.

Ani gasped. The cup of special chai rattled on his tray. This must be the elusive Satyajit Dey. He had almost begun to think of the man as a myth.

"Oori baba, you must be Satyajitbabu, who gave Pahari a chance?"

"Oh, so you know about that," affirmed the tall man, with a smile that would have ignited a Bunsen burner. His Bengali was so tonally sweet you could have dipped rasgoolas into it.

Satyajit Dey was not being impulsive. He was in the business of spotting talent. And this boy was indeed gifted. His inbred devotion, which had enriched his song, was not the kind that could be simulated. He was what was termed theatrically, a natural. "Well, you don't have to give up your job here. Come to us in your spare time, and try it out. If you think you can adjust to the gruelling work and the long hours, you can join permanently. What do you say? "

Aniruddh coloured. As if there could ever be a choice between holding a dishcloth and a harmonium! Was he deserving of all this, he, who had killed a man? "It is not that, Babumoshai. I am too speechless to respond. Would you really give me such a chance?"

"I've already offered it, haven't I?"

"If this is indeed true, and if I am not dreaming, how can I thank you, Moshai?"

"Don't. First prove yourself, and this episode, as not a mere fluke. Once past that, it is your luck, and maybe it will be I who will thank you, who knows, hein? Think of the incredible timing. Perhaps it was meant to happen." He sipped his tea. "This is definitely the best sandesh in town."

"If you will tell me where to come, babu."

"Ah, yes," and the imposing man ordered the cook to fetch him a pencil and paper. That God-fearing person could sense the subtraction of the café's entertainment, not to mention one hand short again.

"Here, get someone to read this for you and give you directions. It is about two-and-a-half miles from here, in a busy street."

"It is alright, Babumoshai, my friend Shabbir will bring me, as I am new to Calcutta."

"Yes. Just ask at the door to see me."

Directly after Deybabu left, Aniruddh took off for Attaribai's. He couldn't wait to share this information with his older friend. The paper with the address was held high as he ran, as if he were flying a kite.

ROUGH CUT

The hoarding atop the imposing entrance proclaimed that Kalamahal Theatres would soon be playing Manmatha Ray's "KARAAGAR".

The familiar magic of the cinema-house rustled them. Instinctively they knew, that once past that great door, they would be transported as if by some space vehicle, into a new and wondrous world. Trembling with anticipation, Aniruddh and Shabbir, finding the door of the theatre closed but not locked, stepped around the alpona at the entrance and pushed it open gently. It made a creaking sound. On their higher stance at the entrance they stood, under the eave of the regal box seats, peering from behind old velvet curtains down past the slanting rows of seats. In front, on an elevated stage, two people were talking in grandiloquent voices and exaggerated gestures, an unwritten history in their tone. Behind them, four men stumbled around propping up a canvas of a painted temple. In a sunken pit at the foot of the stage, some musicians sat tuning their instruments, giving Aniruddh goose pimples with a couple of off-key notes. From some dark spot in the auditorium, Deybabu's voice reverberated.

How could they not be affected by the aura and aroma of the place? The well-worn leather seats, the ghosts of past spectators, the echo of imaginary applause, the piquant smell of the arras, an anticipation in the weft and warp of the darkness creating its own illusions? They stood in thrilling immobility, mouths half-open.

And thus they would have continued, frozen in time and tableau, if something feathery had not scurried over their feet.

In the semi-darkness a man's silhouette began to form. As the figure broke into their vision, all they could make out was thinning silver hair, and eyes so bright they might have belonged to a suspended cat.

An elderly man, holding a broom in his hand, was the object of their disturbance.

Kaku .

No one knew Kaku's real name. Yet in Kala Mahal Theatres he held a position of reverence, for his age and for those experienced eyes,that for half a century had witnessed historic portrayals in this hallowed place. No ordinary sweeper had ever been held in such high esteem. Ever since the Bengalis began to use theatre as an effective means of protest against British rule, Kaku had seen enactments powered by frustration, motivated by anger and scathed with satire. For ages he had stood in the wings, then shuffled down after the matinee, back bending further with time, to clear up the aisles for the next show. Now he firmly regarded these two gawky intruders, one with bands of hair across his balding pate, slight craters from some old smallpox lingering on his face, and the other short and dark, with hair in need of an immediate combing. They were standing with their jaws hanging down and committing according to Kaku's ethics, the ultimate offence. Disturbing rehearsals.

"And who, pray, gave you two sons-of-donkeys permission to stand here watching what is none of your business, hein, hein? Baulo?"

Slightly intimidated by Kaku's dominating, manner, Shabbir, in the humblest of tones, said they had come to meet Dey-da.

"Horses eggs! And do not address him as Dada. Mind, he's Babu or Moshai to the likes of you. Now, out! Out, before I use the broom on your backsides, and I will if I have to, don't doubt for a moment that I won't."

Neither entertained that illusion. Mustering up courage, Ani said in firm tones, "It is Deybabu who called us. You have no right to speak to us like this. We may well ask *you* what authority you have to stop us."

Kaku bristled. This was the ultimate insult! "Do you not understand Bangla, or do I have to talk to you in the King's English? O.U.T! Do you hear, scoot, vamoose, disappear, vanish!"

Unwittingly, he was committing what was his own interpretation of sacrilege.

Satyajit Dey sprang out of his concealed seat in the auditorium, his face scowling with annoyance at the interruption.

"Now what is this disturbance, Kaku? Can't you see I'm trying to rehearse here? "

"Beg your pardon, sir. But there are these two persons at the gate, making fake claims that they know you. I was just trying to get rid of them, sir."

"And maybe they do. Now that you've disturbed me already, send them up here where I can see them."

Shabbir nudged Aniruddh into the circumference of light. It was more the vibrations emanating from Ani, than his dark brooding face or his hair rippling like sand dunes, that made Deybabu recognise the washer-boy from Das Café. He gestured to Ani to come closer. With a flourish of his hand, he ordered silence and instructed the harmonium player to rise.

"Come, sit here on the harmonium, lad, and play something nice and folksy, something of the soil."

Aniruddh recognised the shrill, operatic type of harmonium generally preferred in temples and jatras for its loud tone. He touched his fingers first to the black and white keys and then to his forehead, bowing silently to Ma Saraswati for her blessing. Slowly and softly at first, he began the taans of his song, an example of 'shyama sangeet'. Then he opened his throat and let the notes soar. Thoughts of Ma, of Pujari Babu as he beamed from the sanctum sanctorum, of severed friendship, misplaced childhood, agitated youth, of Paro and Shubir perched in her lap, spread through the song with an additional pathos. His voice reverberated in the dark auditorium, edged by a yearning for the life he had left behind. It filled the corners and seeped into the crevices of the theatre with its clear and full strength.

There was total silence when he had finished.

As he opened his eyes in slow motion, all he could see was a blur. Then, gradually, objects began to limp into the blur. An actor on stage hugging his knees, the temple backdrop with its garish colours, the sombre silhouettes of figures in the orchestra pit.

And all around, an engulfing silence.

Into that silence then, tiptoed a solitary clap. It was the harmonium player. The sound of his lonely applause was a salutation from one artist to another.

The clap was overlapped by another, then another, as people moved and a murmur of appreciation buzzed among those present. As the boy had sung, Deybabu had moved from his supine position to a sitting stance and finally shifted to the edge, clutching tightly at the armrests. There was something unique in the boy's voice, something extra-sensory. But there was no point in telling him so. With his youth, praise would only go to his head. And swollen-headed artists were a dime a dozen in Calcutta, all aspiring for knighthood.

"Er…that was quite..shall we say..good?"

"Thank you, …Moshai," Aniruddh added, as an afterthought.

Satyajit stroked his chin like an imaginary beard. He did a mental calculation. "Well, young man, I called you for an audition. And now, if you like, you can get a job here in the theatre. You sing in the chorus, solo, whatever is required, you play in the orchestra, and if need be, you compose. For this, you will be paid the sum of twenty rupees." He lifted a hand to silence the exclamations. "But for this princely salary you will be expected to put in all your time here. There are no working hours, so necessarily you will have to give up your job at the café. Is that agreed?"

Ani nodded, more out of a gasping incredibility than comprehension.

Satyajit was playing a hunch, but who said running a theatre was only art? His company had till now enjoyed only a moderate success. Something untapped in this boy might contribute to its notability.

"Do I start from tomorrow, Sir?" enquired Aniruddh.

"No, you start from right now". And, as Ani turned to go, he called out to him. "Ai Khokhan, what's your name?"

"Aniruddh Krishna Ganguly," replied Ani.

"Aniruddh Krishna Ganguly, meet me after rehearsals. Backstage. In my office."

"Yes, Sir!" the younger man replied, almost in military fashion, his eyes shining. He started towards the exit, where Shabbir waited for him with dissolving apprehension.

"I'll be damned," exclaimed Kaku, as the boy walked past him. This time, it was *his* jaw that was hanging open.

Shabbir came to the café where Ani still worked late nights so he would be allowed to sleep there, and announced in that lazy singsong way of his, that he had some stupendous news. His placid face offered no clue as to the enormity of his announcement. But then Shabbir would be quite unruffled were he to be granted special audience by the King of England himself.

"Arre miya, there is a new kind of phillum come to Calcutta. Everyone is talking about it. You know that phillum we saw at the Star the other day? The silent one? No sound? Well, this one has people speaking in it. It is called ALAM ARA."

"You mean you can actually hear them speak? Dialogue, as in the theatre?" asked Ani, in sheer wonder.

" So I am told. But miya, should we not go and find out for ourselves?"

"I have an off-day after four days. Could we go and see it then?"

"Why not? It is running at the Chitra, on Cornwallis Street. Bhai, yeh karishma toh dekna hi hoga!"

And they went. And with practically the whole of India, became part of a mass romance. They had gone to hear actors talk, and returned hearing them *sing.*; it was as complete an artistic experience as they could desire, the ultimate entertainment. Later, with 'talkies' like SHIRIN FARHAD and INDERSABHA, and their interminable number of songs, they were hooked in totality, captured for life. Prisoners of Wonder.

He was late. Rehearsals would have begun for the new play, and Satyajitbabu, intolerant of unpunctuality, would be furious. But the rain had held him up. It fell heavily in diagonal lines of excellent monsoon pedigree. He shivered, tingling wet despite the fact that he had travelled part of the distance by tram from the café. Rubbing his palms together to warm them, he walked down the aisle towards the stage. His attempt to arrive there unnoticed was sabotaged by a timorous sneeze, which immediately caught Deybabu's attention. Amazing ears the man possessed, thought Aniruddh, he could have picked up a snake's fart at a fair distance.

"Aniruddh, you're late. And why in heavens are you looking like a wet chicken? Don't you possess a damned umbrella?"

Kaku spoke up for the chastised Aniruddh. "If the boy possessed an umbrella, surely he would use it. Everyone knows he's saving up money to buy a room for his family. So would you, if you could see beyond your script...sir." Under his breath, he muttered something about not everyone being a fortunate big-shot director who owned a theatre company. For in the eleven months that Ani had been there, he had endeared himself to everyone in the company. People had taken to calling him Khokhan, the name by which Deybabu had initially addressed him. But he had made his most ardent fan in Kaku, who, after his initial brusque manner, had become an admirer and supporter of the not-so-voluble teenage singer.

"Really, Kaku, why couldn't you tell me earlier? Why wait for him to almost catch pneumonia? Here, take these two rupees, and go buy the boy a sturdy umbrella." Kaku took off in unabashed glee, looking as smug as a woman who'd just tricked her husband into buying her a diamond necklace. Ani was touched enough to dive immediately for Deybabu's feet. The towering man, a trifle embarrassed, dismissed his largesse with casualness. "Can't have my singers with sore throats. Now, go on, borrow something from the costume department and get into some dry clothes. You've held up rehearsals long enough".

That year, with the monsoon having severely teased his lungs, was to inflict Aniruddh with his chronic bronchitis. But then, he was trying to save every penny towards a home for Ma and Paro and Shubir. His intentions, of course, were governed by so many Ifs. *If* his mother would come to stay with him, *if* she had forgiven him for the offence she mistakenly thought he had committed. *If* she hadn't died with humiliation. *If* Nazrul had managed to tell her the actual facts. No one back home even knew where he was, or even if he were alive. Unless Rehmanmiya had written. But Rehmanmiya, a man of few words, was not so big on correspondence. Perhaps one day he could go back, when India was free and the British had left. He had come to realise how youthfully foolish he and his friends had been, intense and passionate but impulsive and hotheaded, nevertheless. Studious Runu who appreciated everyone else's terrific idea, Dhiren who ranted in the intense night, Nazrul, whose sobriety anchored their collective zest from taking off like a hot-air balloon. Independence was not gained by boiling of the blood, but by careful planning. Before Gandhiji's non-cooperation and Civil Disobedience movement and tactics of non-violence and its comprehensive national effect, their raid on the armoury appeared like a romp at a school picnic.

The plot being constructed around Ani's 'kirtans', Deybabu scheduled their new play to coincide with Vijaydashami, when religious fervour and cultural consciousness reached a zealous peak. True to Deybabu's expectations, Aniruddh's powerful singing impacted on a public that was sensitive to music and particularly vulnerable to a collective ardour at Pooja time. His passionate singing drew unprecedented crowds, which listened and returned home completely entranced. Soon Kalamahal became the new Mecca of the cogniscenti.

Deybabu's hunch had earned Kalamahal Theatres its first truly commercial success.

Pleased, he announced a raise in Ani's salary, incurring the displeasure of his music composer.

"This is not fair practice, Dada," he protested. "Just one play old, and already drawing a high salary. This way, by the end of the next season, he will be earning as much as I."

"My dear Moshai," explained DeyDa, "this is the theatre, not the ICS. There is no hierarchy here, only talent, and the measure of success. Otherwise Kaku would have been our highest earner."

He spoke deliberately in English, not wanting Aniruddh to understand what was an extremely sensitive discussion.

"Kintu, Deybabu.." began Mastermoshai.

"Speak in English, please," interrupted Dey.

"Very well," continued the chief musician, "you can't equate a raw lad from the village with an artist like me. Doesn't experience count for anything?"

"Doesn't talent count for anything, either?" countered Deybabu. "That's why I respect him, not because he rings in the rupees and annas. The feel for it has to be within you, like a blood circulation. I know many tutored musicians who cannot point out an off-scale note."

Mastermoshai bristled with slight at this oblique indication. He was about to say something terribly acidic, when Ani walked timidly out of the wings to resolve the issue by expressing that it was completely alright to annul his raise, if it so pleased everyone.

"After all, sir, Mastermoshai is older and senior," he said in fluent English, in continuity with the discussion. "I am only a poor boy who has a great deal more to learn."

Deybabu gave him a sharp look, like a knife slicing through fruit. With tremendous composure, he slid his hands into his kurta pockets, and said, "So, you speak English. That means you are educated. Then why did you give the impression that you were a village bumpkin?"

"Sorry sir, but everyone just assumed it, sir, because I am from out of town. So they all spoke to me in Bangla. But I am from a small town in East Bengal, which has a proper school from which I matriculated. There's even a British garrison there. I..". He stopped abruptly, afraid he would reveal more than necessary. His hesitation did not escape the notice of Deyda, whose observation was legendary. "What grade did you pass out with? Do you have any certificates?"

Ani looked downwards at his sandals and contemplated the precarious position into which he had unconsciously manouvred himself.

"See me in my office tomorrow morning. I want to hear more of this," Deybabu ordered.

Aniruddh was tempted to run away. What explanation could he possibly offer for not having proper certificates, if he had, indeed, come to the city for work? Why had he opened his big mouth, and not remained a poor, illiterate boy from a village? What had prompted him to mention the English garrison in front of an astute man like Satyajit Dey? Now, as Runu would have said, his goose was well and properly cooked, if not overdone.

He stood outside Deybabu's door in trepidation. The man's stern, authoritative demeanour intimidated him. But rationalism prompted he could not afford to lose this job. It was not just the money. It was work that he loved. The tabla's *theka*. The dulcet notes of the sitar. The constant drone of the tanpura. This was his world now; a world of make-believe. A world peopled by characters who had become familiar to him__Pankaj-da the make-up man, who with his bag of paints and powders, false beards and spirit gum wielded fantastic transformations; Govind Prasad the costume-in-charge, who could convert a two-bit actor into a mighty emperor; Benoy Dasgupta the script-writer who put words into the mouths of modest men that made them strut the boards with grandiose rhetoric; Kalibabu the props-painter, who with his Panchatantra depiction of trees brought a village into a few square yards of city hall. He would apologise, beg, grovel, provided he could just stay on. Everything was so in place.

He heard Deybabu's stentorian voice commanding him to enter.

"So, young man. We have a lot of things to talk about, don't we? What else have you been concealing from all of us, besides your very proper English accent? You say you come from a small town. I presume you could have got employment there. And Kaku says you have a family back home that you want to bring to Calcutta. Why leave them and come miles away, when you are already settled there?"

Aniruddh cleared his throat. "There's more opportunity here, sir."

"And also more competition. An education, and no mention of it. A matriculation, and no certificate. No going home in the hiatus, as others do. A British garrison in your neighbourhood." He glared at Ani over the rims of his spectacles with the grimness of a hangman. "I want the absolute truth now. Are you a refugee from the law? One of those young insurgents running around the state wanted for petty crimes? Or a freedom fighter, or what?"

The sternness of his concentrated intensity made Ani shudder. Feelings, like when his Principal had once reprimanded him in front of the whole school, tripped with a loose-stomach fear over the edge of his poise. Deybabu rose swiftly from his chair and put a heavy arm of consolation around the boy's shoulders. The gesture of sympathy was the last straw for Ani. The sealed barrage of his grim secret broke, releasing all the suffocation, the tortured concealment of his act, the days of desperation and hours of shrivelled loneliness. It was like opening a bottle of ginger ale. Once the stopper was off, it came gushing out, jerky spills of fear and frustration. The spiel of the killing, the escape, the confusion, the bitter separation from the family he loved. Throughout his spasmodic narration, Deybabu remained absolutely quiet, a giant bulwark listening with patience and sympathy.

The narration over, Aniruddh looked at the older man with apprehension. Deybabu's face, chalk-like and unrevealing, gazed steadily at him.

"What will happen now, sir? Will you turn me over to the authorities? Will they hang me like those corpses like tangled kites on the trees?"

Deybabu sighed. "My dear boy, I think if you hadn't felt you could trust me, you would never have told me all this. And do not have any fear that I will turn you in."

Aniruddh slumped into the chair with relief. Deybabu rubbed his fingers over his face, locked into some idea that was taking shape. Aniruddh waited with tremendous assuagement. Then Deybabu began to speak.

"When I was a young boy, I was very inspired by how my elders were using the theatre as a medium of protest against the British regime. Of course, the English imposed all sorts of bans and censorship on plays. But it was still a way of revolution, more oblique and less violent. I think inwardly, I always wanted to continue their fight. Running around the countryside killing people is not the only answer, though yours was a matter of self-defense. You are also a man of art; yes, after what you have told me I cannot call you a boy."

He cleared his throat. "So maybe together we can do something as part of our contribution. Your story has given me an idea. Why don't we make our next play a musical, based on your experience, and intersperse it with songs of nationalism? It's a readymade plot with topical potentialities. Can you manage to write a rough script, which I will later edit, and add songs? Of course you'll get some extra money for your efforts."

Aniruddh stared at Satyajit Dey, wonder and gratitude like twin neon signs in his gaze. Not only would the man cover for him, but also give him this wonderful opportunity! It was enough to canonise him in Aniruddh's eyes.

"But Sir, what about Mastermoshai? He will not react kindly to this arrangement."

"Don't trouble yourself on his account. I call the shots here, and if he doesn't appreciate the idea, he is free to leave. I know that he has been secretly making overtures to Calcutta Theatres. So, take a few days off, work at home, and come to me when you've finished." He began picking up his papers as a sign of dismissal.

Aniruddh rubbed his eyes, and left the office without a further word.

A man, Deybabu had called him. He suddenly felt nine feet high.

SILENT FILM

The day he scribbled the last word in his script, an elevated Aniruddh returned to the theatre. The excitement of being part of a creative process accelerated the pace of his feet. He rushed down the aisles, past the stage and the green rooms, straight to Deybabu's office at the rear, and in his excitement entered without knocking.

Seated in the high-backed chair behind the desk, was a woman. She seemed about twenty years of age. In a heart-shaped face, perfectly matched eyebrows rose upwards like two birds in flight. Beneath them, dark, lustrous eyes thickly lashed, shimmered like black marbles. Her mouth was half-open, as though she were about to frame a word. Kiss-curls danced around the margin of her cheeks, and from her right shoulder a thick braid, like Shiva's serpent, loped around her left shoulder.

Aniruddh saw a woman, crisp at the contours, fairness of brow breaking like a dawn through the night of her tresses, eyes enlarged with curiosity. A woman with heart-stopping beauty in her simplicity. Stunned by her comprehensive attractiveness, his initial breathlessness graduated to annoyance at the sight of her sitting smugly in Deybabu's chair.

"What do you think you're doing, sitting in that chair as if it belonged to your father?"

The girl darted him a sharp look, taking in the boy's true indignation. She lowered her eyes, smiled an amused smile as if she were in no hurry to answer, then began making a great fuss over the frill at the edge of her sleeve. With an exaggerated flapping of eyelashes, she said, "Maybe it does."

Aniruddh gasped at her impertinence. Such boldness could only mean she was an aspiring actress, especially with all that *nakhra.*

"Auditions for the new play start next week. Didn't you see the notice at the entrance? But don't waste your time, there's not much part for a girl."

"Notice? Oh, I didn't notice." She blinked at him coyly.

"Ai, girl, I don't like your impudence."

"But *I* like your style. *You* must be Khokhan." Eyes, rested in discovery, fixed on him with a new meaning. "Kaku can't seem to talk enough about your marvellous voice."

"You must be Khokhan," he mimicked. "Don't try to get around me, understand? Now, get out of that chair at once!"

"Tch! Tch! Annoys you that someone is sitting in your boss' chair? You can complain to him. Ah, here he comes."

Deybabu's face darkened the observation window in the door. With a great stride, he loped in. His face creased happily at sight of Aniruddh.

"Ah, such Providence! I wanted the two of you to meet."

"As you see, we already have, Baba."

BABA?

Why am I always behaving like the proverbial village idiot, thought Aniruddh.

"Ah, sir, I did not know you had a daughter," he said, in a voice as deflated as a gone-limp penis.

"That's because Suchitra has been away to England, studying drama. Thank God she's back. I wanted to tell her about you and the new play, but then all she could talk about last night was seeing ALAM ARA in Bombay. She was fascinated by *The Jazz singer* and *The Melody of Love* in London, but she couldn't believe we had our very own indigenous sound features. Well, now she's back, she'll be managing everyone else like she manages me. As a matter of fact she'll help you with the script, you know, historical details, and things like that. Won't you, Ma?"

"If the great writer feels he needs help." Her eyes were teasing.

Aniruddh stared incredulously at Deybabu. Here he had been talking about nationalism, and he had sent his own daughter to England to study? With astonishing clairvoyance, Deybabu parried the question in Aniruddh's eyes.

"Don't look so shocked. I know exactly what you're thinking. But why blame Poor William Shakespeare for what his descendants do, hein? Besides, I'm against British rule, not British education".

"I saw ALAM ARA too," was all he could think of saying, for Suchitra's' direct gaze was fluttering over him like an insect. Sheepish with embarrassment, he looked down at his feet, noting with unrelated observation that his toenails needed cutting.

"You know, it's Suchitra's ambition to make a picture one day. She's always had this dream of having our own film company. A sort of graduation from the theatre."

Aniruddh looked up sharply, seeing similar sparks in her midnight eyes as those that lit up his own within a cinema hall.

"And so we will one day. I'm convinced of it, Baba. Especially now we have our own in-house music composer. And story-writer, too, I believe."

"Yes, all we need is our own in-house finance. Only forty thousand rupees or so," said Deybabu sardonically.

'So don't get lured away before our turn comes, eh, Aniruddh-babu?"

Saying which she flung in his direction such an indescribable smile, that Ani made an excuse and fled.

Matwali nainonwali

Suchitra took an active interest in the construction of the play. She had a flair for the funny lyric, and an instinct for the right word in the right place. Her physical proximity, however, disturbed Aniruddh, especially with that bold way she had of looking directly into his eyes, saying silent things fearful to interpret. The full volley of their dark and intense scrutiny made him aware of a reciprocal feeling of attraction. Often, when their fingers touched whilst exchanging papers, he felt a tremor go down his stomach and continue shamefully down to his loins.

He became conscious of his first feelings of sexuality. The sensuousness of her walk, the folds of her sari rippling like a clement waterfull over the cliffside of her slender hips as she moved up and down the aisle, riveted his gaze to her body. Sometimes, her pristine shades of off-white smouldering with underlying reds, she appeared unexpectedly in western dress, wearing a frilly blouse over a straight long black skirt that stopped gingerly over the roundness of her ankles. She would pile her hair thickly in an informal bun over the top of her head as she talked, her words flying away like unwanted scraps of paper as he watched it unloose and come tumbling down the slope of her neck in a black avalanche.

But he kept his feelings well under control. However powerful his attraction, or her awareness of it, she was his boss' daughter, and he hoped never to forget that. And so, in spite of the treacherous thump of his feelings as she stepped briskly up the three stage steps to enact a scene for a performer, he manifested no reciprocation. He allowed instead the riot of her thoughts to romp on the wasteland of her own desires.

Prem ka pushp khila man mere

Affronted at being upstaged by an inexperienced boy from out-of-town, Mastermoshai left predictably in the middle of the play. In his time, however, music had been more of an accompaniment. Ani's style was different in that it was intrinsic to the play, significantly blended and overtoned, full of the choral sounds of the feeling of a nation. Unwittingly, he had made the songs follow the parallel in cinema, so that they became as important as the dialogues or the performances, and as indispensable.

'BANGER PRATAP' opened in the winter of '32. A lump as large as a watermelon rested, squarely over Ani's stomach. The success of their previous play had ensured a full house. The newly begun art of criticism meant the presence of critics in the auditorium, resulting in additional flutters. The reporter from Sachitra Sisir and another from a Kallol group paper, were sitting in the front row.

To destabilise matters, Suchitra, cool as a summer resort, continued attempts to make close connections. His own concentration had become a 'shunya'. As the curtain rose, he was paralysed. Sitting in the wings, he could see people in the first row, some fanning themselves with programmes, others sitting forward in anticipation. But then his fingers, of their own accord, found the right bars. After the first half-hour, as the audience appeared to respond, he felt spurred on by a newly discovered confidence. By the interval the lump had dissolved, replaced with an exhilaration as the fact unfolded that they had a hit. The taste of success, like the first sip of alcohol, filled him with a new and heady sensation. When the play was over, the audience rose like a wave, breaking with thunderous applause.

It was obvious that the patriotic songs had stirred them when a sole voice, like a court bailiff's, shouted JAI HIND. The rest of the audience soon picked it up, and the refrain reverberated in the theatre, a choral echo accompanied by rhythmic clapping.

With the evaporation of first-day jitters, the cast, streaks of make-up in the process of removal, moved about backstage in an excited melange of colour and costume. An English helmet, a sadhu's saffron robe, a waiter's uniform, hugged each other in jubilation.

Deybabu, looking taller than usual, beckoned to him. Suchitra nudged Ani who was still frozen to his spot with incredulity, and pushed him in her father's direction.

"This is the young man you wanted to meet", said Deybabu to a noticeable personage with a round face and peaceable expression. The man, in his thirties, was dressed casually in dhoti-kurta, with a cotton shawl draped around his shoulders.

"Let me congratulate you. After so long have I heard a voice full and strong. So much talent, and not yet twenty, Satyajit tells me. Bhai, you must let me borrow your gifted musician in the break before your next play."

"Why not, provided the word is 'borrow'. Who can say no to the great Kazi Nazrul Islam?"

Aniruddh swallowed air and was unable to speak. Why had he not been informed that the reputed bard of East Bengal was to be present? Deybabu thumped him hard on the back, a slug of a congratulatory slap. Kaku, who had deliberately eavesdropped on the scene, croaked and spluttered.

Walking home at night with unbelieving steps, he deliberated on the evening's events. No praise from a hundred admiring people had registered on him as the one sentence from the illustrious poet. He, an unknown runaway, a waif, a struggler, to work with the man he had admired from childhood! Whose Nazrul Geeti they had included in their minstrel repertoire!! Incredulously, he sat down on the pavement under the light of a gas-lamp. When the numbness began to seep like an ebbing fever out of his bones, his eyes clouded with large tears that poured down silently at the sheer honour of it all.

There was no doubt about it. He had begun to have feelings for Suchitra. And he knew that she was attracted to him. Significant messages came from those dark eyes. Like everyone else, he admired her intelligence, and appreciated her boldness in working in a medium where not too many women ventured. Yet, in the next few months, he concertedly avoided her company, unless it was work related. He could not for a moment think of indignifying the daughter of his benefactor. In the hiatus, he went away to the Megaphone Company of India to work with the famous poet.

Aniruddh's flair for choral music, leaning vastly on the repertoire of the minstrel days, found a ready response amongst the public, which derived a sense of unity in group singing. A sense of unity was exactly what the country needed right then. He even acted in a play with another group, using his East Bengali dialect to give comic tones to a character.

He was increasing his work experience, and proportionately, his income, enough to surrender his refuge in the cafe and hire a room for himself. On the first floor of a dilapidated construction he had sufficient place to sleep and keep a few possessions. Through prison-like railings, he looked down upon the busy-ness that went in and out of Central Avenue and moved either towards the cool, classy Esplanade or the grimy density of Sealdah Station. He thought of the unknown places that had become to him now well-known and familiar; the domed monument of the Victoria Memorial, the red-bricked Writers' Building, populated by pen pushers of the Administration; the G.P.O. erected on top of the Black Hole of Calcutta; the Museum built in the earlier part of the last century.

Most of his spare time he spent in the company of Shabbir, his first urban friend. Whenever time allowed, they escaped into the dark confines of the Empire or the Star. Ani would interpret the dialogues of swashbuckling English adventures for Shabbir. Sometimes they saw Saratchandra's classics on the screen in New Theatre productions. The fascination for the magic of the medium with its nexus to music increased after he encountered the fascinating voice of Kundanlal Saigal, and mushroomed into a passion as Saigal became a national icon.

The bitter scars of the separation from his family were now beginning to heal. He prayed and lived for the day he could get them to Calcutta.

The minute the curtain fell on the first day of the renewal of the play, Aniruddh started down the stage steps to mingle with the audience. He was annoyed when he felt a fan tap his shoulder, presuming it was Suchitra. Turning around sharply with a retort, he stared straight into the beady eyes of Attaribai. As usual, her lined face was camouflaged with make-up. Ani's face broke into a smile of genuine pleasure.

"Don't look so shocked," she said. "The connection between music and theatre is like courtesan and customer. Why, even our type of music, the thumri and khayal, is linked to public performance." Years of paan-chewing spoke in her voice, adding to the huskiness of age.

"Shabbir cannot stop telling me about your achievements. It seemed quite unbelievable, so we came to see for ourselves. Quite some success you've gained in this short time, kyon, young man from the village? And not only at work," she twinkled, as Suchitra's curiosity became visibly pretty on the periphery. "We see you starch your kurtas. Quite a bhadralok at this young age, and scarcely any hair in your moustache. Perhaps if we had heard your voice at home, we would not have let you go."

"Oh, Ma, I am not so young as that. In fact, I am almost twenty."

"Oh, that is old, indeed. I had married off a young brother at that age, janab."

She tittered, revealing brick-coloured teeth.

Ani beamed, bending down to touch her feet. After all, his ship had found its anchor in the haven of her house. "As for singing, you may command me any day, it is your prerogative, Ma."

Attaribai crinkled at his address. A nautch girl got called by many names, but hardly that!

" Surely we can prevail upon you, with old associations that grant us the right, to compose a little something for us, haan?" Naughty eyes executed a coquettish wink, and her raucous cackle was not unpleasant.

"I will be there this Sunday. Besides, it is long since I paid my respects to Mamujaan."

"Shabbir has told me about your interest in the ghazal and that you are learning our language. There is a new poet who comes to recite his verses at our doorstep. It is amazing how he has transferred the junoon for the mehbooba to junoon for the country," saying which she rapped him with some delight on the head with her fan, almost in the manner of a blessing. With a stylish swish of her satin sharara, she executed a graceful turn, and her lean, old body disappeared into the crowd.

Aniruddh did not wonder now why girls from good families were sent to the tawaifs to learn the graces. These women had manners and dignity that shone in the rarefied air of their environment.

Suchitra glared at her vanishing back with undisguised envy. Who was this woman to whom Aniruddh had given so much attention? Was she some wealthy Begum with a penchant for toy-boys? Oh dear God, did Ani have this thing for older women? Piqued, she swiveled and walked away, completely forgetting what she had come to say to him.

From the sidelines, Kaku watched this drama with interest. He noticed Suchitra's petulance with an undisguised fear, understanding with the wisdom of his years, its disturbing significance. Over the past few months, he had developed an almost paternally fierce possessiveness for Aniruddh, appreciating his cleanliness and purity for the special virtues that they were, bowing in unexpressed devotion to the miracle of his voice. But now, to Kaku's stupefecation, Aniruddh had manifested a defiling acquaintance with a woman whose very perfume reeked of her profession. Yet, like any other person who loved, he sought justifications for Aniruddh, but was filled with dread at the frantic swing of rejection in Suchitra's plait.

Nibaah ulfat ka in do nazukon se
Sakht mushkil hai

Abdul Karim the potter, black-edged with exhaustion, stepped off the train at Howrah Junction. He had come to Calcutta with a double purpose. One, to attend his niece's marriage, and the other to find a groom for his daughter, Rukhsana. Rukhsana, sweet-scented and delicate, was like a champa blossom with hidden fragrances. She deserved a groom whose handsomeness would match her beauteous charms, and the choices in a city were far more than back home in the outskirts of Barisal.

Once the wedding ceremonies were over, he spoke of his requirement to his brother-in-law, Karamat Ali Khan.

"And I have just the boy for you. My cousin's son. They are a Pathan family from Bhopal. The boy is tall and striking, sturdy and ruddy complexioned. His name is Al-Nasir. I think he and Rukhsi will make a perfect jodi, Bhaijaan. But there is only one problem. The boy is a 'miraasi'; working in the theatre. So much his mother tried to make him understand, but no, the new madness of the bioscope is on him; some day, he says, someone will make him a hero like John Cawas."

"But is the boy good-charactered? Will he take care of Rukhsi? And what kind of salary do these actors earn?"

"Enough to support a wife and a family; twenty-thirty rupees a month, I think. And I can vouch personally for his temperament and his honourable disposition. Look, I have an idea. Why don't we go and see him in the show? It is the most popular play in Calcutta right now. That way, you can appraise him without anyone's knowledge, and if you don't approve, nothing is lost."

The next evening, they set off for Kalamahal Theatres.

Abdul Karim looked around in awe at the carvings on the wall, its leit-motif of tragic and comic masks, and its grand red-and-gold velvet curtain. By the interval, he was on the edge of his seat. For by then, the plot as it unfolded gripped his attention, with its similarities to an event that had taken place in his district almost three years ago. In a bizarre parallel, the protagonist had run away after having dishonoured a girl. Here, however, the play offered another option. Back home, nobody had linked the boy's escape with the murder of the angrezi officer because of the hype about his romance with the Muslim girl! It had devastated the boy's poor mother. Assuagement had come only when her daughter had married Pranoy the flute-player, whose wife had died in childbirth. With no one to take care of the day-old child, it had been a convenient arrangement, especially when Pranoy came to live with the old widow. Gaining a new son had mitigated the disgrace that had come upon the family.

Abdul's attention was drawn back to the stage with a hefty nudge from Karamat Ali. "See, see, that is Al-Nasir, in the captain's uniform. So fair, he's ideal to play the Englishman. After their bow, all the players will sing the main song in chorus."

The audience now added their voices to those of the chorus.

"Look what he's done to your country,
Look what he's done to tradition,
Look what he's done to you.
He with the white face
He with the blond hair
He with the eyes so blue."

But Abdul was not looking at the handsome Al-Nasir. His eyes were focussed on the face of a young lad, a face distinctly familiar. A lad who had been the frustration of Abdul's fellow-Muslims for escaping their wrath at his defilation of a Muslim girl. Tch, such goings-on in the swamps, if Fazlu were to be believed! His moustache had grown a bit thicker, his body a touch fuller, but the face, the hair, had not changed in the past three years. A nagging suspicion had been distracting him throughout the play like a painful memory. It was, with certainty, Aniruddh, the widow Konkona's son. The boy who had been talked about, besides everything else, for topping the matriculation exams, many thought posthumously.

Abdul Karim sat cross-legged on the verandah of the house of Konkona, ignoring the offered cane stool. He did not enter the main house for fear of offending her sensibilities as a devout Hindu. These divisions were understood and respected with a fair amount of sanctity in Barisal. Whatever strange-faced God she prayed to was about to reward her now for her devotion. Amidst loud slurps of tea and an abundant insertion of dramatics, he recounted his tale. He finished with an obstreperous intake of breath, flushed with the importance of such a significant revelation.

Konkona fixed him with a straight and stern eye, her face never letting go of its characteristic serenity, and asked matter-of-factly if he had spoken to the boy who he had thought was her son.

"No, Didi, but I am certain it was him. I reasoned that since he had run away for some specific purpose, I might frighten him by approaching him in this sudden manner. Mind you," he coughed, clearing the phlegm in his throat, "I did consider going to Fazlubhai with this story first. But when I saw in that theatre the facts, they appeared more logical than the tale of Taslima. And Taslima is happily married, soon to become a mother. Why dig up old skeletons? What a better turn to the story, that your son should be a freedom fighter instead?"

"Indeed, I owe you many thanks. For the rest of my life I will be indebted to you, if that *is* really my lost son. After all, you did perceive him from a distance," she suggested practically.

Baba, this woman was made of stone or what? "Only one way to find out, Didi. In fifteen days, I return to Calcutta to formalise the engagement of my daughter. If you send your son-in-law with me, then he can make his identity pukka."

She nodded.

After he had left, she sat very still. Suspense fluttering, fears diving and re-surfacing. She sat motionless, too afraid lest any movement, any wisp of elation, crumble her known and familiar equanimity. Was it probable that the son whom many, except herself, had given up for dead, had been located in some undefined space? Was it possible that he might return, that she might one day touch the dear and familiar mounds of his shoulders, sit him in front of her and rub mustard oil into his thick black hair? She pondered the potentialities of Abdul Karim's suggestion. Pranoy, with his lack of aggressiveness, was not the right candidate for the job. She had a better idea. That afternoon, she sent summons to the three other friends of Aniruddh to see her urgently that evening.

The sunset was a riot of fluorescent oranges and mauves, a blazing backdrop to the meeting. A summer sunset, full of a promising tomorrow. It brought its departing glow into the verandah where they were assembled, presided over by Konkona's austere presence.

She came, without fuss, to the point.

"So, which of you is going to tell me the truth?" was her stern command.

"About what, Mashi Ma?" enquired Dhiren, in genuine innocence.

"Do not pretend, all of you. For three years, I have borne the indignity of Ani's sudden, unexplained departure. I have taken heart from the fact that He who takes care of everything and everyone, would look after him as well. Now, I know my son. I know that he regarded women with high respect and lowered eyes. And he would never have misbehaved with any girl, especially not his friend's sister. So, there was some other reason for his running away so sudden. I waited for one of you to tell me the actual story. But you kept your secret and your distance. I did not ask you myself, afraid as I was that your answers would be coloured with the Englishman's blood. Days passed, then months, and I suffered with a terrible silence. And now, after so long, I have news of my son."

Dhiren made an undefinable noise through his open mouth, an abrupt one-note clarinet burst. Runu began pressing her feet with stepped-up hurriedness. Nazrul turned his face outwards, towards the slowly settling darkness.

"I am waiting".

In a soft voice, Dhiren, intrepid spokesman for the trio, explained. "It isn't that we wanted to conceal anything from you, Mashi-ma. We all, including Ani, thought it wiser that you should know nothing, in case someone questioned you."

"Did you think that I would break before some Englishman's questioning? That I would give my son away with the effects of a little torture, perhaps?"

"No, no, Ma," replied Runu, summoning all his stoic patience to counter her recriminations. Though her voice was level-toned, he could not face the accusation in her eyes. "It was agreed that we would speak to you only after he had informed us that he had found suitable accommodation and means of living. Obviously he doesn't trust postmen, or he would have written. In case of an emergency, we knew he could be contacted through Nazrul's maternal uncle, who had sheltered him."

"So it is true then, what I have always feared. All your fervent foolishness caused my son to kill."

"But Ma, it was not wilful, it was in self-defence," protested Runu.

"After all, it was for the country. And my last information from Mamu, sent by some underground worker," informed Nazrul, "is that he has moved out of his house, and gone to live somewhere else. That he is well, and also earning. Since six months, however, there has been no further information. We are sorry, Ma, for the pain we have caused you."

"For almost three years you hid this news from me, his mother, and let me believe the worst? I do not know if you are really Ani's friends, or his enemies."

"But Ani's message had been that he was saving up for a house so you all could come to live in Calcutta. And only then were we to break the news to you. Perhaps we should have told you earlier. Yet, we have kept our promise to look after you, Mashi-ma. Though, ever since Pranoydada came to stay here, that responsibility was handed over to him. Aniruddh does not even know of Paro and Pranoy," said Dhiren.

"But I cannot wait any more. Now that I know where he is, I want you to go and meet him. I want you to touch him and bring his essence back to me. Only then, will you be forgiven. Now, who will go?"

Runu released a laugh. "Bas, Ma? You are indeed merciful. I will go. Nazrul's sister is heavy with child, and Dhiren's father is not well. The school where I am teaching is closed for the holidays. Just tell me his whereabouts."

"You leave in two weeks on a bus with Abdul Karim, the potter."

"I will give him Maamujaan's address," said Nazrul.

The meeting was over.

Konkona finally permitted herself a sense of relief. She had never, ever, let herself lose control to experience any sensation of excitement. What she felt at that moment was the nearest that she could get to it.

Suchitra paced up and down the aisle, annoyance in her strides. Her large, luminous eyes were darkening with frustration. The long Shiv-serpent braid was intermittently being flung back in a gesture of petulance, whilst the gold hoops of her earrings danced a samba of pique.

Aniruddh was late.

Aniruddh was NEVER late. She had been told that, when not frying fish at home or spending his time in one of the many cinema halls in the city, he was in the theatre. Apparently there was nobody else in his life except that odd-looking musician friend of his, unless you counted the hennaed biddy flirting with him the other evening. Maybe he'd gone to see her…well, what do I care where he goes or who he sees, anyway? Why should I care at all, me, England returned with a degree in drama? What was so special about him to keep him constantly in her thoughts ever since that prelimnary meeting? He was short and dark, eyes stirred with inspiration no doubt but otherwise quite indiscriminate, nose rather flat, lips tending to wideness. His hair, of course, was a definite plus; all those affluent waves giving him that artistic appearance, as if his Samson intensity vibrated in his hair. Besides, when he started to sing, he emanated charisma in magnetic waves. Dimensions seemed to move and inter-change. There was an aura about him which promised success, flared around him like potential greatness. The thought of it made her smile unconsciously, a lingering smile, hesitant to break into fullness. Deciding that she could no longer continue in this emotional limbo, she made up her mind to confront him with the amorphous condition of their mutual feelings, and of her certainty that he reciprocated her restless attraction.

From his vantagepoint at the entrance, Kaku observed her mindless pacing. Nowadays women were so transparent; no subtlety, so much frenetic demand and graceless obviousness, unlike…But Aniruddh had this effect on people, especially women. He'd seen their faces frozen with foolish expressions when they listened to him sing. Kaku hoped Ani would have more sense than to get entangled with the boss's daughter. For surely that would mean the abrupt withdrawal of the ladder of success being held so securely under him by Deybabu. Though there were many rungs upwards and ahead of him, Kaku was convinced that Ani would one day climb them invincibly all the way to the top. He would be a name to reckon with in the field of music, as sure as the cough in his chest. Provided Suchitra didn't swamp him with unreasonable passion.

He saw her now, frowning at her father's pocket watch. Arms banded tightly around her waist, she resumed her frenzied march along the aisle. It brought to Kaku's mind the possibility that perhaps Ani was ill with his bronchitis and his anxiety exploded into a spasm of coughing, relieved only by the sight of Aniruddh stepping briskly down from a rickshaw.

Like an arrow from a bow darted Suchitra, flying down the entrance stairs, rustling Kaku with an annoying breeze. In a swoop she flung herself on the pavement beside Aniruddh, touching the street like an aircraft landing. Aniruddh had scarcely paid off the rickshaw-puller when, propellers still rotating, she began to blitzkrieg him with questions.

"Where have you been there's scarcely half an hour left for the show to begin the musicians are waiting Baba is looking for you and...." she gulped, inhaling audibly, while Kaku gaped at her in astonishment. Horse's eggs! Kaku knew that Deybabu was not in the theatre, but gone to meet with a Marwari businessman regarding finance for his next project. Bah! Women these days were so ingenious with fabrications, they could market the stuff!

He watched tensely, as a small circle of drama seemed to ring Suchitra and Aniruddh. He, touched with the anxiety and concern in her eyes, was overcome with an invading sense of belonging. The grammar of her facial expressions was so easily parsed, so unmistakably comprehensible. A powerful bond locked them in that single moment on the steps, making him gaze into her eyes with confused intensity. What she perceived in them filled Suchitra with a sudden and uncontrollable shyness. She looked away hastily, reddened by a tumult of emotion. Questions and answers careened in the small space between them. Aniruddh unwittingly lifted a hand with the intention of touching her shoulder, but before his fingers could curl over the puffed sleeve of her blouse, old Kaku had shuffled down the stairs to execute some necessary intervention, demanding an explanation for Ani's lateness. "Why this worry, Kaku? I'm perfectly fine, as you can see. I had just gone to look over a place that was supposed to be going cheap."

"And was it suitable?" enquired Kaku, now very much in the arc of focal authority. Aniruddh addressed him, but his gaze was riveted to a point two stairs higher where two eyes, half-hidden, half-shy, were peering at him over Kaku's shoulder. They made a simple if entrancing illustration, a Tagore poem.

"Well, the room was big, but my requirement, as you know, is minimum two rooms. I have a marriageable sister, she would need her privacy." They began to climb the stairs. "I definitely need a puja ghar for my mother. Then I want to be close to the theatre, and in this area accommodation is expensive. I don't want to get them here till all conditions are absolutely comfortable," said Ani, as the trio made its way up the stairs, accompanied by Kaku's nasty wheeze.

They had barely reached the top stair when Kaku suddenly halted, clutched at his chest and collapsed in a faint, his face a gargoyle of pain.

Do naina matware tihaare, hum par zulm karen

The situation between Suchitra and Aniruddh remained unresolved because of Kaku's condition. Four days later, Deybabu summoned the cast together, and informed them that Kaku was suffering from advanced tuberculosis, and that he had arranged for him to be sent to a sanitarium in the hills near Darjeeling.

In an earnest voice he pronounced, " Kaku is the seniormost member of our family. He deserves all our care, attention and respect, for he is not a sweeper, but an institution. I would appreciate, therefore, if we could contribute whatever we can towards his treatment. And not just financially. We must try and go up to the hills to see him, for as far as I know, Kaku has no one to take care of him. The best part of fifty years he has lived here in the theatre, and the best medicine for him would be to be in touch with it, through us."

Despite the fact that he dealt with the process of dramatics, Deybabu was not one to make a demonstration of emotion. Deeply affected, he turned away to conceal his feelings. Yet at most they would have been seen through a haze, for there was not a dry eye in the paraplegic quiet of the theatre.

It was precisely at this moment that Runu stepped through the beaded curtain of Attaribai's establishment, and asked to see Rehmanmiya.

Ai qatibe-taqdeer mujhe itna bata de
Kyun mujhse khafa hai tu, kya maine kiya hai

SIDE TRACKS

Calcutta being Calcutta, with its quintessential ethos practically unchanged despite the passage of time, the play had been seen by every art aficionado and culture vulture in the city. It had been widely discussed amongst the intelligentsia and the literatti. Twice, the Governor had threatened to close it down for showing the murder of an English officer. But in the end, it was left untouched, being merely an inset to the larger picture of what was happening in the country. The political climate was stormy, and winds of unrest blew hotly over the plains fanning bonfires of revolt. Several leaders were spearheading movements in various parts of the land, and the ruling foreigners were hopelessly outnumbered in their efforts to control riots. The Indian National Congress, a force now to reckon with, was clamouring for self-rule. Still recovering from the ravages of the First World War, the British realised that non-cooperation and civil disobedience were eating like dry rot into the stronghold the East India Company had built up with such wile and guile. The Indians were no longer a people to be intimidated by bans and boycotts. It would not be much longer before the tidal waves crashed the banks and the ancient citadels and ramparts came crumbling down.

The play was a fleabite by comparison.

'Banger Pratap' was showing successfully through its second run, though now the houses were not so full. When the curtains dropped, Aniruddh managed to slip hastily out through the exit at the rear, which opened out into an alley. Ever since the day those unmistakable signals had crossed between him and Suchitra, the day that Kaku had collapsed, he had made a concerted effort to avoid her. He maintained a comity equally with her as with any other member of the troupe. But he realized that first his own feelings required sorting out. Admittedly, his attraction towards her was more than just physical. But was it love? And was he mature enough to handle this emotion, and was he ready for any kind of commitment?

He knew however, that his primary priority was getting his family to Calcutta, and only after that could he think of anything else. When he was ready he would talk to her, on an equal level.

He could comprehend her perturbation at his actions. Stolen glances in her direction had underlined her obtunding lightheartedness, frowns creasing her forehead, puzzlement in those ebony eyes, confusion in her decelerated walk. But entering into a relationship at this point was for him committing professional and personal hara-kiri. So lost was he in his deliberations, that he did not see the figure right in front of him, enveloped by vaporous aureoles from the gas-lamp. Ani's steps were arrested by powerful emanations of feeling, a parabola of love that seemed to link him to the figure. Frantically, the features gathered to colligate like parts of a jigsaw puzzle, forming into a face from his childhood.

The likelihood of Runu being on the pavement of a Calcutta street was as much as that of a Martian's descending onto the Maidan. Indeed, he could have been mistaken for one, standing there as if in the triangular downward beam of a hovering spaceship. Aniruddh wanted to exclaim, but seemed to have misplaced his voice. Contrarily, a hundred questions stumbled onto his knotted tongue. He was overcome by a desire to sit on the ground, to feel it flat and firm beneath him, an action solid enough as opposed to this floating sensation that tingled through each vein. But all he could do was freeze and stare. The two friends continued to look at each other, Aniruddh in dumb shock and laryngeal failure, and Runu with such love, that Ani thought he had died and was facing God. Miraculously, his voice came alive, sounding as from a distance, and he could hear the words 'Maa go, Maa go,' as if a ventriloquist were speaking for him, that too, with little success. Then Runu stepped out of the orb of light, and the two friends clasped each other in an embrace, the warmth of which was a conversation in itself. For several seconds they stood, feeling the solid reality of their meeting within the structure of their arms. Then they moved away, their hands still on each other's shoulders, looking at each other, Runu in relief, Aniruddh in disbelief.

"You look filled out, bondhu," said Runu softly, breaking the silence.

"When did you start wearing glasses?" was the first thing that occurred to Ani.

"Since I began to teach in the local school".

"Oh, so now you're a professor? I should have known. And am I supposed to call you Sir, or what?" They both laughed. "When did you come here, and why didn't you let me know? Nazrul could have contacted me through Rehmanmamu." Aniruddh's voice was suddenly apprehensive about the reason for Runu being here, and fearing the worst, he asked, "Has something happened, Runu? Is Ma…?"

"She's fine, don't worry. As a matter of fact, I'm here on her instructions."

"You mean she knows now…?"

"Look, are we going to stand here all night and talk, or are you going to be a good host and feed me something?"

"Damn, I'm sorry. Suddenly I'm famished, too! Come on, I know a place which is open till late. Surely tonight calls for a celebration." Overjoyed, he slapped the back of his taller friend, and in a gesture of extravagance, hailed a passing tonga.

At Das's, Aniruddh was greeted with jolly familiarity, and a great amount of riling for his success.

"Big man, eh? You're well known in these parts obviously. Is it the proximity to Rehmansaab's place, or the play about which I have heard so much from him?" asked Runu with a studious expression, as if his friend's success was purely an expected corollary to his talent.

"Na re, I am just a struggling musician. Do you know, I used to work here, serving at tables and picking up soiled dishes? *Jhoota* plates and cups. Me, a Brahmin! Necessity, my friend, is the grandmother of compulsion. But first, tell me, how are things at home? Was Ma very crushed by my take-off?"

"You know your mother, Ani. She has a tremendous capacity to bear. People came to the house after you left, some full of true commiseration and some of curiosity, but her composure built a wall between them. She hid herself behind a silence that discouraged discussion. She parried inquisitive comments about your reprehensible behaviour with dignified quietude. I think she knew that you must have had a very good reason for going off, and that it had nothing to do with Bulbuli. She never asked us because she was inwardly afraid that it had something to do with the murder. But once she said to me, 'If I've brought him up right, he will be able to fend for himself.' But you know how it is in small towns, things are magnified into dramatic proportions. Everything is made into an issue and discussed with much rhetoric and wringing of hands. But to those who brought to her doleful declarations of your possible demise, she answered in a steady voice, 'better a martyr than a traitor'."

"And Paro and Shubir? Does his cough still get worse in the monsoons?"

"Ah, Paro. Paro is married now, Ani."

"What! Married? When? How? And was I truly given up for dead that they could not wait for her brother to return?"

"Let me quote your own words, bondhu. Necessity is the grandmother of compulsion. You remember Pranoy, the boy who played the flute? His wife died in childbirth, and there was nobody to look after the baby. Since Paro and he spent so much time together, the elders suggested it, and Paro was willing, so it was all arranged expeditiously. But you will have no regret when you see them together. She looks radiant, and has no desire beyond caring for Pranoy, and the baby, a little girl they call Moon-moon. They live in your home now, and since there was someone to care for Ma and Shubir, we didn't inform you. We couldn't write. The postmaster, as you know, is an angrezi stoolie. One glance at your name and address, and you would have been a fried chicken."

Only the thought of Paro's contentment helped mitigate Ani's regret at not being present at his sister's wedding, an occasion he had thought about so often and planned with such enthusiasm. Especially when Runu emphasised how their glow exuded and touched others with peace.

"I've come to take you back, Ani. It's all died out. The murder investigation has been forgotten, and Taslima is settled. Also Abdul Karim the potter, who spotted you at the theatre, cleared up the misunderstanding with Fazlukaka. So, you actually made a play out of your adventures? Amazing! I have to see it."

"Tomorrow's matinee. First row, my friend. But after that.."

"No buts, lekins, kintus. After that you're coming home with me. Memories are short, and each new event obliterates the previous one. Everyone at home is waiting."

The prospect of seeing his family again tempted Ani for a moment, sending a thrill through his body. It had been three long years! But then, better sense prevailed.

"Much as I would like to, I really cannot, not right now. I have commitments to fulfil. Do you know I'm working with Kazi Nazrul at a gramophone company?"

"Now why does that not surprise me, re?" exclaimed Runu, who had always had tremendous confidence that Ani was fated for great things. "But I don't understand why you cannot come home."

"Several valid reasons. Deybabu for one. He has shown faith in me against many odds and much opposition." Not to mention Suchitra, thought Ani. But it was premature to tell Runu about her.

"I can't just walk off without giving him some kind of notice. And there's Kaku, dear Kaku, who's dying in some distant sanatorium. He needs me now. But you know, Runu, ever since I earned my first anna, I have been saving up to buy a house with only one aim in mind---to bring my family here. At home we practically pay no rent, just a couple of rupees, but it's more expensive in a city. Maybe seven-eight rupees. And to buy one's own house, for me, is something of a dream. But, by the grace of Durgama, it won't be long now. The moment I have something suitable, I will send you a wireless at the post office under a code, and you can send me a return message c/o Khokhan at the theatre. It makes more sense to get them all here instead of my going back. Here I have an identity, and also, hopefully, a future. Here, we shall leave behind the past, start afresh in our new life."

"And in that house, will there be a small corner for me? I'll lie there quietly and keep out of your way as much as possible, I promise." The thought of letting his childhood friend go out of his life now that he had found him again was suddenly unbearable.

Aniruddh smiled, a smile like a new spring day, full of warmth and expectation. "And what are brothers for, if they can't share the same roof, even if the goddamn thing leaks in the rains? The present one on my head does just that, and you shall sleep under it tonight and regret that you ever came to find me."

"Never that, no, never that, re. And you'll let me stay, mai ri?"

"If you promise not to recite Hamlet in your sleep."

On this optimistic note of anticipation, Runu returned home the day after, there to await his friend's intimation. His tour of Calcutta could wait for his next visit.

For the next few days, Kaku's deteriorating condition left Aniruddh hardly any time to contemplate house hunting. When the show closed, Ani moved to the sanitarium to take care of him. He spent every possible moment with Kaku, rushing to his bedside at the slightest sound. He managed to feed the obdurate man where the nurses had failed; he dribbled juice down those dry lips, as Kaku's eyes stared fixedly at him with expressions that challenged translation. Aniruddh was the sole person in the troupe with no family responsibilities, who could spare time away from the city and move up there to care for the grizzly, endearing old man. In the past year, an inexplicably close bond had developed between him and dark-faced, blunt-nosed Kaku, two lone persons who ostensibly had nobody to call their own. No one else came to tend the white-haired man, no cousin, no uncle far related, no friend. He looked so solitary, lying frail and helpless in an unfamiliar ward bed, expectorating blood, coughing till his chest ached and beads of sweat grew finely on his forehead.

Thrice Deybabu made a trip up to the hills in his second-hand Austin. He came primarily to settle financial dealings, and never stayed long, for the sight of the decaying old man moved him to misery. Once Suchitra accompanied him, but Aniruddh tactfully avoided any eye contact with her. This was neither the time nor place to settle matters of the heart.

On a wet, rainy day, when the monsoon tortured the hills and whiplashed the conifers and the clouds descended so low that they came in through the open windows, Kaku died. That rankling chest stood still. The raucous, gasping breaths lay unfluttering within that bony ribcage. The pillar of Kalamahal Theatres had collapsed.

A gloom like a giant's shadow encompassed the entire theatre. No stagehand, no musician, no crowd scene extra was unaffected. With mute salutation, their eyes returned time and again to the entrance doorway, where Kaku was wont to stand, keeping strict vigil during rehearsals. They missed his stentorian voice issuing declarations like some dominating patriarch. No one had ever minded his crotchety comments. They all knew the affection that stood solidly behind.

When the Shradh rites had been dispensed with and Kaku's ashes swallowed by the waters of the Ganga, Deybabu summoned Aniruddh into his office. Despite foreknowledge of death, nothing had prepared him for this state of utter emptiness. Suddenly, there was nothing to do, no medicines to administer, no forehead to stroke a troubled Kaku to sleep. Kaku had gone to sleep forever.

"Sit, Aniruddh. There are some things I have to speak to you about, things that lie buried within this theatre, like old costumes in trunks."

And Deybabu began to talk.

Of Kaku, and Kaku's youth, when Kaku's father had been a flourishing tailor for the English memsahibs, and his mother an expert Kantha embroiderer. One day, Kaku, whose real name was Buddhadeb Dasgupta, had come to the theatre, and his life had never been the same again. He had come, seen, and been conquered, irremediably smitten by the leading lady Mumtaz Jehan.

"I was barely ten or eleven years old," he continued, "but I still remember she was fragile and beautiful, as if made of porcelain, chosen as Anarkali for her graceful dancing and her wistful expression. Kaku was enamoured, totally hypnotised. He never missed a single performance after that. Each day he came, and finally, touched by his silent dedication, the lissome beauty began to reciprocate his feelings. But Kaku's father would never give his blessing to a girl of another faith, that too, an *actress.* He wanted no descendant of his to be a hybrid brat, child of a cheap performer. Frantically, he began searching for a suitable bride for Buddhadeb. Mumtaz tried to convince Kaku to marry according to his father's wishes. But he was obdurate. The girl was distraught; the grace went out of her dancing. Buddhadeb loved her even more fiercely for her spirit of sacrifice. So, it occurred to her that the best solution might perhaps be for her to disappear from Kaku's life. One fine day, she vanished and was never heard of again. Some said she had gone back to her native Bihar-sharif; some even mentioned suicide. Buddhadeb was devastated, and to spite his father for his high-caste attitude, left the house and took up a job as a lowly sweeper in this very theatre. Not believing the rumours of her suicide, he hoped fervently that one day his Mumtaz would return. But days passed, and then years, and she did not come, and Kaku grew old and grey and still hoped and waited."

"And what about his parents? Did they never come to take him back?" asked Aniruddh, shocked at this revelation of a calescent desire with a most unlikely candidate as protagonist.

"They tried in vain. But Kaku never stepped through the portals of his home again till the day both his parents were tragically killed in a fire in their shop. Only then did he go back, for he always held it against them that they had considered their good name and respect and religion above their son's happiness. This indeed is a story more dramatic than anything this stage may ever have witnessed."

Aniruddh sat motionless in his chair. Who could have believed that cantankerous old Kaku had been a man of such strong feelings? How well people managed to wrap themselves in layers. Here was a story of an ordinary man whom everyone had taken for granted, yet one who had had the legendary stuff that heroes were made of!

More significantly, he wondered why Deybabu was revealing all this to him right now.

"Aniruddh, the day before I drove Kaku up to the sanitarium, he requested me to have my lawyer draw up a legal document, a will. He knew that he was dying. He also knew that you were looking for an adequate house to bring your family to Calcutta. So he entrusted me to supervise the legal handing over of his house to you after his death."

Aniruddh stared at Deybabu in astonishment. Kaku had owned a house? He was so much a part of the theatre that Ani had assumed he lived there.

"Yes, it all sounds incredible, doesn't it? Everyone knew he had a special affinity for you."

Tremendously overcome by all that a magnanimous fate was dealing out to him these days, struck dumb with the incredibility of the narration he had just heard, Aniruddh felt the acute embarrassment of tears gathering inside his eyes. The most befitting answer he could think of rendering, was silence. There was no alternate way he could imagine of saluting such a tragic legacy that had ironically transformed his dreams into incumbent reality.

"I know how you must be feeling, Aniruddh. We all loved him, but he loved always in a special way. And you must respect that. Don't cry for him. He has gained his peace at last. Perhaps in the last days, he had begun to accept the rumours that Mumtaz had committed suicide. I think the thought that he might be re-united with her soon gave him strength to bear his suffering."

Aniruddh recollected that special light in the dying man's eyes.

"It was good of you, Ani, to spend so much time with a lonely, old man. God bless you for giving him some semblance of belonging before he died. He didn't have much of a life; at least his end was meaningful."

Aniruddh sat, a figure in a tableau, gazing out of the window at the rectangle of overcast sky. He could almost see himself projected there, suspended somewhere between earth and heaven, floating in an ether of disbelief. As though he were watching this happening to someone else, some character on celluloid in a New Theatres tragedy. If you are somewhere out there, Kaku, my Messiah, the big man who made my small dream come true, if you can listen to the salutation of my heart, thank you. Dear, humble, munificent Kaku, thank you.

Wonder and gratitude trickled in a slow drip into Aniruddh's consciousness, along with the incredulous but alleviating realisation that the day to send that telegram to Runu had come, much, much sooner than he had anticipated. The relief of that knowledge began to cut into his grief with the axe of lightness.

Panchi re kahe hot udas.
Tu chod na man ki aas.

The two tongas came slowly down the road. With a taut pull at the reins, the tonga wallah brought the victoria to a halt at the theatre entrance. In the vanguard was his mother, Pranoy, Paro, and Moonmoon, aged three. The one with Runu and Shubir and most of their baggage, followed closely behind. Ani watched his family dislodge with a mixture of apprehension and delight. Finally, the day he had been eagerly awaiting had arrived, closing a chapter of suspense and struggle. He had fixed auditions for Pranoy and Paro with Deyda and he was confident that Runu would procure a job as private tutor in some noble household, or perhaps an academic post. They could together look forward to a more comfortable life. Indeed, with a combined income of almost two hundred rupees, they might even manage some accoutrements of luxury.

With a sense of joy at the reunion, he stepped forward to assist his mother.

Her hair was speckled with gray, but her face had the same serenity that he had left behind almost three years ago. He bent down to touch her feet. She caught his shoulders to raise him, an unexpressed blessing. The truth was known; explanations were unnecessary. She surrounded her most favourite child with a warmth and security that only a mother's embrace can give. Not given to demonstrations of a maudlin sort, Konkona brushed aside a solitary tear that had somehow found its way to the edge. But the others dissolved into a tearful show of emotions, an expended agony in the salty flow.

Runu sighed. Sighed not just for the end to closeted weeping, but for the time of reconstruction. Scars had to be healed, hopes to be fulfilled, happiness to be restored. It was Life's cycle. Happiness was followed by sorrow, sorrow by happiness. On the wheels of the world they chased each other, their rotation required for progress, for conducting the business of existence.

Konkona glanced upwards, her attention pulled to the top of the stairs at the theatre entrance. Leaning against a Corinthian pillar stood a woman. Arms folded across her waist, long, thick braid dangling like a challenge, she was watching this family reunion with interest. Konkona was mesmerized by her eyes. Eyes with the night in them. Konkona shuddered, wondering how long and dark that night might be.

THEATRE COMPANY

Kaku's house. Four square rooms around a central courtyard. Sepia photographs of ancestors on the walls, well-oiled men with anointed foreheads and chaste women with covered heads. They glare in soundless protest at the full stop to a line of cutters and seamstresses. Plaster-peeling walls with gaping holes demand concrete fulfillment. Silent windows look out at the world. Lancet doors with broken hinges bear testimony to a man's solitariness.

Into this setting strolled sound, bringing alive the dead walls with resonance. A child's tantrum; a teacher reciting Shelley, a conch full-blown at prayers, the mellifluous practice of a flute. The clatter of pans in the kitchen.

The walls rejuvenated with face-lifting paint. The windows smartened up with new polish. The ceiling smiled down at the colourful, oily reed mats on the floor. And Kaku's spirit, filled with oblique happiness, slanted an aura of shanti into the once-empty monument to the memory of a frail danseuse.

Ek bangla bane nyara
Jismein rahe kunbaa saara

Aniruddh, his mind uncluttered, now began to focus on the new play, a doomed romance entitled 'Raag-Anuraag'. His mind was pullulating with innovative ideas. It had been scripted by one of Deybabu's writers who had migrated to Bombay to join the developing film industry there.

"How would it sound, Sir, if we introduced violins in the sad scenes?"

Deybabu's disapproval punctured his enthusiasm.

"The sarangi is perfectly suitable, Khokhan. Why bring in a western instrument?"

"The sarangi is so stereotyped. The violin's plaintive tone will melt more easily into the heart. Besides, what you once said about Western education could also be applied to Western music."

Suchitra's support of Ani's suggestion was so instantaneous, that it startled her father. "He has a point there, Baba."

"All that loud sound was required for our previous subject, but this is a *romance.* It needs to be treated more subtly." suggested Ani.

"Exactly." Suchitra agreed, comprehending perfectly. She bestowed on him a smile beatific enough to suggest more than just an agreement of ideas.

Satyajit glanced sharply in his daughter's direction. Suddenly he observed the way she looked at Aniruddh, the bewitched slant of her eyes and the satiny sheen of their resting on his face. The unusual illumination of her skin came vividly to his notice, and he realised there was an enhancement about her, an augmentation of self as if the spokes of her being moved with some unexplained energy. This was a new Suchitra, more smooth and honeyed, vibrancy resonating like a sole sitar in an empty auditorium. He noticed too, the way she called his name, as though each time she said 'Aniruddh', she was calling him twice. He seemed to pick up something in the yin and yang of their connection that disturbed him. He filed it away for future analysis. Work needed his primary attention at that moment. He was see-.sawing with reservations and the desire to keep an open mind about newness. Theatre did demand courage and conviction, and sometimes calculated risk.

"Well, perhaps we should experiment with the ideas of young minds. Though personally I am quite satisfied with the existing style of dramatic music which suits the manner of our dialogue delivery."

Suchitra's face was effulgent with happiness, and Deybabu was afraid it had to do with more than just the modifications to the play.

Aniruddh composed songs with a quality gentle and soothing, like a drizzle after a dust-storm. His background score wove its emotional threads through the paisleys of the story. Pranoy's flute blew its wounded breaths into the scenes, and Paro's beautiful voice lent its exquisite sadness to the heroine's doom.

They generally practiced at home, leaving the theatre free for rehearsals. This arrangement did not please Suchitra at all. She longed for Aniruddh's company as much as the heroine in the play pined for her lover. When Aniruddh *did* appear, looming large on her horizon like a glorious sun, he was inevitably accompanied by the shadowy cloud of Runu, who seemed to have replaced Shabbir as Aniruddh's Siamese twin.

Yet, something in their exchanges made her feel an emolliation, as if unwittingly he was discarding his chainmail and shield. A concomitant softening towards her put a flourish in her steps and rainbows in her daydreams. Besides, with Pranoy and Paro around, Aniruddh was more open, more accessible.

She hoped fervently that this augured well for their future.

Satyajit Dey was disturbed by what he had seen in his daughter's smile. He had reared his motherless child with more liberty than the climate of the time permitted. He wanted his only daughter to grow freely as a human being, to be independent enough to make her own choices. But was independence the same as wisdom? Her next step might be precarious to the balance of arrangements that he and his childhood friend, Birendranath Chattopadhya, had made for her and Biren's son, Uttam. She and Uttam were childhood friends and the two had been meeting frequently in London, where, after successfully graduating from the University of Calcutta, he was now studying engineering. The day he returned to open his own firm of civil architects in Calcutta, they planned to announce the engagement between their two children.

Now here was an unknown musician sounding an off-key note in this well-orchestrated scheme. Not that he had anything against Aniruddh. He was a decent, talented boy, and would evidently go far. It did not matter that he lived in a modest house bequeathed in charity, whilst Suchitra lived in an ancestral mansion in the suburb of Tollygunge, or that he was not, like Biren, a member of the Bhawanipore Club or The Royal Horticultural Society. But he wondered about this unequal partnership. Then again, would Suchitra find in a mechanical man a companion more suitable than an artist who wrote poems and was conversant with Tagore and Ghalib? An artist who had the dark and brooding tempest inside him that gave him more interesting shades than a soft-spoken builder whose mind would be all slabs and pitons and girders?

Perhaps, he ought to wait and watch. Yet he was afraid that it was already rather late for just watching.

"This is the shortlist of the auditions," said Suchitra, handing over the paper to her father.

"Did you find someone suitable?"

"Well there is one girl who seems appropriate for the role of the sister-in-law. Her name is Bela Bhattacharya. There's that kohl-edge of meanness around her eyes. Given that none really has the experience, we'll have to try someone raw."

"So many girls suddenly wanting to join the theatre! I wonder if the glamour of the talkie has something to do with it, and if they consider this as a stepping-stone to the screen. After all, so many films are just extensions of plays nowadays," remarked Satyajit.

"It's all thanks to Durga Khote. Her example is bringing out more girls, that too, from good families. Meanwhile, let's check out this Bela for the role. Her strident voice should make for some good theatrics."

Bela's shrewish nature was ideal for the negative role. A woman of garrulous temperament and transparent ambition, she didn't take long to make her presence felt in the company. Her dramatic gesticulations were meant to draw attention, her fluttering fingers reining in an audience as she tossed them about.

It was unfortunate that the person most drawn towards her was Runu. If the adage of 'opposites attract' held true, here was a classic example. Mesmerised by her chattiness, the way in which she executed each word with a brashness and her total lack of inhibition that conversely appealed to his own shyness, he would stare at her ceaselessly, open-mouthed and breathless. Slumped invisibly into a theatre seat, he would watch with controlled excitement the flamboyance of her body language as she strutted centrestage. It looked like Kaku's story all over again, reconstructed decades later, except that this time the heroine was more farce and less poetry.

Runu's fascination could not be concealed long from Aniruddh. His responses were so unusual to the complete simplicity of his temperament that his tripping pauses, his fading speech as Bela loitered around or sometimes inside him, became to Ani as noticeable as a new film hoarding.

The two friends finally confided in each other their developed and developing romantic urges.

"Why don't you reveal your feelings to her, my friend?"

"Am I that obvious?" asked Runu anxiously.

Ani picked up the violin he had been practising on.

"You're as taut as this violin string. One flash of the bow, and you'll breathe pure music. Perhaps if you express yourself, reveal all to the fair and frolicsome damsel, she might tell you what she feels."

"Which will probably be contempt. Her vibrant nature must consider me to be a dull and hapless teacher-type. It is bad enough I shall be rejected; I shall also become the butt of the company jokes."

"And in the looks department, you are not exactly Rudolph Valentino. Ish! I am afraid you are banished to a romantic limbo, Runu."

"And what about you? Why don't you speak to Suchitra? It's no secret how your eyes search her out. And from what I notice, you, at least, will not be disappointed. As Shabbirbhai says, this silent film has gone on too long; it is the time of the 'talkie.'

"All in good time, bondhu. Let this play finish. By that time I'll be almost twenty-one, a good age to marry. If it's a success, I shall be established in my own right as a composer. With its extended orchestra, this play has become an experiment of sorts. If it doesn't work….. I might just be the musical laughing stock of Calcutta. Just look at her, Runu, she's so dynamic. Look at the energy in her thoughts, that jangling power in her actions, her entire personality echoes with confidence and celebration of herself. You remember that passion we all shared in Barisal, that desperate desire to do something for our country? I see that passion in Suchitra, pulsating in the strength of her arms, the conviction in her speech. I always imagine her in khadi, leading a procession of women, shouting slogans of protest. She deserves better, and when I fit into that bracket of better, I shall speak to her of my feelings."

Once Aniruddh had completed the musical score and left the notations for his musicians to follow and practise, he began to spend most of his spare time at rediscovered Attaribai's, which had become a focal point for the meeting of poets and radicals. Here, he romanced the ghazal. The ghazal as an art form was an echo of the richness of his yearning. Its peculiar rhyming of qafia and radeef synchronised with the rhythm of his feelings. The milieu of intellectuals seemed his natural company, where he could debate and discuss with pizazz. Ironically, it was here that he learnt 'tehzeeb', polishing his provincialism into a more classy urbanity. He could feel his mind opening like a flower. He began to be aware of a process of evolving, and it infused in him a progressive confidence.

Man ki aankhen khol, baba, man ki aankhen khol

The new play opened to a mixed response. Something was different in the entirety of its presentation. Deybabu had expected this. People are generally comfortable with the familiar sounds of years, secure in the net of habit. But Kalamahal's reputation now insured an audience. There were people who appreciated the new sound and hoped it meant a change of tune for the theatre. He did not see failure in his innovation; instead he enjoyed an artistic satisfaction as the music complemented the intensity of the story, enhanced by the pure drama of Paro's voice. One of her songs was much appreciated:

'We are two banks of a river, so close, and yet so far
I am a speck of dust, you a distant star.
We may walk the same street
Yet our steps will never meet
This world has a match
Our dreams fire will catch
And like used paper crinkle, burn and char.

Written by Ani as a reflection of his own feelings, expressing the situation between him and Suchitra with its lyrical double-entendre, it skimmed along the shores of emotion, floating on a dense sadness without sinking into a maudlin marsh. The song mirrored itself in Suchitra's glistening eyes and allowed her a nebulous glimpse into the preserved secret of Aniruddh's feelings.

Satyajit realised that the play's sound waves were lapping the shores of acceptance when a complete stranger walked into his office and introduced himself as a representative of the Gramophone Company of India. Deybabu's normally serene eyes sparked a degree of interest. "I'll come straight to the point, Deybabu," he said, business-like, "we are interested in cutting a record of instrumental music with your flautist."

Deybabu's eyes reverted to their sereneness.

"And why have you singled out only Pranoy Biswas, may I ask?"

"It's his flute. So much larger and longer than the conventional instrument, and with a unique richness of sound. I hope he is not under singular contract to play for you."

"None of my artists are bound to me exclusively. So you may approach him directly, if you wish. But please see that it does not interfere with his performances at showtime."

When the man had left, Deybabu sighed, bowing to his disappointment.

The publicity ensuing from the record transformed Pranoy into an individual performing artist. Sometimes, when Paromita accompanied him with her golden voice, it was difficult to discriminate where her voice left off and his music began. With the money he received for the record Pranoy bought a gramophone, an instrument with a large horn-like contraption.

Konkona's initial reluctance at leaving her hometown had swiftly dissolved before the practical aspect of the move, and now with the thought of the rightness of it, she smiled her beatific smile and launched herself with additional zest in grateful devotion to her gods.

From her vantage point behind the box curtain, Suchitra watched the interplay of flirtation between Bela and her father's assistant, Bankim Bannerjee. It had not taken long for a calculating woman like Bela to latch on to the vulnerable points of the unit, and Bankim's was his weakness for the opposite sex. Kalamahal's unwritten rule forbade involvements amongst the cast, so Bela kept inside that lakshman rekha of interpretation. But by hinting at a promiscuous dalliance in the grammar of her eyes, she procured his extra attention towards herself and her performance. Bankim's interested response was evident to the intimate coterie. Aware of Runu's hopeless infatuation, Suchitra prayed desperately that he would not get hurt. The woman would vampire-like attach herself to his simplicity, suck out his innocence and tear him up, screed by screed. What perturbed her right now also was how to resolve her own inchoate relationship with Aniruddh, to translate in words the emotions that quivered beneath their surfaces.

She dropped the velvet curtain, which fell heavily upon the scene downstairs.

Dapper in his pinstripe Bond Street suit, the man twirled an unlit cigar between his fingers. From his gelled hair and his fashionable chain watch to the tips of his immaculately polished shoes, he looked perfectly the Brown Sahib, a term used in the city to typify those men who fell into neither category of British nor native, but oscillated somewhere in between

"So! Mr. Dey! I hope, you will consider our proposal, with interest! I am sure, that it will be, to your advantage." His opening speech was punctuated with an exclamation mark after every two words.

"Definitely, Mr. Ghosh, very definitely. But you do understand that the story being co-written by one of my assistants now working in Sagar Movietone at Bombay, I have to procure his permission. Then I will study the financial aspect. But, tell me, sir, I thought New Theatres was only interested in doing Saratchandra and Tagore."

"Of course, of course, but we are always in search of other properties. Let Madan fancy foreign adventures! You will agree that no Bengali worth his kaalajaam would be truly satisfied, unless he was given something emotional, something philosophic?"

Mr. Dey did not disguise his surprise. Mr. Ghosh laughed an inaudible laugh that fluttered his adipose chin.

"I know. I know, exactly what you are thinking. But, I say, do not judge a book by its cover. My fancy clothes should not mislead you. Under them I am as Bengali as you are."

"If you say so. But, sir, what exactly is your interest in all this?"

"Mr. Sarkar has had a couple of failures, but we, his friends, are willing to finance dreams! And a certain difference in your play drew the interest of Mr. Debaki Bose, our director. I suppose you have heard of him?"

"Who hasn't? "

"Mr. Bose had been recommended to see your play. He did appreciate the music, perhaps, because it was not theatrical? In the film, too, New Theatres composers will carry forward the same style."

"You mean you won't require Aniruddh?"

"Perhaps in the manner of an assistant."

"You can convey to Mr. Sarkar that I shall be in touch with him shortly. Perhaps at the studio, as it is quite close to where I stay."

The door opened, and Suchitra walked in.

"Ah, my daughter Suchitra. This is Mr. Ghosh." Deybabu's flourish of introduction seemed to say many things.

Mr. Ghosh eyed Suchitra with peppered interest. She was pretty enough to be an actress herself.

"So! We shall await your response. I hope, we shall be doing business together, Mr. Dey."

Suchitra made a moue at the back of the departing guest.

"What was a man like that doing in our small little office? One would have thought that he would be more comfortable on The Royal Calcutta Golf course, sipping jasmine tea and talking of handicaps." Suchitra's eyes suddenly brightened. "Hey, Baba, was he interested in sponsoring our next play by any chance?"

Satyajit turned an inscrutable face to his daughter. But in a second, his eyes were twinkling.

"It was something better than that, ma."

"What could be better than…gosh! You don't mean..?"

"Exactly. Something that you have been waiting for, my dear daughter. Filming our play, Raag-Anuraag! It appears romance is on the commercial cards right now, ever since the fantastic success of SHIRIN FARHAD and the popularity of Kajjan and Nissar."
"And of course, you're going to accept!"

"After I consider the other proposal." He said it so calmly, that it took a few seconds for Suchitra to register what he had said.

"What other proposal? You mean you actually have two? Baba! Oho, I should have known you were just teasing." Light faded from her face, like from the earth after sunset.

"No, honestly, Ma. Would I lie to you? This Mr. Ghosh is connected with New Theatres. But yesterday, I had a visitor, one Vimal Kumar. He is from the Bombay film industry. Only, he was interested in taking Aniruddh to work for him."

"But that's simply wonderful. It will be an excellent opportunity for him to present his talent on a broader scope. Imagine how it will be to hear at the end of a gramaphone record his voice announcing, 'Mera naam Aniruddh Ganguly.' A record that perhaps an entire nation might hear. Not just a restricted Calcutta audience."

Like two fireflies, her eyes reflected pride in expectation of Aniruddh's future fame.

"That's all very well, but have you considered it means we will lose our talented composer and singer?"

"Oh, Baba, surely you will not be so selfish," said Suchitra, her face clouding. "It's a chance in a million for him!" She tossed her plait across her shoulders.

"New Theatres wants the *play*, not the music. They will compose their own songs," replied Deybabu. "R.C.Boral and Mr. Pankaj Mallik and even Timir Baran are so firmly in the seat there, that were Aniruddh even to be asked to work on the film, being an assistant is all the future he can expect. Therefore, we have to weigh the opportunities carefully. Perhaps, he should decide for himself."

Suchitra's next words were born, like an accidental child, from pure excitement.

"Please, let me be the one to tell him, Baba. I want to break the news to him and see the very first expression on his face. Please, please?" Her eyes danced in jubilation.

Dey stared at Suchitra, his eyebrows lifting just a fraction. An aura of light was glowing all around her like a phosphorescent second skin. Her face was shining so brightly, that he could not look at it, like one cannot look at the sun. For a second he hesitated, then with words in slow motion, he said, "If, it's all that important, to you, ma-go."

He watched the light in her face breaking into prisms. She touched the colour in her cheek. The subtlety of her father's words was not lost on her. But she was not ashamed of her feelings. It was time to pull out from buried realms, emotions that had been banished there by diffidence.

"Yes, Baba."

Those simple two words, uttered with silken softness, spoke intended volumes.

Something shattered inside Satyajit. Perhaps it was a dream.

"You must do, then, what you think is best, child."

She nodded, turning swiftly, blessed by the endorsement of her father, leaving the office and its occupant in a state of turbulence. Some of it she carried in her, as she ran up the aisle towards the theatre entrance.

Satyajit hid the disappointment on his face with his hands.

But it was *her* life. He had trained her to be responsible for it. And he could not renege on his own compromises.

Less than an hour to go for the evening's performance. Why had Aniruddh not arrived? Suchitra's entire system was tied up in knots a Boy Scout would have been proud of. Bombay! The city of dream factories! Where Wadia, and Ranjit, and Imperial manufactured fantasies! She could almost reach out and touch Aniruddh's success, like you touch a forehead for fever. This offer would equalise the differences that she understood held him back. Now that he would be going away, surely he would make some presentation of his feelings? Here were two wishes for the chance of one! Imagination spun in her mind, like grain in a chakki, producing the fine powdery substance of happy dreams. Her entire body vibrated with a high-voltage electric current, so that she was charged like a full battery.

Across the road, she spotted him alighting from a rickshaw. Her heart tumulted, anticipating his astonishment at her news. She streaked down the steps like a comet, her sari pallu its flaring tail. In her little window of focus, there was only Aniruddh, and Aniruddh alone. So intent was she in trying to capture his attention that she didn't realise she had stepped over the kerb.

The hooded Vauxhall coming down the road was slow; unfortunately, her own speed was not.

About to cross, Aniruddh was arrested by a bloodcurdling scream, as the figure of a woman catapulted into the air and fell in a terrifying leap back onto the macadam road. The raucous screech of halting tyres resounded in his senses for what seemed an eternity. The flowing lines of traffic ceased, sound and motion arrested. Pinpoints of people froze; then moved magnetically into a circle around the spot where the woman had fallen. The circle grew, adding ripples to the fulcrum of the accident. Aniruddh pushed passed the burgeoning mob whose protests began to soar into a deafening roar, scratchy and screechy. Their fury was targeted at the Englishman whose car was the culprit.

He swam past the outer circle into the vortex, pushing and thrusting this way through, till he heard someone say, 'Be careful, you'll trample her. Move away, give space, move.' And above the virulent Bengali, a single voice said distinctly. ' Oh Ma. Oh Ma, it's Suchitra-di!'

For a second, he was immobile and blank, as if he had floated away and was staring, from a distance, at his body turned to concrete. His senses seemed to be running away from him, and he struggled desperately to get them back_his sight, his hearing, his mind in separate parts. Then someone slammed into his back, and he came together again. His gasping eyes looked down at the figure lying like a broken doll on the ground. He took in each terrifying delineation; her sari bunched up at the knees, one leg, its fine hairs detailed against the fairness of the skin, entangled in the spare tyre along the car's running board, a rounded knee, neck turned at a precarious angle. His eyes encountered a red stream under her body, as though sindoor from her hair were being washed away.

He heard a voice shouting, "I know the girl, I know the girl," and it was his own voice, crackling with panic, as a sympathetic wave parted to give him space. Shocked faces looked at him with concern. He bent down to pick up the unconscious woman he loved.

"Be careful with the neck, you," shouted the Englishman. "It looks like it's bloody broken."

People from inside the theatre dashed out of the building, drawn by the noise and the commotion. An agitated Deyda, urging them to go back in, followed. Astonished faces, shocked faces, turned back at him. Deyda stared, appalled, at the sight of Suchitra in Aniruddh's arms.

"What do you think you're doing?" he demanded.

"There's. ...been an accident." Aniruddh barely managed the words.

Satyajit Dey gasped in horror, hearing the words but not registering their meaning, not connecting his beloved daughter who but moments ago had pulsated with so much energy, with the twisted figure being carried aloft by a shaken Aniruddh.

"There's still a pulse," exclaimed the Britisher, characteristically litotic. "Hurry up, let's take her to the hospital. I'm sorry, but she came dashing down in a frightful hurry right into my car. It wasn't my fault, old chap."

Aniruddh placed Suchitra gently in the vehicle. A hundred faces jostled, trying to peer in. He made to follow, but Deybabu put a hand on his shoulder. Gazing at him with dead eyes, he said, "It's okay. You go, manage the performance. The show must go on."

The show must go on? What kind of a heartless man was Deybabu to expect his crew to carry on sailing when one of them had just been thrown overboard? Was he so insensitive to think that

Aniruddh could sing whilst Suchitra lay in some impersonal ward unconscious, perhaps even dying? God, he shouldn't be thinking like this. Suchitra wouldn't die. She would pull through; she *had* to. She would survive; maybe with a couple of broken bones, but survive nevertheless. She was a fighter. Afterwards, he would tell her how he lay awake nights re-living the moments when their eyes met with intimate significance. And now that he had a steady job, a status, even a home, he could think in terms of offering her marriage. This would really please his mother; a Bengali daughter-in-law of good birth. With a mind of her own, one of the new breed of Indian women.

The show was over. A half-hearted, dragged-out performance, anxiety adding to its already potent pathos. But neither Bankim nor Benoy, who had forcefully accompanied Deybabu, had returned with any information. The strained cast made straight for Deybabu's house, a solemn collection of stagehands, prompters, actors, musicians, all moving as one mass of tension.

They found the house in darkness. Only the street lamp burned, throwing a bizarre shadowplay on the walls. On the steps sat Ramdeen, Deybabu's old retainer who had brought up Suchitra since she was a baby. With unshed tears moistening his old eyes, he sat like Michaelangelo's Thinker, as if he had been sitting there for centuries.

The group settled down to wait with him; some on the stone steps, some standing outside the gate, some hanging on the railings like strings on the trellis around a pir's mazaar, symbols of hope and prayer. Pranoy, who had sent Paro home to deliver the news to Konkona, stood clutching his flute tightly. The moments ticked by; tick, tick, each second dripping down the hourglass, dropping into silence as nothing came down the quiet street. They spoke in whispers; spoke of seeing Suchitra coming along in plaster and bandage, coming along unconscious but safe. Ramdeen kept flicking an old towel on and off his shoulder, as if the everyday action would anchor him with a sense of routine. The gas-lamp on the street hissed, killing hundreds of buzzing moths with its dragon-breath.

Well past midnight, the hooded Vauxhall came down the road with the slow motion of a hearse. Faces were tense in the darkness, as the car braked to a halt on the pavement outside the gate. Aniruddh gripped Runu's arm tightly. Deybabu alighted first. His face was like sculptured marble, expressionless and cold. From stunned forehead to leaden feet, he looked the bearer of sad tidings. With the single action of shaking his head from side to side, waiting breaths and frantic thoughts sank with the sensation of inevitable doom. He stared at the expectant group without recognition. An overwhelming panic choked Aniruddh's throat with bile. He felt himself rise, then fall back into his body. Runu's glasses misted, images breaking into squares like blocked-out faces in newspaper photographs.

Not a leaf stirred, not a breath exhaled, not a word was dropped into this nightmarish tableau.

Then Deybabu, breaking the stillness, moved a step forward, supported by Bankim and Benoy.

The silence shattered with a lonely shriek. Ramdeen, jerking upwards, ran frantically and fiercely towards the car.

Suchitra lay pale as a waxwork, her body shrouded in a white sheet. Beautiful, warm Suchitra, her lustrous eyes closed forever. With broken, tortured steps Aniruddh staggered towards the car, supported by Runu. Through the mists of his daze, he could see her eyelashes absolutely still in her pretty pale face. Closed down upon the candlewax cheeks like the flap of an envelope. Those eyelashes would never flutter again at him, shielding her dark, luminous eyes with their world of hidden meanings. Her lips would never move to voice the crowd of thoughts that had jostled in her mind or the subjugated feelings in her heart.

"Don't cover her face!" exclaimed Deybabu, speaking to Aniruddh, looking at him with accusing eyes. "Do you want her to suffocate? Can't you see the poor child is sleeping peacefully?

See how they have tied her hands in such a brutal manner, stuffed cottonwool into the poor child's nose. Free her hands, Ramukaka. My baby rests, re. Be careful with her, her neck is broken."

These dislocated words followed her into the house, as Deybabu stumbled behind the people carrying his daughter's body. They put her down on the cold floor, ice upon ice. A wail rent the air as one of the girls let out a piercing sound. The sudden loudness of the cry seemed to cut into the general state of shock. Realisation began to seep in. As if the colours of the world had turned into one negative reel, people, like shadows without form or substance, slid mechanically into the motions one performs for the departed.

For once, even Bela's amplitude of speech had tapered into compulsive silence, her fingers locked over her mouth like a grill. Aniruddh stood in a corner, incredulous, wondering if he was in some horrible dream, and that daylight would bring relief that this had not happened. He would open his eyes in his home, and sigh, and thank God it was not true, then leave for work as usual.

This was the woman he had loved; full of fluctuating emotions that only he had had the power to bring to the surface. But he had avoided eye contact and deliberately not read her body language. He had been hesitant, scared, and righteous. So many things had remained unsaid; words smoky and intense, flashes of bright phrase, words lingering for a moment like frozen breath upon their lips, then blown away, vaporous. A bridge had stood between them, uncrossed. He had been such a fool. And the irony was he had considered himself so wise! And now there would never be another chance, no second opportunity, for having repudiated what Destiny had offered them once.

The show was over.

He stumbled into a corner like a sleepwalker, fitting into the angle where two walls meet, sliding down onto the floor.

The refrain from his song buzzed in his mind. "Though we walk the same street, our steps will never meet."

Suchitra's footsteps had risen above the street and floated away somewhere, leaving his footsteps alone.

As the night began to break into shredded light, Pranoy sat on the steps, blowing into his flute gently. He played a slow and lingering Bhairavi, and the sound from his flute resembled a human wail.

She burned like incense.

The pristine off-whites melted in the heart of the fire, the passionate reds outlined its flames.

She became just a deeply-entrenched but perishable thought, a vivid, golden calendula in a bed of memories.

After the cremation, Deybabu retired into solitariness. His face was a blank memo-pad; as undistracted as a penance-seeking sadhu in meditation, impoverished of everything but a quiet grief, resigned to a deserved karmic status.

Though he ordered the performances to continue, he never came to the theatre again. He greeted sympathisers like strangers, received condolences wordlessly. Mr. Ghosh came and went, unrecognised. His friend Birendranath orbited for days, but Satyajit stared at him as if he were no more than a spectator at one of his shows, and Uttam's telegram like it was some old piece of paper with scrapped dialogue. He walked around the house like a zombie, roaming in the alleyways of his memories, refusing the food that Ramukaka unswervingly placed before him. Yet, sometimes, Aniruddh felt his eyes sharply upon him, figuring out something. It puzzled him. But of this he was certain, that one day Deybabu's train of grief would halt at some strange station, and he would step out like a tired passenger. And Aniruddh wanted to be there, to receive him at the platform when it happened.

Morning after morning, he returned and waited patiently. But Satyajit Dey maintained his 'maun', wrapping his grief around him like a shawl. The show closed down. After a while, people stopped coming. But Aniruddh came with unabated constancy, knowing full well that the wall of stony silence had to crumble. On the lobby wall he hung the picture of Suchitra that the prop artist Kalibabu had painted of her, capturing wondrously all her vitality, and garlanded it with fresh flowers everyday. Touching her painted face, he would will it to come to life, to let the red-tinged cheeks flesh out in his palm, as though by praying hard, he could imbibe a little divinity into his fingers. Even on canvas, her eyes were expressive enough to appear to be talking to him, her pink smile spreading specially for him. And their exchanged looks told their story, read by a wizened Ramukaka, and sometimes, unobserved, by a graven Deybabu, watching from behind a frayed curtain a great distance away. _

Dukh ke din ab beetat naahi

THE TALKIE

"You cared for her too, didn't you?"

It had been so long since he'd heard him speak that Aniruddh almost never recognised Deybabu's voice. In astonishment Aniruddh swiveled, and came face to face with him, dressed in just a dhoti and a short-sleeved vest, looking strangely out of place in his own home. He, too, was gazing at Suchitra's portrait, as if he had lost her for a while and found her again, encaptured in oil.

Aniruddh paused, stunned. Of all the words he had thought Deybabu would first speak coming out of his samadhi-like state, these were not what he had expected. Yet, somehow, it seemed right, as if there were some unmentioned connection between this sentence and Suchitra's death that had to be resolved between the two. Some hidden, drowned nexus that would come floating up on top of the water like oil.

There was no time for denial, or self-justification. In any case, such a moment of absolute significance had to be honoured with nothing but the truth.

"Yes." There was a simple dignity in the solitary word. "But I never spoke about my feelings…sir."

"I know," interrupted the older man." He spoke hesitantly, slow words that seemed to drag out of him. "That is the inference I have made in these past few days. In the beginning I hated you. I blamed you for all that had happened. But then I reasoned out that it wasn't your fault. It was the uncontrolled excitement of her own feelings."

A question appeared in Aniruddh's knitted brows.

With gradually strengthening words, Deybabu continued, all the simmering language of grief bubbling to the surface, the long silence spilling out in fractured syllables.

"That day we had been approached to make a picture of the new play. She wanted to be the first to tell you. Unable to curb her child-like exhilaration, she must have dashed across..and.." His voice cracked and splintered.

Aniruddh reached out a hand to the older man, a hypotenuse to his collapsing right angle. Deybabu seemed to gather his separate parts together, as though sympathy embarrassed him.

"I didn't want to overstep the lines, sir. I never did anything to.."

Deybabu held up his hand. "I know, I know. I should have realized that you had too much honour. For some time I had been suspecting her feelings; I just didn't evaluate them seriously. But that day I was sure. And I had made up my mind that I would speak to both of you after the show. I only wanted her happiness. After all, she is.. I mean..was.. my only child. Do you know, she was prepared to lose you, just so that you could progress? The offer from New Theatres might have included you in the package deal, but I was against the idea of sending you there. Bombay was the place for you, we were both agreed on that."

Aniruddh was taken aback at this revelation. He had so misjudged the depth of her emotions. He wondered if he, trundling his pushcart along the road of life, would ever have been capable of such sacrifice.

"I have been thinking these past few days, if you would perhaps fulfil her last desire. For the peace of her soul. There's nothing left in Kalamahal. What will I work for now? It was all for Ma. But you, your life lies ahead of you. She wanted your success so desperately. Go to Bombay. I have friends there who will help you. Promise me you won't refuse. Aniruddh, promise me!" His eyes sparked momentarily, as if searching a reason to live.

Aniruddh stared unblinkingly at the senior man, and marvelled at his greatness. He had been the indirect cause of his daughter's death, yet the man had no remonstrance, no bitterness, no acrimonious outburst of reprehension. Just a simple request for the happiness of his daughter's departed spirit! This man was nothing less than a saint! Before goodness of such titanic proportions, how could he not have the grace to agree? Besides, he owed it to Suchitra. He could no longer stay in the company now, knowing what Deybabu knew, and being a constant reminder of what he had lost. Fate had set his feet in motion again, forcing him to run one more time.

He nodded in affirmation.

Deybabu sagged in relief. His face lightened, and he glanced at his daughter's portrait. He must have imagined it, but it felt as though Suchitra smiled.

"Thank you, Ani," said Deybabu, simply.

He made to turn away, looking exhausted, as if the whole scene had been too much of a strain, as if he wanted to get back into the grief that accepted him without explanations. Aniruddh, wanting desperately to continue the unprecedented intimacy that had been established between them by Deybabu's use of his shortened name, held out a hand and touched his arm gently. Deybabu hesitated, then looked at him with so much surface pain. A sound surprisingly like a sob escaped Satyajit. Then he moved forward and held Aniruddh close to his heart, as one would embrace a favourite son. At last, the dam of restraint broke and the suppressed feeling of days gave way to racking sobs, as his large frame heaved on Ani's small shoulder. Unashamedly, and without constraint, both men wept.

Ani's intentions were received with reservations. Pranoy and Paro expressed reluctance to uproot themselves considering they had only just settled down. Besides, Pranoy had established himself as a concert artist, so it did not affect him much if the theatre closed down. Runu, too, thought it a foolish idea to gad off to another city without a job and begin the struggle all over again.

"But Deybabu will give me a letter of recommendation to someone he knows in a film company. Once I have a job, I can always look around for other prospects. In any case I am not asking you all to make the move. I'll go ahead, and once things are organised, I'll send for you."

"Ki korso? You can't always be 'sending for your family' Ani," advised Runu philosophically, "You have experience now, and any other theatre will give you employment. Why go to Bombay, so far away, away from your roots, your culture?"

"So what's wrong with putting down roots in Bombay? And what other theatre will progress now in front of the talkie? The stage has a dim future, unless it comes out with some new and dynamic techniques. The scope is so restricted compared to the boundless parametres of celluloid. We have to look at things practically. If I don't move on, perhaps I may just remain an accompaniment to Pranoyda. I don't want to be just a tabla artist.The best opportunity is *now*, when so much experimentation is going on. Studios with electric lights and sound systems; who knows we can start some method of parallel singing that will end listening to the off-key notes of actors who can't speak their dialogues, let alone sing."

"Ani. Your head is full of sawdust. Look at you speak! What do you know of these matters?" exclaimed Runu.

"No bondhu, my head is full of dreams. I have been finding out about these things, reading the papers and magazines. I know about Dundiraj Govind, about Dadasaheb Torney and how he would have been the pioneering producer of Hindi movies had not his SAVITHRI been washed out in the printing process. I have seen the exciting techniques of trick photography in Phalke's KALIA NAG. Everyone is learning, like your little students."

"I think it's a crazy idea. Even if you want to do this, what is wrong with remaining in Calcutta? You're almost getting a job at New Theatres."

"Because Bombay is going to be big, bondhu."

Except for Ma, who understood that it had to do with Suchitra's death and her now long night of eternity, the others sulked, thrusting

Aniruddh into dichotomy. Deep in her maternal heart, she knew that some spark within him had dimmed, and what he needed was a change of atmosphere. A struggle to re-establish himself would keep his mind occupied. He was young; and with the transience of youth, he would soon forget.

He escaped into the realms of fantasy, seeing one film after another with his old friend Shabbir. He saw a re-run of YAHUDI KI LADKI, a re-make of CHANDIDAS where his heart wept at Saigal's singing, and a new production of Ranjit's called GUNSUNDARI starring the fabulous Gohar. He felt a strong connection between himself and the screen that he could neither deny nor ignore. Like a flame in the wind, his decision tossed one way, then another. Most times, the practical platitudes of his family anchored him to a rationale that expressed in staid tones, the lunacy of haring off to a city several hundred miles away with neither job nor support of any kind.

Fate, in its persevering game of patience, eventually played its hand. Deybabu informed him that Bankim had also decided to take his chances in Bombay, and two together could go it better than one. Aniruddh's wayward thoughts now crystallised into a firm decision. He iterated that nothing ventured was nothing gained, and quoted the example of Dadasaheb Phalke, who had sold his effects, even his wife's jewellery, to buy a camera and study the art of cinema in England.

"And look what he achieved! You have to be a little mad, a little daring to chase your dreams," he proclaimed.

The others thought him crazy and stubborn. Only his mother encouraged him, hoping that the change of scene would help him exorcise whatever spectres were haunting him, and rid him of his lethargy and loss of direction. Runu finally admitted with a sense of fairness that the thought of separation from Bela might have coloured his opinions, and was actually pleased to have his rival Bankim out of the way.

Taking leave of Deybabu was the toughest, but then Aniruddh understood that to fulfill his mentor's wishes, Deybabu had to let him go in every sense.

On a cool evening, at ten minutes past five, he and Bankim boarded the Bombay Mail and chugged out of Howrah Junction on a journey of adventure that could prove them either prophets or fools.

The year 1934 was drawing to an end.

YEH HAI BAMBAI MERI JAAN

Horse-driven tongas. Clanging trams. American cars. It was not unlike Calcutta. But there was an electricity in the air that had nothing to do with ohms and volts. After alighting at Victoria Terminus, where red-shirted coolies with dirty turbans and cactus stubbles clucked them on, they boarded a tram to Parel, the district where Mithun Chatterjee stayed at the house of his friend Utpal Dasgupta, in a one-room tenement building near the Hindmata Cinema. As the tram jerked along, Ani felt he was riding on the throbbing and thriving pulse of the city. He could see myriads of lights; shining from tiny squares in clone-like buildings that lined the road. Lights that moved along with them on the route edged by great, old trees that appeared more ancient than the one in the Botanical Gardens back home. Lights that passed the famed Novelty Cinema, where on 7th July 1896, co-incidentally the date of his birth, six of the very first two-minute motion films in the world made by the Lumiere brothers had been shown to breathless Bombay audiences.

When the tram paused at a stop, Ani gazed out of the window, reviving with the electric rejuvenation the city sponsored. At a traffic light, he saw a car sliding in beside him on the road. A plumpish arm curved along the rim of its window. In the light that spilled out from the tram, he could have sworn the fair and beauteous woman inside was the sensational Nadia. He must be in heaven, if the stars were so close. But before he could distract Bankim from staring at a young woman in a Punjabi dress, the car lurched forward and moved away.

The tram sidled on. There was an efficient boarding and dislodging of people that spoke of a well-ordered civic sense, an off-loading of evening-shift faces at places with names like Byculla and Chinchpokhli.

They reached an area where dark and brooding chimneys spiked the sky.

"We're nearing the place now," informed Bankim.

Hungry and exhausted, they found Utpal's place, down what Bankim described as a 'shonkirno gali,' only to discover a lock on the door. It was nine at night. Accustomed to the irregular hours of entertainment people, they knew there was nothing to do but wait. They had spotted what Bankim referred to as an Irani restaurant on the ground floor, and porting their sparse baggage, they trudged downstairs to dine on omelette-pao and crisp mutton samosas, then shuffled up the three floors, past the smelly common toilets to his room again. Night dropped a chessboard of lights and shadows in the common corridor of the chawl.

Way past midnight, when Utpal came whistling along and made to open his door, he stumbled upon prostrate figures blockading his entry. Swearing under his breath, he kicked viciously at the reclining forms.

"Ai, get up you devils. Only my place you found to drop your drunken selves at? Go litter someone else's doorstep, you sons-of-owls! Sprawling anywhere as if it was your father's property!"

Aniruddh and Bankim rubbed sleepy eyes. Warily Bankim rose, and asked if they were addressing one Utpal Dasgupta.

"And what is it to you if I am?"

"We have come from Calcutta."

"So? A hundred Bengalis come from Calcutta every day. Do they choose my doorstep to lie down on?"

"But Aniruddh and.."

"Aniruddh..Wait a minute.. I've heard this name somewhere."

"Deybabu said..."

"Ah! Of course I remember now. Satyajitbabu wrote about you. Not to me, but to Mithun Chatterjee, *my* ex-room-mate, *his* ex-story-writer. Why didn't you say so in the first place, you sons-of...oh, sorry, don't mind me. But look at you both; you look dead tired, and here I am abusing you instead of asking you in. Mithun-da himself is living on someone else's mercy, so you are welcome to park your butts at my royal palace which is grander than the Viceroy's residence!" He swept his arm in a grandiose gesture, as though granting them entry into the Diwan-e-Khas.

Utpal's ten-by-twelve ft. room would never have won a prize for tidiness. Clothes littered the floor; dirty utensils lay in a corner looking sorry for themselves. A towel had caked on the window bars. But for two tired men, it might have been a grand suite at the Taj Mahal. They spread themselves on chattais on the floor, and within minutes were dead to the world, and certainly to Utpal, whose rhapsodic snores they were too beat to hear.

Utpal proved himself to be a warm-hearted host. At first light he was up, and had put together a meal to the best of his ability for the still-weary travellers.

"Bachelor cooking, bondhu. If I can eat it, so can you. It's not food for an emperor's table, but it's never given me a stomach-ache. Today you folk relax. I'll go out and talk to a couple of people I know," he advised, with a grand air of importance.

Utpal was true to his word. Three days later, he had arranged an interview for Aniruddh with a composer at Ranjit Movietone. "It's just to play the tabla, mind. I know boss, it's music direction you seek. But lafda kya hai, here you do what you get, and later do what you want. It's important first to get a foot into the door. And to earn your dihadi. What?"

"I'm not expecting miracles, Utpal-da," said Aniruddh quietly, amused at his host's odd style of talking Hindi. To one accustomed to the pious Urdu of poets, it sounded most peculiar.

The first step he took into the studio, overwhelmed him with a sense of awe as he walked through, as if he were stepping not through a wicket gate, but a magic door into another world. This was it then; the embryo of fantasy, the cocoon that nurtured the butterfly. The spun silk of stories, touched by the wands of directors, cinematographers, actors, composers. As with the stage, he noticed the aroma so special to a studio; the smell of greasepaint, of brightly-painted props, of excitement that went straight up the nostril like snuff. It was something that he couldn't put into words, a feeling of undisputed grandeur that affected the light boy as much as the leading star.

There was a loud honking outside the gates; an Aston Martin drove in and halted just inside, near the main office complex to the right. A gentleman of about forty stepped out of a door being held politely open by a chauffeur. The sun glinted off his glasses, and his dark face acknowledged the salutations of a couple of extras in monkey costumes. He walked up the stairs to a row of executive offices on the first floor. Although his clothes made him look like your friendly neighbourhood bania, he had an air of confidence, almost haughtiness. A man evidently conscious of his power and position.

"Who was that man, Utpal-da? Seemed like a big shot, nahin?"

"And why should a big shot not look like a big shot? That was Mr. Chandulal Shah, the owner of this studio." His voice lowered. "Rumour goes that he's having a fling with Goharbai, his heroine. Lucky bastard!"

Aniruddh saw all this, and something else besides. He saw how everyone had greeted him, kowtowing and submissive, and he determined that some day people would salute him thus, and he would possess a swanky car like Mr. Chandulal Shahen-Shah.

Jhandey Khan, the composer, recognising his innate skill, employed Aniruddh immediately. He knew the taals; the sixteen count teen-taal, the six-count dadra, the complicated eighteen-count kaherwah. He could play the dholak, the tabla and the pakhawaj, and at just twenty, had experience and style.

For the next four months, Ani played the tabla on the sets, and listened to leading stars struggle to sing. His hands flew like doves on his instruments as he rehearsed with the actors. Songs were recorded on the sets along with the dialogue. Two days ago, his harmonium had been loaded on a 'thela,' and pushed along behind the camera and a microphone for a sequence involving a streetsinger. Often, he expressed to Bankim that, with the discovery of sound, some system could be developed whereby someone else could sing for the actors and they could just move their lips in synchronization. No longer then would they have to stop and re-start if a cow moo-ed, a crow cawked or a car honked to intrude into the sound track. Surely there must be some way to also avoid listening to off-key voices in discordant accents.

That day it was a scene with Goharbai and Billimoria. Aniruddh had still to get attuned to many peculiarities of Bombay, and one of them was this way of addressing women. Whereas up north it was considered a suffix for mujra girls and madams, here Bai was, strangely enough, a form of respect.

During a light change he sat cross-legged, humming to himself, his leg shaking frantically with the beat. Suddenly, he noticed a man beckoning to him. Since he was a perfect stranger, Aniruddh presumed it was someone else he was addressing. He turned around, but saw no one behind him. But when the man continued to stare at him, he was curious. Who, me? his eyes seemed to answer, and the man nodded.

Aniruddh approached him gingerly.

"Hey you, have we met before? I seem to know your face."

Aniruddh smiled in relief. "That is not very likely, sir. I am new to the city and hardly know anyone."

A man sitting alongside him laughed out loud. "When Vimal says he knows you, he probably does. His memory for faces is legendary in the film world."

"Then certainly this time it has failed, for I have just now come from Calcutta, and definitely never met you before," replied Aniruddh, pleased to be making a record of sorts.

"Calcutta... Calcutta, now why does that ring a bell...oh yes, I've got it! Raag-Anuraag! You composed the score for that, didn't you? You sang and took a bow in the end. I knew I couldn't be mistaken." He didn't even wait for Ani to confirm. For Aniruddh, just the mention of the play made him move in separate parts, as the past invaded the present and cut him in two. "Then what is a composer doing playing tabla like an ordinary musician? Arre, Samantbhai, you remember when I went to Calcutta last year for some work with Madan Theatres? I chanced to see this play, and the music was so...so different. I had approached Satyajit Dey to request him to send you to Bombay. Then why did you not approach me?"

Aniruddh related to him what had transpired with Deybabu, and the tragedy as it unravelled in Aniruddh's grave artistic voice touched the two listeners, highlighted by Aniruddh's deeply felt personal pain.

"So, obviously, it must have slipped his mind. Anyway, come and see me tomorrow at the office of Sagar Films, that is, if you are not required here. We are midway through planning our new film, and have not yet chosen our music director. Perhaps the big boss might consider you. Ask for Vimal Kumar. Of course, there is no guarantee. It depends on how you impress him."

Aniruddh understood that here was a statement that could aptly be applied to the world of films. There was no guarantee. It was all a matter of success and failure, and a very thin line ran in between.

"Utpal-da, today I shall accompany you to your studio," announced Aniruddh in a matter-of-fact voice.

"Why, Shriman Aniruddh Krishna, you too want to ogle the fair-fair beauties like Bankimbabu here, eh?"

"Nahin baba, who needs these distractions? I have a career to concentrate on, a future to build. I have been asked to see one Shri Vimal Kumar there."

"And why would one Shri Vimal Kumar, who just happens to be one big Marwari businessman, who just happens to be one big financier gun of the film industry, want with the likes of a modest tabla-player? The face of a film star you do not have. So tell, tell, spill all."

"They want to try my tunes for their new picture."

"Hey hey! Hey hey! Out of the sky such offers do not fall into the laps of newcomers to Bombay. So what's the big secret?"

"No secret, baba. He heard me once in Calcutta. That's all."

"*That's all!* That's all? That's fucking plenty! And if it's true, if you are not spinning one grand tale, then better wear your best clothes. Pant-shirt, you know. Big-big sittings are going on these days. Mr. Nauroji will be there, too, and he likes smartly dressed people. Western-dressed, mind you. In your dhoti-kurta you will look like some stupid village boka."

"But Utpal-da, I am not ashamed of my national dress," protested Aniruddh.

"Perhaps, but Mr. Nauroji likes the Western style, and in Rome, do as the Romans do or get fed to the lions."

"Mr. Nauroji?"

"Now he will ask, who is Mr. Nauroji? And I will answer, he is a prosperous man who made a fortune importing and exhibiting foreign stunt films. He is also financing the film industry. It is said that he is on the Board of Directors of Bombay Talkies, but I am not so sure of that."

"Bombay Talkies? Is this a new studio?"

"Brand new. And most modern. Way out in the suburbs, in Malad. Of course you don't know where that is. That's the new studio that Mithun is joining. Which is why he moved to Goregaon, to be nearer."

"You mean the man who co-scripted Raag-Anuraag with Deybabu? Perhaps he can get me a job there."

"Perhaps he can get me a job there? He hasn't been able to get *me* a job there. Who are you? Aniruddhbabu, do not forget your status. You and I are part of a large floating population called 'strugglers'. Bujhle? The road for us, Moshai, is paved with rough stones, not gold."

Aniruddh hung down his head, feeling adequately admonished. The moon's proper place was in the sky, he thought.

Utpal saw his eyes lower, and continued as if the interlude had not occurred.

"Now, what was I telling you? See, always you interrupt. Ah, Himangshu Rai. Himangshu Rai, who studied filmmaking with the Germans, runs it like a corporate office. It opened last year, with its own cutting, editing and rehearsal rooms all in one compound. This makes work easier for poor assistants like me instead of running here and there. But where will I get work in such a studio, tell me? And here is this new boy, having appointments with big big people. Lucky bastard."

Utpal directed him up to the first floor to the executive offices, pointing to the polished door of the committee room where the bigwigs sat in conference. "And be careful with Nauroji. Mr. Nauroji, is, how you say it, a sharp cook." Cookie, thought Aniruddh, but didn't interrupt Utpal-da. "Can't mistake the door, boss. One mile away you can smell the stink of that infernal pipe he smokes. Anyway, best of luck," he said good-humouredly.

Aniruddh knocked timorously, an almost inaudible sound like a discreet cough, and was bidden entry. The overwhelming smell of tobacco was thick like English blankets in the room. Aniruddh gazed around with apprehension. Had his desire for achievement not been so powerful, his fears would have made him turn on his heels and scramble. Three men sat around a desk covered with papers and teacup stains. Vimal Kumar he recognised at once, looking brisk and affluent in his sharkskin trousers and diamond cufflinks. The pipe that he caressed from time to time like a woman's body identified Mr. Nauroji, who resembled a sophisticated gangster, with his smart Saville Row business suit and gelled hair. A monocle held by a silken black cord was affixed over an eye that glistened like a new knife. His ruddy complexion glowed with finance, and over the rim of his pipe bowl he glared at Aniruddh with a mean and snobbish look.

Before he could open his mouth, Vimal Kumar spoke up. "Ah, here he is. The boy from Calcutta I spoke to you about." Of course, he didn't feel the necessity to introduce the third person to a poor little hopeful like Aniruddh.

"Does he have any experience, or training at all? He looks much too young," said the Third Man. Nauroji grunted like a hungry bear.

"Since you've recommended him, Vimal, we'll hear him out," Mr. Nauroji remarked, as if doing Vimal a jolly big favour. But the look of appraisal he gave Aniruddh very clearly indicated that he considered this short, dusky lad completely without potential.

Without any waste of time, the Third Man came straight to the point.

"Our next film is a mythological," he said, a shade more kindly. Mythologicals rang in the cash returns. "So sing us a bhajan that you've composed personally."

Aniruddh cleared his throat, and began to sing, whilst Mr. Nauroji made a great fuss with his pipe cleaner. When Aniruddh had finished, the three men looked at each other. Nauroji stuffed his pipe between his clenched teeth and drew a great puff, as though making some kind of valid statement.

"So, what did Mr. Nauroji have to say?" enquired Utpal-da solicitously, at dinner.

Nothing." replied Aniruddh, never a one for untruths.

Seeing Aniruddh's crestfallen face, Utpal-da launched into a massive morale-lifting effort.

"Never mind. There are other avenues. Pass the fish. Besides, the news that I have to give you is so stupendous, so stupendous, it'll knock you out of your fucking wits."

"So, tell us. As the Urdu poets say, My goblet of patience is spilling over," said Ani.

"First pass me the rice dish. Goodness, how I survived before you guys came. That shit I cooked for myself was only fit for the toilets. Ani, you make a decent macher jhol; if we're ever out of work, we'll open a bloody restaurant."

"Utpal-da, stop dallying. What is this news?"

"In a moment, brother, in a moment. Where is the rush? You are here and I am here, is it not? What good is it if a man eats a satisfactory meal, and doesn't burp, for God's sake?."

"Utpal-da, why didn't you ever marry, if you're so hopeless with the domestic angle?"

'See, see? What poor memory this poor boy has? Good thing you are not wanting to become an actor; you will never remember your lines. Did I not tell you about our great tribe of strugglers? Strugglers, bondhu, can't support wives."

"What about us? You supported *us* in the beginning." "Yes, but for how many days? One? Two? Wives you have to support for a lifetime. No wife when in strife. Besides, you are my statesmen." "Statesmen? But Utpal-da, we're not in ruling or administration." "Always arguing, Aniruddh, always arguing. Aren't you from my state? That makes you my statesman. See, made me forget what I was telling you. Then you will accuse me of dalliances." Dilly-dallying, guessed Ani, but knew better than to open his mouth before Utpal-da's generous nature.

"You were telling us about something fantastic?"

Utpal rose, emitting a great sound from within his stomach that might have been a belch from the neighbourhood mill chimney. Leisurely he washed his hands, making a big Pontius Pilate production of the act. Aniruddh shook his leg with vigorous impatience. Seeing their restiveness, Utpal embarked on a hyphenated Sohrab Modi laugh that reverberated in the tiny room, lending his announcement shades of drama. "Ani, oori baba, Ani! You are a man of vision indeed. You always said didn't you, that we should have a parallel system of singing? Well, we've done it! We have cracked the bloody technique of recording a song *outside* the studio. New Theatres has made an epic-making breakthrough! Or is it epoch-making? Whatever, this is history, bondhu, musical history. "

Aniruddh stared at him incredulously. "Shothi? Has it really happened?"

"It's absolutely true. It's the buzz of the studios. The name of the film is BHAGYACHAKRA. According to its director Nitin Bose, it might possibly be the very first experiment of its kind in the world! And that is not all the news I have to give you. Tomorrow we go to see a producer from Kolhapur, who is planning to shift into the Hindi stream. Now tell me, does this not deserve celebration?" "Very definitely. Which is why we have already brought some 'Kalajaam."

Utpal regarded the two sharply. "Acchha, you already knew about this, hein? Saala,wanting to make a fool of your Dada?"

"No no, Utpal-da, far be it that we should steal your thunder," replied Bankim." But Ani has got the job."

"What? Now you are stealing my lightning also. You mean at Sagar? Why didn't you tell me before, you son-of-an-owl? Looking so dejected as if it were the end of the world? Face hanging down between your balls!"

"That was just pulling your leg."

"Now you are beginning to trick your elders? Mai ri, is it all pucca? Contract and all? Did you sign.."

"On the dotted line. In block letters. I still have to develop a signature, you see."

"You bloody horse's tail! You are..."

"I know."

"What?"

"A lucky bastard."

The Maharashtra Film Company had been established by Baburao Painter, and was financed largely by the Maharajah of Kolhapur. It made mainly mythologicals, and had an edge over the other studios in that it was more organised. Bengal was heavy on literature and romance, having readymade stories in the works of Saratchandra and Tagore. But in the west there was more emphasis on historicals and mythologicals, and several versions of the Ramayan had already been made.

All this Utpal-da explained to Aniruddh as they rode in the tram for their interview. "See, Hindi films have a larger audience, and so they want to switch. But Shantaram, Fatehlal and Damle are doing excellent work in Marathi. Their films are very popular and technically superior. But naturally, they want to reach more people. Larger audiences mean larger gains. Simple mathematics. And speaking of mathematics, let me do all the talking. They've signed you for horseshit at Sagar."

"Naturally, Utpal-da, they're giving me a break; I was hardly in a position to bargain."

"Positions are not there, Ani, they have to be made. And sometimes they are made by pretence. So, just act. Act knowledgeable. Act pricey. Act *established.* Don't fall into their laps like a ripe strawberry."

"You mean plum."

" See what I mean? Don't show off your high education to me. Show it to those sons-of-donkeys."

"Yes, Utpal-da. Whatever you say."

At the hotel they were informed that the producer had had to leave for Poona suddenly, but that his production manager would have a preliminary meeting with them. In the room they were greeted by a man in dhoti and black overcoat, a white turban stretched tightly across his wide forehead. Off-white sandal paste marks encrusting his forehead like a dry snakebite displayed his religious bent and augured well for the mythologicals. Thick, dark moustaches added to the impression of a provincial army subehdar. Aniruddh imagined him issuing stern orders in the court of Shivaji. It appeared that Atmaram Joglekar was deeply afflicted with permanently blocked sinuses for, time and again, he would snort noisily like a frisky thoroughbred before a race.

"Well, well, well," he remarked, twirling his hirsute adornment with a flourish. "So you're the lad who's signed Sagar's new film."

"So I am," replied Ani, calling upon his acting experience at Kalamahal to pose as a confident maestro. "I believe you wish to discuss the music direction of your proposed film with me."

"So we do, so we do. Adventure story. You know, brave deeds, horse chase sequences, helpless heroines, that thing. Slipping in patriotism. Want strong, operatic music. You did theatre work in Bengal?"

"So I did, so I did," replied Ani, in Atmaram's style of duplicated speech.

"Of course, we have many artists who have done impressive theatre work in Maharashtra, but you have been recommended. You can handle this? Are you not too young? And are you conversant with the Hindi language?" He snorted.

"No problem. He knows Urdu like he knows Bengali," put in Utpal-da swiftly, acting the wheeler-dealer to perfection. "And a big studio like you can have no trouble paying his salary, three hundred rupees, plus all expenses when he comes to Kolhapur for story sessions, etc."

Atmaram-bhau went into a rhino-snort of great astonishment. "Three hundred? Daylight robbery! Even big heroes get paid only five hundred rupees. What newcomer gets this kind of money? A hundred and fifty."

"He is no ordinary newcomer, Bhau. He is a big name in Bengal. Already he is being talked about in the circles as a man of unique talent. We have got feelers from Bombay Talkies for a big contract, a long-term contract. And once he signs that, he is their man. Even if he does just one film with them, his price will go up. Don't go by his appearance. You know that geniuses come in small packages."

"Bombay Talkies? New-fangled studio in Malad? Rubbish!"He rolled his 'R' in emphasis. "Himanshu Rai works with foreign technicians. Why he should take comparative newcomer?" Snort.

Ani was thankful Utpal had engaged Atmaram in direct conversation, because his jaw fell open. What the hell was Utpal talking about? He was about to interrupt with a remark of pathetic honesty, when Atmaram, with an agitated twirl of his moustaches, continued. "Three hundred I am not authorised to clear. Himanshu Rai! Bombay Talkies! Hah! Kai Tari Sangto."

Utpal-da then played his next hand. "Look, Bhau, if you really want to do business, then perhaps we may settle for twenty-thirty less. He is not greedy; he wants to do good work. Quality work. And you are quality-conscious people, no?"

"That we are, that we are. Will talk to my superiors first. Then contact you at Sagar. You are not on permanent contract with Sagar, Aniruddh?"

"As yet the contract is for one picture. But if they are pleased they may put him on their permanent payroll. That is, if he does not accept the Bombay Talkies offer first," Utpal answered.

"Utpalbabu, why you not let Mr. Aniruddh talk for himself? You are his manager or what?"

'No, Atmarambhau. I am his friend."

A week later Utpal got a message that they would be agreeable if Aniruddh would nod for two hundred rupees a month. Aniruddh nodded.

"Ani wants us to go to Bombay. He writes that he's already rented a comfortable house with a hall and two bedrooms in a good area called Shivaji Park," read Konkona proudly from her son's letter.

Pranoy's reaction was edged with irritation. "But Ma, we're settled here as far as work is concerned. You know that Paro has even sung for this playback thing. And we can't always live on Ani's bounty, on Ani's whims. We have our own identity," replied Pranoy, chafed at this constant thing about going to Bombay.

"That's exactly it, Pranoybabu. It seems you are quite known there for your flute-playing. Many have heard your gramophone record. He has offers for you too, for playing the flute in some films about Lord Krishna," she twinkled. "Besides, this playback singing has attracted many more people to the industry, he says. There is a whole secondary industry coming up of singers, musicians, recordists, lyric-writers and composers. There is so much work, and now is the right time to cash in on it. Otherwise, other inexperienced people will step in and it might be too late."

"So? With all due respects, Ma, I have a niche here, I can even claim some fame. I have a family. Ani has no responsibility; he can chase after rainbows."

"At least I must go then. For I, too, cannot always live on your bounty, and these money orders do not necessarily come in time."

Paro's quiet, non-interfering self became articulate.

"Ma is right. We are one family, and we have pledged to be together. After all, Ani has gone through so much, the scar-tissue will not heal so soon. He is alone there; he will need us."

"Alright Ma, I will think about it," said Pranoy, with a great effort at calmness. Konkona regarded him with bothered eyes. "I promise," he added.

It was eventually Moon-moon's refrain about her AnuMama, sweet-voiced little Moon-Moon with the dimpled chin whom he could refuse nothing, that finally tilted the balance. Finding himself hopelessly outnumbered in the vote count, Pranoy was prevailed upon to finally sigh and agree. He asked Runu if he would hold the fort in Calcutta. "Just in case we are forced to come back," he added sceptically.

"Do not be concerned. We will take care of everything. We will look after your house as if *it were our very own*," answered the new female entrant into their family.

Like a flashing Cyclop eye the train's beam slashed the station, and came to a halt with an asthmatic wheeze, exhaling a great cloud of steam.

"You look to the right, and I'll search the other side," said Ani to Utpal, who made off immediately in the opposite direction. Almost towards the end of the platform he espied the waiting group. They made a neat family portrait, ready, steady, click. A middle-aged woman with a mien of such serenity that it broke your heart; her more youthful duplicate with the aura of a cool summer moon; a straddling tall man who had the body of a wrestler, a sober lad aged eleven, and a cherubic dimpled four-year-old girl with the most delicious smile. His face crinkled with welcoming pleasure.

"You must be Ani's mother. Pranaam," declared Utpal, and dived straight for her feet. Konkona patted his head in the customary reciprocation. She stared into the face of this cheerful young man, whose thinning scalp hair seemed to be fiercely compensated by the obdurate stubble on his cheeks. Yet his rough edges did not lack warmth.

"Bless you, son. Was Ani too busy to come?"

"Busy? Ki bolchen? Baba, he would have given six months salary to be here, Ma. He's somewhere down the platform. Your son could not be distinguished in a bunch of dwarfs, let alone an infernal crowd like this. Ah, here he comes, the little big man."

With a great amount of fuss, Utpal began to gather the pieces of baggage together, allowing Ani and his family a sentimental reunion. Little Moon-moon squealed with delight at beholding her Maama, and Pranoy, looking every inch the Babumoshai in his sedate dhoti and kurta, greeted him with sobriety. Shubir had not grown much taller, and it seemed that both brothers were destined to remain short and dark. Paro resembled their mother more and more. She had the same cool surfaces. "Ma, this is Utpal, without whom I would still be walking the streets in the day and sleeping on some post office verandah at night."

"Oh yes, Ani wrote about you. You have been like a messiah to my son. How shall we ever repay you?" Her smile was beatific.

"By feeding me with proper home-cooked fish till I grow fins. Although your son is not half so bad. He cooks some decent prawns and pumpkin, and a satisfactory dohi-maach. And as far as gratitude is concerned, forget it. We are all instruments of karma. Perhaps I had to repay something which your son did for me in his last life."

"Where's Runu? Has he not come with you?" Ani asked.

An embarassed silence seemed to grow around them.

Finally Pranoy cleared his throat and said. "He had to stay back. After all, the house has to be looked after, at least, till you decide what to do with it."

Ani was satisfied with that explanation.

At the house, a pock-marked man with almost circular eyes was waiting for them on the porch.

"It is the manager from Sunny Cinetone, where we had that meeting last week." said Utpal. He, Ani and the visitor went into a quick huddle as Pranoy ported the baggage into the house.

Within five minutes, he had departed, having obviously delivered a brief and brisk message. As he left, Utpal broke into his characteristic chuckle, which, in this sober and restrained company seemed as out of place as a tango in a convent.

"Aaha. Your footstep into this house is indeed auspicious, Mother. We shall lunch in a hurry, as important men do, and take off immediately to negotiate a very significant contract. Your son shall be bound to this important studio for three years, and be paid the sum of three hundred rupees a month as salary, or I'm a dhobi's ass. Come on, my friend, we have work to do. Keep your pen ready, and practise your signature on the way. Wah! Wah, wah!" His exclamation was worthy of a veteran stage actor.

The others adequately gasped. It was not everyday that one was offered a fortune. Konkona regarded this newly acquired son with a generous dose of indulgence. Obviously his colourful temperament was going to fill their house with brightness.

"Bombay's going to be our home now, isn't it, Ma?" asked Shubir.

Wisdom flows from the mouths of children, thought Konkona.

It was on the day that Utpal took Pranoy and Paro to enroll Moonmoon in a nearby school that Konkona spoke to Aniruddh about Runu.

"You have to hear me out with patience, Ani." she began. "Runu has got married."'

Aniruddh almost choked with shock. "That's impossible. Runu would *never* get married without me. Why is everyone determined to marry without my presence?"

"It had to be done in a hurry."

"Why? What was the urgency? And who did he marry?" asked Ani, warily.

"He had to marry Bela."

"What do you mean *had to?* Not that he would have complained. He was fond of her, that I know."

Konkona found it awkward to have to speak of such matters, but he had to be told, and Pranoy had stated emphatically that he wanted nothing whatsoever to do with this sordid tale.

"She was… with child. He had wanted to write to you, but I advised him that it was wiser to wait and tell you personally. You with your hot blood, you might have reacted and done something foolish."

"You don't mean..". Ani was sharp enough to get the connection. She had been flirting with Bankim at the time they left, against Kalamahal's principles.

"Bankim! That rascal! That abominable, cowardly…. I'm going to break his legs. Thank goodness I'm not sharing a room with him now." Black images danced before his eyes and his murderous expression terrified Konkona.

"He knows nothing about this, Ani. She only found out after the two of you had left. With her constant sickness, she had become too weak to travel to Bombay, and even then she was not convinced he would do the honest thing by her. She almost went to one of those quack women in Bada Bazaar to get rid of the baby. Anyway, who are we to judge people or question the ways of the gods? The fact is that he saved the honour of the woman he loved. He had always felt that Bela with her bubbly nature would consider him too boring. Now he thinks of it as a reward for his devotion. Treats them both as though they were made of glass. Finally, a lonely orphan has found his own family."

Aniruddh's anger dissipated in front of her calm and careful reasoning.

"Well, if you say that he's happy… He always had a soft spot for her. Runu would himself have quoted Shakespeare who said that all's well that ends well."

"Who is this Sheshappa Aiyyar?"

"Just someone I'm fond of."

Aniruddh smiled softly. Dear, sweet Ma. She was not very educated, but she was so wise. And as always, she had been right.

Ismail 'Sunny' Choonawala was not the kind of person you would have expected to be heading a major studio. He would have been more at home in a stock exchange screaming madly down a telephone line, calculating wildly about commodities and shares. First-born son of a highly successful third generation trader family who had moved to South Africa, he had early figured the tremendous commercial value of making films if handled with the correct financial attitude. So, carting a considerable amount of capital from his hometown, he had moved to Bombay, investing in a concern that would make films in a not very expensive way, thus retrieving considerable gains. Eponymously, he 'lagaoed choona' wherever it benefited him, and went about recruiting new talent which would work cheaply and deliver value for money. He was ruthlessly frank about the fact that he was in the business, not for his invisible interest in the fine arts, but to make money.

"Welcome aboard the ship," he said to Aniruddh, the day the latter joined up. "I want you to meet Imtiaz Ali Khan, your First Mate, as it were. I have brought him down especially from Lahore to direct our new film. So, you two men chat and get to know one another, since you'll be working together."

Aniruddh politely regarded the other man, a dreamy fellow just a couple of years older. He had a picaresque air about him, a kind of roguish politeness like a good-hearted buccaneer. You couldn't have called him handsome, but his face glowed with intensity. His features could be generally classified as broad. A broad forehead, broadly spaced eyes that looked at you with unabashed curiosity, and a broad, stocky frame on which hung surprisingly well-formed muscles. In short, an intellectual's face on an athlete's body. But then his smile broke, crinkling his eyes with warmth. And Aniruddh took to him at once. Accustomed to the cheery communication of Bengali neighbours, he had been disheartened by the phlegmatic attitude of the mill workers in Utpal's chawl. But his intuition prompted him that here, perhaps, he might find a close friend and associate. Imtiaz, too, instinctively liked this new composer with the wavy hair and the reputation for talent. Ismail, watching carefully, noticed this exchange with immense satisfaction. Good vibes between his crew always meant good work. Good work hopefully meant the happy plus sign in the cash book.

Imtiaz suggested they could go down to the studio canteen to discuss the story. "Good idea," corroborated Ani, "it's time for tea anyway."

As the duo walked out of the office into the waiting room beyond, Aniruddh stopped dead in his tracks. It was as if he had been suddenly punched in the guts with a heavy hand. He felt his heart trip. For, sitting on the leather sofa, her graceful fingers delicately gripping her crossed legs, was the most beautiful woman he had ever seen. The effect remained with him for long afterwards, making him rather breathless.

In the café, Imtiaz looked him squarely in the eyes and said, "Gorgeous, isn't she? She has this effect on people," he winked. "B-Grade, mostly. Which is why you never recognised her. Though she plays the second lead in his current venture, Sunny-saab wants to sign her as heroine for our picture. Her name is Priyanandini, and she has the most captivating eyes in the industry."

Dil se teri nigaah jigar tak.

Meherunissa

LEADING LADIES

She finished her matriculation exams on a balmy December day. Trudging behind Shamim, her older-by-two years brother, Meherunissa smiled back at the friendly sun. Scattered wisps of candy floss clouds dotted the postcard-blue sky. Relieved at the completion of this scholastic phase, she was determined not to pursue her studies even if her mother insisted on her going to college. No more books and midnight oil, or essays on Journeys by Train or Autobiographies of a Suitcase. She would not tax her mother further, she decided, as she walked towards their one-room residence in Byculla.

Depression and dire existence hung like cobwebs over the doors of this Central Bombay district. Weary faces of a daily grind appeared behind window-bars. Yet Meherunissa's spirits were buoyant. Her feet, though encased in soles stretched well beyond their limits, tripped along without a care. Her skirt was a couple of inches short of orthodox Muslim requirements. But knowing the tough struggle Rehmatbi had undergone to send her to a convent school, she had not insisted on the expense of a new uniform. She considered herself fortunate just to have received a proper education, that too, in times when it was highly unnecessary for daughters from poor homes to be educated at all. Especially for this one, the neighbours whispered, with those grey-green eyes, devastating dimples and divine complexion unfettered by veils or virtue of coyness. The thick volume of curly hair and that sashay as she walked down the mohallah were enough to make a saint blaspheme. Any 'pirs' amongst her ancestors had better be praying for her salvation.

But Meherunissa had no care for neighbourly disparagement. She tolerated their resentment as sure as she understood that the combined beauty of her elder sister Kulsum and herself was not just their envy, but also ambivalently, their pride. Ever since she had attained marriageable age, her sister Kulsum with the droopy eyes and the skin like a summer dawn, had been inundated with matrimonial offers from the Khoja community. Most of these were from wealthy Kutchi business families whose desire to showcase a good-looking daughter-in-law quite overlooked her financial status. Strangely enough they were all from widowers or men who had said 'talaq, talaq, talaq' to former wives. Her mother had seriously been considering the proposal of a middle-aged property owner, a widower with two children. Who knew whether a younger but poorer man would make her happy? At least it was certain that a wealthy man would keep her in comfort. So within a few days, the terms of the marriage would be finalised.

Mehrunissa hoped it would happen soon. For she had a secret. Savouring it was a delicious taste, like a foreign chocolate or forbidden fruit. Her mind went back to last week's conversation with her best friend Sarojini, her daydreams wrapping themselves around her warmly like an equatorial belt. Yet rationally, she knew that the fruition of the idea had as much possibility as India becoming independent next week.

If only Mithima would agree. There was a flood of If Onlys ready to drown her dreams. Once Kulsum is married I'll broach the subject to my mother. The relief of feeding one less mouth might make her more receptive to the idea, which otherwise, would definitely be buried under the debris of her volcanic ire.

Saro had entered the class in high-voltage that day. Beckoning her into a corner, she had said conspiratorially, "Mehru, can you promise to keep a secret?"

"Aichi Shapath," confirmed Mehru in Saro's Marathi, holding a fold of her neck between forefinger and thumb.

"I've been offered to act in a picture."

"What? Do you mean like Sulochana and Zubeida and that Ayodhyacha Raja heroine Durga Khote..."yelled Mehru, excitement getting the better of discretion.

"Sshhh. Do you want the whole school to hear or what?"

"Does it matter? In a week's time we're going to be out of this place. So, are you going to accept or not?"

"Keep your voice down, Mehru. If the nuns get a whiff of this, they'll think I'm wicked."

"Rubbish, dearie," exclaimed Mehru, borrowing Sr. Mary Matthews' favourite address. The sisters are too busy with exam papers to bother."

"That's true."

"But tell na, really. Migosh, my best friend an actress!"

"No, yaar. When this producer, who stays down my street, approached my father, Baba said he'd rather die than see a decent Saraswat Brahmin girl become an actress."

"Ohhh!"

"Not so bad if you hear what I have to say next. I told this producer that I have the most beautiful friend. So if not me, would he give her a chance?"

"Really? And who is this friend?" enquired a little-bit-jealous Mehru .

"It's you, stupid."

"Me? Are you crazy or what? Your Baba and my mother are made of the same stuff. Na re na, I can't even think of it. Next thing, I'll be under house arrest."

"Don't just dismiss it, Mehru. At the most your mother will say no. Have you any idea how much an actress earns?"

"No. How much?"

"A fortune! Something like four-five hundred rupees a month. And Ruby Meyers, she is contracted for as much as Rs. 3000 per picture, or so I've heard from my uncle who runs a photo studio where she shoots her stills."

"So much?" Mehru's beautiful eyes opened wide. "But Saro, I don't know anything about acting."

"And you think I'm Greta Garbo? The director will show you how to act, silly. You have to just imitate him."

"But am I pretty enough? And I don't have thin-thin eyebrows like them."

"Now don't dig for compliments, haan."

For the rest of the week Mehru floated on a magic rug of possibilities, banking up a great heap of hopes.

The stink hit her nostrils as she entered her lane. The drain that ran one side of the narrow alleyway was a frothy off-white, proof of the recent washing at the community tap. She sidestepped a banana skin, almost walking over a little boy happily defecating into the drain. Aquamarine flies buzzed around his tiny arse, loaning a bizarre sense of colour to the tan and ochre.

Stooping through the low doorway, she entered the modest room to find her mother squatting on her haunches in front of the earthen 'choolah', patting bhakris made of bajra with amazing speed between her calloused hands. Clothes were strewn all over the room like Kamatipura whores, asking to be picked up. With a great sigh of relief, Mehru flung her books onto the single charpoy.

Rehmatbi lifted her eyes from her tawa for a reprimanding moment. "Don't throw your books like that," she snapped. "You know how much they cost? If they tear, you won't get any value from their second-hand sale. Then they'll only be fit for the kabadiwallahs who under-weigh and undervalue everything. How did your paper go? Here, sit and eat whilst the rotis are hot. Shamim, any luck with the job-hunting today?"

"No, Mithi-maa. I spent my last anna in the tram, as I was getting late to pick up Mehru from the centre."

"Wah! What luxury! And are your legs so weak and your age so advanced that you can't walk some distance? Back in Bhuj we walked several miles a day without complaining, and now my son will waste money on riding in modern vehicles like tram-vram?"

Shamim pretended to look shame-faced at this matriarchal outburst.

Rehmatbi concentrated hard on eating her brinjal-and-potato vegetable, brow creased in exasperation. The foolish boy had spent their last anna, her elder son Esa was not due back from his job as salesman in a crockery shop till late. She would have to borrow from the neighbours to prepare the evening meal. Her second son Suleiman was probably playing gooli-danda in the back alley with other unemployed twenty-year-olds, or working the buses picking pockets. What a life! She had lost her lissome beauty bearing these children, been widowed early when her husband died leaving her with no savings from his job as a grave-tender and five small children to raise. Moving to Bombay from her native Cutch when Mehru, the youngest, was still an infant, she had trained on the job at the local maternity hospital. Her breasts still abundantly flowing with milk, she had doubled as midwife and wet nurse for high society women. With their frilly British nighties and fancy underwear and their paranoia about sagging breasts, those delicate specimens would hand over their bawling infants to her to suckle. Night after night she had shushed babies to sleep with lullabies and a tug at her nipples. Her skin had faded, her once-green eyes dulled to a metallic grey, her hair become thin and lax. She had educated Esa in a madrissa, and put Shamim and Mehru through school. Kulsum, at a tender age had had to take care of the house and the smaller children. Esa, her first-born, had grown up to be a sober lad, spending his leisure times in prayer and piety. He said namaaz daily and kept rozas like a devout Muslim.

But her middle son Suleiman, an unbridled horse, had not allowed himself to be reined in. Just as Suleiman distressed her, Shamim disappointed her. With his head full of dreams about these new-fangled moving pictures that corrupted the pious, he demonstrated no inclination to learn any trade. Brightness in her life came from her two beautiful daughters; Kulsum with the colour of fresh roses in her cheeks and the darkness of magrib in her eyes, and Meherunissa with shining teeth like chandelier crystals and matching tinkling laughter. Kulsum's beauty and talents in the kitchen would fetch a good bride price, she thought, spreading her mat for an afternoon nap. It was night duty at the hospital again. It would be a big relief once these two girls were settled. As for the boys; Esa, thirty in another two years, would have to marry soon. Allah knew what sort of wife he would take, but she would then have to stop expecting him to bring his entire money home.

Once the girls are married, she sighed, I shall go for Haj. As for these boys, Allah Maalik.

It was a week after the wedding. The quawalli singers, had finished at dawn with a superb 'naath' that had many going into a religious frenzy. The Kadri family was thankful to the bridegroom who had paid for their services. The ceremonies over, Shaukat Hussein had taken his bride Kulsum to his large house in Sewri. The alliance of a wealthy widower with a girl from a poor family is always a convenient adjustment. Not only is the bride a good and frugal housekeeper, but, in return for certain comforts, she willingly takes care of her stepchildren.

Rehmatbi had however, during the rites noticed the lustful stares of the mohallah men towards her Mehru who had looked most fetching in an emerald green sharara. Only when Mehru was dispatched to her in-laws' home would she allow herself to relax.

Unmindful of her mother's thoughts, Mehru had restless ones of her own. How to tell her mother, and when? A week had gone by and she hadn't had the courage to ask. Saro had told her yesterday that the producer had liked her photograph immensely, but would not wait forever.

Finally, she decided the best time was just before her mother left for work. If she didn't approve, there would not be much time for theatrics and hopefully, by the time she returned in the morning her anger would have abated. And if the night was peaceful, with no emergencies or deliveries or bawling brats, who knows she might even have a positive response.

When Rehmatbi took her odhni off the hook before leaving, Meherunissa said in a subdued voice, "Mithi-maa, can I talk to you?"

"Daughter, you have a bad sense of timing, Can you not see I am leaving for the hospital? I'm late already, and I have at least a fifteen-minute walk."

"It'll only take two minutes."

"Out of which you will spend one fidgeting and whimpering. Come on, say it quickly."

"Mithi-maa, I've been offered a job."

"What job-vob? Why should a girl with three burly brothers have to work at all? I'll soon get you married into a good family like your sister."

"It's not a permanent kind of job, Mithi-Ma."

Rehmatbi fixed her daughter with a look so stern that the poor girl's heart began to palpitate. She was convinced that if her mother had lived in the time of Clive, a different history would have been written for India.

"And what kind of a job would that be?" she asked, voice heavy with iron.

"It's not what you think," retorted Mehru hastily. "It's an offer to act in a talkie."

Rehamatbi paused heavily before replying. In those few seconds Meherunissa wished some Fairy godmother would whisk her away to the North Pole, or somewhere equally inaccessible.

"And what makes you think that there's any difference between what you're saying and what I'm thinking?"

"But Mithima, I could do well and become famous like..". It was pointless making a comparison. Mithima would never have heard of Durga Khote.

"And they pay well, too. When I finish the work I may earn a thousand rupees! Mithimaa, we can eat mutton daily and not extend our hand before our neighbours.? And you can take a tonga to work; why, you could even give it up altogether if I succeed...."

Rehmatbi lifted a hand for silence.

" Enough! It's bad that Shamim is inflicted; now he's given you this sickness too. Do you know what evil lies in this line of work? No decent girl goes around flaunting herself in so immodest a manner. Where did I go wrong in bringing you up that you should even think of such a thing!"

"But Mithimaa.."

"No buts! Even talking about these moving pictures is a sin. Besides, your two minutes are over."

She walked through the door and down the lane without a backward glance, leaving Mehru's tremulous hopes in shambles.

Five minutes later, Shamim walked in looking mighty perplexed.

"What happened to the old lady? Didn't answer my greeting. Just carried on muttering as if she hadn't seen me at all."

Mehru turned away to hide the tears stinging her eyelids.

"It wasn't anything," she murmured.

"It has to be something. Either the bloody British have raised the price of sugar again, or Suleimanbhai has been locked into a remand home, or perhaps some lafanga tried to be smart with you. By God, I'll break his neck; just tell me the motherfucker's name."

He twisted her round to face him, and was surprised by the glisten in her eyes.

"It's nothing of that sort. I got this offer to act in a picture, and Mithimaa refused. She wouldn't even consider the economics."

" Lo, sun lo baat. Here, I'm desperate to get into the line, and my little sister gets an offer on a platter. Who is this by, anyway?" "Some neighbour of Saro's.. But I can't defy Mithima."

"The question is, do *you* want it?"

"More than anything else."

" Then we'll just have to convince her, won't we? Think of it, Mehru, a better place to live, like Chembur, perhaps, and one of those foreign motorgaadis, fame and fortune. Now do make me a cup of tea; when you're a famous actress, I can boast that you once used to fetch my chai."

"Don't count your chickens, Shamimbhai. It's not going to be easy to persuade her. Now, if you want tea, go borrow milk from the neighbours."

Shamim rolled his eyes in mock disgust, and went out the door. His desperate efforts to put his toe into the doorway of the film industry had just received an extremely unexpected boost. He gazed back and saw Mehru framed in the window. Such a symbolic shot, he thought; Mehru looking out at a new life that awaits her beyond the end of the lane, beyond its squalor and its un-toilet-trained children.

As darkness progressed over the comparative quiet of the children's ward, Rehmatbi stole a few moments of introspective reflection. She was still seething with Mehru's outrageous request. The daughter of the pious bhagat who had tended a pir's durgah, paint herself like a common whore, and sing and dance like a mujrewali? For shame! She had heard some films went to the extent of showing kissing; Khuda khair kare, these actresses were no better than sophisticated prostitutes! Mehru had been educated so that she could take her place in some decent family, where her virtues and her learning would earn her respect. She turned her side to face the wall. A thousand rupees, she had said; how much was so much money, an unseen, unimagined amount? She barely earned fifty or sixty rupees, if you counted the tips. Four grown children to feed, and her sons good-for-nothing!

Her bones felt weary. Maybe I should consider the advantages, she pondered. It had been an uphill struggle most of the time; going hungry to bed, pretending she'd eaten at the hospital, so her children could sleep with full stomachs; wearing hand-me-downs of wealthy patients. And what if she was depriving her favourite child of fame and luxuries, which she perhaps, deserved?

The confusion exhausted her mentally. Maybe I'll think about it tomorrow. Kulsum's wedding was so exhausting. Yes, tomorrow.

She dozed.

Morning smoke was rising from the mohallah hovels as Rehmatbi shuffled her way home. Of late, her breathing had become slightly laboured; often at nights she woke with a feeling of suffocation. She prayed fervently the dirt and smoke of the chawl had not given her some dreadful disease like tuberculosis. She could not afford treatment at a sanatorium. But she would speak to Dr. Habib at the hospital. At least, medication there would be free.

Only Shamim was at home.

"Where is your sister?"

"Gone to Saro's. Some boy is coming to see her, so she was asked to come and help."

"Your sister should have so much sense as her friend, instead of this actress-vactress dreams. Make your house, have children, but no; she wants to earn a bad name and ruin chances of a good marriage."

"What, Mithimaa, this old-fashioned talk I do not expect from my bold mother. Good girls from high-caste families are also going into this line now. It's a job like any other. After all, you work in a hospital where there are men too—doctors, wardboys. If Mehru joins films, it will just be another field. That work is harder; stand in front of harsh electric lights, or in the glaring sun, repeat the same scenes over and over again. But you are entertaining millions, making so many happy."

"Prostitution I call it---entertaining them and making them happy. Ah, there you are Suleiman," as her middle son stepped into the room, chewing a neem stick with sadistic glee. "And where has my dear son been breaking his bones earning his daily bread?" Suleiman, his hawkish nose gleaming, beady eyes shining shamelessly, laughed a villainous laugh. " You two are a pair; get off your butts and find work today, or I shall put a fistful of chillies in your backsides to speed you up!"

Suleiman's ruffian hair bristled. He nuzzled his mother's cheek with a bark-like chin, rough with a two-day stubble. "Mithimaa, give me one rupee, and I'll be off to look for kaam-dhandha."

"I will give you one kick. Did Esa eat something before going to work?"

Nobody cared to answer.

Rehmatbi rested her head on her frustrations, and sighed.

"Breathe deeply," Dr. Habib instructed.

Rehmatbi inhaled. With a frown of concentration, the good doctor detected the wheeze in her chest.

"It's a touch of asthma," was his diagnosis. "You will have to take it easy now, Rehmatbi. Short working hours, no night shifts, some breathing exercises, and daily steam inhalations. As you know, no cure exists. Only care. So, nothing cold, no fried delicacies or heavy sweetmeats." He wagged a finger in warning. "Forget your halwas and samosas and you'll be fine. Here, give this prescription to the compounder. And I'll re-arrange your working hours."

Halwa, thought Rehmatbi, as she shuffled her way to the dispensary. Who eats that stuff anyway? And samosas, nicely filled with mince, are a luxury only during Ramzan or wedding banquets. No night shifts, less working hours meant less money.

A basket of fruit greeted her when she arrived home; big, juicy tangerines, a healthy watermelon and a dozen full-bodied bananas. Beside it, on the little table, was the delectable sight of rich-orange Karachi halwa. Dr. Habib's warning lurched in her vision. She turned away. Ya Parvar Digar, Suleiman had looted a hotel!

The culprit in question was reclining on the floor, sprawled on his lean bedding. He recoiled at the accusation in her sharp eyes.

"Ya Khuda…Mithimaa, do you think I have sold my Imaan? These came from Kulsumbai's, brought in a fancy firangi car by a driver. I have asked him to teach me how to drive a motorcar; then he will get me a job also."

"That day be praised when it comes. I am warning you, the doctor has cut my working hours and that means less money. If I can't feed you any longer, you will have to leave this house and fend for yourself."

Oranges and lemons! Rehmatbi neither wanted to accustom herself to their taste nor live indefinitely on Kulsum's bounty.

When Shamim returned in the afternoon, she took him aside.

"Tell me Shamim, something about this film-villum business. How is it managed?"

Shamim waxed eloquent on his favourite subject.

"You act out a scene. There is a camera taking in all your action." With both palms raised flat and vertical before his face, Shamim wandered around the little room with a mock camera. "It imprints the images onto a reel. The reel is fed into a projector. The projector throws the images onto a screen. Till last year these images were quiet, but now there is a sound system by which you can hear them speak, and…just a minute. Since when did you develop an interest in all this?" he asked suspiciously.

"Just like that. I was wondering about the repercussions if I had let Mehru become an actress. Not that I'm thinking of it, no. But what would the neighbours think, or Kulsum's in-laws? And who will marry her if she dances around like a nautch girl?"

"Oh Mithimaa, actressess don't just sing and dance, they play all sorts of roles. They can be housewives, or college girls, or even play a goddess from the Hindu mythology. What is indecent about playing Seeta or Parvati? And if our Mehru had joined, and of course, I'm not saying you'll let her, she would have moved in a better society. Imagine Mehru having tea with a Maharani? On the contrary, joining the film industry would improve her prospects of marriage. She will be well-known, who knows, some prince of some big state may fall in love with her. Here what does she have? The gully goondas? And worse fate, if some mawalli type influences her, she with her innocent little heart, and she runs away or something? Where will your good name be then?"

Shamim stirred his cup of dialogue with some necessary dramatics. Rehmat appeared considerably influenced. For hours she pondered the cogent points of his argument. She thought about Mehru's extraordinary beauty and the spark in her eyes. What if Suleiman's muscular ethics were not frightening enough to protect Mehru from some foolish romantic influences? If Shamim could be allowed to work in a studio, why not Mehru? Just because she was a girl? Hai Allah, what had she been thinking, she, who had herself worked all her adult life?

Mehru was not worldly wise; she knew nothing about the jungle out there. But with Shamim's guidance and Suleiman's protection -. Besides, a time limit could be affixed. A couple of years, and then marriage was a compromise that could be amicable to all.

The next morning when Mehru returned from the community tap after the day's washing, Rehmatbi motioned her youngest daughter to come sit by her. Mehru was instantly apprehensive at the gravity of her mother's brow. But when Rehmatbi stroked her delicate fingers wrinkled from the washing chore, she relaxed. Rehmat contemplated those fair, frail fingers and wondered if they were intended for rings and manicured splendour.

"Look, Mehru, I have given what you told me the other day, some thought."

" Really, Mithima?" asked Mehru hesitantly.

"And I have decided to let you try your hand at it, for some time, mind you. Maybe a year or two."

Mehru was incredulous. "Do you really, absolutely mean that?"

"But first you must listen to me seriously. You have to beware of the hunters out there."

Mehru nodded, sobered by the text of her mother's speech.

"When your father died, I was still quite young. And to be sure there were many men who were willing to support me in return for favours granted. People began to look at me like appraising meat in a butcher's shop."

Mehru's face adopted an expression of sheer incredulity to conceive of her mother as young and desirable. She now discerned the faded traces of a beauty that once must have quite shaken the buttresses of men's control.

"But I was not going to be any man's chattel, I decided," continued Rehmat. "I was fiercely determined to be independent and single-minded in bringing you up the way I thought was right. I struggled and starved, and let nothing upset my perseverance. Remember this, Mehru, when a woman is strong and fearless, and stands up dauntless against the wind, then men stop trifling with her and start looking up to her instead. Are you understanding what I am trying to say, child?"

Mehru was not exactly sure if she could identify separate parts of her mother's logic, but she was more than certain she had grasped most of the gist. She tried to look adequately philosophical, if that could convey her comprehension.

"I have built up a reputation for myself through the years. If you think that you can hold your own out there, then go ahead, and may Allah shower you with success. All I ask is that you do nothing that in one swift stroke will cut down that carefully constructed good name."

Mehru promised, with all the sincerity and sobriety of a sixteen-plus-some-months-old. Somewhere in her young mind, the words of her mother poured in like wet cement, and hardened into one of the unforgettable edicts of her life.

Jhulna jhulao

DREAM FACTORIES

In the Kadri household, there were mixed reactions to the announcement that Meherunissa was to become an actress. Esabha grumbled that they were inviting a definite ticket to hell. Poor Esabha; hardly anyone paid heed to his mutterings. Suleiman, a great deal more voluble and vociferous, threatened to break her legs if she ever brought the family a bad name. Kulsum was afraid her in-laws would not permit her to associate with them now. Shamim, eyes blinded by the light of arc lamps and solar reflectors, considered it an invaluable opportunity for himself. Rehmatbi spent many rueful moods contemplating how she had allowed herself to be swayed by a breathless moment and the sight of a watermelon; how she had let the disappointment in her daughter's grey-green eyes skittle her prudence to the desperate state of a whim.

But as the routine of their daily existence swirled around them, soothing them into acceptance, many compromises were arrived at.

Esa's fears were tempered by the knowledge that joining films was not a necessary reason for excommunication. Suleiman's simmering fury, when placed in the refrigerator of greed, quickly set into an avaricious jelly. That he would become the brother of an actress might also gain him some clout with Amina, the lusty wench who worked as an ayah in a well-to-do home in the neighbourhood. Kulsum's husband, whom she fondly called Saajan, was too content to look beyond her rosy cheeks.

In the quiet of the night, a wheezing Rehmatbi sank herself on the pillow of surrender, covering herself with the sheet of relief. The fact that she was handing over responsibility to a daughter instead of a son, gave a delicious flavour to her mouth, like savouring a paan full of gulukand.

Symbolically, Mehru's maiden film was titled AZAADI KE DEEWANE.

'HAI HAI HAI shrieked Rehmatbi, when Mehru returned from her first day of shooting. Her cheeks were scarlet and lipstick made a bloody gash of her mouth. Her eyebrows had been shaved to an indiscernible line. To make matters worse, she was dressed in satin pajamas, her hair plaited into two semi-circles looped behind her ears like a brass knocker.

Rehmatbi beat her breasts. "I must have been insane to have permitted this. These filmwallahs have turned her into a cheap street woman!" she proclaimed to all who could hear, and there were plenty crowding the door for a first-hand glimpse of the mohallah's pioneering rule-breaker.

Speechless with horror, Mehru rushed to the community tap to wash the muck off her face. It took all of Shamim's elocutionary powers to convince his mother that the red colours were darkened to emphasise the features which came across as black and white on the screen. It took at least a week before Mehru worked up the courage to inform her mother that she had been christened Priyanandini, a Hindu screen name. By that time Rehmatbi's fears had toned down to resignation. Never having heard of Shakespeare, she decimated the dramatic eloquence from his famous line into a shred of practicality. "What's in a name?" she said. "Do I stop you from going to midnight mass for the Bada Din? And do you not celebrate Diwali with Sarojini? You may be called Salma, Sandra or Sunita, what's the difference? That you are still my daughter is an unchangeable fact of nature."

Rehmatbi's nightmares soon dissolved into a soft-focus dream when her daughter placed in her wrinkled hand the sum of rupees hundred and fifty, her first advance installment of pay.

"Let me serve you, lord and master, with my body, heart and soul. Grant me but a small corner in your house, where I shall lie quietly. But do not scorn me, or I shall die." The man addressed turned away in contempt. He looked in the opposite direction, offering a perfect profile. "Hmmmmph!" he grunted. "How I regret the day my parents tied me to an unlettered girl like you." He stood still, and the woman regarded him with an upturned face. A single tear meandered down her cheek. The scene froze into a tableau.

"Cut!" yelled the director.

The giant sound stage exhaled, sagged, and relaxed. The woman rose, wiping away the single stream of glycerine from her fair cheek; the man turned and stuck his tongue out at her, making her chuckle sweetly. One by one the arc lamps dimmed, leaving a blinding afterglow. Two massive fans in diagonal corners came on with a swoosh. Muffled whispers graduated into audible chatter. The lofty doors were flung open to admit a gaggle of fans and a few stagehands into the cavernous indoor studio set. The clapper boy changed the words on his board with a chalk: DO AKSHAR. Scene 37. Take Two.

The director flopped his massive frame into the chair reserved for him, wiping the perspiration from his brow. His assistant materialised with a handy soft-drink bottle stoppered with a marble.

"Sirji, lemonade. Acchha shot hua, sir. Shall we can it?"

"Can it. No retakes."

Wasn't a great shot, the director contemplated. This new girl the producer had hired still had to mature at acting, in spite of being two years in the industry. Neither was her dialogue delivery great, but what could you do with the kind of sound system they had, Big studios like Imperial had the Tanar Sound system and foreign technicians to operate it, but lesser production houses had to make do with the work of Indian technicians still learning the craft. So at best, the voices came out in a slow drawl, and the intonations of theatre still hung, like bats, in between the words.

But this one, when she looked at you with those gorgeous green eyes, she could melt your heart. What a face! That natural rosy complexion required no rouge or pancake. What was amazing was the chameleon quality of her eyes; humble one moment, fiery the next. No wonder the producer had signed her for another underproduction film where she played an empress. Of course, she had an excellent public relations promoter in her brother, who circulated her still photographs with oily mobility. And another ruffian brother acted as buffer between adulatory fans and promiscuous advances.

He beckoned his artists, and began explaining the next shot, emoting it with dialogue and action. The dialogue director rehearsed their lines. "Shot ready!" screamed the assistant with great importance. It was a signal to chase away unwanted people from the set. The heavy doors were pushed shut like the strong gates of a fortress, and the soundstage was sealed. The make-up man dabbed a wet sponge on the heroines's face, retouched her lip-paint, and Priyanandini took up her position for the next take. The hero ran a comb through his well-gelled hair till it shone like the paint on his newly-acquired automobile.

The lights came on in all their glory and heat, but none present felt any discomfort in their excitement.

"Silence!" yelled the director, his face stiff in concentration. The set settled into resolute soundlessness. No one moved. People were scared to breathe lest the sound of their exhalation be picked up by the sensitive boom suspended from above. "Camera on! Start sound!" then staring hard at the artistes, he said, "Action."

Matwaale nainonwaali, ghungrale baalonwaali

BOLD AND BEAUTIFUL

Saro's father is dead!" were the first words Rehmatbi conveyed to her when she returned, after a long outdoor stint at Khandala.

"What! When?"

"Almost a week ago. We didn't know where or how to inform you, otherwise at such a time…"

"How?"

Suleiman piped in with the rest of the information. "The British found out he was using his bank to fund the freedom fighters. They sealed it and confiscated the deposits. The shock and the humiliation made him kill himself by hanging from a fan."

"I must go to her at once." Mehru dumped her baggage and ran down the lane.

Sarojini dissolved into a paroxysm of weeping at seeing Mehru for the first time since her tragedy, but controlled herself soon.

"What are you going to do now?"

"First we have to leave this house."

"I would have taken you to mine, but it's already crowded, and Aai may not adjust in one room, that, too, of a Muslim household. I have now rented a flat at Shivaji Park, but there is still a month for the present tenant to vacate and hand over the place. Once we are there, you are welcome to stay with us. There is enough accommodation there for two kitchens."

"That is really sweet of you, Mehru. But it is already arranged for us to move in with my uncle, the one who has the photography shop at Dadar."

"And what about your marriage?"

"Oh that. I'm seriously considering terminating my engagement. This boy is so possessive. Don't do this. Dress like that. He even objects to my talking to my male cousins."

"But Saro, nobody else will marry you then."

"Who cares? I am quite capable of earning my own living. There is still the offer of films, even after two years."

Two months later she dramatically broke her engagement, creating history by being the first girl in her community to actually reject a boy.

"I have accepted the offer of The Maharashtra Film Co. at Kolhapur to star in their next film. I play Seeta. Someone from their company saw my photograph at maama's studio and approached us. Maama was livid, of course, and would hear nothing of it, but for once Aai stood up for me."

"But how did she give her permission? Won't your community reject you, and your relatives disown you?"

You know I was giving tuitions in a decent family, teaching English to the children. One day the father, finding me alone, tried to molest me."

"Ohmygod!" What did you do then?" asked Mehru, shocked at this primary revelation of lasciviousness.

"I scrambled around the house clutching my sari tightly whilst he chased me like a wild bull, but finally managed to run out the door. When I told Aai, she was in total agreement that lechers could as well be found in the most respectable, high-caste homes. So why blame the film industry? Besides, where are these community members and relations now? Except Maama, nobody came to help us in our time of need. You know, Mehru, this situation has made me conscious of one thing. You must always live for yourself and be responsible for your own joys and sorrows. Who knows if we ever have another life? "

"Saro, this means we shall be colleagues, perhaps co-star in a film. How exciting!"

"That is not all, my dear. I have met a man, most dashing and different, whom I have decided to marry. His name is Kumarsen, and he has just returned after doing a course in cinematography in Germany. He has modern ideas. He has no objections to his wife becoming an actress."

Mehru hugged her friend and sighed, and wondered when and if, she would also meet a man so 'modern'. A woman had the right to dream and desire, to discover the fulfillment of her hopes in her own way and by her own standards. She liked Saro's statement about being responsible for one's joys and sorrows. It echoed inchoate feelings inside her own heart, and the more she thought about them, the stronger they became.

"I've signed a film with Surendra and Bibbo, Mithimaa. They are big stars. It's called PRIYATAM. It's the second lead, but it's the big bracket. We can order new furniture, and I can buy a motorcar. Suleiman is driving now, but of course I'll want to learn eventually."

They were sitting in the verandah of their new home, enjoying the salubrious sea breeze. Rehmatbi could breathe more easily now away from the dense air of the mohallah. She sat contentedly contemplating the changes in their lives. Esa was married to a frisky, young girl whose hair fell below her knees, and who had a great skill for cooking paaya and biryani. She was only sixteen and carrying their first child already. Rehmatbi fearing her shrewish tongue, was relieved when Esa moved to Mohd. Ali Rd., closer to his place of work. Suleiman had wed his feisty maidservant Amina, and retained the Byculla accommodation. Shamim stayed with them, but occasionally went to Poona to work with Prabhat Films. Personally, the glamour of her daughter's career affected her not the least, though comfort-wise it was a sea change in her life. Mehru now employed an orphan from the jamaatkhana to do the domestic work, giving Rehmatbi a much-deserved rest. The dear old lady had graduated to wearing English lace on her 'pachadis', and entertaining her ex-neighbours with generosity.

"Allah ke vaaste, what kind of a name is Bibbo? A patient at the hospital had a cat named Bibbo."

"She is a plump, matronly actress, and many think I would have suited better in the leading role, but then I cannot sing, and she can."

Priyanandini's performance as the unrequited lover in PRIYATAM fetched her many kudos, and in 1936 she signed a film as the heroine opposite Master Vinayak. By that time, playback had been introduced, and Mehru's one-scale singing was no longer a disadvantage.

While the rest of the country crested a wave of patriotism, with morchas, demonstrations, women's councils, civil disobedience, and demands for a more active part in the Administration, it was business as usual in the mercantile town of Bombay. Cotton markets flourished, commercial establishments carried on their work side by side with the efforts of the great freedom fighters of Maharashtra. In the setting of 'tinsel town', women like Devika Rani and Durga Khote had made a rebellious entry and carved an impressive place in the cine world. With their beauty, histrionics and dignity, they embellished a hitherto disparaged medium with grace and decency. Though in the absence of censorship, clinches and kisses were not an uncommon part of the script, they were no longer stigmatised by vulgarity or cheapened by voyeurism. Top actors and actresses gained acceptance in high society, fraternising freely with royalty and senior British officials. This new breed of women, which included Saro, re-christened Sukumari, thrust cigarettes into fancy ebony holders and blew smoke rings in the company of males. They adorned racecourses wearing embroidered French chiffons and satin puff-sleeved blouses, and glanced knowledgeably into racing guides.

Mehru, too, in her sequined georgette saris and gold heeled sandals, permed hair and painted nails, moved in this set as if to the manner born. Her beauty and inherent grace, as well as her intelligence, were her passport to the circles of the crème de la crème. Her beauty blossomed with her success, and one flicker of her kohl-lined eyes often reduced strong men into babbling idiots. But she was neither conscious nor vain, and the indelible memory of her mother's words strengthened her awareness of her self-respect. She never wore costumes that raised eyebrows, or indulged in minor flirtations with her co-stars on the sets.

Rehmatbi's peace and prosperity, as she surveyed her comfortable surroundings, as she gazed across at the sea in its summer serenity, as she regarded the mini Austin parked outside the gate, prompted her to arrange niaz at the jamaatkhana. Between her and Kulsum, blessed now with her second child, a cherubic daughter called Zeba, they often donated money to the Aga Khan orphanage. After all, Allah had been so merciful, and a good Muslim always gave 'khairat'.

Main ban ki chidiya banke ban-ban ghoomoon re

Mehru sat on the sets of TOOFANI SOWAR, a Sunny Cinetone stunt film, trying to decide what to gift Saro and Kumar for their second wedding anniversary and the birth of their daughter, Malini. She and Kumarsen had eloped, braving scandal and her uncle's wrath. Saro had accepted her film offer, and till now had played Sita in so many films that it felt as if she had never removed those bracelets of flowers from her wrists or the gajra from her topknot.

It was in between shots on the last schedule of the shoot, and there was crazy activity inside the soundstage. False jungle trees with canvas leaves, part of the previous dismantled set, loomed in a corner like green ghosts. Mustiness swirled like a morning mist, adding its odour to greasepaint and perspiration. Instructions flew around like darts. Frustration at wasted minutes, which to all on a Sunny film spelled over-budgeting, was like a virus affecting everyone's concentration.

But in her corner Mehru relaxed, going over her dialogue silently, fingers playing with a ringlet. Suddenly, a magnetic force told her that someone was watching her with a powerful concentration. She turned, drawn to the origin of the disturbing vibration. Her cool, green eyes locked with the dark intense ones of a dusky man standing beside the gigantic studio fan.

He was a stranger, and he was staring at her in unabashed fascination. She was used to being looked at; but there was something daringly different about the way this man was fixing his eyes on her. His expression was one of surprise, as though strolling down a dark tunnel he had stumbled, like Alibaba, upon a cornucopia whose sparkling gems had blinded him. His hair fluttered gently in the fan's breeze, lifting off his neck and giving him an adventurous appearance, as if he stood proudly at the prow of a ship. This was not the ordinary stare of the stargazer; it was a bold bandit stare. Bewilderment darkened her eyes, as she realised that in spite of registering her answering reproach, his eyes did not move away. It was as if watching her was his own special experience, exclusive and private despite the presence of spot boys, light-men and camera assistants.

Mehru snapped her eyes away. Her forehead creased in a speed-breaker frown. But against her volition, her gaze kept returning to him repeatedly. She was rattled by a plethora of emotions. Annoyance was getting pleasurably mixed with an unexplained shyness. Her self-confidence was attacked by undisciplined glances that seemed to be branding her with ownership.

Disturbed by the rocking of her well-maintained equilibrium, Mehru requested the director to order all visitors off the sets. Some people left, filtering through the sieve of reluctance. But the man remained, transfixed, somewhere in the penumbra of awareness beyond the lights. She was glad when the shot was ready, and once she had taken her chalk-marked place, he was no longer in her mind. When she returned to her chair, he had disappeared. Good, thought,

Mehru. Banished and vanished. She let out an exhalation of relief, and felt strangely unburdened.

The next day he was back, his presence as irritating as an itch. Gazing upon her with unblinking continuity and that charismatic storm in his eyes. She found it unsettling. Ignoring it with all her might, she concentrated on her work. His presence, however, became unmistakably felt, day after day, a series of dashes and commas and semi-colons, but no full stop.

Then, suddenly, one morning, he was not there.

Mehru had grown so used to his presence, that his absence stuck out like an irregularity in a cardiogram. When, by the lunch break he had still not turned up in his accustomed place, curiosity got the better of her. She summoned her hairdresser to enquire from the director's first assistant, the identity of the regular visitor.

"Who? That dark fellow who's hanging next to me this past week?" asked Kamalbhai. "Arre, he's Aniruddh Ganguly, the music-director of our next film. Today he is having a sitting with Imtiazbhai, our new director from Lahore. Supposed to be a talented Babu-moshai. He was an insurgent or something. Vimal Kumar has brought him from Calcutta, I believe. But why are you so interested, my pretty?"

"Chal hatt re," parried Bertha, and moved back to Priyanandini with a coquettish swagger of her hips.

"Baby, he's composing the score for Sunny Saab's next film. Today they are having the sitting."

So that's why he was away, and that's why he had not been shunted off the sets with the other visitors. Making music, huh? He shall be made to face it, now. Petulantly, she decided she was going to make him dance to his own tune. Perhaps influence miserly Sunny to get him off the film even.

Yet, next day when he re-appeared, the mere sight of him contrarily sent a surge of relief through her entire being. Inadvertently, a smile overtook her lips.

Perhaps it was an emotional response. Perhaps just a feeling of satisfaction at the reconstruction of a familiar scene.

But on the periphery of the set, standing in half-light and half-darkness, Aniruddh saw the smile, and fell uncontrollably, desperately and fatally in love.

Main kya jaanoon kya jadoo hai

Ismail 'Sunny' Choonawalla sipped elaichi tea in Priyanandini's drawing room, and tried to convince her to sign his new picture.

"This stunt film is a quickie. But the next film is a powerful emotional drama with a solid role for you."

"Drama is not what I want now, Sunnysaab, what I want is a break. Look, I've been working four years nonstop, and I need rest, perhaps a holiday. I'm not a machine!"

You are, thought Sunnysaab. A goddamned moneymaking machine!

"What holiday, Mehru," interpolated Suleiman. "How nicely he's asking you. How can you refuse? After all, he's our old producer."

Mehru looked at her brother sharply. What difference did it make to him? The more she worked, the more money he could sponge off his mother. And Mithimaa? She had not reminded her daughter once of the time-limit clause. Mehru understood why. She no longer had to extend her hand before Esa, whose shrewish wife demanded all his salary on payday. And a distance existed between her and Amina, Suleiman's henna-headed wife, whose vinegary tongue added no sweetness to family life.

Ismail tried to impress Priyanandini with his weighty star cast. "I know, Nandini, you are getting heroine's roles now. But this is a powerful second lead. Leela Chitnis and Jairaj; how can you refuse a top-notch billing like that? And your role of the other woman, who is a dancer, means you get most of the song picturisations. Aaahaha, what songs Aniruddh Ganguly has made. 'Payal mori baaje,' and the other song which has a line just for you, 'Mere matwale nainon se chalke mast khumaar,' wahwah, .."

Mehru interrupted his musical digression. "Who did you say?"

"Jairaj and Leela Chitnis. Imtiaz is recommending this new girl from Gujerat called Sardar Akhtar, she has a nice, earthy voice, good for a dancing girl; maybe I will take her then, but you are the classic choice for the seductress, so.."

"No, no, no, no, the music-director, Ismailbhai, who is he?"

"Aniruddh Ganguly. He's a new boy from Calcutta. I have snatched him from Sagar Film Co."

"I'll do it," said Mehru, with such readiness that poor Ismail was stumped. Despite his tremendous coaxing she'd been refusing adamantly, and now, all of a sudden, an unexplained acceptance! Well, these actresses were a whimsical lot. Understanding women was not his job; all he wanted was to get Priyanandini to sign on the dotted line. He drew out the contract from his bag, and removed his new Schaeffer pen from his pocket. From the corner of his eye, he saw the smile spread across Suleiman's features. Nasty old swine, he thought. Thank God he's not *my* brother.

I don't care if she thinks I'm a lovesick fool, thought Aniruddh. But, standing inconspicuously at the muhurat, letting the hubbub of the event rise and fall before him like a stormy sea, he was powerless to take his eyes off Priyanandini. All he wanted to do was to stand there and let the intoxicating effect of those eyes destroy him.

He was not unaware of the magnetic compulsion that kept pulling her in his direction. The responses he was receiving from those gorgeous eyes made everything poetic and intense in him rise up and suffuse his being with arias of sweet melody.

Priyanandini, too, was conscious of those powerful eyes stalking her. Without knowing how or why, her eyes would turn and fix themselves on the exact spot where he stood. Through a roomful of people, strong vibrations reverberated with their awareness of each other and an imminent fruition that awaited the first, the barest sign without any embarrassment.

When the traditional coconut-breaking was over, she knew, that not being in the inaugural shot, she must leave. Aniruddh Ganguly notwithstanding, it did not befit her status to be hanging around when the camera was focusing on another star. She had an image to maintain, and images were what the movie business was all about. So, when a little fuss was being made over Aniruddh, the new kid on the block, she gathered her nineteen years of grace and prepared to leave quietly.

Ismailbhai, quick to notice her slipping away, waddled behind with a box of sweets, his huge buttocks swaying from side to side.

"Arre, Baby, have a peda at least before going. And do me a favour."

"I thought I already did that by agreeing to act in your film."

"Kya Nandini, tum bhi. Didn't I tell you it was the role of a lifetime?"

"So every producer says. Now, tell me what is it?"

"Our composer lives in the lane next to yours. Please, Baby, drop him home. I will really be obliged."

It's the other way around, she mused, but all she did was nod regally. She justified her swift acquiescence by the affirmation that condescending to the request of studio heads was tantamount to obeying a fatwah.

Aniruddh neither smiled at her nor offered a greeting. He slid quietly in at the back, whilst Suleiman, miffed at the newcomer's audacity of not sitting up front, drove off with a furious change of gears. The ride in terms of distance covered not five miles, but an entire age. The two occupants of the back seat were excruciatingly conscious of each other's presence, of the recollection of the electric moments in the studio that had preceded these. Every few seconds Aniruddh and Priyanandini turned to each other, searching for hints and suggestions. Using glances for words, they managed to communicate in a language lovers have understood for centuries, but to which no specific translation has ever been realised. Aniruddh understood with an indefinable clarity that what he had had with Suchitra was merely the bud; this was the opening of the flower. Somewhere in the misty future, this woman had been waiting for him. Whether drying her hair in the sun, or lining her magnificent eyes with kohl, folding a stray garment or getting rain-soaked in the monsoon's first drizzle, her every moment had been filled with an anticipation of his possession. He gazed upon this woman sitting beside him, this woman of such exquisite beauty that you could not look at her too long lest it blind you, and he knew that this next moment of blended agony and ecstacy was his destiny. If he lost it, he would lose an entire world.

In one dashing, daring act of courage, he covered her hand with his.

Priyanandini gasped, her face turning the colour of the inside of a peach. But though breathless with blushing confusion, she did not remove her hand.

Thus they rode, one hand simply over the other, warm with a clan oath, understanding unmistakably what would entail. When Aniruddh alighted, Priyanandini realised that they had not exchanged a single word. Yet, suspended in their interim space, an entire conversation had taken place.

Love at its most youthful, its most frenetic, is a passion whose intensity no barometer can measure, a depth that cannot be defined. Love is a hunger and a thirst that only the sight of the beloved can satisfy, when every gesture or change of expression is annotated in the mind. Love that neither Aniruddh nor Priyanandini had ever imagined they would have the fortune to experience as they stole moments away from the world's prying eyes. Time was siphoned from story sessions, borrowed from make-up mornings, pilfered in rehearsal rooms where in the grand solitude they clasped each other, afraid to breathe lest it shatter the magic of the moment. Time was spent hatching schemes to evade Suleiman's vulpine vision as he monitored each situation. Efforts were made to avoid being recognised as they strolled on the beach in an early morning rendezvous, and heard the breaking waves echo the majestic surge of their heartbeats.

Such passion consumed the two and held them in a still-frame, apart from the rest of the world. In a sneak-away hour, they often sat incognito at the Five Gardens at Wadala, far from their normal circuit, where Mehru, in nationalistic khadi would not be recognized for the glamorous star. There, sitting like any other courting couple under the panoply of trees, they would talk. Or rather, Aniruddh would talk. Having so much more to recount in terms of experience, he was the more loquacious. Whilst Nandini picked at blades of grass, he would tell fascinating tales of Barisal, of his theatre days in Calcutta, of Suchitra and the affair that had almost been, of his mother's strong character. Acutely aware of her own shortcomings, Priyanandini felt niggles of apprehension about measuring up to the standards of that paragon. As compared to Konkona's calmness, her own temper had gone missing many a time at the discovery of Suleiman's extortions from producers or Shamim's attempted negotiations of dates or prices.

So preferably she listened, for Ani had a way of conjuring up images with sheer elocutionary prowess. His poet-at-heart would temper narrations with couplets from Ghalib and quotations from Tagore, and on a magic carpet of words he would ferry her to lands where Attaribai's nautchgirls twirled with timorous anklets, or British soldiers rode a storm.

Anyway, what could she tell Aniruddh of her family story, which was hardly a fairy tale? For his talented sister and brother-in-law, she had conniving brothers and sisters-in-law who could put Cinderella's stepsisters in the shade. Perhaps her mother's saga matched his mother's own, but she humbly mentioned it not. A fatal mistake. But then how many relationships have been wiser only in hindsight?

So Mehru, sitting on the sands of Chowpatty, gazed upon the majestic mansions of Marine Drive, whilst Aniruddh had his legs massaged with mustard oil by a masseur and spoke of some day owning a big house and an American Buick and a cottage at Lonavala. She coloured her dreams with his and overlooked the smell of the mustard oil, which she hated. She thrilled when he called her Babesie, a diversification of the address of 'Baby' for the heroine, and teased him by calling him Ani-honey, which he found distasteful.

She knew that Aniruddh was nowhere near even the least handsome of her heroes, but when he regarded her with those soulful eyes, he seemed the most handsome creature on earth. Their feelings embossed their work, as they struggled to give their best for and to each other, and to prove their combined worth to the world. The films they worked in together were hits. 'Hit' being the quintessential by-law in the industry, they were often paired as a lucky combination.

To them both it seemed providential that they had met on the sets of TOOFANI SOWAR, a name that could, in their case, be suitably applied to Cupid.

Woh jo hain mere man mein samaaye,
main bhi un mein samaaoon

BLACK AND WHITE

Aniruddh's early morning beach perambulations had not escaped Konkona's shrewd notice. Her son was not the sporty type, he had the inherent indolence of the Bengali who prefers to live by a multi-functional pond. Her astute mind wondered if perhaps at the back of it all was a girl. When questioned, Paro confessed ignorance. So did Pranoy. Nothing had fazed his passion for his flute; neither the relocations nor the bioscope. Having too much self-respect to live on Aniruddh's bounty, he had started taking on disciples to feed his family. His music dissociated him from most things, least of all Ani's affairs-de-couer.

Curious, she followed him one morning. She saw him pass through the gate in the wall that divided the building from the beach. He sauntered southwards, anticipation in his pace. The sun was just beginning to warm the glass sheet of the sea; overhead gulls squawked and circled. It was the time of morning just before the city woke to the cacophony of its daily sounds. She saw him pause, and pluck a champa off a tree whose branches extended beyond the wall.

In the shimmering sandy distance, a figure came into view. All Konkona could discern was a slim girl in a red sari, little wisps of hair flying around her forehead. Aniruddh met up with her, and the two walked towards an outcrop of rock against which they sat.

Konkona hid behind the slim trunk of a coconut tree. Then, to her absolute surprise, she saw Ani pin the champa in the girl's hair, and place an arm around her slender shoulders. The tenderness in the act reached across the sands to her. Her son had apparently moved much beyond the diffidences and doubts of the Suchitra phase.

She spoke nothing of this to Aniruddh. If it were serious, he would approach her himself. If not, the affair would fizzle out with the ephemeral quality of youth. She was not against these minor liaisons, which were sometimes necessary for the process of maturing. Like all people gifted with patience, she decided to wait and watch.

But Aniruddh's morning walks continued with undiminished regularity. An amplified restiveness preceded his departure and when he returned the serenity surrounding him was beatific. He sat to work with inspired zeal, and the tunes he composed were so sweet and soulful, that Konkona was convinced that anything that generated such results could not be harmful for her child.

For his part Aniruddh resolved that Suchitra's history would never be repeated. Perhaps with his initiative, Suchitra might have derived some happiness before she died. One thing he had learnt from his past. Opportunities should not be allowed to slip through your fingers leaving nothing in your palm but regret. If he had not grasped Priyanandini's hand in that fateful moment, perhaps they might never have got involved. That one moment had changed their lives and yielded so much happiness for more than one person; the two of them, their producers and hopefully the public.

Mehru was returning from her beach rendezvous, a smile on her lips and peace in her heart. Her brother Suleiman stood some distance away, reflecting on the reason of her beatific expression. There was gossip in the industry about her and the Bengali composer who lived in the next lane. Messing with a boy was bad enough; if it was a Hindu boy, he would kill him.

Suleiman's scheming mind had no intention of letting go of the golden goose. If she fell in love with some silly boy who took her away and all that lovely money with her, Suleiman would have to find alternate means of livelihood. Esa's wife's miscarriage had given Amina pregnancy-fright, making her adopt a daughter,

Fehmida. What Suleiman did not know was that Amina, having got herself pregnant whilst whoring in her ayah days, had gone to a quack in Pydhonie to get the baby removed. Her tubes were now damaged to the extent that she could never have another child. The bottom line was that Suleiman now had three mouths to feed, and his own appetite was large enough. He decided that the best person to influence Mehru was Rehmatbi. So he began a concerted campaign to fill his mother's ears with stories of his sister's indiscretions.

"Lie, lie, on those comfortable sheets, Ammi Huzoor. Why should you worry about what your daughter Mehru is up to? So much independence you have given her. Coming when she likes, going where she likes. Do you know what she is doing these days?"

"And what exactly, my loving, providing son, is the real meaning behind all these sarcastic words?"

"I am trying to warn you. Mehru is flying like a kite. If you don't rein her in, she will ruin herself and your good name. She forgets her dialogue on the sets, and bunks shootings. Who will give her work if all she gives them is trouble?"

"Ah, so that is really what is upsetting you, that you will lose your chance to skim money off her earnings!" retorted the sharp lady. "Let me tell you, I will be the happiest person if that day comes, and may Allah bring it soon. Then she can settle down, and live a decent life like her sister. So carry your tales elsewhere; they will have no effect on me."

But her indifference only further fired him to expose this 'hanky-panky' between his sister and the dark-skinned composer from Bengal. Like a turkey buzzard he waited, to swoop on some odd suspicion, some moment to catch them red-handed and present the fact before his mother. However, his recent reprimand had taught him that a sense of timing was crucial to the imparting of vital information if the desired result were to be achieved.

So he waited for a Sunday, when Esabha and Gulsakkar came over for their weekly visit. His conniving nature had diagnosed a temperament similar to his own in his sister-in-law.

"Esabha," he said, as gravely as he could. "Have we not all been brought up as good Muslims?"

Esabha nodded with matching gravity. "Yes, but all of you do not read the Quran as much as you should."

"Perhaps, but do we not go regularly to the jamaatkhana and hold faatiya and niyaz? And does not Baima support Ismaili orphans? And Mithima contribute generously towards the rehabilitation of the Sunni widows?"

Rehmatbi, pleased with this reference to her philanthropy, wondered where all this was heading.

"Why then is Mehru cavorting with a kaafir?"

A scandalized silence stilled the air.

Before further rebuttal, Gulsakkar intervened hastily, "But that's her job." Having two well-placed sisters-in-law whose good-condition cast-offs she acquired, and in whose kitchens she greedily ate 'khichda' and 'dal-gosht', it terrified her that perhaps Suleiman was suggesting Mehru quit films.

"I mean in real life, Sakkar Bhabhi, not in reel life. For the past few months she's been running around with this Bengali boy. Ani-Moshai, he's referred to as. You know the saying about ishq and mushq. Tell me, is it a co-incidence that they have signed so many films together? Even the producers are cashing in on this loving 'jodi.' Could she not find a good Muslim boy? That director Imtiaz, for instance? Esabha, you must speak to her."

The good Esa's cheeks flamed. His sister having a 'lafda' with a worshipper of idols? Bringing shame on their family and ignominy to the small community of Aga Khanis!

"Where is she now?" he demanded to know.

"Allah jaane. Does she tell? Comes and goes like a man whenever and wherever she pleases. I warned Mithimaa. This comes from giving a woman too much freedom, not to mention education. Just because she is earning…"

"And her brothers aren't," piped in Rehmatbi, who had been listening all the while in stoic silence. "You are dependent on her for your job as her chauffeur, and Shamim has left his work in Poona and is sitting at home, playing cards with the boys in the lane. Esa, you are the only one who has a right to talk. It is certainly not correct for her to be associating intimately with a kaafir. But at the same time, you can't gang up against her when she is not here to defend herself."

"You see how Mithimaa always speaks up for her."

The subject of their debate walked in just then, dressed in the trendy Lila sari which had been set in vogue by the dancing star Lila Desai. Her mood was mellow but her eyes were brilliant. The bubble of euphoria quickly burst at the sight of her family gathered in a grim conclave.

In a voice as light and fluffy as a newly beaten egg she said, "What is this war council, bhai and bhai?" Then, seeing no reaction to her light remark, she went serious too. "Don't tell me someone died?"

"Yes. Our respect and good name," said Esa solemnly, not commonly given to fancy dialogue.

"What do you mean?"

"Where have you been gallivanting all day?" snarled Suleiman, impatient to get to the point.

Mehru shot a dagger look at her older brother.

" Suleimanbha, I don't have to report my movements to you."

"See, see, how she talks to her elders. It is her guilt speaking in this offensive way. Mehru, just your earning more than us does not give you the right to talk to us like this. Saali chinaal, I will have to beat some sense into you it seems." He lifted his hand to strike her.

Rehmatbi clutched his arm.

"Do you think hitting her is going to solve the problem? And will you raise a hand on a grown-up girl? Let Esa speak to her. At least his speech is more dignified."

Mehru's eyes were awash with tears of humiliation. How dare he call her a slut when he had no shame eating the crumbs off her table?

"Alright. Let Esabha ask the harlot why she is blackening her face with an idol-worshipper."

Mehru's face coloured with anger. Rehmatbi scowled at her middle son. The old woman still had enough command in her demeanour to silence a man like Suleiman.

"Listen beta," began Esa in his benign, fraternal manner, "how long are you going to work in this film line? Mithimaa had said two or three years, but it is much past that limit. We think it is high time that you settle down. It will be hard for us to find you a husband, now that you are well known and also educated. At Kulsum's time we never had any problem. Look at her example; two lovely babies and how happy she is. Perhaps we will have to consult Mrs.Chagla; she may be able to find someone suitable in her society, one who will not object to your new Hindu name."

"Enough," interrupted Mehru, her fury burgeoning beyond control. "I am tired of hearing about Kulsumbai's happiness, Kulsumbai's status, Kulsumbai's money. Is happiness gained only from marriage? And is marriage the only qualification for respectability? Tell me, have you heard any scandal about me in the film line? But do you know what Baima's neighbours are saying about her? That she is bored with her much older husband, that the old man does not satisfy her? That she's making eyes at her Yehudi tenant and worse still, that her daughter Zeba looks the spit image of the Jew? And if my marriage is such a burden to you, then stop troubling yourself. I shall find a husband on my own."

Whilst even Gulsakkar blushed with embarrassment, Esa's face turned a dark shade of purple.

"Tauba! Tauba! I wish my ears had turned deaf before they were exposed to such scandalous words. I told you not to educate this girl. You see now, how the shaitaan speaks through her tongue. Allah! That decent girls should talk of such things in front of their elders. Today I have ruined my Imaan. Come on Sakkar, I will have no part in such shamelessness."

Suleiman was tongue-tied. All he had expected was for Esabha to give her a mighty good scolding. Seeing his ploy turning in a different direction, he decided retreat was the best strategy for now, and followed Esa out. At the door, however, he hurled poisoned darts of obscenities at her, making Mehru tremble with a spasm of hiccups. She ran into her room and dissolved into loud sobs of frustration. Such confrontations upset her with their indigestible taste of unpleasantness.

Wise Rehmatbi thought it best to leave her alone. A strong reason to avoid a talk with her was that she, too, had heard these rumours about Kulsum. With what face could she argue with Mehru? Khuda khair kare, she could feel an asthmatic attack coming. She swallowed a pill, and lay down for it to take effect.

When Shamim entered the house, morose at his loss at cards, he was greeted by powerful static; evidence that the room had recently witnessed some electricity. Mithimaa appeared to be asleep, her *pacchhdi* covering her face. He sauntered into the kitchen to salvage lunch leftovers, but all he saw were empty pots, and a couple of stale rotis wrapped in oil-stained muslin. He peeped gingerly into Mehru's room. She was lying face down on the bed, her body heaving with sobs. He tiptoed in, thinking he would ask her what was the matter, but his brotherly intentions wavered at the sight of a ten-rupee note thrown carelessly on the dressing table. Temptation sent a little vibration up his spine. Hell, the least he deserved was a proper lunch. Mehru's consolation could wait till later.

He pocketed the ten-rupee note, and walked across to the Irani restaurant on the corner of the main Cadell Road. After making a meal of six crisp Irani samosas, omelette-pao, and a plate of baked custard, he still had enough for next afternoon's game.

Kuch na sujhaye, jiya ghabraaye

The next morning Mehru decided that, notwithstanding the repercussions, it was time she confessed all to Ani. She knew her brother was quite capable of executing his threat. Her depression showed in her red-rimmed eyes which Aniruddh was quick to notice. Her whole demeanour was subdued, like a low blood pressure.

They sat on the sands in silence for a minute, looking out at the long outcrop of rock that cut the border of the sea like a natural jetty. The tide was low, like the atmosphere. In front of them, an elderly man taking the air ambled past with a walk like a stammer.

"Babesie, what is the matter? Have you been crying?" He gently put an arm around her shoulder, speaking in a whisper lest he break the fragility around them. The concern in his voice made Nandini sigh. She wanted to say so much, but the weight of the words inside her was heavy. The memory of Suleiman's abuses paralysed her vocal chords. Suddenly, she put her head down on her grasped knees and began to weep. Tears rocked her body and wet her forearms and she sniffled loudly between breaths.

Aniruddh had never seen any woman cry. Both his mother and sister were so in control of their emotions, that he was totally flabbergasted about dealing with this alien situation.

"Oh God, don't cry, Babesie, whatever happened between yesterday and this morning? Tell me, for heaven's sake." He pulled her face up and began to brush the tears off her cheeks, as though by flinging them away he could expel her sorrow. He stroked her hair, uncaring if anyone watched. Soon the tempest of her pain began to abate, and she was about to tell him the whole nasty episode of the day before, when a shadow loomed over them, shutting out the sun. Aniruddh looked up to see a road-roller of a man towering above them. The typhoon in his face threatened to break and blow them apart. With irate strength, the man yanked Nandini up, twisting her arm in a vicious grip that made her scream in pain.

"Hey you, what is the meaning of…"

"You shut up, *haraam ki aulad*. And this *saali raand*, I am going to teach her a lesson she will never forget." He strung his fingers through her hair and with unbelievable force, wrenched her up and started to drag her so that her body heaved along the beach, feet furrowing deep troughs in the sand. A passerby stopped, shocked at this violent spectacle slashing the morning quiet. Aniruddh tried to rise, and slipped. By the time he recovered his balance, the man had dragged her some distance. He chased them, his feet shovelling jets of sand behind him. He caught the man's arm, desperately trying to shake his grip off Nandini, but the man was too strong for him, and shoved him off with an abuse. Aniruddh glimpsed the hair bristling on the man's solid forearms before he fell back on the sand. Even in that state of shock, he realised that the man was too big and burly for him to fight. He lunged at him in desperation, but the stronger man slapped him viciously across the mouth.

Aniruddh boomeranged onto the sand. The single curious passerby got joined by another, then another. Then Mehru, still shrieking with agony, yelled, 'Leave it, Ani, he'll kill you, Go! Go!' The terror in her voice was vibrant enough to halt him in his tracks. He stared at their retreating figures in sheer horror, the slap stinging his mouth.

Knowing the futility of winning against the heavy-set man, he stood speechless with frustration, oblivious of the crowd that had collected. Damn! he thought, stomping his feet again and again in the slippery sand, his humiliation and inability to defend her raising heat behind his eyes. Never in all his life, in all his experience or exposure, had he witnessed a scene as distasteful. His Bangla refinement could not conceive of treating any woman in so indelicate a manner. From where he came, women were treated with respect and called Maa, not dragged along the ground by abusive cavemen. A second skin hovered around him, tense and vibrating. Heaviness hung on his shoulders like an army overcoat. Behind him, the crowd dispersed at this abrupt end to the matinee.

On reaching home, he struck his harmonium with such anger, that Konkona, usually never distracted from her pooja, stopped blowing her conch, and stared at him in puzzlement.

Beyond the sea wall, the tide began coming in.

Suleiman dumped Mehru in front of his mother as though she were a sack of goods. Rehmatbi looked up clucking with disgust, and put down the lace she was tatting. What new drama was her son going to unfold?

"What is the meaning of this manhandling, Suleiman?"

"Why don't you ask her? Haven't you been told often enough how she is bringing disgrace on us? Blaming Kulsumbai for nothing! Ask her what she was doing khule-aam on the beach with that saala black Bengali? She might as well become a streetwalker. She's certainly behaving like one. Why doesn't that haraami defame some silly Hindu girl? Did we protect her so in the mohallah, to let her blacken her face with that ugly dark man? Talk about Beauty and the Beast!"

Rehmatbi struggled to maintain her calm. Pointless letting the situation gain the upper hand over her asthma and blood pressure. Better to grip it by the horns, and settle it once and for all. First she had to get rid of this bull in the china shop. Esa had washed his hands off the matter; Shamim didn't give a damn. It was for her to decide as the head of the family.

"If you have said your piece, Suleiman, I shall handle it from here. Now go home to your wife. The studio car is comimg for Mehru. You won't be required today."

"But Mithimaa.."

"You understand Kutchi, do you not? I think I said, go home."

Suleiman averted his eyes from the forceful steel in his mother's look and pulled at the collar of his black coat salvaged from a burn-British-goods bonfire. He wore it regularly with khakhi half pants, like a uniform. Showing yellow-stained teeth, he snarled at his mother.

"This is justice, indeed. I get a reprimand for trying to salvage the family honour, and she will get an embrace and loving pardon. Of course, why should you want to upset the golden hen? After all, you can't make omelettes without eggs, can you?"

He flicked back the strips of unruly hair from his forehead, and left, the scowl on his face darkening into a storm.

All this while, Mehru had sat on the floor with her back pressed against the wall, eyes shut against images of the preceding ugly scene which kept replaying in her mind. Rehmatbi shuffled into the kitchen and brewed herself a cup of strong masala tea.

"He's gone; you can open your eyes now. By closing them, the nightmare doesn't vanish. Life is made up of unpleasant things. You have to stare them in the face, not avoid them."

In slow motion Mehru's face relaxed, the blank tautness easing out into lines of such pain that Rehmatbi's sternness fast dissipated.

Gently, she asked,"Is it true, beti, what Suleiman said?"

Honesty had always been Mehru's sterling quality. Moreover, she had no intention of lying to a mother who had vested so much trust in her. Slowly, she nodded.

Her confession stung Rehmatbi like a slap.

"Ya Allah!" she exclaimed.

But Mehru was quick to correct the perspective. "It's not as indecent as Suleiman describes it. This morning on the beach, he was only comforting me because I was upset about yesterday's events. On the contrary, Aniruddh is pure and gentle. No one could be more caring or concerned. Esabha is indifferent, Shamim doesn't bother, and Suleiman is out for all he can get. A father's love has been denied me. What can I do if Aniruddh makes me feel needed? So what if he is not handsome, when he is so gentle and kind?"

Pragmatic Rehmatbi was more concerned about practicalities than in a litany of purified emotions.

"But will he marry you, child? Or is he merely amusing himself with you? After all, you are an actress. You know how actresses are thought of. People love them and leave them, but few marry them. Unless they are rogues out for money."

"Mithimaa, we've never discussed marriage as yet. He is a Hindu, after all, and opposition is expected from both sides."

"Why did you conceal all this? Being clandestine makes love sordid. You are an educated woman, of strong character and capable of knowing your mind."

"I was afraid of Suleiman's reaction, and see, how right I was."

"But, child, if you want to get married, then go about it the right way. This house is yours, and you put food on the table. It would have been a different thing if your brothers were supporting you. Think about what I have said. Now, go wash your face. Don't you have shooting today?"

"But, Mithimaa, he may not convert. Don't you mind that he is a Hindu?"

"If you say he is a good man, that is all I care."

Happiness came out on Mehru's face like the sun from behind a cloud. She wrapped her arms round her mother's neck and hugged her tight.

Embarrassed by such demonstrations of emotion, Rehmat ordered her daughter off for a bath. But it set her wondering if perhaps their family would have been happier had it been more demonstrative. In her sons she had lost hope; Suleiman, in particular, filled her with shame that he had been born from her womb. Mehru, with her honesty and generosity, her lack of hypocrisy, was the queen in this conniving pack of cards. She had always known that Mehru would never settle for an arranged marriage. She wanted comfort; but she needed love more.

She hoped the boy earned enough to keep Mehru in the luxury to which she had now become accustomed. When the belly was empty, this fancy love-shove flew out of the window on speedy wings.

When Mehru emerged, Rehmat knew with an unmistakable clarity that the sparkle in her daughter's eyes was the sum total she wanted for every following consequence.

Through the trellis pattern atop the wall, Konkona espied a face, a sweet early morning face glowing with anticipation. She smiled to herself at this blessed beginning to her day, and continued to pluck flowers for her morning pooja. But as the figure came nearer, a red sari came prominently into vison and Konkona was struck by déjà vu. The morning walk rendezvous girl! When the girl paused opposite their house and glanced in the direction of their windows, she was sure. Her heart marveled at such classic beauty; densely green eyes, clear complexion, near-perfect lips and a nose of exquisite pride. However had this girl become attracted to her son, who wasn't generously endowed with good looks?

She walked up the few steps into their ground floor flat. Shubir was getting ready for school. Aniruddh was pacing the floor with a fury that threatened to wear off the mosaic.

"So, you are planning to take today's walk inside the house itself?" she asked, with a teasing tone.

Aniruddh looked up sharply at his mother's uncharacteristic playful air.

"The weather outside is simply divine; perhaps you should go have a look. The sea is almost at our door."

"That's impossible. There are two buildings between us and the beach; besides, it should be low tide now," answered Aniruddh ill-temperedly.

"See for yourself. The tide must be pretty high."

For want of anything else to do, Aniruddh strolled out. He was shocked at the sight of Priyanandini hanging about outside looking much like a lost doe from the Panchatantra. Hastily, he crossed the street.

"I didn't think you would come after yesterday," he whispered.

"It's alright. Everything's fine now. That was my brother; he was upset about our meetings. In a way it's good that it happened because everything came out in the open. I've cleared everything with my mother, and she said you should meet me at home instead of like this, chupke-chupke."

"Really? But that's wonderful." Mehru could see the tension draining out of Aniruddh. "Look, we can't talk on the road like this. You have a Sagar Movietone shooting today, isn't it? But tomorrow evening I'll come over. But first, I have to settle some matters with my shrewd mother, who, I suspect, sent me out deliberately. Can't imagine how she knew. In any case, it's time we resolve this situation." He touched her cheek, and nodded to her to go.

My sentiments exactly, thought Mehru, as she turned away. In fact, it was a leap year, and she wondered if *she* should propose to him first. She walked a few steps, then turned back to look at him. He was staring at her retreating figure with so much tenderness, that she knew without a shadow of doubt that she wanted to spend the rest of her life with him.

Piya Milan ko jaana

Aniruddh looked through saris in the shop at Matunga, which dealt exclusively in Bengali wear. Dhakais, Balucharis, Shantipuris of every hue were laid out on the counter for his approval. Finally he chose an exquisite white Tangail with delicate red and green motifs. He thought it fitting that Priyanandini should be dressed in a Bengali traditional when she came to meet his mother for the first time. He would present her with it when he met her mother this evening.

Strolling along the road, he glimpsed a small shop tucked away beneath a stairwell. The bright lights blinking off its neatly arrayed glass bottles seemed to lure passersby like Circe's sirens. On an impulse, he stepped in. Colours in all the rich hues of gold confronted him. Mellow honey, iridescent amber, incandescent bronze, a darker shade like the heart of a chocolate, and cream like sunshine on a dewdrop. The little bottles of 'attar' seemed like *mini* containers of magic potion. Hesitantly, he asked the henna-bearded salesman for the best in jasmine scents.

"My favourite flower," he ventured in terms of explanation.

The salesman smiled at him. "We keep the finest," he said, proffering a miniature beauty for perusal. "Pack it nicely, please," requested Aniruddh.

"A gift for someone special?" asked the salesman.

"Very special."

Sundar naari, pritam pyari, Pyari chab dikhlaaye
Naina raseele, baanke kateele, Chadi nain ladhaye

Aniruddh hung around at the head of Priyanandini's lane, waiting for her to return from the studio. It struck him that since they lived in the same neighbourhood, their romance might have been a boy-meets-girl-next-door one, even had they not been in the same line.

Round the corner, her Mini-Austin came into view. It rambled down the lane, coming to a stop at the end of the alley where the road met the beach. Nandini alighted with the elegance of royalty. Aniruddh was filled with the wondrous feeling of possessiveness for this beautiful woman. Only after he had seen her wolfish brother depart, did he walk with slow, measured steps towards her residence. His heart beat fast at the thought of seeing Priyanandini for the very first time in the location of her home. Nandini informal would be delicious, as delightful as Nandini all made up and ready for the set.

The door was opened by a grizzly woman in a long flowing gown. A dupatta of fine muslin enclosed her shoulders and a conspicuous wart at her chin sprung a bouquet of gray hairs. Before she could ask his business, Nandini appeared speedily from a room, smile pearly perfect.

"Mithima, this is..er.."

"I understand." The addressed lady opened the door wider as a sign for him to enter.

Priyanandini's face flushed a nice admirable rose, and Aniruddh tentatively settled himself on one of the upholstered sofas, in front of which a V-shaped vase sprouted paper flowers. He was aware of a huge armoire with a garishly painted peacock on the front that blocked a wall on one side, and in a corner a hat-stand festooned with dupattas stood like a colourful Maypole.

"So, first tell me your name, son. All I know about you is that you are a Hindu."

What an odd remark to open one's conversation with, thought Aniruddh, but shrugged, giving her the benefit of senility.

"His name is Aniruddh", offered Priyanandini timorously.

"Let the boy speak. Doesn't he have a tongue in his mouth?"

Priyanandini looked chided.

"And what do you do for a living?" Rehmatbi addressed Aniruddh with a directness that dispensed with formalities.

Priyanandini coloured, embarrassed at this obvious matrimonial questionnaire. But Rehmatbi thought it futile to circle around the point. If he wanted to marry her daughter, it was of the highest relevance to know whether he could support her.

The old lady's no-nonsense directness discomfited Aniruddh. But he was here and there was nothing to do but answer the woman's question, considering he was halfway to making her his mother-in-law.

"I make music," he said, tersely.

"That's all very well. But what do you *do* for a living?"

"Exactly what I said, Ma. I make music."

"So, you are a mirasi or a quwaal perhaps?"

"Not exactly. You know, the films your daughter acts in? Do you see people singing songs in them? I compose those songs, even sing in them."

To Rehmatbi, whose comprehension of her daughter's work was a little above a fraction point, the boy's statement made not much sense. She tried another tack.

"And are you paid well for this music-you-make?"

Priyanandini almost choked. Even *she* had not dared ask Aniruddh what he got paid. But by that time, Aniruddh was cruising along with Rehmatbi's flow. What the hell, she was a mother; it was the type of question she was expected to ask.

"Not as much, perhaps, as your daughter. But enough to support a family." That, he knew, was the crux of this grilling. "And I don't have a car as yet, but I should be getting one shortly," he offered as an afterthought.

Rehmatbi expelled a satisfied sigh, which didn't escape the concerned couple. "Well then, you go ahead and talk to Mehru, and I shall make you a cup of tea."

Her smile, as she disappeared into the kitchen, was tantamount to a blessing. Offering him tea was acceptance.

Ah, *as much as Mehru,* she mused, and a car on the order list. She decided to serve the wheatflour halwa she had conditionally made earlier.

Somewhere along the edges of his notice Aniruddh realised that Nandini's mother had called her by a strange name, but the twinge of discomfort dissolved as swiftly as icicles in the sudden sun of Nandini's smile.

Rehmatbi returned with tea and a saucer of freshly made halwa generously sprinkled with nuts. It made an instant connection with Aniruddh's sweet tooth. Thinking it necessary to deliver some kind of approval to the proceedings, Rehmatbi embarked on what was an impromptu presentation of a code of conduct.

"And in future, if you wish to meet Mehru, you must come fearlessly to this house. It is not good for children of good families to meet secretly like this." Again Mehru, is it some kind of family name, Aniruddh wondered? The old lady continued without allowing Aniruddh to put in a word. "And you mustn't mind what my son Suleiman did on the beach that day. He's a rough one, but he was only being protective. You would have reacted the same way had it been your sister."

Her noisy slurps of tea resounded in the silence that followed.

Aniruddh put his cup down with a rattle. Suleiman? Her son? But that was a Muslim name! He looked away in shock, and for the first time, on the opposite wall, a picture of the Kaa'ba at Mecca came glaringly into focus. Right next to it was a telling portrait of the Aga Khan.

The knowledge hit him like a brick. Priyanandini, his beloved Priyanandini, was a Muslim!

Suddenly everything seemed unreal; including her name, which must obviously be one adopted for the screen. Why had this never occurred to him? Her actual name must be Mehru-something.

"…..is falling."

"What?" he asked, his mind far away.

"I said be careful, son. Your tea is falling."

"What is it, Aniruddh? You seem so distracted," enquired Mehru.

"I just remembered that I have a rehearsal I completely forgot about."

What love does to a man, mused Rehmatbi, sipping her tea noisily from her saucer.

"I'm awfully sorry, but I must leave at once."

He wanted to be far away from here, alone in a place where he could think, and that too, clearly and calmly. Away from her concerned eyes that would otherwise drown him.

"But finish your tea at least."

"I have to rush."

The teacup clattered on the table. He went stumbling out the door in a state of shock, leaving both women completely baffled as to the abrupt amputation of the evening.

SAIGAL FACTOR

Aniruddh weaved down Cadell Road like a drunken man, striving to condition his mind to this startling knowledge. The picture, the old woman's attire, the names! Priyanandini was an Aga Khani, a Khojah! Oh Ma!

He had nothing against Mohammedans. In Barisal, they had existed side by side carrying on a similar, but distinctly separate existence. The vivid lacuna between their religions allowed no overlapping of their lives. Hell, one of his best friends had been a Muslim, but there would never have been a possibility of his ever marrying Nazrul's sister! Then how could he ever expect his mother, she with her beads and her brass icons, with her jaap and her meditation, to ever accept into her house of holy thakurs, the daughter of a beefeater? Undoubtedly the Kalma was out of place in Konkona's spiritual dialogue with her brocaded gods.

Of their own volition, his steps found their way to the beach. Here, in solitude, he hoped to find a reasonable solution to his chaotic thoughts. In less than an hour, his world had done a somersault, his crystal hopes shattered into infinitesimal pieces.

It was darkening, and he sat down on a little rug of twilight sand to sort out the configurations of his discovery.

In the current application, any alliance between him and Mehru-Priyanandini was doomed to their spending their lives in separate lanes. It would be prudent if he banished into the ravines of oblivion that lovely countenance, those pensive eyes and those darling dimples. Their union was not to be; there were no Hamlet options. Their love had been sheer poetry; but life was practicality.

With some semblance of rationality, he deduced that it was unfair to dump on his hopeful mother a daughter-in-law who smeared greasepaint on her face and danced for other people's entertainment; who spent most of her time *outside* the house than in; who prayed to a faceless God and whose caveman brother swore in objectionable parlance. Indeed, as Runu would have quoted, he and Priyanandini, or Meherun, or Meherbanu, whatever her name was, were a pair of star-crossed lovers. How he longed for his friend's practical perspective that would superimpose a frame of reality on a picture whose colours were beginning to run. Why had he never pondered repercussions or equations? But he could not have done otherwise; such were the primordial designs of love.

He *had* to forget her. If her eyes invaded his mind by bouncing uninvited onto its darkened screen, he would expel them from his thoughts. He was sure if he concentrated on nothing and converted himself into a cypher, he could do it. He tried it, closing his eyes in emptiness and listening only to the sound of the waves foaming at their nightly mouth. The vacuum made him conscious of the weight at his fingers, and he realised that the packet he had intended to gift her was still in his hands.

He smiled an ironic smile. So much for the exotic thought of the attar! Wasn't attar frequently used by Muslims? She probably had bottles of the stuff lining her dressing table.

In his mind the foetus of a poem began to take shape, and in his native Bengali, he delivered, as it were, a requiem to their relationship:

I, on this bank, you on the other side
In between the river flows
Oblivious of the separation caused
To meet its sea, the river goes.

Like two birds on distant trees
I hear your call, and you hear mine
But never destined are we to meet
Though we may make music divine.

Pain clanged at his heartstrings; the pathos-enshrouded songs of Saigal floated by, filling him with a sadness so profound he could not convert it into tears. He clasped his knees in his arms, and rested his head on their fold. For not more than two minutes he succeeded in blanking out everything. But suddenly it all galloped back into the silence of his mind; the tenderness of her touch, the smile in her eyes, the scent of a promise so sweet it made you cry. He contemplated that no more would this very same sand bear the prints of their proximity, nor their eyes gaze out at the vastness of the sea, nor their faces feel the friendly touch of the lonely morning breezes. No more would she sit on a public park bench half-covering her face to become incognito, revealing only eyes full of a mystique that sometimes startled a passerby.

Overcome by a sense of finality, he stilled his mind by an exercise of rationale. He could not live without Priyanandini; but he could not live with her either. The pain would have to be treated with the ointment of reality.

The solution came to him in terms of such simplicity, that its practicality was an anesthetic. Yes, it was time he told his mother to search for a suitable bride; a traditional Bengali girl who cooked shoshur-bhata maach with the right measure of mustard, and who celebrated Durga Puja with all its perfervid splendour. One who would chant by her side in the mornings and blow the conch with hopeful aplomb, and garland her gods with strings of golden beads. This would be the ultimate sacrifice in honour of the mother on whom he had once inflicted a great and silent pain.

Having given a somewhat balanced segment to his turmoil, he walked homewards. With quiet resolve he concealed the packet containing the sari behind the kurtas in his cupboard. He had to begin to forget; right now was as good a time as any. Suchitra had found solace in death; Priyanandini would find it in time and youthfulness, and like the climax of one of her films, label THE END to their glorious affair.

Outside, on the waves, the moon's reflection broke into fragments.

Chah barbaad karegi, humein maaloom na tha

At Ismail Choonawala's wrap-up party, a double celebration along with the birth of his daughter Daisy, Mehru's eyes followed Aniruddh as he mixed with the rest of the guests. Still trying to find an answer to his peculiar behaviour the other day, she was further baffled by his avoidance of meeting her gaze. Her intelligent mind, however, whilst observing his indifference, failed to analyse its cause. For the past many days, he had neither come to her house nor sought her out in the studios. Was it because her mother had come on too strong the other day? Had he not understood that Rehmatbi was only a concerned mother, uneducated in the niceties of small talk?

Her abstraction caused her to spill a little sherbet on her expensive Chantilly lace sari, creating a local stir. People gathered around her with wet napkins and suggestions. But Aniruddh maintained his distance, speaking with tangential concentration to Imtiaz Ali, proffering neither solicitous enquiry nor curious glance. When the stain had been successfully removed, she looked up in his direction only to find him gone. He had left the party without a single exchange. Her heart distended with disappointment.

The next morning she walked along the beach, hoping that he might be waiting for her, as was his wont, although the requirement for their rendezvous had been obliterated by Rehmatbi's official endorsement of their relationship. Contrary to her hopes, Ani was nowhere in sight, and she crossed only the old man who daily shuffled along in semi-colons.

Two weeks passed without any word from him, confirming his desire to avoid association. It dawned on Mehru with a terrible clarity that she was confronting a good, old-fashioned rejection. She had been jilted, shredding the confidence with which she had endorsed his character to her mother.

The enormity of her sorrow was felt excruciatingly by the older woman. But she wisely refrained from speaking to her daughter, not wanting to rub salt on fresh wounds.

Mehru's baffled anguish compounded, hitting her eyes with unspoken grief.

Young love, at its happiest, may not be difficult to hide. But young love in torment is impossible to conceal. Mehru moped around in suspense, bestowing on her acting a dimension of tragedy so far absent from her earlier performances. It was a dimension that grew from the finer lines of experience and earned her commendability as a tragic actress. Her audible sighs created an aura of almost contagious sadness.

Aniruddh, on the other hand, gained his composure much faster, having been tutored earlier by Dey-da's instruction on the show going on. He immersed himself in his work, composing tunes of exquisite but gentle pain. His music, with its profusion of violins with their woeful notes and the haunting refrains of Pranoyda's lonely flute, began to be recognized as a new and distinctive style apart from the prevalent operatic tabla-harmonium mode.

From work he would come straight home and to Konkona's immense surprise, lock himself in his room. He became sullen and ill tempered. His only merciful retreat was his Sunday visit to distant Malad, where Paro and Pranoy had recently shifted. There, whilst Pranoy played the flute and he listened to his sister's marvellous timbre, he would find relief, pushing away the sight of his mother's puja room with its awesome reminders of what a difference, a difference in religion could make.

Viewing the general untidiness in his room, Konkona realized that not only had Aniruddh become abstracted and uncommunicative, but also rather careless. Industriously, she set about clearing up things and putting his cupboard in order.

Behind his kurta shelf, her hand encountered a paper packet. On emptying the packet she discovered quite unexpectedly, a Tangail sari. She stared at the green and red motifs with some amazement. What was a sari doing in the middle of some very masculine apparel? Couldn't possibly be for her; she only wore white as befitted a widow. Perhaps it was for Paro, or, could it perhaps be for the beach rendezvous girl? She realized that Ani had not been to the beach now for several days. But once or twice she had glimpsed the girl trying to peep into their windows, big, wistful eyes peering through the trellised jaali.

Something heavy seemed to still weigh down the packet, and putting her hand in she withdrew a bottle of strong-smelling scent. Now she was convinced it was for the girl on the beach. Then why had he not given it to her? Maybe they'd had some sort of lover's quarrel. That would surely explain Ani's sullenness, his not noticing that she sometimes put sugar in his curd instead of his favourite patali 'gur' which they had brought in plentiful all the way from Calcutta.

She wondered if she should talk to him about it, and whether that would be right. In the end, she decided to wait and see if he would broach the subject with her, or if some development would just naturally bring it out into the open.

And, as destiny would have it, it did.

Unpredictably, the very next day itself.

Fresh out of kalonji to temper her fish curry with, Konkona decided to amble across to the grocer. Her mind still rotating around the fulcrum of Ani's behaviour, she waited for the bania to weigh notorious-looking red chillies for a woman who had the appearance of a kindly witch. Beside her stood a more bullish male version of her, carrying her profile in such facsimile, that he was obviously her son. He was firing words like salvos at the harassed grocer.

"Come on, you lazy character. We haven't all day. Don't you know your wares are meant for the house of a famous actress?"

The older woman fixed her son with a razor look, then resumed her inspection of the grocer's weighing. Grunting, he glanced up at Konkona, and his expression changed to unconcealed disgust. Poor, curious Konkona wondered why he was so angry with the rest of the world, and wished he would remove that curious dragon stare. She lowered her gaze, for it was not cultured to stare at anyone or even be stared at in the way he was doing.

What happened next took her completely by surprise.

"Look Mithima," he pointed, " this is that kaafir's mother."

Konkona looked up. She was taken aback at the smouldering viciousness in the man's eyes. Certainly she had never seen him before, and wondered at the reason for his ire.

"See, how she stares innocently, as though she knows nothing. Tell her to instruct her son to keep away from my sister. Does he have no women in his community that he lusts after the women in ours? Ai, you Bengali whore,..'"

"Sshhh, Suleiman, have you lost your sharafat completely?" Rehmatbi interrupted. "Don't know what to talk and where!" She turned humbly to Konkona and apologised for her son's irrational behaviour.

"Forgive him sister; he is hot-blooded and not very wise." Saying which she pulled her son away as if he were a mentally challenged child needing guidance.

Konkona, dazed and doubtful, turned away, her kalonji forgotten, and traced her somnambulist steps back home. Her mind had been bombed out by this verbal missile, ears flaming with his vituperative abuse.

At home, she sat on a chair to figure out the reasons behind this absolutely unprovoked attack. Recalling his words, which came back to her frantic and fragmented, she tabulated certain facts to achieve a cogent conclusion.

1. The man had insinuated Ani was involved with his sister.
2. Since they were shopping at the local grocer, they obviously lived in the neighbourhood.
3. The slip of a girl who had been haunting the front lane also lived close by, and it was safe to assume that she must be the sister in question.
4. The woman had addressed her son as Suleiman.
5. Suleiman was a Muslim name.
6. Oh Maa, therefore, the girl with whom Ani was involved was a Muslim!

With sudden clarity, everything began to fall into place. Konkona's confusion dispelled to crystallise the situation in bold black and white. The unhappiness that Aniruddh wore on his forehead, his unsmiling face laminating his acceptance of a destiny of unfulfilled love, his abrasive attitude symbolising a frustration, clearly spelt the truth. Comprehension illuminated the dull stretches of her mind like a bright light on a dark street.

Understanding her pious and devout outlook, Ani had known with certainty that a Mohammadan would not be acceptable in her home. This had been the core of his dilemma and his subsequent surrender. Yes, surely this must be the answer to a conundrum that had existed around his figure these past few weeks.

Poor, poor Aniruddh! Her heart ached for her valiant son, running away all his young life; first from the clutches of a British justice, then from Suchitra's proffered feelings, and now from his own. Even if the girl's family had protested, he could always have married her and brought her into his home, if he had thought she would be welcome here. He would not have thrust the gifts for her into the back of his cupboard, or his feelings for her into the back of his mind. Worst of all, he had not divided this pain with anyone, neither with her nor Paro. Bottling his feelings within himself, he had let his anguish pour forth into those wistful songs he composed, which made others cry, leaving his own eyes ironically dry.

The rest of the day she ruminated the situation with a clear and calm mind, for Konkona was not given to impetuosity. The sight of her son's sombre face when he returned that evening firmed up her decision as strongly as cement fortifies a wall. She concluded that she must match his sacrifice equally with one of her own. It was a very selfish mother who would place her own superstitions above the happiness of her child.

Next morning at breakfast, she inaugurated her discussion with the casual enquiry.

"Son, we are doing comfortably now, aren't we?"

"Well, there's much more to achieve, Ma, but yes, you could say we are comfortable. Of course, once we have the car, we shall be in an exclusive class. But why do you ask? Are you in need of money? In that case, you know you only have to ask."

"No, my son, I have much more than I need already. From a shanty in a backward town to a solid two-bedroom apartment by the sea in one of the most progressive cities of our country; what more could I ask? But it is not of material things I speak. Are there not emotional needs to fulfill?"

Aniruddh stiffened; the mention of emotional needs made him disturbingly conscious of where this was leading. He looked down at his omelette with focus, minutely inspecting the pieces of onion and wondering why some were tinged green and others pink, as though by cracking this culinary puzzle he hoped to achieve some solution.

"Are you listening?" queried Konkona, feeling tension electrically charging the atmosphere.

"Whose emotional needs are we talking about, Ma? I, for one, am quite satisfied with my life. I have you and Paro and Pranoyda, and there is Utpal-da and my friend Imtiaz Ali. We have all grown pretty close over the past two years."

"You know very well I am not alluding to those ties. You need a woman to bring colour to your life. Don't you think it's time you married? You're twenty-three; at your age your father already had two children."

"Yes. Yes. Of course, marriage is necessary. After all, the family name has to be carried forward? In fact, it's the right time now. I have an extended contract with my studio, and some sort of name in the industry. So, Ma-go, why don't you search for a nice Bengali girl? She can assist you in the kitchen, and blow your shankha whilst you chant."

"I was referring to a companion for you, not for me. My thakurs are all the companions I want at this age. As for the girl, I have found one."

Aniruddh started. What? Already? She **had** been fast! Abruptly, Konkona returned from the bedroom with the brown paper bag. "This is the girl I want for you; the girl for whom you bought these gifts."

Ani's expression blurred with awkwardness.

"You should not have gone through.."

Konkona answered with the rectitude expected of her. "Believe me, I was not prying; I happened to chance upon it."

Aniruddh remained silent, a trifle abashed at the way he had spoken to his mother.

"You have stopped your walks on the beach, Ani. You have had a quarrel, perhaps?"

This couldn't be happening, thought Ani, appalled at his mother's deductions. But her suggestions would not survive the acid test of truth.

"Ma, you don't know what you intend. Let it be." He felt embarrassed talking such matters with her, but he was glad she had initiated the discussion and somewhat relieved it was out in the open. Perhaps now, he could bury the whole thing under layers of tradition.

"Yes, I do. What you are trying to conceal is that she is not of our faith or community, are you not?"

He had to admit, his mother never failed to surprise him! Aniruddh had no way of understanding how a woman, who spent half her time in the kitchen and the other half in prayer, could possibly have derived knowledge of Priyanandini or the fact that she was a Muslim.

"But how could you possibly know?" he asked, shock disturbing the rhythm of his words, so that they came out like the fluttering wings of birds.

"Who knows how the Lord organises things? When he wants to lead you somewhere, he charts a way for your footsteps."

"No, Ma. She is of a community that will not be acceptable to you. That is as sure as I am your son."

"You are sure of that only because I say so. And if I say she is acceptable to me, who are you to object? She is a Mohammedan, that I have found out. But if you have taken her into your heart, why cannot I take her into my home? If I am not raising objections, me, the sole hurdle to your happiness, why should you?"

Aniruddh looked incredulous. It took him a while to emerge from his verbal paralysis and actually frame a sentence.

"Ki bolchen Ma? Do you mean that?"

"No, I am having a cruel joke at your expense. Silly, I cannot wait for you to bring the girl home. From afar she looks quite pretty. Up close, she must be some beauty, hein?"

Ani regarded his mother with an expression that was a fraction over admiration. Perhaps it was worship.

A laugh, like a fast teen-taal tabla beat, came from his throat, dissolving the lump that had been resting there for the past many days. He had surrounded himself with gloom, with negativity, and it had all been blown away by a brief breakfast conversation. For the first time after a long gap, Konkona saw her son smile. The worry eased from his brow, and his shoulders appeared to lift in relief. Inside her she felt a beatitude that convinced her she had done the right thing.

"Go give her this packet, son. Inside I have added a small box of shindoor. So, I hope this will speak simply and shortly of your intentions."

Bereft of words, Aniruddh gathered his notation papers together and prepared to leave for work. On impulse, he bent down and touched her feet, the only way he could express the gratitude he felt. His mother was indeed a truly remarkable woman, one of a kind.

Kisne ye sab khel rachaya

KABHI KHUSHI KABHI GHAM

The putative topography of love's terrain has been universally declared as rough and rocky, so Aniruddh was not expecting it to be a silk and satin job to placate Priyanandini. [He would always think of her thus.] He was prepared fully for verbal outbursts, repulses, a slap-in-the-face, throwing a fit, tantrum or something more concrete, but hopefully not an irrevocable rejection. It took him all of three days to discover the location of her current shooting, for after the way he had treated her, he could not just politely ring her doorbell and expect her to respond amicably to a proposal.

She was in the middle of a take when he spotted her, wan and woeful, enacting a scene co-incidentally, of a woman whose love is being repudiated by the hero. Her distraught expression, obviously reflecting her true-to-life predicament, made Aniruddh wonder how much of her performance was really acting.

When the arc lights dimmed, and the fans whirred on, he watched her sink into a chair and call for the make-up man. A spot boy stood ready with a cup of tea, that ever-refreshing beverage of most filmwallahs. From somewhere in the darkness, the summoned make-up man materialised with a bottle of glycerine, his instant tears. He stood before her with his tray, hand mirror and the indispensable wet sponge.

"Wipe the sweat from my forehead, Pandhari, and touch up karo,' she ordered. Aniruddh watched the man work deftly on her face. He caught his eye, signalling to him that he wished to speak to her. Apprehension throbbed nervously in his breast.

"There's someone to see you, Baby," said Pandhari softly.

"Who is it? I don't want some inane fan to come and disturb the mood I've built up."

Without looking back, she held the mirror at an angle to see the person's reflection. Both hand and mirror went into freeze, as she saw Aniruddh's face smiling back at her with a cheeky calm. Now I'm seeing his face everywhere, she said to herself. God, I must be losing my senses. She dabbed her face hastily with a puff, hoping to powder away the apparition.

"There's someone to see you, Babesie," and at sound of the familiar address, the mirror descended onto Pandhari's toes. She swung around and stared squarely into his eyes.

Pique got the better of incredulity, as lightning burst from her eyes and dazzled him.

"What do you want? I'm not giving out any autographs."

"Madam, I had no intentions of disturbing you,' he said as soberly as he could, looking every bit an errand boy in distress. "I only came to give you this." He offered the paper packet with as much care as if he were handing her the Crown Jewels.

"Alright, so you've given it. Johnny, take this to my driver and instruct him to keep it in my car." Obeying her royal command, the spot boy vanished with Aniruddh's peace offering. She pulled her pallu over her shoulder with agitation and walked regally across to the opposite side of the set.

Aniruddh knew this was not the time and place to tackle her with the most significant moment of their lives. Yet he had preferred to make the first move in a place public enough for her not to react with a justifiably mad outburst. Because his Priyanandini would prototypically create a scene not in the script, instead of dissolving into feminine tears. But that was what drew him to her, for he didn't care for weak women.

The die was cast; or should it be the ball was in her court, and he would have to await some kind of response from her to hopefully carry forward their love story into a happy ending.

Riding home in the car, her hand encountered the brown paper packet resting coolly on the seat beside her. In her anger she had all but forgotten it. Fumingly she placed her hand within, feeling something damp. She withdrew a packet of wet leaves containing the most exquisite mogra buds. Their fragrance at once filled the interiors of the car with a heady scent. Mogras_her favouite flower, no, *their* favourite flower! She held them close to her face and inhaled deeply.

Then Fury overcame sentiment. How dare he! How dare he maintain a stony silence, a frigid distance, and then appear out of the blue trying to bribe her fragrantly back into his arms!

There was more in the packet; she pulled out a sari, woven in the finest cotton with motifs of ethnic splendour. It was so different from the floral georgettes that she was wont to wear. A soft moment of appreciation for Ani's taste interrupted her annoyance. If I were with him, she mused, I would switch to wearing paithanis and patolas. But I'm not; she collected herself. Nor will I be influenced by ethnic palliatives. She thrust the sari inside and made another discovery of a delicately engraved silver box around which a note had been tied with auspicious red thread. She opened it to read a single line: 'Give me a sign that you are prepared to listen, and I will explain everything.'

Explaining everything, Ani-moshai, might just take up a lifetime! What cheek to presume that one guest appearance would convert him again into the hero of a romance that he had caused, by willful neglect, to sour into a tragic tale? To expect the fragrance of jasmines to eradicate the pain that he had placed within her heart? He had the nerve to reappear after three months and think that they could carry on from where they had left off! Just like that? Well, he could stew in his 'macher jhol' for a while!

The car braked to a halt before her gate, and she quickly thrust the packet's contents into the bag before Suleiman's curiosity questioned her feverish face.

Indignant with Ani as well as herself for having succeeded in thawing, even for a moment, the feelings she had placed in cold storage and the memories she had refrigerated into mental ice cubes, she threw the packet into a chest of drawers. It was her firm determination that Mr. Aniruddh Ganguly was getting no 'sign' from her, whether in print or in Morse code or in eye language, for a pretty long time to come. He would pay for the hurt he had caused by wallowing in some hurt of his own.

Udi hawa mein jaati hun

For a whole week Aniruddh waited expectantly, but all was quiet on the neighbourhood front. There was not a word from Priyanandini. His patience abated, and hope, too, began to evaporate. She must have been hurt more than I had estimated, he figured, for her pride to hold out so long. Priyanandini, his glorious butterfly with a damaged wing. He was about to be punished for what he had done in all good intention.

Finally, it was his mother's cajoling that persuaded him to make one last-ditch effort. Like she said in her provincial wisdom, he had given her the wound, he must provide the salve.

On a Sunday, when she generally had an off, he espied her car still parked at the kerb, and prepared to face the fallout of her indignation. Marriage proposals were, as the pundits said, for better or for worse. Plunges were taken to either drown, or swim through underwater fantasia.

Her doorbell jangled raucously. The door was jerked open by Priyanandini herself, still-existent rancour expressive in the act. Eyes, registering surprise at first, smouldered on to a fiery glow.

He attempted a smile.

"You? You!" came her double exclamation. "Why are you darkening the doorstep that you last departed as if a posse of devils were giving chase?"

"I..er..I've come to see..see... your mother!" he said, the stutter which interfered at moments of stress surfacing as he uttered the first thing he could think of.

"What could you possibly want with a simple old lady like her?"

"If you ask me in, perhaps I could tell you. It's a little difficult explaining with a threshold between us. Perhaps you may ponder the irony of how an open door is such a barrier."

"There's nobody home. So, it's not *proper*," she proclaimed in tones that would have made the Victorians proud.

Aniruddh laughed heartily, an amused laugh that brought his eyebrows together.

"What, the indomitable Priyanandini afraid of what society would say? Apprehensive of a 5' 7" not too strong young man whom she can knock down with one sweep of her eyelashes? I must have got the wrong house."

He turned to go away. A sound like a dry twig snapping underfoot came from behind.

"Come in if you must. But be prepared to wait some minutes. She'll be home shortly."

"Tell me, Babesie, who are you really afraid of? Me, or yourself?"

"Don't call me that. What do you really want?"

"Truthfully? To taste some of your mother's delicious wheat flour halwa."

"What do *you* have to celebrate that you come to sweeten your mouth at her door?"

"Perhaps I have, and perhaps I don't. Time will tell. Or maybe you." His voice was velvety as he stepped closer towards her.

"Don't you dare come near me," she screamed hysterically, flailing her arms to keep him at a distance, "I'm not interested in anything you have to say that could not have been said three months ago."

"But I was in such a dilemma, sweetheart. My mind was confused, and I had to sort out some discoveries."

"Don't call me that. I suppose I couldn't have helped you."

"You don't understand, Babesie."

"No, of course I don't. I'm a fool, you see, totally lacking in the brains department. So if I couldn't understand then, what makes you think I'm more intelligent now?"

The tenderness of his smile only made her madder. For want of words, she began to hit out at him with her fists, muttering and calling him a damn fool son of a Bengali peasant.

"That's the first time a curse sounded so sweet. How about my teaching you some choice ones in Bangla?"

"There are plenty in my native tongue, and with a brother like Suleiman, that part of my vocabulary is quite proficient, thank you."

"You are welcome to practice them all on me. God knows I deserve it."

"I haven't been wasting my time; the most acrid variety has been fired at you in absentia, damn you."

"My God, Babesie, do you think I've not suffered at all? That I'm devoid of feelings because as a man I cannot easily cry?"

"Then you must be a masochist if you went on enjoying it for so long. And you cannot expect me to consider extenuating circumstances just because you come here bearing gifts like... like the Magi [here Mehru's convent slip showed], and I should forgive and forget because I'm susceptible to bribes. Here," she said, procuring the packet from the drawer in the armoire, 'here's your precious gift! Go give it to some homely Bengali girl who'll bow her head at your every command and bore you to hell." She flung the paper packet at him with such vehemence that it ricocheted off his chest and clattered to the floor with a reverberating clang.

The bottle of attar was saved as it landed on the sari, but the silver box rolled onto the floor, spilling its contents all over the many-coloured mosaic. The sindoor splayed like martyr's blood.

Mehru stared mesmerically at the auspicious powder all over the white and green mosaic, then met Aniruddh's stricken look with eyes that dilated with splendid shock. Goodness, she had not remembered to check inside the box at all! Had this been then, Aniruddh's concept of a proposal, and had he come here despite its symbolic though mistaken rejection?

Silently, he began to gather the scattered powder with the edge of the paper bag, his eyes downcast with disappointment. Absentmindedly Mehru bent to brush off the redness that clung to the rims of his sleeve, knowing how pristine white he liked his kurtas.

Aniruddh's proximity to the gravelly powder then erupted in a violent sneeze.

"Oh dear," began Mehru, but before she could say a further word, her olfactory organ answered his sneeze with an equally strong one of its own.

Then they were both sneezing in tandem, almost choking with the in-between laughter that spilled forth at the oddness of the situation. And before they knew it, they were in each other's arms, touching with the desperation of a long separation.

Suddenly Aniruddh pulled away, "Do you know that this might possibly be the first ever allergic reunion in romantic history? Come to think of it, why don't we ever connect such mundane realities to lovers? As though Romeo had never been spotty with measles or Juliet had a running nose, or that Shirin snored and Farhad farted?"

Her laugh tinkled in the room like the prisms of a chandelier. Her eyes shone, obliterating the weeks of dullness with a glitter that was as much happiness as tears.

'Then why, Aniruddh, why?" Her seriousness was silken.

"Nandini, the day I first came to your house was the day I first discovered you were a Muslim. We had never spoken about such things before because they probably never mattered."

"My name, Priyanandini; that must have caused the misunderstanding! But of course, that's not my real name. Since everyone now calls me that, with the exception of my family, I never.."

"Precisely. And since we were thinking marriage, there was one highly important factor to be considered; my mother. Being a Brahmin and a woman of piety, it was not possible for me to cause a defilation, don't take that personally, in her puja room or her kitchen. Accepting that our union was ill fated, I thought it best to make a neat amputation, and to keep the cleavage bloodless meant avoiding a face-to-face with you. Taking her point of view completely for granted, I never once considered venturing her opinion. God knows how she found out about us, literally she says it was the 'way of the Lord', but my mother mixed her black and white and accepted the grey. She says her son's happiness comes first, and there's no need for sacrifices. She's given us her blessing. She is one great woman!"

"And what about mine who had accepted you without even meeting you, which is why she gave you the third degree that day?"

"So now we have maternal permissions, Miss Priyanandini, perhaps you could tell me your real name?"

A rare coyness overcame the heroine of this romantic tale. She trembled and said diffidently, "Meherunissa. And by the way Mr.Ganguly, does the symbolism of the sindoor stand for what I think it stands?"

"You bet your daily installment it does, Baby!"

This, then, was the tableau that greeted Rehmat's eyes as she stepped into her living room. Her daughter and that strange Hindu boy on all fours on the ground, scraping something off the floor. A clucking sound escaped her practical lips.

"My floors need extra scrubbing or what?"

Startled by the sound of her voice, Mehru lifted dewy eyes and stared without focus at her mother. Rehmatbi was not sure if the redness in her face was a blush or the reflection of the red powder strewn on the floor. With a sigh she hung her pacchhdi on the maypole.

"So are you going to remain frozen there forever or do you intend to show some respect to your elders?"

Both sheepishly rose. Mehru busied herself brushing the powder off her sari.

"Mithima..

Ma.." they began in tandem.

"Mithima, why don't you prepare seera for our guest like you did the last time?"

"Why? I only make seera when it's cold, raining, or a special occasion. And the sun is shining brightly outside," she said pointedly.

"But what if it's really a very special occasion?"

Rehmatbi's eyes glowered like coals. This had better be good. She was not going to make a fool of herself a second time round. Her stance caused both matrimonial incumbents to huddle in silence, one waiting for the other to speak up first.

"Well, I'm listening."

"Would you be terribly displeased if you were to acquire a Hindu son-in-law, Ma? My mother has given her consent."

Allah ka shukra hai, the boy spoke up first. If Mehru had done so, she would have thrown the boy out for being a spineless idiot. The smile that divided her lips caused multiple creases to break up her face. Her wart quivered.

"I'm not terribly thrilled with my Muslim son-in-law anyway. A joroo ka ghulam, ek number ka. Why not try a Hindu one, haan? Provided you can lasso this fiery, flashy filly. On that condition, I'll accept."

"That shouldn't be too hard for a krantikari who's even been in jail."

"Well, I hope he has no intentions of repeating that performance. Instead of standing there, Mehru, sieve some flour. Kismet ki baat hai, I brought home some Karachi halwa from the jamaatkhana."

"What's Karachi halwa?" asked Aniruddh's sweet tooth.

"Just the stuff, my lad, for a celebration."

Hasinon ki jitni tehardaariyaan hain

Suleiman spat furiously at the news. Annoyance at the thwarted attempts to get rid of the Bangla-moshai compounded his frustration, but with Mithima's concurrence, and his sister's adult status, there was really not much that he could do except boycott the wedding. Esabha made a proclamation whose eloquence was wasted because of disillusioned mumblings and the fact that no one really listened. Shamim wondered if a composer brother-in-law might just be advantageous to further his own career. Kulsum, busy with her babies and her beau, showed no special point of view. Being particularly fond of her sister, she was just happy that she had chosen to marry at all. For Mehru in particular, what was of crucial importance was that Aniruddh chose not to raise any objections to her continuing in films. Ma was there, and their combined incomes could now afford the employment of domestic help to manage the running of their home.

Mixed reactions were equally prevalent in the other house, as was natural to an unprecedented Hindu-Muslim marriage. But the admirable control of the Ganguly women was such that no scenes, objections or excessively verbal discussions ensued. A stoic surrender, a low-key acceptance, a practical attitude marked their preparations. Although happy in her brother's happiness, Paro often wondered what ripples had occurred in her mother's placid mind, what emotional compulsions had prompted her acceptance and at what cost. For Konkona neither initiated nor encouraged discussion on the subject. Only Shubir was visibly excited, and informed friends, teachers, neighbours and all those who cared to listen that he was to acquire a 'Bou-di.'

The two mothers-in-law met to discuss the wedding plans. They were a study in dramatic contrast. Rehmatbi, dour-faced and hoarse-voiced with asthma, with a predilection to prolific mohallah-style swearing; Konkona temperamentally docile and delicate, prone to poojas and penances. When dress and ritual posed a problem, it was agreed by general consensus that the best possible recourse was to a civil marriage. The affianced couple, eager to tie the knot before a change in mind, professional hurdles or social hassles upset their plans, thought it best, too. The familial climate was affable, and before possible storms blew everything away, they applied at the court registrar's.

And so, whilst the struggle for Independence changed colours in the background maintaining its pre-eminently red motif, a Hindu and a Muslim were united in matrimony by a British Justice of the Peace.

The year was 1937. Ten years later, in the havoc of 1947, such an alliance might have generated violent, perhaps fatal, responses.

Babul mora, neihar chooto ri jaaye

Priyanandini and Aniruddh

THE GREAT STUDIOS

Mr. and Mrs. Aniruddh Ganguly, along with their witnesses Utpalda, Prannoy, Imtiaz Ali, Shamim, Saro and her husband Kumarsen, removed to Aniruddh's house for the wedding lunch after the simple ceremony that united them.

The patio was decorated with alpona, the doors and windows fringed with garlands of jalebi-coloured marigolds. As communal compromise, a combined lunch had been cooked by the women of the two families; chodhchodhi and fried bekti, a delectable biryani aromatic with saffron, fish steamed in banana leaves and 'baked' in sand.

When all the guests had departed, Konkona, carrying an attache case, took her son aside.

"Ani, I am planning to stay a few days with Paromita and Prannoy."

"But I've just got married, Ma."

"Shei toh! All new couples need privacy. It will give my new daughter-in-law some time to get used to the house without having a mother-in-law hanging around. Besides, her mother has agreed to take care of your food. You have servants now; so be kind and give me some time with my daughter and granddaughter." Her smile was so affectionate that Ani, happy at her consideration, agreed amicably.

Meanwhile, in the bedroom, Rehmatbi had been giving Mehru a last minute talk on 'pleasing her husband'. Finally she too left, giving her reassuring pats on the back, making Mehru wonder if 'pleasing her husband' was going be an ordeal that all women have to bear, like childbirth and menstruation.

But here we must begin, along with the new phase in our heroine's life, to address her as Priyanandini, or Nandini shortly; for she had adopted her screen name as a permanent one. She was now Priyanandini Ganguly, Hindu wife.

Alone at last; the all-time favourite post-wedding sentence.

Nandini showered and changed from her heavy silk sari into an imported lacy nightgown, which Bertha had procured from an Anglo-Indian railway officer's wife. She sat in front of the dressing table, opening out the pins that had held her profuse hair in a 'jooda.'

And that was how Aniruddh saw her in that first moment of privacy. That everyday simple act of unpinning her hair brought home with heightened significance that this woman was now his, to share his life, his room, his bed.

His sudden introduction in the mirror made Nandini pause. She was suddenly aware of their being alone in a way they had never been before, of a vital change in the equation of their lives.

Eyes locked together in the mirror image, he walked towards her reflection with slow, measured steps. For a pulsating moment, he stood behind her in a freeze shot. The heat of his breath made a frosted circle on the surface of the glass. Then he began removing the pins in tandem. His touch was both warm and chilling, and the comprehensive aura of intimacy made her shudder.

Her hair rushed downwards darkly, framing her porcelain cheekbones. In contrast, her shoulders were light on white silk. Mesmerically he gazed at her shoulder blades, sharply right-angled to her slim neck. With light feathery strokes he began to caress them, sending tingles up her neck and down her arms. The old-fashioned frame of the mirror threw up their montage sharply as his fingers splayed along the top of her lush and creamy breasts. Never for a moment was that electrifying eye contact in the mirror lost, as they watched their actions being played out vicariously by reflected characters. Aniruddh slid his hand upwards and cupped her chin; then that dynamic eye contact snapped as he tilted her face upwards. Her eyes took on a deeper green, like the shades of an ocean bed viewed through a glass-bottomed boat. He bent down and kissed the mystique shut, as though it were too beautiful to behold. Moist lips traced her nose and came to rest stunningly on her lips. She gasped; and in that open-mouthed second, his tongue slid inside and interplayed gently with hers, two snakes coiling around each other in hunger and ecstacy. Sweetness began to melt inside her like warm honey. Slowly, without her realising it, his hands were inside the lacy neckline and cupping her breasts. Beneath the froth of lace her breasts rose like two magnificent swans, and her heart throbbed madly, triggering a vibration lower down in her body.

He can do what he likes *with* you, Rehmatbi had advised, but she had mentioned nothing of what he could do *to* you, thought Nandini, as she felt her breasts tauten. Gently he lifted her, guiding her towards the four-poster with its embroidered sheets and frilly pillow covers. His hands strummed her nipples, guitar-like, swamping her with the discovery of her own sensuality.

Then they were side by side on the bed, straining for closer contact, their movements tutored by the instinct of their desires. Over his shoulder Nandini incongruously espied the falooda-pink ceramic rose on the footboard, behind which blue wall-water floated. *Do whatever he teaches you,* her mother had said, but Nandini discovered that the art of making love was not a lesson, but came naturally in the desire to please and be pleased. With his index finger he played a sonata on her thigh, till she felt a diminutive sun rise up somewhere under her navel, a kundalini heightened by cosmic warmth and light.

This was nothing like the painful experience she had been anticipating. Perhaps it would come later.

"Please, Ani, you will be careful," she blushed, as if he could be gentler than he already was, holding her as if she were made of porcelain "it's my first time, you know."

Aniruddh paused in his symphonic administrations to rest his head on his palm and look down at her with infinite tenderness. "Goodness, Babesie, what a co-incidence. It's mine, too."

Then their bodies were moving in a rhythm that comes naturally to a composer, a rhythm into which Nandini flowed like a tributary into a river.

When the sun set in her navel, Nandini threw her head back upon the pillows with a deep sigh. All energy seemed to drain from her, as if someone had switched off a light within, and placed her in the lap of peace and serenity. Their *coming* together was all the pain and pleasure that defines the agony and ecstacy of young love. What surprised her was her own response, doing things naturally instead of with preconceived notions, feeling neither shy nor embarrassed.

They slept blissed. It was darkening when Nandini awoke. The twilight filling the unfamiliar room disoriented her. For a moment she imagined herself in some strange hotel room on location. Then warm breath fanned her cheek, and gazing at the man sleeping heavily at her side, she recalled the day that had been. This man was her husband, with the social license to sleep beside her and the emotional capacity to arouse in her never before experienced sensations. Strange, she had shared a room with four other people, but besides the floor space they had shared little else. She wanted all that rectified now. She wanted to multiply an extreme closeness with this man, to reimburse their children with love and happiness and contentment. For her part she vowed to interest herself in his music, to learn Bengali, to bond with his mother.

Filled with these good intentions, she extricated herself from his leg and found her way to the kitchen. The servants had been given a holiday to accord privacy to the couple.

Juggling two cups of tea, she returned to their bedroom, she placed them on a side table, and tried to shake her husband awake. Her husband! Oh, how she loved the sound of that! She savoured the word on her tongue, rolled it around like a lemon drop, as she gazed at the sight of Aniruddh sleeping so satiatedly on the rumpled sheets.

Aniruddh stirred and looked at her with half-closed eyes. Seeing Nandini's flushed face and tousled hair, he imagined himself in a dream. If that were so, he had no intention of waking up. He gripped her hair and pulled her towards him.

The tea on the side table cooled. The bowl of mogras floated fragrantly on the dresser.

Appropriate to the circumstances of their union, the couple held their reception on a studio set. Long strings of garlands dangled from the scaffolding, the Mole Richardson arc lights lent brightness, and the giant floor fans swished cool air around the invitees. There was Chandulal Shah accompanied by his heroine Goharbai; Himanshu Rai with the gorgeous Devika Rani, internationally acclaimed for her beauty. Vimal Kumar, Nauroji, a deputation from Prabhat, Saro/Sukumari with hubby Kumarsen, Zubeida and Zebunissa, dapper Jairaj and petite Lalita Pawar from the silent era, Leela Chitnis who lived a few houses away, rubicund Sunny Choonawala and robust Imtiaz Ali, and Dalsukh Pancholi who was visiting from Lahore.

There was a satisfied buzz that Nandini would not be quitting films after marriage. Pretty women were hard to come by, and harder than that, pretty women who agreed to work in films.

These then, were the dreamers and seekers, experimenting with the embryonic medium. They were on a journey of discovery. By a process of trial and error, they would mark the road for future dreamers. Exultant in their common experience, they were the chosen few, looking to part the waves.

Soon they settled into a daily programme, both leaving for work together, generally in Aniruddh's new Austin with the ventilator in the roof, and when they returned in the evening they were never too tired to entertain. They were charged with a new energy, two triumphant spirits complementing each other and completing themselves. They were like joyous waves of the sea moving with a blue light, imbibing great quantities of ozone love; or many-hued birds soaring high enough to hear the music of the spheres, the whisper of the raindrops. They were bright like mustard flowers in winter, sharp as the tang of salt spray. Nandini could no longer recollect any life before Aniruddh, before the loving way he had of suddenly looking at her.

Around their happiness many people gathered. Their home was open house for men like Utpalda and Imtiaz, and the poet Narendra Sharma and the shair Safdar 'Aah'. Occasionally, someone would bring over a bottle of Scotch, and Aniruddh began to appreciate its heady taste just as much as he enjoyed the inebriation of a tipsy success.

It was almost a year before realisation struck that Ma was still at Paro's.

On being questioned about her return, she deftly waived aside protests by saying Moon-moon needed to be taken care of now that Paro's career as a playback singer had taken off. Besides, Nandini was a good surrogate mother to Shubir and domestic affairs were being taken care of. She no longer had exclusive rights to the house; it was now Nandini's home, too. Aniruddh left it at that; he was worried about her possible objections to the consumption of liqour in their house. Any amorphous doubts that she might have made a graceful exit leaving the fort to be womanned by a Mussalman daughter-in-law, soon frittered away.

For Nandini announced that she was pregnant.

Aniruddh's jubilation was unbounded. At 24, he could be considered moderately successful, had a beautiful wife he loved dearly, a house even though it was rented, a car, money beyond his dreams. Now he was about to become a father! What more could he ask for, except a healthy child?

In July 1938, a son was born to them, and they named him Pradeep, light of their lives.

Hum, aur tum, aur ye khushi, ye kahkahe, ye dillagi,
Chitki hui hai chandni, hum, aur tum

The cherubic child managed to endear himself to one and all. With his round, plump face, his father's dark, curly hair, and his mother's green eyes and deep dimples, he was a great favourite with both his grandmothers and the delight of his 'kaka' Shubir. But astonishingly the most remarkable affect he had was on the hitherto black sheep, Suleiman. At sight of the child the diabolic bull-man was reduced to soft mush, and his dialogue metamorphosed from the growling delivery of swear words into nonsensical baby chatter. The poor confused child always had his uncle's stubbly cheek being rubbed against him, but in the universal way in which babies understand affection, eventually established a rapport with this fierce homosapiens. It was Suleiman who surrendered his daily duty of driving in favour of Pradeep's airing in the Shivaji Park grounds; it was Suleiman who held him in his arms and cooingly made him listen to the sound of the breakers. There were general speculations as to how long this sentimental streak would last. But everyone was unanimously relieved at this temporary reprieve, and the transformation of Attila the Hun into Mary Poppins was accepted blissfully for however long it would last.

Nandini, who had retained her figure despite the birth, went back to work under the arc lamps. Her face was a little fuller, but she seemed to have become more beautiful, if that were at all possible. Motherhood had added an aura to her face. As for Aniruddh, he was upwardly mobile, and if his alliance with Nandini had proved lucky, [he had signed four films after his marriage], the year of his son's birth saw six releases of films with his music direction. He started to work with the top singers of the time like Amirbai Karnataki,

Zohrabai Ambalewali and Rajkumari. His home became the confluence of rhythmic rivers, and regular gatherings included aritsts like Waheedanbai and Jaddanbai, and Saraswati Devi of Bombay Talkies, through whom he developed friendships with women like Devika Rani and poets like Pradeep. He was content with this amazing sangam of the commercial and the intellectual, which filled his stomach and satisfied his soul.

1939 saw the outbreak of war on the European continent. The rumble of guns and the blitzkrieg of battlefields, the rhythm of boots marching on the hearts of nations, the clash on the ground and in the skies indicated a drop in production in Bombay's film world. It meant proportionately lesser availability of imported raw stock though more availability of themes, as war crept onto celluloid. Social messages now began to replace the much played-out mythologicals, and the horrors of war, the abolition of untouchability, the ravages of famine, became optional concepts. Consciousness of film as a powerful medium of social reform saw a new type of genre emerge. Nandini did a major role in a film about the harmful effects of drinking, and the titles of Aniruddh's films gradually began to shed their eclectic American captions.

In 1942, Imtiaz Ali Khan spoke to Aniruddh about starting his own production company.

"But, Imti, isn't it too big a project for you to handle? Times are lean, finances low. If you go out on a limb, you may just find yourself crashing to the ground. Don't you think it's safer to stick with employment and let someone else take the fall when a film bombs? Excuse the phrase; it must be the effect of the war."

"Amman Ani, you know Sunnysaab. He's only interested in returns, never in art. You and I are a different set, yaar. If *you* co-operate, I can manage the finance part. But the people interested in extending loans still desire names that matter in the studio line-up. So, can I expect your help as a friend and as an artist?"

"Bhai, you don't have to ask. I completely agree that it's stifling to work with Sunnysaab. But my contract with him expires at the end of the year. After that, I'm all for the cause of meaningful cinema. And let me give you some names of people who are keen to nurture the medium. They are all artists of theatre that my seventeen-year-old brother Subir associates with; a new breed of thinkers and radicals who will work with us less for money and more for fulfillment."

"Amman yaar, I am touched by your reference to 'work with us'. Let us vow today to work always with each other; whenever I do a film, you will score the music, whether you are contracted or not."

"Then let me make an amendment. I shall obliterate this contract system from my side. Perhaps I shall start a new trend of freelancing. After all, times are changing. Have you thought of where you will build your studio?"

"I won't have the money for a studio, just for a production company, but I intend to buy land in preparation for establishing one. I've seen a place in the suburb of Bandra; it's going cheap because it's a little hilly there. But beggars can't be choosers."

"Then let's just pray choosers don't become beggars. It is my 'dua' that you should achieve great success and become a cinematic legend."

"Inshallah."

Duniya rang rangeeli baba, duniya rang rangeeli

GOLDEN ERA

It was after Imtiaz's epic film on the great spirit of Indian womanhood, that Ani had a most unexpected visitor. Standing three steps below him in the incredible morning was Ambika Devi, known to a few and adulated by millions. Reputed to have features that would proudly adorn the face of a coin, she had mysteriously gone into retirement after her very first film achieved legendary popularity. Ambika had preferred to settle down with the dynamic producer of her film, the formidable Rai Bahadur Durgadass, who owned the second largest studio in the city. Durgadass had been something of a fop, and smoked smelly cigars in the style of a Hollywood mogul. True to his foreign predilections, he named his company Shooting Stars when everyone else was affixing theirs with Cinetone or Talkies. His studio had introduced the current matinee idol. He had still been enjoying the overflow from his super-successful film starring his wife, when unfortunately, he died in a plane crash on his way back from England with new suits and the processed prints of his next film. Leaving Ambika Devi in control of his vast business empire, his fortunes, and his production company. The industry grapevine had it that though Ambika wasn't as successful as her husband, visitors to the studio office preferred the fragrance of her Chanel No. 5 to the stale cigar smell that had hovered like a fog during the Rai Bahadur's era.

Ambika was an enigma to some and a snob to many, purely because of her reclusivity. She drove around in an American Chevrolet with black tinted windows and gave audience in her studio office to only the few who worked with her. She rarely attended film functions.

And now here she was on Aniruddh's doorstep, looking as fresh as the crisp December morn. His stammer justifyingly appeared as he invited her in. When she said in clipped tones, 'Ah, the boy from East Bengal,' he became embarrasingly conscious that he was clothed only in a banian and lungi. Whilst he excused himself to become more presentable, Ambika Devi looked around the drawing room and noted its leather sofas, the ornate dresser that took up most of one wall, and wondered if the painting atop the sideboard was original Jamini Roy, a painter who had recently held a successful exhibition in London. Placing her purse gracefully on one of the walnut side tables, she inhaled deeply the scent of the flowers that wafted across from the mogra trellis in the balcony.

Aniruddh returned in western attire; a natty multi-crease trouser and shirt.

"So, you're Aniruddh Ganguly," she said pointedly, giving him a careful scrutiny.

"Perhaps I looked more like Iqbal the butcher earlier," he replied, wondering why on earth everyone said this to him as their opening sentence. Maybe they expected some Babu-moshai with betel juice dripping at the corner of his mouth, humming refrains of Rabindra Sangeet.

"I didn't mean to be offensive."

"Please, neither did I. It's just my complexion, the essence of us East Bengalis."

"I want you to do a film with Shooting Stars," she said without fuss.

Not one for the small talk, thought Aniruddh, appreciating her direct approach.

"Impossible right now, madam, you see I just signed a contract with Nauroji to do two pictures at a stretch, and the underlying clause is that I don't work outside till then."

Ambika Devi was not accustomed to being refused. Furthermore, she had never heard the word impossible. For a brief second, her eyes flashed.

"Think about it; signing a film with us will bring you straight into the 'A' pictures bracket, much above the level of Choonawala and Nauroji."

"But Nauroji is my mentor," he parried, "I can't be disloyal to him."

"A creditable virtue, loyalty. But nevertheless a foolish one."

"That's a chance I have to take, madam."

She was intrigued by this little man who had the guts to say no to her.

"Perhaps we could circumvent this legal hurdle if you composed under an assumed name."

"It's a possibility," he said, with an air of non-commitment.

Her beauty smote him between the eyes. Her alabaster skin glowed with freshness and fragility. "I would like to work for you... for Shooting Stars, if that can be arranged."

"Then be at my office tomorrow morning at ten."

"Impossible. I have a rehearsal."

Impossible twice in one minute was beyond Ambika Devi's vital endurance. With sudden intensity, she leaned forward and commanded, "Cancel it."

Her ominous tone left Aniruddh with no option but to agree. Besides, he couldn't really be rude to a lady, especially one like her, enthralled as he was by her mystique.

She rose, turned on her smartly shod heel, and departed regally without formal leave-taking.

For a long time Aniruddh stood staring at the indentation in the chair that she had just vacated. The majestic Ambika Devi had actually sat across him in his humble abode. Her perfume still lingered heavily, proof of her presence.

Utpalda had been right. This was an industry of images. The celebrated actress, the intriguing woman, the ultimate femme fatale of the thirties, was as hard as polished nails. And he wasn't referring to the manicured variety.

For the first time after five years of happy domesticity, he felt attracted to a woman.

Ye kaun aaj aaya savere savere

He was met outside her office by her secretary Jamnadas, a business-like Gujerati who had worked with the Rai Bahadur and was known for his fierce loyalty.

"Madam is awaiting you. Madam is very keen you work with us. Madam has very good judgment." It was obvious his world revolved around the sun of Ambika Devi.

The lady herself was ready with the papers, professional to her pedicure.

"I knew you would come." Clipped tones as usual. "You have thought of a substitute name?" she asked, straight down to business.

"Yes," he answered, observing her with his direct gaze. "My brother-in-law, Prannoy Biswas."

"Good. Then we can dispense with the formalities like payments, etc. I have signed up Amirbai Karnataki to sing the female lead songs."

Aniruddh's Bengali eyes flashed annoyance, a rare sight for Ambika.

"It is convenient, madam, your taste agrees with mine. But I do not like to be dictated to about which singers are suitable. To use a market phrase, I know my onions. If we are to work together, I would like to be clear regarding such matters. Suggestions, yes; interference, no."

Ambika Devi's pencil-thin eyebrows rose almost to her hairline. Nobody had spoken to her thus. She secretly admired his cocky confidence. A man who knew what he wanted, and was not afraid to speak his mind. She had met few like him.

When he departed, he left his charisma behind. She inhaled it deeply like an aphrodisiac. For a change, Ambika Devi was affected more by a man than by the imminent dissolution of her company. An occupational hazard that had made her *go to* Aniruddh Ganguly, instead of summoning him. As she had rightly estimated, it had overwhelmed him enough to come straightaway, drawn by the spell of her personal approach.

Jamnadas saw Aniruddh out of the office. When he returned to the sanctum sanctorium, it was to see Ambika's face flaming like a forest fire.

"Perhaps he is a bit mad, but it is fine, madam," he said in pacification. "One hit, and the company will stabilise. Our star will stay, and not go to the rival studio. Vimal Kumar's advice was good, nahin, madam? Pull Aniruddh Ganguly up into the high bracket and watch him deliver. What foresight that man has, madam. He is a financial genius."

Ambika Devi inhaled sharply, her sari pallu flying away with her feelings. Then she beckoned to her secretary. Drawing his hand to her breast, she made him squeeze it tightly. One by one, he fumblingly opened her buttons, and put his mouth to her hard, erect nipple. Slowly his tongue rolled over her gorgeous mound, and he began to service her in the way she had taught him as part of his confidential secretarial duties.

Aniruddh had turned her on. Her orgasm was fast and furious.

One song did it.

It tore out from the rehearsal room and swept all over the country like a whirlwind. Expressing the thematic content of the rich-poor divide, a subject which Aniruddh knew well having experienced both worlds at close quarters, its lyrics cocked a snook at the affluent who remain isolated in their castle residences, and rejoiced in the condition of the poor who live contentedly in their beloved bylanes. Since most of India fell snugly into the category of poor, the general public celebrated the song like a festival. Audiences clapped with it in the theatre.

Dancers floated to it at weddings. Choruses raised its words to the sky.

And Ambika Devi smiled her regal smile all the way to the bank.

No song had achieved such phenomenal popularity since last Devika Rani had cooed 'Main ban ki chidiya' in 'Acchut Kanya.' It not only secured Ambika Devi's tottering concern, sparing it a humiliating liquidation, the potentialities of which had been known only to a close few, but also catapulted its composer right to the top as the most sought-after music-director in filmdom. For despite the surrogate name, it was an open secret about who had really scored music for the film.

Some important consequences occurred thereafter. Aniruddh signed a five-year contract with Shooting Stars at a revised price he commandeered, with no obligation to exclusivity. Attracted by the leftist ramblings in the lyrics, a man named Khwaja Ahmed Abbas was drawn towards him, shaking Aniruddh's socialist leanings out of their dormant state. His response to the man's intellectualism resulted in a lifelong friendship. Abbas brought along with him other like-minded people, most of whom would conjoin in the Indian People's Theatre Association, and ripples in Aniruddh's cultural river extended to cover a wider intellectual circle.

He was aware of strong sexual vibes that emanated from the savvy producer of his first statistical hit. But though Aniruddh was conscious of his new standing in the industry, of his power as a music broker who now held the careers of singers, musicians and lyricists in his hands, he firmly kept lust at a distance.

For he loved his wife dearly, and that's the way he wanted it to stay.

When Pradeep was four years old, Nandini conceived again. It was good that she had only one major outdoor stint left for Master Vinayak's film. She would try and complete it before she began to show. It couldn't be postponed because once the rains set in, all units would immigrate indoors.

The location was for five days at Alibaug, and though she could have come and gone daily, she decided to stay on location along with the rest of the crew. Commuting everyday would have meant being up so much earlier. Pradeep was in the hands of an efficient Goan nanny. Besides, she could do with a break from Ani's daily soirees that sometimes overwhelmed her with their weighted intellectuality.

It was a jungle adventure. Tents were erected on the site to house the artists and technicians as well as a travelling kitchen. Sister-in-law Gulsakkar accompanied Nandini. Being childless, she was free to tag along with Nandini and enjoy vicariously the many-splendoured pleasures of a life of glamour.

On the last day, the director approached Nandini with the day's schedule, and asked if she knew how to ride.

She was immediately apprehensive, wondering if it were safe in her condition. But pregnancies being the most heavily guarded secret in the industry besides love affairs, Nandini wondered if she should tell him. Her mother had warned her not to speak to anyone about it because of the evil eye; especially not to Gulsakkar in case the childless woman cast some resentful shadow on her state. Once her stomach extended, the child would have grown strong within her womb and developed its own destiny.

So Nandini decided to risk silence; and was gratified on being informed that she had to ride sidesaddle, and trot but a few yards.

She took her perch on the horse, which seemed docile enough, and waited in the centre of a cleared space for her signal to move. The solar reflectors blazed; it was a good day for an outdoor. On the sound of ACTION, the horse trainer clucked, motivating the horse forwards. Two more steps, and she would be out of the camera's frame according to the marking.

Just then, a coconut on a tree above broke loose and landed on the horse's rump. The horse, interpreting it as a signal to move faster, sprinted into a gallop. An unprepared Nandini screamed in terror as it went hurtling into the bushes. Reedy thorns and cactus spines raked her feet as the horse bumped across scraggly bushes. Only her desperate presence of mind, born of a sense of self-preservation both for herself and the child within, prompted her to pull tightly at the reins. The bolting horse came to a staggering halt, neighing loudly and frothing furiously. Behind her was a trail of devastated plants and a stunned crew. The unit members rushed after her, jumping and crashing through the stamped-out undergrowth. Nandini sat motionless on the still horse, its reins now safely in the hands of its trainer. Head bent, breathless with panic, she throttled the screams at the base of her throat, lest the horse bolt again. The men helped her off the horse, supporting her shocked sides between them.

A group of startled jackdaws went fluttering off the trees with obstreperous cries into the disturbed jungle.

They quietened her and put her down on the camp cot in her tent, with Gulsakkar hovering around like a fretful bird. They served her glasses of iced water and stroked her head till she appeared visibly soothed. Once the excitement was tempered, they even discussed the bad comedy of the coconut's timing. In any case the cameras had been whirring and captured the shot; the rest would be taken care of by the London-trained editor.

The shot was done; so was the damage. When Nandini left the location she began spotting, by the time she reached home the blood was spurting in rich, red dollops, carrying in its clotted hearts, her baby.

After the miscarriage had been dealt with medically, Nandini lay in confined and compulsory bedrest thinking only of the enormous ravages of her stupidity. If only she had had the guts to tell her director, he could easily have managed long shots with a duplicate. But no; she had wanted not to make a fuss, it being the last day on location of a big picture with Master Vinayak as hero. Multitudinous stabs of regret pricked her soul. She lay dull and desolate, neither appeased by Ani's mumblings about destiny nor his consolations about more children in the future. A miscarriage is traumatic in itself, but Nandini's was compounded by her apportioning all blame to herself. It had been one moment of carelessness, one moment of negligence, one moment between preserving a life and terminating it. Face streaked with the outlines of tears, she branded herself a murderess; she beat her breasts in self-reprimand. The weeds of remorse grew over her body and threatened to choke her very will to live.

She vowed to quit acting because she saw this as Nature's Nemesis. Where other women stayed at home and cooked and crotcheted and embroidered handkerchiefs, she had sought to venture out of four walls and carve a destiny of her own. Now Providence had wreaked its revenge.

She moped around the house aimlessly, longing for her husband's company, but he was too busy. Her mother moved in to take care of her, but what she really craved was Ani's pampering. Her husband was always off to rehearsals and recordings now that SS had launched a big production about the Quit India movement. Of course the film was his brainchild; it was he who had given Ambika Devi the idea based obliquely on his Calcutta play. These days the two were always huddled in story sessions. This time the heroine was a dancer, and her stage shows gave plenty of opportunity to fill the picture with songs of patriotism. The timing for such a film was absolutely right, now that Indian soldiers were dying on lonely, foreign shores, participating in a war for a nation whose rule they were frantically striving to overthrow.

She developed a paranoical attachment to her son. She learnt new recipes and calculated household accounts to the last pice. Though as a working person she could understand Aniruddh's commitment to his work, her desire to have him around her became a obsession. Aniruddh realised that some occupation had to be developed for her. But what? Acting was all she had ever done for the past ten years. Films were her solitary interest.

He decided to finish this important film first and do something about her later.

Ho dukhiya jiyara, rote naina-

"TAQDEER KA FAISLA' was a contrast to the previous film in that *all* its songs became a national rage. This time Aniruddh had outdone his previous performance. He had beaten his own record, and finally had no rival but himself. Each song was a jewel by itself, but the ruby that flashed brightest was his song about the British leaving the Indian shores. Such was the potency of its nationalist flavour, the aroma of its swadeshi spice, that it attained the level of a national anthem. Its regimental rhythm marched into the hearts of the people, stomping into their lives to add its potent flavour to the resounding call for self rule. This time it was the youth that was fired. Students paraded to its beat. Left-Right. Left-Right. Onward Indian soldiers.

To Ambika's unbounded joy, the film attained unprecedented popularity. In one theatre in Calcutta alone, it ran for a phenomenal hundred and fifty weeks. In Lahore, it had a house-full exhibition for one whole year. This time, people of high society hummed it as much as the man on the street bellowed it.

Accolades, adulation, newspaper reviews, personal appearances, throngs, fans, fuss. Aniruddh ran the gamut with aplomb. His prowess with words made good copy. The nation's most celebrated composer was heady with the knowledge that one swing of his baton, one stroke of his harmonium, had wielded the power to bind the nation. He was the acknowledged Houdini of popular music.

Suddenly, the people and the press sat up and studied his career. They noticed that he had been the first composer to use a full-fledged orchestra with western instruments as early as 1937, thus laying the framework for the modern film song.

With producers lining up outside his door, he felt that now he could afford to build the house he had so long dreamed of. For starters, he purchased a large plot of land in the prestigious Hindu Colony, and the day he signed the deed was the most exhilarating moment in his life. For it not only qualified his newly-acquired status, but also marked the distance he had travelled from his small county home miles away in East Bengal, a home which now felt as if it were floating weightlesslessly on some distant planet, part of a long-forgotten dream or another life.

Door hato ai duniyawalon
Hindustan hamara hai!

Of all the fan mail Aniruddh received, the most precious was from Runu, a letter that expressed how Aniruddh's talent had finally vindicated Runu's confidence. Their childhood bond would always remain despite distances or silences. His daughter Chandrika was eight years old, and Bela was expecting another baby. There was to be a change in his life, now that he had been offered the post of Principal at a college in a small town of Madhya Pradesh, which he hoped would define a rise in material benefits. Also, Runu confided, proximity to the theatre was always pulling Bela in that direction, and though there was nothing wrong with acting, [even Bou-di practised it], Runu's academic career and an actress wife did not jell. A Principal needed sobriety and discipline to set a good example to his students. So he was glad of this offer and could even consider a trip to Bombay with his entire family.

Meanwhile, some decision had to be taken regarding the house that belonged to Aniruddh.

So much had happened in his life since Calcutta, that Aniruddh had all but forgotten about his home in that city. When he discussed it with Nandini, she felt it was best to dispose of it. By now Kaku's'spirit would be at rest. An empty house in a faraway city was an encumberance, to rent it logistically more difficult. To stay there on a casual visit didn't make sense at all, for now they could afford an hotel.

Aniruddh agreed with Priyanandini. He could always rely on her for prudent and practical decisions, which, he claimed were due to her Bania ancestors in Bhuj. He wrote to Runu that he would make a trip to Calcutta and would he, in the meantime, find a buyer for the house?

In his new avatar of celebrity, he decided to fly, with a stopover in Delhi, a city that he had not yet seen. So much was happening there, now that the war was over and hopes for a hand-over of administration were high.

With a sharp sense of excitement, Aniruddh boarded the DC-3 on his very first flight.

Lutyens' Delhi was a unique revelation for Aniruddh. Here was the scenario, so in contrast to his adopted city, of a society coloured obtrusively by the British Raj. Most people lived in white-pillared houses with sprawling lawns large enough to house a regiment. Maharanis and princesses flashed diamonds, ivory cigarette holders, a Rolls Royce, an occasional toy-boy or two, and dropped snippets of summer vacations in Monte Carlo. They played canasta and croquet, and went riding on the Ridge with viceregal secretaries and British memsahibs, accompanied by an entourage of syces, grooms and weatherbeaten retainers. In their capital residences, tea was poured from silver teapots, whilst anorexic cucumber sandwiches were munched on with delicacy.

Addresses were of crucial importance here; and association was encouraged or discouraged by the governing factor of where you lived. If you stayed at distant Patel Nagar, it was villifyingly bourgeouis. In Bombay, nobody bothered whether you lived on Malabar Hill or Bhuleshwar.

Everywhere he went, whether at political soirees or on the party circit, the probability of Independence monopolised conversation.

Aniruddh shopped at Queensway and in the white colonnaded Connaught Circus. He paid homage at the mazaar of Amir Khusrau, a poet he had become acquainted with in the mirrored parlours of Attaribai's establishment. He strolled in the leafy Lodi Gardens, and walked the cobbled paths around Humayun's tomb.

In the evenings, he was entertained by people who made fawning comments about the film industry, about Bombay's famed Marine Drive, its reputable theatre run by Prithviraj Kapoor, the previous year's harbour explosions, and the recent introduction of an intense hero named Dilip Kumar. For the first time Aniruddh experienced the limelight with singular excitement. He realised Priyanandini was not there to share with him the spotlight's glare. He was somebody, apart from the husband of a well-known actress. He was Aniruddh Ganguly; recognized, sought-after, an entity on his own merits. From the backwaters of Barisal he had arrived in the spotlight of national recognition! The realisation added a dash of swagger to produce a heady cocktail.

On the day before his departure, the C.P.C.I. distributor of Shooting Stars invited him for an informal dinner in Chandni Chowk, to see the flip side of Delhi. After visiting the house where Ghalib had lived, they arrived at an ancient haveli situated in a narrow, crowded lane called Kinari Bazaar.The old and smoky residence was clutterd with objets d'art and a gaggle of gawky Jains, Mathurs and Sharmas from Kucha Patiram and Sitaram Bazaar, eager to toast their eyes on the celebrated composer of Bombay. Film personalities were not a daily sight in Delhi; occasionally, a Noorjehan or Surendra was glimpsed at an opening at the Moti or Jubilee Cinema, but a film personality up close was rare and fortunate.

After the gastronomic delights of Punjabi cuisine, Aniruddh had to digest the. Tandoori chicken and mattar-paneer by enduring an amateur entertainment of jarring singers, which was not just a strain on his ears but also on his intestines. Politely and painfully, he sat throughout the pathetic performances. Except for a teenaged boy introduced as Suraj Prakash Mathur, who sang a bhajan with devotional depth, they were monotonously unimpressive.

Fortunately, the evening was redeemed by the final singer who sang a Saigal number [didn't they all, Saigal being an icon for all aspiring crooners]. The tall, exceedingly good-looking man named Rajan Gupta had an unusual timbre, delightfully nasal, and an expression of pathos reminescent of the cult figure. With a mixture of relief and pleasure, Aniruddh rose and personally congratulated the young boy who had given a fillip to the wilting evening.

"That was really very good, lad," he pronounced, and as the boy beamed, he was accosted with a sense of deja vu, as he saw himself in Dey-da's place and the hopeful in his.

"Dada," the young man continued, conscious of Aniruddh's Bengali status, "could you help me to become an actor if I came to Bombay? Any role would do, however small."

"Arre bhai, I'm not a producer-voducer. But if you should wish to sing, then we could perhaps try in that direction. You need training to chisel your voice, to give it modulation and maturity. Playback singing is more difficult than acting; you need emotions *plus* a good voice."

The boy's face fell; Aniruddh tapped him encouragingly on the back. "If you ever come to Bombay, contact me," he encouraged, puffing up with philanthropic largesse.

Ai dil-e-beqarar, jhoom

The plane from Delhi to Calcutta navigated a turbulent path, but once past the air pockets Aniruddh was pensive. I am not a producer, as I told the Delhi singer, but what's to stop me from becoming one? Nandini and I both have the experience; in tandem we could do it. The pasteboard castles of the studio sultans were crumbling. New Theatres was facing closure; Bombay Talkies was about to split into two factions. After the death of her husband Himanshu Rai, Devika Rani had struggled to maintain the empire her husband had built, but unlike her contemporary Ambika Devi, she had not been so lucky. Though it was she who had discovered the fruit seller Yusuf Khan aka Dilip Kumar, her current superstar Ashok Kumar had been snatched away by the splinter group. Ambika Devi herself was riding piggyback on the success of his music. And though he had got the kudos, she had made the moolah. Imtiaz, too, had done extremely well as an independent producer by hiring the space and equipment from defunct studios. They had made a second hit film based on the Bengal famine, and presently he lived in a swanky bungalow at Worli, right beside the sea. His new studio was coming up on the land he had bought in rocky Bandra.

The era of the independent producer had begun.

Of course! It was the ideal solution for Nandini's restlessness. With Pradeep in school, taking up production in her capable hands would keep her occupied in a proffession she understood.

By the time they landed at DumDum, he had already designed a logo. A Saraswati sitting atop a dholak, and guarded on both sides by tanpuras, would signify the promise of good music.

Calcutta was one big nostalgic trip. Many things, however, had changed in the ten years he had been away. Chowrangee had gone commercial. Das had closed down; in its place a greasy petrol pump reared its mechanical head. Attaribai was dead. Where once coquettish dancers had twirled, accountants and clerks now poured over ledgers and files. The subtle seductions of the mujra had disappeared; women blatantly advertising their trade walked the streets of Shona Gachi. Only the cinemas remained from his past; reminders that he had once stood at their fringes.

Memories lurked at every corner and confronted him at junctions; pain blunted by time now opened up like an old wound. Thoughts sidelined by struggle and pushed away into some icy corner of the heart peeped out, beckoning him from worn-out windows. Here it seemed that time stood still on a pinpoint and space was frozen into a tableau; only he had moved on.

It would be painful, but he had to see DeyBabu. The once towering man had shrivelled and become frail, his vitality eroded by a grief gnawing at his faculties like a cancer. At the unexpected sight of Aniruddh his eyes brightened. He had been following Aniruddh's career meticulously; every article, every cutting had been fastidiously filed. His trembling soul glowed with pride at Aniruddh's achievements. Both men were struck by a common thought. Suchitra would have been so happy at his success today.

But if Suchitra had lived, thought Aniruddh with irony, perhaps he would never have gone to Bombay. His talent would never have been discovered, leave alone acclaimed. It would have faded out in stale compositions for an obscure theatre or remained imprisoned in the inky cells of stanzas that no one would have read. Sadly, both deliberated the weft and warp of Destiny's pattern. Things happen because they are the precursors of things that are to happen in the future, a telescopic sequence of cause and effect.

Gham diye mustaqil,
kitna naazuk hai dil ye na jaana,
hai hai ye zaalim zamana

The time together passed heavily. So, though Aniruddh promised to visit again, he never went back. Old times weighed down his heart, cutting away at the edges of new interests. They had shared so much in the past, but that past now had gone into an unrecoverable time zone.

The high point of his trip, of course, was the reunion with Runu. Dear, unchanged Runu. As simple, sober, sincere and serene as he used to be, smelling of happy childhood times. In contrast to Runu's pragmatic attitude, Bela was loud in unnecessary praise. 'Chandrika's Kaku' she told all and sundry; 'we have known him since childhood'; 'he sits everyday with heroes like Ashok Kumar'; 'he's giving music in two Dilip Kumar pictures'. Although Ani could see Runu squirming at her obsequiousness, he felt secretly flattered with such attention.

The sale of the house completed, Aniruddh said he must leave at once.

"Why this hurry? You have come after ten years, stay a while longer."

"No, Runu. I must go for many reasons. You see, the industry is changing. It's not like before, when talent was rare and technicians were few. Only the bold and crazy ventured in. Now it's opening up. There's this new boy Naushad Ali. He's good. He's *competition.* In this line, to be around is a phrase that is to be taken literally and also metaphorically. Besides, construction on my house has begun, and though Nandini does supervise most of the work, I can't leave it entirely to her."

"You mean Bou-di deals with things like bricks and mortar?"

"Yes. She *is* a remarkable woman. Why don't you make a trip to Bombay, bondhu? Our new house will have plenty of space."

"Perhaps we will. Once we move to Bina."

The two friends embraced warmly before parting at the station, Runu making a final proud appraisal of Ani's new sophistication. Then Aniruddh boarded the train.

He was alone in the coupe, as few Indians could yet afford to travel first class. He had deliberately chosen this mode of travel to compose along the way songs for his new film with the dapper Motilal as hero.

The whistle blew.

Suddenly, the door to the compartment was flung open and breathlessly a girl rushed up the carriage steps. A coolie had barely stuffed her trunk onto the lugguage rack when the train began to hiss and nudge forward. The girl fell back on the berth as much with relief as with the jerk.

The busy images of Howrah Junction began to whirl past; kiosks, red-shirted coolies, Wheeler's Book store, room-signs, station-signs, cars parked open plan along the platform; then the cries of hawkers, the mumbo-jumbo of waiting passengers, the tinny clatter of trunks got drowned in the clanking percussion of the wheels. Picking up speed the train moved onto a maze of tracks selecting its trajectory.

From the corner of his eye, Aniruddh observed his travelling companion. Of medium height and wheatish complexion, she was what could be described as buxom, the type that would bloat abominably after marriage eating desi-ghee aloo parathas. Dark eyes were framed by two eyebrows like taut arrows. Dressed fashionably in a short white taffeta kameez embroidered with black sequins, she twirled and un-twirled a black net dupatta between her fingers, randomly biting on its tasseled edge.

He was raked by big, black eyes staring directly at him with unconcealed curiosity. Although accustomed to being stared at, nobody had glanced at Aniruddh in this brazen manner, like a prize exhibit at a slave auction.

After a while, she removed a magazine from a carpetbag and began to read. Over the well-thumbed edition he could see her eyebrows drawing together till they almost formed a straight line. Two eyes emerged suddenly over the top of the magazine, catching him in the act of appraisal. Embarrassed, he looked away. It was dark, and he could perceive the images of their reflected movements in the window.

He saw her put the magazine aside and reach for a basket on the rack. Taking out a tiffin carrier and dismantling it expertly, she spread upon a plate a couple of parathas and bitter gourds and some pickle. With delicate movements she twirled a paratha into a roll and was about to take a bite, when she paused.

"Excuse me, ji. Would you like to share some food?"

Startled at her forwardness, Aniruddh glanced at her disparagingly.

"No thank you. I have my own food, and besides, it's too early for me to eat," he replied, staring out of the window.

She shrugged. He began to hum as a tune formulated in his mind, a Tagore ditty that he placed within the framework of the train's motion. His leg shook like a metronome.

"So I was right, ji. Surely you are *the* Aniruddh Ganguly, famous music director."

"I don't know what you mean by *the*, but yes, Aniruddh Ganguly is my name. Why?"

"Because, you see, here is a picture of you in the magazine. And your name was on the card outside. Two and two makes four, nahin ji?"

He looked at the girl more closely. Her eyes were the colour of burnt milk. Dark Indian eyes, lined generously with kohl.

"Would you be kind enough to sign on it, ji? What they call, autograph?"

Her eyes seemed to bombard him with their direct gaze. Aniruddh nodded. It paid to be polite to a fan. Quickly she dived into her carpetbag and withdrew an expensive Parker pen. Ani looked at the picture. It had been taken at a muhurat. There he was with his arm around Imtiaz Ali, beaming for the cameras.

"Whom shall I address it to?"

"Ramola."

"Ramola. That sounds nice and musical," he said, scrawling his name across his picture. He seemed to be floating into conversation against his own volition. Perhaps her black eyes were putting a tantric spell on him." What kind of music do you like?"

" Folk. That is why I like your compositions, ji. You see, I am a dancer, and I have small troupe. We are presenting the folk dances, and just now I have done a show at a club in Calcutta. Now we are on our way to Nagpur to perform at royal function."

No wonder her hands fluttered about like a pair of peacocks.

"You look young to be heading a troupe by yourself. Where are the rest?"

"Travelling third class. Myself, I have been dancing since the age of thirteen, which was nine years ago. My parents were from Multan, but may their souls have peace, they are both dead. Having struggled long, sometimes I pamper myself with chota-chota luxuries like travelling first class. And then you never know whom you may meet in first class, hain ji?. Dekho, here I have met you, a famous man."

She was impressed by Aniruddh and not hiding it.

Struck by her forthrightness, or was it her naivete, knowing that most women would have given a right arm, painted nails and all, to conceal their age, he changed his mind about the dinner. She sprang up to collect her food paraphernalia and laid it on a spread newspaper between them on his berth.

"Karelas I hope you like. Don't spoil easily. So they are best for journeys."

Bela had packed some puri-aloo, two pieces of fried fish and three varieties of sandesh, plus some savoury snacks.

"Good you have changed the idea about the dinner,' said Ramola joyfully. "Long journey, no? Why not pass it pleasantly? You will be surprised how much you can talk to a complete stranger."

Aniruddh slid into relaxed conversation with her before he could take cognizance of the fact. Her grammar betrayed her not very high education, yet her knowledge was amazing. Her folk music acquaintance covered many states, to demonstrate which she sang a heer of Punjab and two lines from a 'ghoomar' of Rajasthan.

Her Multani-mitti voice was strong and earthy, a timbre he loved.

She quizzed him about personalities like Devika Rani. Aniruddh told her she was an elegant and beautiful woman. "And Ambika Devi?"

Aniruddh asked her to come closer. "I'll tell you a secret if you promise not to tell anyone." Suddenly he was feeling very important. "That woman knows what she wants and how to go about getting it."

"Really? She looks as if the makhan would not melt in her mouth."

Maintaining proximity, she asked him flirtatiously, "How much do you charge?"

"Why? Are you some informer of the Income Tax department?"

"Nonono, I have a project in mind about choreographing Krishan Leela. Maybe I will sign you to make the music."

He whispered the amount in her ear. She gasped.

"Hai Ram! So much! I can't afford, baba. Maybe some time in future."

"Maybe."

Dinner dispensed with, they lapsed into an easy silence.

The steely scissor of the train chugged on through the darkness, cutting the distance. The silver-sharp moonlit lines of the rails sprinted alongside in a neck-to-neck race. Black spheres of trees whirled past like planets in another universe, orbiting in the opposite direction.

Aniruddh sighed. Suddenly, a weight dropped on his shoulder.

Ramola had fallen asleep, the movement of the train making her slump against him, one hand flung casually over his thigh.

For a few seconds Aniruddh went into shock. Since the eight years of his marriage to Priyanandini, he had never been so physically close to another woman.

Now the intimacy of the scene disturbed him. He became acutely conscious of the closetted setting. The girl and him alone together, her hair spread on his shoulder, eyes closed, lashes dark over her fair face. Her dupatta had fallen to one side, revealing a tantalising view of the top of her breasts. They were so close to his lips; he had only to bend slightly to...

Dear God! What was he thinking? It was the lurching of the train, arousing him with its rhythmic motion. He stiffened so as not to let her nearness disturb him. But he felt like a floating cipher. The only area of sensitivity was under her hand, lying heavily and perilously inches away from his crotch. Involuntarily his eyes were drawn back to her breasts, twin golden apples of Eden. Was he going to bite?

He looked outwards, away from her, but the window reflections only served to heighten his excitement. Temptation was a blue glass film.

Ramola moaned; a muffled, sensual sound that seemed to spike through his genitals. The thought came to him suddenly that it was so long since he'd last had sex. The trauma of her miscarriage had made Nandini apprehensive about physical relations, and most times he had come home too late and too tired to even think about it.

Aniruddh actually now saw, like the rare sight of a flower opening its petals, Ramola's breasts tauten and stretch against the taffeta of her kameez. Was she having some erotic dream? Her nipples appeared to stand up and point, like bullets. Bullets that were going to blast away his equilibrium, his integrity and his fidelity to the woman he loved. He tried to shrug himself away, and switch off the compartment light.

But the slight movement was his undoing. As he moved, Ramola fell forward into his lap, her mouth shockingly near his penis. Damn! He made a final Supreme Court appeal to his good sense. His mouth was dry. He felt himself harden. Don't do it, something inside his head warned. But then his libido took over. He reached forward and put a hand tentatively under one breast. She gasped in her sleep and stirred sensuously, one leg opening and closing like the pleats of a concertina, stoking the fire that was increasing hotly inside his trousers. Aniruddh double-checked that the door was locked, including against his own conscience.

The shutters were down, and through them daylight streamed in stripes onto the compartment floor. Aniruddh struggled to open his heavy-lidded eyes. Then the sight of the lugguage on the opposite rack hurtled the events of the previous night into his consciousness. Oh Maa, what had he done? His mouth smelt like a vulture's crotch. His entire body reeked foul. It took him some moments to realise it was the odour of guilt.

He looked around for the girl. From the sound of running water, she was apparently in the attached bathroom. He thought about last night. He figured he had neither raped her nor had she succumbed. But then she was a full-blown-grown woman, and from her experienced response last night it was obvious she knew exactly what she had been doing. In fact, he wondered how much of it she had orchestrated. He had heard his colleagues talk loosely about women who got a kick out of sleeping with celebrities. Fame fucks, they called them. But while he listened, he had kept himself away from this syndrome.

Until last night.

What he felt guilty about was that it had been so easy. He had felt safe, knowing she would not upset his life.

Ramola emerged from the bathroom, her face fresh and newly washed.

"Good morning, ji" she crowed in a voice as chirrupy as a morning hen.

Aniruddh groaned, wishing he could rewind to the moment she had stepped onto the carriage.

"You are feeling bad about last night, kyon ji?" She towelled her hair vigorously, rubbing it dry with frantic motions. Her unfenced breasts jiggled. "What for? Sex is beautiful thing. You are hungry, you eat no? You have feeling to have sex, you have the sex. It is nothing to hang your head down in shame."

Aniruddh felt worse. All he had done in his frenzied desire was to tunnel into her like a locomotive.

"Yes, you are right. I did not get the satisfaction." God, the woman was a bloody mindreader.

"I like to have the fair dealings, kyonji? Give with one hand, take with the other. Hisaab kitaab barabar. So, we will make up for it now, hai na?"

Aniruddh unlocked his eyes from her coquettish irises.

"I am not asking you for the love-shove no? See, that is the trouble with you married people. You want to get it over as soon as possible, then fall on your wives to convince yourselves that it is they who you really want. Arre, men fool themselves. All they want is sex. They will put the picture of Ruby Meyers on an ugly woman's face and bang away. So take it step by step. Enjoy."

Aniruddh was as much surprised by her burst of vocabulary as by what she did next. Sitting beside him, she took his limp penis in her fingers and began to administer gentle, caressing strokes. Aniruddh shifted, but she pinned him down. Fingers deliberately soft, she played with his foreskin till he was limp no longer. All the resolutions, the self-denigration of a few moments ago began to melt like icecream in the heat, flowing into a creamy, lusty substance. He struggled to get up, but she pushed him back.

"But I haven't brushed .." he began to protest.

"So what? Morning is the best time for sex. Your day will be fresh and full of energy."

"Please, don't.." She silenced him by putting her mouth over his. Her kiss tasted of toothpaste. Her hand never left his organ. Crucially, her breasts strained towards him, brushing his bare chest up and down along with the motion of the train.

Her entire body language was a statement. She was not ashamed of her sexuality, but revelling in it.

"Today I must enjoy, too," she whispered into his ear, nibbling at it with a wet tongue.

"How?' he asked.

"Let me show you," she replied in her husky voice.

And she did.

And he was startled to realise how much easier it was the second time round.

The train steamed into Nagpur at 1630 hrs, almost an hour late. Ramola began to gather her things together, rejecting Aniruddh's offer for help. He felt somewhat sad at their parting. He had never before celebrated sex like this. Unadulterated, if adulterous, sex.

"At least have tea with me in the refreshment room."

"Thank you ji. But my troupe will be there. We are, as it is said, two ships that cross at night. Still, I will not say goodbye. Agar 'Taqdeer ka Faisla ho,' we may meet again."

She stepped down, and was sucked into the vortex of travellers.

Aniruddh lay back on the berth for a satisfied while. He had never met a woman like her, so blatant about her own satisfaction. Who could tell what destiny had programmed, and when those two ships would cross again, by happenstance, some other night?

Jawani ye bharpoor, dilkash adaayen

NEW DISCOVERIES

Ah. It was good to be home, back with the familiar touches and smells. Which fool had said familiarity bred contempt? Familiarity bred *comfort*. That night he made passionate love to his wife. He practised on her the wonderful pleasures Ramola had taught him, surprising both of them with the discovery of new erotic delights and erogenous zones. In the end, they rolled away from each other with slumberous satiation.

Nandini thought, how my husband has missed me.

Aniruddh thought, how damned right Ramola was.

"Saro and Kumarsen came to see me whilst you were away," Nandini told him the next morning."They brought the hero from your new film 'PEHLA PYAAR'. They didn't know you were out of town. We need to get a telephone installed."

"We'll do it for the new house. It's only a question of a few months. What's he like, this Abhijeet?"

"Well, he has a winning smile, and flashes his eyes a bit."

'Hmmmm. Not attracted to him by any chance? You know what they say about the seven-year-itch?"

"Excuse me! I thought that applied only to men," said Nandini in mock indignation.

Aniruddh looked away, guilt flushing his face. Nandini misunderstood the gesture, thinking she had upset him.

"Come on, Ani-honey," she said with deliberate sweetness, "I didn't mean anything personal."

Aniruddh considered it best to ignore the conversation, lest he give himself away. Deftly, Nandini changed the subject.

"Abhijeet mentioned that his nephew or cousin or someone would be contacting you about some singing assignment and please to give him a hearing."

"Okay."

He departed hastily for his rehearsal room, leaving behind contrails of guilt that slowly evaporated into thin air.

When the doorbell rang early morning a week later, Aniruddh was struck by an extra-sensory perception that something significant was about to happen. His East Bengali servant Babu informed him that one Rajan Gupta was at the door.

"Rajan Gupta? I don't know anyone by that name. Early morning they come, to disturb for nothing. Tell him I'm still sleeping or in the bathroom."

So much for psychic sensations.

Babu came back. "Saab, he says he has come all the way from Delhi."

The boy has walked all the way from Barisal.

"Oh alright, ask him to wait in the hall."

He tied his lungi tighter. He was still only at home in his Barisal attire.

The boy was waiting at the door. The sun's morning rays had backlit his head crowning him with a halo, and the whole effect was so ethereal that Aniruddh held his breath. He was struck by the look of purity on the boy's face, a face handsome enough to be a film star. The youthful man joined his hands together in a greeting that was almost reverent.

"Namaste, sir. My cousin Abhijeet said that you would see me."

"What about?"

"If you could give me a chance to sing. Anything sir. Even in the chorus."

Mar gaye, thought Aniruddh. Now for some goddamned hero's sake, I have to hear another besura ass. Endure, bhai. Networking was important in the industry.

"You did not recognise me, Sir?" The 'sir' was unsettling him with its memories of Deybabu.

"Should I have?"

"I sang before you in Delhi, at Jain Saab's haveli."

Relief came with a memory.

"Oho, I remember now. The boy with the unusual timbre. Why didn't you say so in the first place, bhai? I thought you wanted to be an actor?"

"I did. But when I told my family, they all advised me that if *you* had suggested I take up singing, then that is what I should do? So here I am, come to take my chances."

"Have you been to any other composer?"

""Yes, two or three. Only then I had the courage to come to you, sir. If you put your hand on my head, surely kismet will smile on me."

Aniruddh had encountered many singer-aspirants before, but intuition prompted him that this boy would be special. Maybe it was his air of openness, the clean-ness of his hopes, or perhaps his sheer humility. His voice had depth, and that depth could be worked upon, chiselled.

"Well, we'll see what we can do. But I would like to give you something very special for your first song. Are you willing to wait, not to grab opportunity, but let opportunity grab you?"

"Surely. Just your saying that is a benediction, sir."

"Then...ah here comes Jasbir Singh, my assistant. Jasbir, yaar, take down this munda's address for future reference whilst I get ready."

Jasbir, a benign Sardar, regarded Rajan Gupta with a happy smile.'"Kyon putar, singer banna hai? Life bana denge Ani-Moshai."

"Is that what he is called... Ani-moshai?"

"Aaho."

Rajan Gupta gave his address, and walked off, wondering at the vagaries of the film industry. Ani-moshai.

Such an admixture of familiarity and respect.

The opportunity came sooner than expected. When Aniruddh was told the situation of a song in, co-incidentally, Abhijeet's PEHLA PYAAR, he knew intuitively this was the right song for the new singer. The lyrics required an extra-dimensional pathos, a quality of the singer's voice.

Rajan Gupta was summoned.

At the very first rehearsal, Aniruddh knew his judgement had been accurate. The base was there, and patiently Aniruddh honed it. He guided and taught, he corrected and rehearsed, till he got the desired effect. He was surprised at himself when at the recording, there were tears in his own eyes at his own composition. The man had captured the Saigal Effect. Not just the voice, but also the spirit.

If Rajan Gupta had not come to meet Aniruddh, he would have sung a few mediocre songs for mediocre composers and been banished to the domain of anonymity. He might have returned to Delhi unheard, unsung. But that meeting had been providential. This one song did for him what that one song in Ambika Devi's film had done for Aniruddh. It catapulted him to national fame.

As it had celebrated the poverty song and the Quit India song, the country paid homage to the tragedy in Rajan's voice. From Qandhar to Cape Commorin, people sat still before their radios, in front of phonographs, and listened to his nasal-voiced hurt. Lovelorn majnus, refuted Lailas, young maidens not permitted to express their attractions, wives sorrowing for negligent husbands, men burning with secret longing, identified with the song and gloried in a mutual sadness.

When the great Saigal died the country mourned. But their grief was mitigated by the acceptance of his successor, Rajan Gupta.

"Don't let all this go to your head, my boy," advised Aniruddh at the function hosted by The Gramophone Company of India, commonly known as His Master's Voice, to felicitate Rajan Gupta on his phenomenal success. "You have a massive task ahead of you."

"And what, Ani-moshai, is that?"

"You have proved yourself an excellent Saigal clone. Now you have to establish your own identity…the identity of Rajan."

"You mean Rajan Gupta."

"No. Just Rajan. That's how you shall be known henceforth. Rajan Gupta sang a very successful song in imitation of a great singer. Now emerges Rajan, a man who can stand on his own voice."

Rajan bent down and touched Aniruddh's feet.

"With your blesings and your guidance, sir, I will strive to achieve that."

Aniruddh suddenly felt two feet taller than the considerably taller Rajan.

Rajan…. thought the singer. I'm part of it now. The industry's queer syndrome of familiarity and respect. Now I must fulfil my promise to the man who made me what I am.

And he did. He went from success to success, and became a musical legend. But that was later.

That evening, Abhijeet paid a visit to the Ganguly residence. Aniruddh had never disillusioned him about the fact that he had chosen Rajan because of Abhijeet's recommendation. So Abhijeet was full of mistaken gratitude, and cemented a lifelong friendship. A considerable part of that friendship was also influenced by the fact that Priyanandini was Saro's closest friend. And Abhijeet found Saro very, very attractive.

If Rajan's meteoric fame made Aniruddh conscious of anything it was his power. He understood that the lines of a future singer's fate were inextricably linked to his and in his palm he held their destiny.

After what he had done for Rajan, his doorstep became the Mecca for all those who aspired to sign their names in the Book of Fame. Wannabes flocked to his door like a gaggle of pheasants; cackling, crowing, clamouring to be heard. As far as the females were concerned his code was simple. Iss haath de, iss haath le. Hisaab kitaab barabar. Ramola had come into his libidinous castle by hacking away the conventional overgrowth and awakening the sleeping Prince with a French kiss.

Aniruddh Ganguly was now a force to reckon with in this burgeoning industry. He had clout, he had fame, he had fortune. He had an imposing building coming up at Dadar, a two-storey mansion. He was a founder member of this business of entertainment. So if he tweaked a tit when some chorus singer missed a note, they laughed. When he fondled a fleshy rump at an off-key junction, they tittered.

Only Priyanandini, in the manner of all wives, was the last to know. Even if she had, she would have been the first to disbelieve. So when Suleiman, whose troublemongering instincts had till now remained dormant, characteristically sneaked into her ears tidbits about Aniruddh's dalliances, she dismissed them as rumours spread by Ani's competitors.

"Don't heed your flesh and blood," Suleiman screeched at her. "One day you will regret, I am telling you."

He was rewarded for his endeavours by being fired from his job as the Gangulys' chauffeur. He took his satyr face away, a gloating Aniruddh staring after him.

Only one person, disillusioned by Aniruddh's new demeanour, started to distance himself from the famed composer. Imtiaz Ali Khan. What he had seen in the early Aniruddh had been an echo of his own desires. There had been a nobility in his mind, a fire in his heart. Now the only fire seemed to be in his loins.

Disillusioned that Aniruddh had fallen prey to the imbalancing factors of success, he began to look for a new personal and proffesional tie. His eyes set upon Naushad, a 'shair' in his own right, a decent and devout man. Most importantly, a fellow Muslim.

After three years, Nandini signed her first film. The relief of finally working was like a spring shower on the arid, parched earth of her spirit. It was the oil she needed to rekindle the flickering lamp of self-esteem.

The familiar sights of the studio with its hangar-like sound stages, the warren of offices, extras and assistants was like manna to her hungry soul.

One thing however appeared to have lost its familiarity. In the make-up room the smell of greasepaint made her surprisingly nauseous. Its odour shimmied up her nostrils and flared out into the nooks and corners of her head, till she was sick a couple of times. But being a professional, she summoned her recovery swiftly and reported to the sets on time.

Here, too, the arc lamps were inimical. They glared like a glass factory furnace and poured heat upon her till her head ached. Presumably, she had got unused to the rigours of shootings. She reached home completely enervated and the smell of the greasepaint came home with her and made her retch again. Disheartened, she realised that the rodents of inactivity had been gnawing and chomping at her hoard of strength.

"I should see Dr. Kapoor about this allergy I seemed to have developed to pancake," she told Aniruddh at night.

Dr. Kapoor, who was physician to half the industry, asked her point-blank when she'd had her last period.

"I don't really recollect, doctor. The new house has been taking up all my attention."

"Then you better wait and watch next month. It's a possibility that this is not an allergy but a bout of morning sickness."

"Oh no!"

"What is this young lady? A pregnancy is generally considered good news."

"But doctor saab, the timing's all wrong! I've just signed a new film. As a matter of fact, I did the first shot only yesterday."

"That's good, because it won't cost the producer much to reshoot one day's work with a replacement."

"But doctor....."

"No buts, my girl. You remember what happened the last time. How can you take such chances again, eh? How old is your son now?"

"Seven years."

"Then shooting is not the only thing you are doing after a long gap. Doctor's orders, dear. Cancel your contract, and take it easy. Understand?"

When her pregnancy was confirmed, she bowed out of the film with mixed regret and joy, recommending an engaging new actress by the name of Rehana as substitute. The newcomer expressed her gratitude in no uncertain terms.

"Don't worry, Baby. You owe me one, as they say in the American movies."

It was time now, thought Aniruddh, to divulge his intentions to Nandini, so that the prospect of setting up her own production house would be the salve to her disappointment. If anything could brighten Nandini's first few months of sickness and hormonal changes, it was the promise of running her own company. It was the calcium and iron her body required.

Meanwhile, with Aniruddh's professional workload increasing, she busied herself with the finishing touches to their new house, and her days became a smorgasbord of curtains, carpets, carpenters, cabinets and curios.

SWEET SUCCESS

The housewarming is everything that should be expected from one of the foremost families of filmdom. Everybody who is somebody is invited. In fact, if some whacky psycho has the freakish idea of putting a stick of dynamite in the stairwell, he will blow to blazes most of the industry's pioneers and render half the major studios decapitated.

The Baniya and the Bengali are truly married in the interior décor, a combination regulated by Aniruddh's ethnicity and Nandini's utilitarian Kutchi upbringing. What symbolises a commonality is the continuous repetition of windows along the walls, borrowing from the outside, light, fresh air and sunshine, motifs of love. A glorious betel-nut palm streaks the windows behind the main seating area.

In a blank space, the logo of the Gangulys' new production company, Jubilee Pictures, has magnified into a sandalwood image of Saraswati sitting atop a dholak, supported on either side by veenas. She seems to have materialized on the bare wall, wearing an expression of indefinable calm.

Colour, glamour, wealth and fame seat themselves as guests.

Devika Rani, who has been taking singing lessons from Aniruddh, looks cool and elegant. The sequined spray on her embroidered georgette sari gleams elegantly as well. The 'Shah' of Ranjit Studios is accompanied, as always, by Goharbai. Ambika Devi, the discoverer of the Aniruddh factor, has made the rare exit from her closet. Her fascination for Aniruddh has not totally diminished despite passionate encounters of the third kind in her closed office. The vibes between them are like taut wires, but nobody is walking around with clippers. A new studio developer from Pakistan named A.R.Kardar looms tall, and Mehboob Khan is greeting everyone with his customary'aadaab'. Saro has come alone, giving credence to the rumours that she is estranged from her cinematographer husband, and is ensconced in cosy conversation with Abhijeet, confirming the news that nowadays they are a couple.

Phani Majhumdar who has migrated to Bombay from New Theatres, Mahesh Kaul and C.L.Kavish make up a sedate corner. They are joined by Khwaja Ahmed Abbas. He has brought along with him two friends, a young fiery poet named Abdul Hai from Ludhiana and an actor from IPTA who impresses everyone as much with his erudition as his good looks. Nandini is so taken up with his chaste diction and the affability of his disposition, that she immediately presses upon him the sum of twenty-one rupees as a signing amount for any film she might produce in future. His name is Balraj Sahni.

The party has its share of gatecrashers. Amongst them is a pair of nubile nymphets who sit starry-eyed and wondrous. They claim to have come with Abhijeet. Out of earshot of his hosts, the hero, too much of a gentleman to blow their cover, approaches them tipsily and enquires if he knows them at all.

"We were in your film 'Pehla Pyaar'. We danced in the 'Allah kasam' number."

Abhijeet doesn't remember at all, but says politely, "Of course. Please, would you enlighten me with your names?"

"I'm Helen, and this is my sister, Gabriella. But my screen name is Pravina, and hers is Indumati. Please, we want to be introduced to Aniruddh Ganguly and to hear Rajan sing."

Abhijeet obliges them.

The sisters are a study in contrast. Gabriella is giggly, sharp and flirtatious whereas Helen is dewy-eyed, coy with a dulcet voice. Aniruddh seems enchanted by the musical cadences in Helen's tone, and spends a noticeable time being hospitable to her. This does not escape Nandini's notice. She, is stabbed by a dart of apprehension poisoned at the tip by Suleiman's diabolical dribblings. But she consoles herself with Aniruddh's oft-mentioned golden rule about illusions. Here it is mandatory to dole out loads of pleasantness and backslap your rival as if he were your closest friend. Aniruddh, she notices, has mastered the art to perfection.

The guests rave about the rich Persian carpets, the deep upholstered sofas, the black-glass dining table for eight in the centre of which a cutglass bowl filled with mogras sits on its own reflection. A grand radiogram occupies pride of place opposite a pumpkin-coloured wall along which an Ikat-draped diwan is banked by ethnic cushions. A wrap-around balcony holds the house in an embrace.

Jasbir Singh decides to have some fun at the expense of his wife, who is standing beneath a wall light in the shape of a leaf.

"Oi Pammi, makhano, move, move. The kodkilli on that leaf is about to fall on your head."

"Hai Rabba," screeches Mrs. Pammi Singh, and runs away from the spot with great alacrity. There is group laughter. For the lizard–on-the-leaf is fake, a baroque indulgence on Nandini's part.

"Oi, Pammiji. Maan gaye. You are a Sardarni to the Kaur."

Narendra Sharma, pristine in white dhoti and silk kurta and chewing the perennial 'paan', recites a poem. Lyricist Prem Dhawan gets up and does a mini-Bhangra, dragging wife Noor to the floor. Abdul Hai, whose 'takhallus' is Sahir, reads with a sleepy drawl from his anthology 'Talkhian' which has been published the previous year. Tempestuous Sitara Devi flares her sari in a dance.

Nandini is distracted from watching Ani fawn over a re-married Devika Rani when Baburao Patel, editor of Filmindia , introduces her to a short but pleasant-faced man named Prannath Sarang.

"He is a journalist like me, and a writer of short stories," continues Patel. Nandini answers distractedly, "Oh, I thought he wanted to be an actor."

The man, flattered at what he considers to be a back-handed compliment, flashes a smile as bright as a 100-watt bulb.

"I hope we shall work together some day," he says, gazing with appreciation into Nandini's emerald eyes.

Nandini, being a good hostess, bestows on him a saccharine smile . Inside her, the baby, aged a pre-natal six months, gives a vigorous kick.

Utpal whispers into Ani's ears that Dey-da is perhaps dying. Go visit him, he advises.

"But only last year I was in Calcutta. I'm upto here," he gestures at his ears, "in work. We've just launched our own production company, Nandini is six months pregnant, and the house is not completely furnished yet. We moved in earlier so the new baby can be born here. Besides, this new boy Naushad, his songs in ANMOL GHADI have become so popular that now he is giving me a run for my money."

Utpal's face dulls like a sudden overcast. He searches in Aniruddh's eyes signs of the man who had earned respect by so selflessly taking care of the dying Kaku. He is dismayed that Aniruddh's environment has so begun to dominate his heredity.

During dinner, Aniruddh stretches his leg under the table towards Helen, sitting opposite. His toes touch her thigh, probing like a Geiger counter. He is not surprised to feel her legs spread apart like the edges of a hand fan.

When Aniruddh brings forth champagne, the suave Motilal, a close friend, enquires if they are about to drink a toast.

"No meri jaan," ripostes Aniruddh, "this is to wash your hands with."

"Sorry boss, ask a stupid question…"

But Aniruddh means it.

Rajan sings.

The nymphets are appropriately goggle-eyed, and stare at everything and everyone.

The next day, the party is the talk of the town. In studio offices, in dance halls, in recording rooms, everyone is talking about the saffron-flavoured biryani, the marble bathtub, the pastel glass tiles over the stairwell through which you can see the sky, the novel finale of washing the guests' hands in champagne.

In the post-war scenario of the industry, to be talked about indicates success. And Aniruddh has begun to feel its syrupy flavour. He does not have a sweet tooth for nothing.

Jhoom jhoom ke nacho aaj, nacho aaj,
gaao khushi ke geet ho o

Saro discoursed at length on the benefits of boarding school. The two friends were having a hen-chat over coffee at a hotel.

"But Saro, how can you send both your daughters away so far, to Mussoorie?"

"It's for their own good, Mehru. I'm shuttling between Kolhapur and Poona and Bombay. I really can't look after their studies. Of course, they're extremely attached to their Aaji, but they need company of their own age. They need to be with ordinary folk, not constantly in and out of make-up rooms and muhurats. They need to learn about grace and deportment and table manners. Knowing the positive effect of the nuns, I'm sending them off to a convent. I can plan my schedule around their holidays so I spend maximum time with them. When Malini finishes her matriculation, I have plans to send her to Switzerland to a finishing school."

"You have a point there, Saro. I think maybe I should consider sending Pradeep away, too. Suleiman's pampering and my cloying affection after my miscarriage are making him into something of a sissy. And talking of busy schedules, mine's going to be hectic with two new babies:- the one in my stomach and the production company."

"Then I know just the place for him. The Shivaji Military Preparatory School at Poona. They'll turn him into a man."

"Saro, can I ask you something frankly? Are you really doing this for your children's advantage, or because it's convenient on account of..you know...Abhijeet? Rumours are floating around."

"As Sukumari I would have denied the whole thing, but as Saro I will not lie to you, Mehru. I married Kumarsen out of a sense of fancy and freedom. He was so handsome, and the idea of eloping was terribly exciting. But he's just..a handsome man. Abhijeet, on the other hand may not be as good-looking. But he's a gentleman. He's caring. I'm living the romance now; all the candlelight dinners and flowers and the close dancing and the thoughtfulness. He fills my insides with sweet warmth, you know, like drinking brandy with honey."

Nandini thought that any man who wanted to romance another man's wife could in no possible way be a gentleman. But then her mores still required the broader spectrum of reality. She had yet to understand that maturity was not living your life according to pre-settled notions, but analysing your self and pathfinding your fulfillment.

"Then let us go next week. I should like to register him before the baby is born. I can visit Shamim, too."

"How is Shamim doing? He always seems in and out of jobs. Doesn't he plan to get married? That might make him more responsible."

"Don't know, Saro. He's back at Prabhat now, working as an assistant director. Perhaps I'll surprise him, if there's time to meet him, that is."

"Maybe Abhi and I can come along too. You can drop us off at Khandala and pick us up on the return. Will you do it?"
"So, this is serious, haan? What do you plan then? Will you divorce Kumarsen and marry Abhi?"

"Can't do that. He's already married."

"What? A married woman and a maried man?"

"Don't sound shocked. Married people are still people with feelings, Mehru. He has a wife in Delhi, but heroes'wives need to be invisible. I may just separate from Kumar and stay on my own."

"How can you live like this Saro? No status, no entity, an ambiguity in society?"

"At some point you have to decide…does it matter? Is society responsible for your happiness or do you owe it to yourself?"

Nandini marvelled at Saro's guts. Being happily married, she could not contemplate living as Saro described, coping with a disapproving society. But why should *she* worry about that at all? It was Saro's life, not hers.

The Western Ghats were a mixed blend of green and brown and purple, resplendantly verdant with monsoonial splendour. Nandini dropped Saro and Abhijeet in the shadows of the imperious Duke's Nose, promising to pick them up on the return journey. The damp mists that float around the crown of hills at Khandala were dissolving in the early morning sun. Cataracts slipped gently down the walls of the hills, slight and thready, like skeins of rippling silk.

Driving up the snaking road that perilously hugged the side of the hill, past the temple where every Ghat-crosser made a silent prayer and threw coins, Nandini wondered if she'd done the right thing by helping the lovers. But once the road had evened out, she saw how easy it was to accept an extra, or was it an extra-extra-marital alliance.

Na toofan se khelo, na saahil se khelo

The school was satisfactory. After the registration, Nandini drove towards Somwar Peth, the market area where Shamim rented a room. A narrow staircase festooned with cobwebs and graffiti-covered walls splashed with betel juice identified it as a lower-class accommodation. The smell of urine and raw onions made her wrinkle her nose in distaste.

The door was opened by a slip of a girl in a ghaghra-choli. Nandini thought she had the wrong address; obviously some Marathi family had residence here.

"Does one Shamim Karamali stay here?" she asked of the frisky girl, whose eyes seemed to dilate at the enquiry. Her buckish teeth suddenly appeared prominent in her coltish face.

Nandini became apprehensive at the girl's silent but obvious fright.

"Answer me girl, Does Shamim Karamali stay here or not?" she shouted impatiently.

The girl gave a gasp, and tried to close the door. But Nandini, fully prepared for such a reaction, was faster. She jabbed her foot in the doorway and despite her pregnant state, strongly pushed it backwards. The girl lost her balance and staggered.

Nandini recognised Shamim's clothes on the hook, and her tone became sharper.

" So where is he and what are you doing here?"

The girl appeared frightened to death at Nandini's authoritative interrogation and began to sniffle and shake.

"He's not here, he's not here," she said quaveringly. "I don't know when he will come back."

" Do you work here?" If she did, she ought to be sacked, for the room was in desperate need of being tidied.

" Have you come from my mother's side? Please, please, you won't tell her, will you? She'll thrash me, what's more my…..". Her words faded away, the fullstop of caution. Nandini said peremptorily, "I will, if you don't tell me the entire truth.."

"Nono, we haven't done anything wrong. We were married right proper in the temple… hey raam, I'm not supposed to tell anybody. They will.beat him to death."

"Who?"

"My brothers, who else!"

Fortuitously just then, the person under discussion made an entry, accompanied by a colleague with myopic eyes and a lopsided smile. He was startled to see his glamorous sister perched so unexpectedly upon a stool, looking as out of place in the bedraggled environment as a marble statue in a hovel. Shocking de Schiaperelli blended with the smell of lentils simmering on the stove.

Nandini came straight to the point.

"What is this girl telling me?" she admonished, astounded that Shamim should have hidden his marriage from the family.

"Alright Mehru," said Shamim, giving the girl a stiletto look. "I guess since she's already spilled the beans, you might as well know. This is Sumangala, and yes, we are married. Suman, this is my sister Mehrunissa."

The girl made a bewildered namaste.

"But why the secrecy?"

"Suman's mother is a rigid Brahmin. What's more, she's revered as a high priestess of sorts. They call her Asha Devi and she's considered an incarnation of Durga. Does that explain everything?"

"Explicitly. If there's a whiff her daughter is married to a Muslim, her credibility crashes."

"Precisely. Sumangala has seven solidly built brothers who will not stop at murder."

"But as far as *we* are concerned, there's already a Hindu-Muslim marriage as precedent, so Mithima would never object."

"But she dare not tell her mother," explained his companion. "So she comes here during the day and goes home in the evening, pretending she's at college. This has been going on for a year."

"This is ridiculous. Some day they'll discover it. And then…."

"Then anything can happen," offered Shamim's friend as optimistically as he could. "By the way, I'm Vasudev Bhatt."

"I'm sorry," said Shamim. "In all this tamasha I forgot to introduce Vasu. He's a colleague at Prabhat and works as choreographer."

The man with the myopic eyes smiled a cute lopsided smile, as if only one half of his face was used to giving expression. Nandini saw a modest shyness in his eyes, and an occasional spark that flashed like a stroke of genius.

"How old is she?"

"Almost nineteen."

"Then that solves the problem. She's an adult and legally free to marry according to the law," she announced resolutely. "She's going back with me. I'll take her to Bombay and her family will presume she's run away, and they won't raise much dust for fear of scandal. There may be, just maybe, a job for you. We're starting our own production company."

"Your own company? That's wonderful, little sister!"

The girl meanwhile had been staring dumbfoundedly at this apparition who had waltzed in and closed the situation in her tight fist. Fear gradually ebbed from her face as she found the lady not hostile but quite in control. But when told of the plan, she panicked.

"Ai ga! Impossible. My mother…."

"Oh don't dither, girl. Should you not be in your husband's proper house? Besides, if you don't go now, you never will."

Something in Nandini's strong, resolute demeanour struck chords in the girl's mind like loud piano sounds. Some overt strength in this lovely personage swept away the dust of her doubts. She felt drawn into the car with a strange sense of compulsion, and quite content to let someone lead her to her destiny. Nandini was embarrassed by her gaze of adoration. She did not know it, but she had gained a reliable fan and ally.

As the Austin moved away down the line of sari and kirana shops, Vasudev stared at its departing dust with admiration in his myopic eyes. "Your sister is quite a lady," he commented to Shamim, who, with a tremendous sense of relief, nodded in agreement.

"Oh yes," he corroborrated, "she's one of a kind. The bold and the beautiful kind."

Ye kaun aaya ki mere dil ki duniya mein bahaar aayi

"This was a silly thing to do," expostulated Aniruddh, on Nandini's return with the saucer-eyed girl. "You don't know what legal problems could be involved."

"For goodness' sake, Ani, the girl is not a minor. She's come with me of her own accord, so I can't be accused of kidnapping. And they're married; they can't go on living in fear forever. Besides, on the way she confided that she's pregnant."

"And you took it upon yourself to pump her with some of your courage, unmindful of the repercussions. Wah! Babesie, wah! But be warned, you brought this on yourself, you jolly well handle it. Anyway, if she is to stay here, she can give a hand to the servants in the kitchen, and help you prepare for the birth. And get her some decent clothes. She looks like a 'ghatan'."

Nandini was stunned at Aniruddh's suggestion.

"Have a heart, Ani, she's not an ayah, she's my sister-in-law now, for better or for worse. I refuse to treat her like some poor relation."

"*What else is she*?" exclaimed Aniruddh, stomping out of the house in a fury, leaving Nandini staring in astonishment. Had he forgotten so soon the dilemma of their own Hindu-Muslim situation? Did his statement now categorise both their mothers, for instance, into the compartment of poor relations too?

A gentle touch on the arm brought her out of her deliberations. Sumangala, not being conversant with English, had not known the exact translation of their words. But this much she had comprehended; that *she* was the context of their argument. She knew, that whatever had made the angry man rush off in a tempestuous fit had been something said by the gracious lady in her, Sumangala's, defence. She also knew by instinct, that an unborn child's well-being mattered as much as that of a human born. And, in her own way she wanted to reach out to this pregnant messiah who had come from the thin blue air into her nineteen-year-old life, and transformed it categorically, all in one day.

Nandini went into labour in the early hours of 21st December. When the frequency of the convulsions increased, she roused Aniruddh, who placed her in their brand new Desoto and rushed her to the maternity home.

Labour was long and tedious, and the birth a difficult one. The expenditure of energy left Nandini considerably drained. Precisely at noon, when the afternoon sun was at its brightest, her daughter was born.

Aniruddh was thrilled. He'd always wanted a daughter whom he could pamper, and who would reciprocally pamper him in his old age.

"She can massage my head and tweeze out all the grey hairs."

"When you're old, she won't be with us," suggested Nandini. But Aniruddh cradled the tiny green-eyed infant in his arms, beholding her with brightening pride.

Nandini's sister Kulsumbai presented a silver rattle to the baby, and observed that she and her daughter Zeba now shared a birthday. Aniruddh watched as she cooed and addressed silly gibberish to the sleeping child and wondered why people spoke idiotically to babies. If they couldn't make sense of sense, how could they make sense of nonsense? He had never been taken with Kulsum, or any of Nandini's relatives for that matter. They were an odd lot; Esa with his fanatical mutterings; Suleiman the Shaitan with his mal-intent; Kulsum, who looked fragile but had a conniving underside; Shamim with his indifference; her psychic mother who hovered around grunting.

"That didn't strike me," said Nandini, too weak for such coincidental observations. "I hope my daughter will be as pretty and sweet-natured as Zeba."

"Why not? She already has your eyes and dimples."

But she might have her aunt's temperament, pondered Ani, as a genetic afterthought.

The insatiable baby cried incessantly, and her wailing demands for milk seemed interminable. Rehmatbi, experienced wetnurse as she was, was summoned to help and manage the large house and its increasing retinue of servants.

Nandini tried desperately to recuperate her strength. The months of inactivity had made her eager to continue the work she had left off for the delivery. By tacit understanding, Rehmatbi got permanently ensconced at Nan-deep, whereas Sumangala was packed off to take care of the Shivaji Park flat. Aniruddh wasn't ecstatic about his mother-in-law being in residence. He resented the fact that his own mother was not allowed to take her rightful place as head of the house. But the silk cushions of luxury enamoured not Konkona; the tassels of which, she claimed, had an irritating habit of getting in your nose.

But really, he couldn't complain. He had the best banners flocking to him, his film TAQDEER KA FAISLA was still running for the second consecutive year at a Calcutta theatre. He owned a mansion he had ardently aspired for, he had presented the nation with Saigal's heir, and now he had this cute little daughter.

His cup of happiness was full.

DECLINE OF THE STUDIO SYSTEM

Yeh jang hui purani. Desh
Azaad hua toh hoye
Sangeetkaar hoon, rahta hoon
Bas apni hi dhun mein khoye.

The struggle for which he had once risked so much, became delinked from India's Independence. For Aniruddh now it was a struggle to defend supremity in his field, as with the bifurcation of the country, an exodus from what had now become Pakistan infiltrated Bombay, making it the major production center of the film industry. Producers, technicians and stars now crossed over from both sides depending on their religion or political preferences. Noorjehan, Saadat Hassan Manto with whom he had worked at Bombay Talkies, and musicians like Ghulam Haider opted to go to Pakistan and pursue their careers there.

Though Bombay had its share of Hindu-Muslim clashes, its communal street warfare, its stone-pelting and bottle-throwing, its silent stabbings in by-lanes, he was away from the horrific history that was being written in blood on the plains of Punjab. He was untouched by the horrendous scenes of slaughter, of the cries of widows and orphans as a bizarre and savage genocide stained crimson the waters of the Indus and the Rabi. It was business as usual in the resilient film metropolis, whose get up and go never got up and went, as more individual production companies became established and the older studios began to crumble.

It was only when Runu wrote him about the situation in Barisal where he had been to cremate his uncle, that Aniruddh felt the repercussions of Partition touch him personally. Runu wrote in detail about the havoc in the city of their birth. The people who had once lived in amicable proximity had now become thirsty for one another's blood. The most horrible news he had to relate was that Nazrul had attacked his own best friend Dhiren and stabbed him mercilessly with barbaric relish.

Safe within the confines of his own solid house, he felt the memories of his childhood come flooding back to infect his Brahmanical consciousness with the virus of hatred against Muslims. With awesome impact he realised he was *married* to one! And though he still cared for Nandini, (she was his wife after all,) his perspective of her and her relatives was never the same after he had read Runu's letter.

This time his cough was nasty. His bronchitis seemed to be worsening. In addition, he had developed a black and ominous rash on the inside of his leg, which itched a great deal. Aniruddh consulted his friendly neighbourhood physician about it. That was metaphorically speaking, as Dr. Bose was an exceptionally grim man who spoke in clinical tones. A compatriot from East Bengal, this competent doctor had studied medicine in Germany where he had wed a Teutonic lady of large proportions and matching grimness. Only the extenuating circumstance of her wearing a sari and sindoor had spared her from antagonism during the war.

"I can give you something for the cold and cough," said the able medicine man, summoning his compounder to dispense the medication from his luminous array of red and green bottles. "But you'll have to see a skin specialist about the rash. Looks to me suspiciously like eczema."

The dermatologist corroborated Dr. Bose's diagnosis.

"I have ointments to cure your problem,' was his serious pronouncement, "but I must warn you that it could get translated to asthma. I leave the choice to you."

"There's no choice, doctor. Music is my profession. If I can't sing, I shall perish."

"Then I suggest you leave it as it is. It's not oozing, and it's in a place that will be covered with your trouser. Of course it will itch a great deal, but you must remember that eczema is highly contagious, so do not, at any cost, scratch it with your fingers and touch any other part of your body. Use a copper coin, like the one-paisa coin."

Aniruddh told Nandini, who agreed that he had made the right decision.

On account of the itchy phenomenon, Aniruddh shifted his bedroom into his rehearsal room, called the Golden Room on account of its yellow curtains, and shared Nandini's room only at night. If he composed till late, he slept on there so as not to disturb Nandini who came home from the studio dead tired.

Everyone in the Ganguly household now took turns at the exercise of scratching Anirudh's eczema with the copper coin. Rehmatbi was absolved from the task due to her age and status, as well as Nandini who spent most of her time at the studio office. The coin-scratching contingent graduated to include singers, musicians, chorus, and aspiring lyricists who would recite their creations whilst their hands worked laboriously at the maestro's legs. After the first two home productions became moderately successful, the procession was joined by a steady stream of struggling actors, directors, dialogue writers et al.

Taking her place in the line with graduating frequency was Helen-Pravina. Invariably when Nandini returned from the studio, it was to discover Pravina at his feet. She could fully fathom why Latika Karmarkar, a talented singer whom Nandini fondly called Do-die-Do in a literal translation of her surname, wore out her Kolhapuri chappals for seva of her guru, who was tutoring her in the techniques of microphone singing and breath control. But Pravina's presence was inexplicable.

The vibes between her and Aniruddh persevered in their unsettling influence. Since the day of Aniruddh's unreasonable outburst when she had brought Sumangala home, she had noticed a change in him. He seemed more extroverted, almost flamboyant, and sometimes sadly enough, veritably unrecognisable.

Pouring over a manuscript for her third production, Nandini was surprised to look up and see a pleasant-faced man standing at the entrance to her office.

"Prannath Sarang? Have we met before?"

The man smiled ironically.

"I attended your housewarming two years ago."

"Oh yes, the aspiring actor," replied Nandini, at vague recollection of his plastic smile.

"Actually, an established writer."

"And what have you written?"

"Several newspaper articles. A book on the holocaust of Partition, which will be going into publication soon."

"Oh," said Nandini, unimpressed. Every writer worth his ink had written about the unspeakable acts of inhumanity during the Hindu-Muslim riots.

"I heard you were looking for a property for your new film. I wondered if you would care to peruse one of my subjects." He pushed a manuscript across her desk and peered meaningfully into her eyes, eyes that had lingered on in his memory.

She had just picked up the bound file when Suleiman rushed unexpectedly in.

"Saajanmiya is dead. Come on, we have to hurry. The funeral is in an hour."

Nandini scrambled out without bothering about formalities with her visitor.

"Who's Saajanmiya?" asked a voice in the sorrowful silence. Nandini turned round sharply at the sound, to see Prannath Sarang firmly ensconced in the back seat of her car.

"What are you doing here?" she questioned sharply, amazed at his audacity.

"Someone died. I figured you could do with an extra pair of hands."

Since he was already in the car, there was no point in asking him to get off.

A grim atmosphere prevailed in Kulsumbai's house where a profuse number of Saajan's relatives had gathered and were beating their breasts with loud wails. Kulsum's married stepdaughter Mariam and her brother as well as her own Zeba and son Sarfaraz stood around, helplessly numbed. In the centre of commiseration sat Kulsumbai wiping her eyes continuously with her pacchdi.

"Oh who would have thought an ordinary fever would carry him off like that?" moaned someone.

"Pneumonia is not an ordinary fever," the tenant Samson tried to explain.

Prannath espied a lissome girl dressed in salwar-kameez standing in a corner, looking bereft and beautiful. Her forlorn air echoed like a swan song. Her eyes, full of frozen tears, were almond-shaped and glistened darkly against her tremulous fair skin. A sharp nose quivered over majestic lips shaped in a perfect Cupid's bow. The romantically inclined Prannath was smitten with her fragility to forget momentarily his fascination for Nandini's eyes.

Someone called to her, and he learnt her name was Zeba.

She glanced up at mention of her name, and across the mournful room their eyes met. The expression on his face was so beautiful, that for the first time since hearing of her father's death, Zeba began to weep.

Aahen na bhari, shikwe na kiye
Kuch bhi na zubaan se kaam liya

VAMPS AND VILLAINS

The clippity-clap of sandals sounding on the stairs brought Rehmatbi quickly to the iron grill overlooking the stairwell. For a home otherwise expensively decorated with imported crystal fixtures, the stairwell was dimly lit by only a 40 watt bulb. If only Mehru would devote more attention to these little details! These servants were good-for-nothing and would lead thieves on a conducted tour of the house, if not for her vigilance.

She had grown feeble, shoulders stooping, her face the texture of old parchment. With her frail eyesight, she could vaguely make out the figure of a woman clutching her sari pleats in order to climb the stairs. She made a face and sauntered back to her room. The bell buzzed. One of the servants came to inform her that 'that girl' had come to see Saheb again.

"Which girl?" she feigned, knowing well who it was.

"That same girl, Mithimaa, who comes for guru seva. The thin one with the two long plaits and the pockmarks. But Saheb is sleeping, and we don't know whether to wake him. What if he gets angry?"

" Perhaps he will be more angry if you don't wake him. Allow her in, but let her knock on his bedroom door on her own. She can take his anger on her head."

Yes, who could tell how these artist types would react? They functioned on moods. 'Don't disturb me, main mood bana raha hoon!' What manner of work was this, that paid you to be moody?

Half an hour later she walked past her son-in-law's bedroom, wondering about the modern methods of this generation that had a 'his' room and a 'her' room. How they managed to produce two children was a mystery! In our time we pleased our husbands each night. It was our duty and their pleasure. Not like these two, sleeping in separate rooms because he might want to get up in the middle of the night and yell sa-re-ga-ma.

Through the slightly ajar door, she could see the girl patiently pressing his legs. The man even snored in 'taal'. He would wake soon enough and holler for tea, then proceed to howl Aa Aa Aa loud enough to wake the corpses in the kabristaan.

It was past ten oclock when Mehru's Hillman honked its arrival. Nandita was asleep, and Aniruddh was out for some film function. But then he was out on his own most nights.

Mehru came in, looking tired but surprisingly elegant in her pale peach georgette sari with a brocade pallu.

"Mithimaa, what's for dinner? Today my artists demanded prawn curry and chicken biryani from Coronation. Those days are gone when the entire unit ate together in the studio canteen. Still, the stars could do less 'nakhra.' They come late on the sets, demand huge payments, bring along a party of relatives whose bills we have to pay. Black money, white money. So much bother."

The expression on Rehmatbi's face pretended it understood everything.

"Anyway, by the time the artists finished there was hardly any left for me. Where's Ani?"

"There's paaya and some of that smelly chodchodi. Your husband has gone for some film function. That girl was here again," was Rehmatbi's summarised itemisation of the day's events.

"Oho, there was an after-release party tonight. Ani phoned me at the studio and I told him to go on without me. Which girl are you talking about?"

"How many take the liberty of walking into his bedroom whilst he's still sleeping in lungi and banian? Really, Mehru, you have this huge room with sofas and carpets and tables. Why can't they sit there? The servants dare not say anything to me, but I see that lewd amusement in their eyes. First time they must be seeing a memsahib going out to work with other men, and a sahib who works with nubile girls behind locked doors."

"Now Mithimaa, Latika comes here only for rehearsals. Do you know she refused to accept payment for my present film? I'm going to present her with a pair of diamond solitaires. Mark my words, she will be a big name one day. What a voice! It flows like water, taking on whatever shape you want. As for pressing his legs, that's only guru-seva," explained Mehru, slipping into a comfortable kaftan.

" Mehru, men are irrepressibly unfaithful. Loosen the hold slightly, and they're off! All those pretty chorus girls hanging about the house in your absence. A little temptation, and lots of opportunity; bas! You may be very beautiful, but better an available ugly duckling than an elusive swan."

"Oh, Mithimaa, you're really reading too much into all this. I've been working since I was sixteen. I'm double that age now. You can't expect me to give it all up and start changing nappies and cutting onions and buying vegetables on a daily basis. Besides, I'm not sure yet, but I think I'm preganant again. With three children, a business and this house, believe me, Aniruddh's not going anywhere."

A pregnancy, thought Rehmatbi, shuffling along. Now *that* is something.

Yet it was a long time before she welcomed sleep into her anxious eyes.

Pregnancies no longer excited Aniruddh. He began to regard them merely as a process of family expansion. With Nandini relaxing her workload, he began to work with Sarang and Shamim on the post-production and background music of their new film NAAYAB. A friendly affection developed between Aniruddh and Sarang, but with Shamim, Aniruddh was always dissatisfied, often reshooting his scenes on the pretext of perfection. Shamim considered it a Hindu prejudice.

As expected, the music, with its folksy, catchy dholak flavour suiting the tribal story, was a great success, and the film had a good initial.

Just after the birth of their second son Upamanyu, whom they called Mannu in short, Runu wrote that he and Bela, along with their two children, Chandrika and Chandan, would visit them in the summer break. An excited Aniruddh pressed upon Nandini the fact that no stone should be left unturned in the entertainment of his childhood friend.

They arrived one morning with half a dozen trunks and Bela's endless chatter. Nandini was dismayed at the quantum of their baggage. Obviously they planned to spend their entire summer vacation here. With a small baby, and their next film just flagged off, she already had her hands full without having to proffer hospitality to an entirely unknown family. Bela's eyes shone at the splendour of Aniruddh's house. Nandini felt sorry for the disconcerted Runu, with his intellectual appearance and predilection for politics. She could see how this attraction of opposites had quickly degenerated into an awkward alliance.

The loquacious, ingratiating Bela had nothing in common with the brisk and business-like Priyanandini. Moreover, her detailed examination of the objets d'arts and graceless enquiries as to their prices smacked of an uncultured upbringing. If celebrities visited, Bela at once took over as surrogate hostess. Often when Nandini returned from work it was to discover that Bela had already ordered the menu for dinner ['But then I know Dada's taste so-oo well] or inspected the pantry and replenished the required articles despite Mithima's protests. [of course, Bou-di, you are so-oo busy. It's the least I can do to help] Nandini refrained from reminding her that the house had run on oiled wheels even before her arrival. Besides, she was always pulling toys out of Nandita's possessive grip and handing them to her children to play with. Her kids rarely handled expensive Bayko sets or golden-haired imported dolls with care.

If Aniruddh noticed anything, he pretended not to. The soft-spoken and gentle Runu never could bring up the courage for reprimand.

Nandini decided that the most diplomatic way to avoid any kind of unpleasantness was to absent herself as much as she could from the scene. So she spent maximum time at the studio, leaving the visiting contingent with its effusive host. They probably preferred it that way, the odd woman literally out. The result was that Nandini became an outsider in her own home, marooned in her room with the baby, and oft neglected in their convivial celebrations.

Returning from the post office one morning, Runu crossed a pleasant-faced man in his early thirties going down the stairs. There was something vaguely familiar about his face with its neatly aligned features, but Runu could only place this paragon when he reached the top and jabbed his finger on the doorbell. In Calcutta he would have recognised him instantaneously; here, in out-of-context Bombay, it had taken some time to guage his identity.

"What was Ashutosh Roy doing here?" he asked Aniruddh.

"That was Ashutosh Roy?"

"He sure looked like Calcutta Movies' blue-eyed boy to me."

'But he said he was some Aziz Masood from Lucknow."

"That is his actual name. But a Muslim hero in Bengali films didn't jell, so they changed his name to be more acceptable to the Bengali audiences."

"But he wanted a chance in my films and I presumed it was for acting. So I asked him to go see my wife at the studio. But isn't Ashutosh Roy a singer?"

"He is a singing star out there, so naturally he'd want a break in an acting role."

"Why don't singers realise that with playback singing now they should concentrate on what they do best? Look at Latika and Rajan.

Both tried to act and fell flat on their faces. I recollect this Ashutosh Roy had a couple of successful private songs before he joined films."

"Yeah, he's an HMV discovery."

"He has a voice like velvet, a most unusual timbre. Run, bondhu, shout at him from the balcony. He might still be walking down the lane, or waiting for a taxi at the end of it."

Runu raced to the verandah, but the lane stretched before his eyes like a roll of empty film.

The industry was still small enough for Aniruddh to locate Ashutosh within two days. He had sent feelers out everywhere, for he was in a frothing excitement to experiment again with a new voice. It was Chaitanya, his ex-assistant, who had graduated to individual music-direction, who accosted Ashutosh when he approached him for a break.

"Arre Azizmiyan, Ani-moshai is looking all over for you."

The truth was that Chaitanya found Aziz's voice too vibrating. The grapevine had it that most of the other music directors had turned him down for the same reason.

However, Aziz's pride had suffered a severe dent because of Aniruddh's arctic attitude, and it took three messages from the maestro to defrost his rejection and make him climb that winding stairway again.

Aniruddh was not so big a man that he would not stoop for his music. He sensed the other man's discomfort, and instantly put an arm around his shoulders with obvious bonhomie.

"You must forgive me for for my attitude the other day," he began apologetically, "but I presumed because of your good looks that you were interested in acting. Now that, you see, is my wife's domain. To convince you further about my sincerity, I am going to give you a song in a current film that is actually complete. But I shall persuade the producer to specially insert a situation for you."

The singer was too much of a gentleman to hold resentment against such solicitousness.

"That is kind of you Ani-moshai. When should I come for the sitting?"

"You are already in the sitting, my friend. We shall move to my rehearsal room in the other wing of the house and start immediately. I'll phone my lyricist to come at once."

"What about the tune?"

"I'll compose it whilst we wait. We shall create a song of pathos for which the silken tones of your voice are ideal. Being a Muslim, your diction and understanding of the lyrics will give your singing an extra dimension. Have you ever considered singing ghazals?"

"Not after my first private record."

"Then we shall work on that. Don't look surprised. I may be a Bengali, but my interest in Urdu is quite ancient."

The moment Aziz began to sing the opening notes, Aniruddh was convinced that this singer had the potential to suit the tragic stories that were currently in vogue. Though he could not take very high notes, there was an unusual tremolo in his voice that added to the aura of suffering. Aniruddh had recently signed three Dilip Kumar films in which the actor played the self-sacrificing hero. And Aniruddh knew with uncanny certainty, that more than Rajan, Aziz had a refined softness, that coupled with Yusuf's histrionics, would make the perfect match for tragedy.

The lyricist arrived. Aniruddh presented him his requirements.

"Give me a song of utter loneliness, and private pain."

The poet nodded and began to scribble. Within minutes, he handed over the 'asthayee.'

'Oh heart, let us away to a place go,
Where there is none, not even a shadow,
No sun to smile, no happiness to greet,
No caravan, no fellow-traveller to meet.'

Aniruddh's fingers flew over the keys in fluttering rhythm like the batting of insects' wings. Then the notes began to flow, soft and silky, gentle and sad as a widow's tears. Aziz started to hum along; then as the tune firmed in his mind, began to sing. But the last note was a little too high for him, and his voice fumbled and faltered. He tried once again, but his scale tipped away from him. Disappointment flung itself over his face like a quilt. He had really wanted to sing under the baton of the great Aniruddh Ganguly, but he was obviously not up to the standard. He considered it wiser to quit gracefully before he was discarded in disgrace, and offered to retreat.

Aniruddh struck his fingers on the harmonium with a jarring sound like a ghostly finale in a thriller film. The notes echoed in the ensuing silence like the hummimg of locusts.

Aziz stiffened. The lyricist shuffled impatiently, crossing and uncrossing his legs with some irritation. He wondered why Animoshai was entrusting an important song from a big-budget movie to an inexperienced newcomer whose voice actually trembled with nervousness. This time, surely he was making a grave error in judgement. Aniruddh tried to gather his control in that vaccuum of time. He was not wishful, however, of discarding his hunch.

"Look, son. This tune I've created is like my child. I have put all my energy and sensations into this composition and I do not like it to be wasted or abused. If you cannot sing it, don't wreck it. I shall change the tune, give you a madhyam raag to suit your range. This much I can compromise. But in return, I don't just want the loan of your voice. I want the very essence of your soul, every moment of pain and passion in your lifetime that you can recollect. Remember, don't struggle to do what you cannot. Rather try and excel at something you can."

Touched by the considerations of his adjustment, Aziz closed his eyes and put his entire imagination into the rendition.

The effect came through in the recorded version. Whereas Rajan's introductory song had suggested a passionate grief, the silky-soft chords of Aziz's voice furled around heartstrings and touched with a gentle sadness. It was as if the listener had drunk from a goblet of sorrow, and was inebriated with a heady sadness that ennobled his soul with the dignity of pain.

His very first song attained nation-wide popularity, establishing a cult-worship akin to that of Saigal's. It was another hit from the now-famed Golden Room. The lyrical notes in that silk-velvet refined timbre did not flow like Latika's river perhaps, but were tremulous like a quiet lake in the moonlight. In moments of solitude, on lonely nights when the sleepless had only the moon and their saddened thoughts for company, Aziz's record would be played on gramophones as listeners felt the compassion of a fellow-sufferer whose voice reached out to supply soothing ointments for their souls.

Kudos once again knocked at Aniruddh's door. His presentation of another talented singer endorsed his supremity and his reputation as the maestro with the magic touch.

Suddenly all heroes were clamouring for Aziz as their ghost voice, and composers were restless to exploit this new sensation.

When Aniruddh re-called Aziz for a new film, he was dumbfounded to discover that his unusual tremolo was 'sadly' missing from the singer's voice. The effort to straighten it out, like thrashing out a curl of hair, depleted the emotion and expression. The song was no longer melody, but a strenuous copybook exercise.

When questioned, all Aziz had by way of explanation was that other composers were advising him to delete it from his voice.

"You fool! Are you determined to do harakiri? Without that rare and distinctive tremolo which is such an asset to your voice you will be just another commercial singing idiot who came and fizzled out like a damp squib! You may be suicidal, but I will not wilfully commit murder. It pains me to see a man deliberately throw away his chance at greatness."

"But Ani-moshai, no-one will take me with the tremble. They all want me to sing like Munnawar Hafiz."

Aniruddh's disillusion sizzled into such an incensed state that he lunged out and struck a stinging slap on the man's cultured cheek.

"Then listen to them and go out and become ordinary."

Shaking with fury and frustration, he stomped out of his own room, banging the door with resounding anger.

Aziz Masood sat alone in the golden room from where his hopes had graduated to such stupendous consequences, holding his face where the imprint of the slap still stung. He was immobile with shock; nobody had slapped him before. Not his parents, his teacher, nobody. After all, he came from the city renowned for its courtesy.

He gathered the remnants of his damaged self-respect and went unsteadily down the winding stairs, his steps slurring like a drunkard's.

Bade be-aabru hokar tere kooche se hum nikle

CHILD PRODIGY

Bela shred supari with a silver 'sarota', chewing betel-nut as she snipped. Aniruddh and Runu, hanging around informally in tehmats and vests, discussed in their native dialect the policies of Jawaharlal Nehru. Suddenly, Aniruddh glanced up to see a man looming in front. He seemed to have materialised out of nowhere, a giant genie with the features of a bear and the body of an ox.

"Hey, who the hell are you and how did you get pass the grill door?" shouted Aniruddh, disgusted at the inefficiency of the servants and concerned about the propriety of his dress.

"A thousand pardons, but the door was open, so I took the liberty of stepping in, Sir-ji."

"Do you make a habit of entering the houses of people whose doors are standing open? Koi hai? I'll cuff these bastard servants. All they do is gossip and drink innumerable cups of tea!"

"What to do when the mistress of the house does not pay enough attention?" intervened Bela with pretended righteousness.

"Damn! Nobody seems to be around. Anyway, since you're in already, state your business."

"Myself Vikramaditya Mehra. I am indeed grateful for your time," he said, in well-intonated Bangla.

God, thought Aniruddh, another one come to take advantage of being a fellow Bengali. A steady procession of compatriots had already been incorporated into the studio hand and chorus singer brigade.

"Are you from Barisal too?" he asked with a considerable degree of sarcasm.

"No Sir-ji, I am from Punjaab."

"Amazing, Punjab is the last place I would expect a Bengali to settle."

"But I am not Bengali. I am 100% Punjaabi, sir-ji."

"Remarkable! How do you speak such good Bengali then?" This specimen sounded interesting all of a sudden.

"My wife is from Assam and speaks no Hindi. So I learnt the Bengali. I have stayed in Calcutta till now, and worked in some bit roles in New Theatres phillums."

He gestured for the man to sit down. The hefty Mehra sat on the edge of a chair, adopting a stance of abject humility.

"Sir-ji, you have introduced many singers, guided and trained them and made their lives. Please, please, will you consider my daughter, and take her under your honoured guidance, sir-ji?"

Exasperatedly, Aniruddh answered that he had some audacity walking into his house with such a request. "Look here, Vikramaditya Mehra, I am not running a training school for singers. There is a music school next door called Rupayatan. Take her there."

"Nono, Sir-ji, you mistake my meaning. She is trained from the age of five, and well-versed in the ragas. Only she is needing the expert touch, to put polish into her singing."

The damned jackass with his mouthful of a name must think I'm running a bloody gurukul, thought Aniruddh. This was becoming quite farcical; this phenomenon of aspiring singers traipsiing into my home and walking out famous with just one song. Should he put it to the test to see if it was merely a fluke? His daughter, eh? Perhaps she might be a pretty pert thing interesting enough for a fling. Her breasts, he would see her breasts and decide.

"Okay, bring her to me. And next time don't walk in unannounced like this. Take an appointment with my assistant Jasbir, or my tabla-player Ramakant."

"But she is waiting outside only, sir. Perhaps you may hear her just now itself, if you have the time?"

Colonel Pickering Runu rose immediately to escort the girl in. "Arre, why did you not tell us before, baba?"

"She was feeling shy, sir," said Mehra, ambitious father of a diffident daughter.

Around the edge of the heavy wooden door appeared a fair, round face, eyes tilted upwards in tribute to her Assamese heritage.

"Come inside, girl. Don't be afraid. Nobody is going to eat you," said Bela in chaperone tones.

The tall girl, of an indefinite age between fourteen and nineteen, stepped around the door. She wore a long floral dress with a bow at the neck. Her hair was pulled back in a luxuriant ponytail. Her eyes had the expression of a terrified deer.

"Come forward, Minoti, and touch the guru-moshai's feet." The girl stepped forward and lightly brushed Aniruddh's toes with feathery fingers.

She was just a very young girl with no boobs.

"Come child," Aniruddh encouraged gently, "sing something. Let us hear your voice."

"Wh.. . .what shall I sssing?" came her voice, just above whisper level.

Spare us, thought Aniruddh, if she sings like she speaks, her voice would be fit only for Leela Chitnis.

Sing the maestro's song from 'Tamanna,' the one that made Ashutosh Roy famous," advised her father.

Not so brilliant a ploy, for it would be easier for him to pick out the mistakes.

The girl cleared her throat. The audience held itself in polite anticipation. She began to sing, softly at first, then, vitaminised with each note, her voice grew stronger and fuller. Her palm hit the sides of her leg with the beat. When the song ended, there was an admiring hush. She had sung Aziz Masood's song on a considerably higher scale and managed it competently enough without stumbling on the higher notes. All heads turned in Aniruddh's direction, awaiting his pronouncement.

"Very good, child, very good for one so young as you. But the emphasis is on 'young'. Your daughter, Vikramaditya, is sweetly in tune, she has an unusual, well-trained voice, I admit. But she has sung this song like a classical exercise in a music school. Film singing requires emotions, you have to suggest in your singing, and for that you must have, either a natural flair, or maturity and experience. So I suggest you come back when you are older. Meanwhile, I'll refer you to Chaitanya, my ex-assistant, who does lighter stuff. He will give her some tripping little songs to sing which will serve as good practise."

The girl reddened with pleasure. This was praise, indeed, from the great man. A visibly happy Mr. Mehra departed amidst a thousand platitudes.

Bela smiled and commented that the girl would probably grow up into a pretty young thing. "So it is good you told her to come back later, hein Dada?" She gave Aniruddh a naughty wink that sent the good composer into a pretty fluster as to her conspiratorial intentions.

Meri qismat ke kharidaar, ab to aa ja

On the eve of Runu's departure, Aniruddh told Nandini he wished to give a send-off party to his friend.

Nandini sighed. "Really Ani, I don't see the need for a formal farewell. They've been here for more than three months and we've shown them the sights, taken them for launch rides at the Gateway of India, escorted them to muharats and premieres and looked after their every need and request."

"Look Babesie, they've come to my house for the first time after their marriage, that too, after so many years. I think that's the least they deserve."

"They've met most of our friends Ani. I'm sure Bela has enough stardust in her eyes to last a whole year before she visits again. She's even asked me for a role in our next film. I'll give her that too. What else can I do? Besides, I have a dialogue sitting in the morning and in the afternoon I'm going to Bombay[as the city area was referred to] to clinch a deal for an office at Opera House. With such a schedule I've really no time to organise a party."

"What do you need an office there for? Aren't you carrying this production thing a bit too far?"

"It's good to have a place in town for official meetings. There are studios in the city, too. What if we're shooting at Central? Really Ani, it's been nice having them and all, but I am looking forward to having the house to ourselves again." Running a brush through her hair and picking up her briefcase, she signalled to Suleiman, who had been re-instated as chauffeur on account of Nandini's misgivings about Pravina, to take the car out of the garage. Secretly she was quite relieved at the departure of that interfering woman and her obnoxious children.

Aniruddh removed to the guest room where they were packing and apologetically told Runu that he would have liked to give them a farewell party, but Nandini had a heavy schedule that day and would not be home to organise it.

"Oh a party!" exclaimed Bela. "But what should be the problem, Dada? What do you have two cooks in the kitchen for? If you phone and invite the guests, I will handle the kitchen and the menu. Isn't it a wonderful idea of Dada's?" Runu considered it rather unnecessary, but Bela's enthusiasm at the thought of a final chance to sit with filmy bigwigs bulldozed his protests.

Nandini arrived home late to find a party under full swing in the brightly-lit drawing room. The character actor Bannerji in the window of the opposite building was peering through the bars at this Bacchanalian conviviality. Utpalda, Chaitanya, Praveena and Indumati, Jasbir and Abhijeet sat around in various positions of informality. The lyricist Prem Dhawan was regaling the gathering with the parody of a Punjabi 'tappa'.

Someone felt her imperious presence and stopped in mid-laughter. His silence was infectious and the laughter petered down to a trickle.

Bela was quick to sidle into the pause. She swayed up to her bonafide hostess and murmured in condensed-milk tones, "Oh Boudi, I hope you really don't mind." As if she cared if I did, mused Nandini. "Knowing you are so busy I thought to save you all the bother so you could just come home and enjoy."

"Of course you did," was Nandini's sardonic reply. "Do continue. Now please excuse me, I have to feed the baby."

Her anger was an exclamation mark. Annoyance left a comet's trail as she strode out of the room. Undoubtedly that woman had done this to show up Nandini's absences from the house as a minus point in Aniruddh's life.

She was still breastfeeding the baby when Aniruddh came into the bedroom twirling the ice in his glass of Scotch.

"Now what was the meaning of that dramatic little scene? Can't I have a party in my own house without your concurrence?"

"Now that you've proved your point, why discuss it?"

"Because I expect you to freshen up and sit with my guests, even if you can"t look after them."

" They're *your* guests, not mine. You entertain them. I just want to go to bed." She placed the sleeping baby beside her and lay down on her side away from him, a signal that the conversation was over.

But Aniruddh hadn't finished. She was his wife; it was her *duty* to listen.

"So now you're playing the bigshot producer. All my friends advised me about not giving you so much autonomy, but did I listen? No, I felt it was important for you to work now that you'd given up acting, so you wouldn't get restless as you'd become after your miscarriage. Now look at yourself, you're becoming self-centred and mannerless. At such times your low breeding really shows up."

Nandini shot up in anger.

"Ani, they say when a man is drunk his subconscious surfaces and he unwittingly speaks the truth. You're just envious that I as a woman have progressed individually in my own field with some success. You didn't expect me to do that, did you? You really wanted me to revert to you with my incapacities. And don't throw my breeding in my face okay? You were pretty much acquainted with my family before marriage. I know you're always comparing us to your precious family of prudes, but at least we're humans, not paragons."

Eyes blazing, Aniruddh flung the glass with fury and force against the bathroom door and swung out of the room. Nandini stared with glazed eyes at his departing back, then buried her face in the pillow and wept trembling tears. Why had Aniruddh changed so? What had become of the caring and considerate man that she had married?

He slept in the rehearsal room that night, a fact that didn't escape Bela's Machiavellian notice. She left Bombay the next day a very satisfied woman. Priyanandini had been snobbish, aloof and condescending. Petty Bela had every intention of giving her a grand funeral, and yesterday had been the first nail in the coffin.

Kisine mujhko mere ghar mein aake loot liya

All couples fight. Married couples, after a certain time, fight specifically. They quarrel over petty things and have uncompromising opinions and sometimes go surprisingly in tangential directions. Occasionally one re-talks by the compulsion of habit or a desire to revert to an accustomed ease that will dissipate the tension hovering in a common space. Invariably the situation resolves itself by the sheer necessity of having to consult each other on matters of daily domesticity.

Thus in the absence of the servants who were out on various errands it was Nandini who had to inform Aniruddh, that he had a visitor.

"Who is it?" asked Aniruddh with a scowl.

"Don't know," sullenly replied Nandini, who very well knew who it was.

"Chase him away."

"He's very insistent. Says he owes you an apology."

"Alright. Ask him to wait whilst I change."

Aniruddh strode into the drawing room to find Aziz Masood ensconced on the sofa. His scowl deepened, becoming almost monsterish. The singer rose, palm raised in an'aadaab'.

"So what makes you return? Are you not satisfied being another Munnawar Hafiz! I have worked with accomplished singers like Amirbai Karnataki and Rajkumari and Parul Ghosh who all sang in their natural voices. Madam Latika has also been convinced to overcome her Noorjehan fixation, and Rajan stopped copying Saigal and adopted an identity of his own. But you, you are determined to destroy the one quality that makes your voice so rare. This, my dear man, is an adventure of discovery, and we are all walking along on the way. If you want to fall down on the roadside, it is entirely your prerogative."

"Ani-moshai, please do not make me more 'sharminda' than I am already. Do not give me a second chance if you wish, but please say you have forgiven me?"

"Audhbhut! Convention would dictate that I should apologise, considering it was *I* who slapped *you*!"

"It is specially because you slapped me! After you did that, I walked for hours along the sands of Juhu. After much deliberation I realised that there had been so much 'ikhtiyar' in your action. If a son does something wrong, a father instinctively slaps him. Initially, I was hurt. I just took time to muster courage to come here. But it is the duty of a son to say sorry to his father, isn't it bhabhiji?"

Aniruddh glowered at Nandini as though not desiring her complicity, but she was too compassionate a person to reserve her comment.

"Come on Ani, do forgive him. The man has apologised. He's genuinely repentant. Anyone can see that."

Aniruddh bristled at her implication that he himself was too obtuse to notice, but the fact that she had spoken to him after several days of silence somewhat mitigated his pique. His features unscrewed themselves from their stance of annoyance. Nandini played upon his dismounting anger.

"Besides, Ani, he's such a shweet boy."

"What schweet-weet! That is for the mishti-shops, but it has no relation to what I expect of him if he has to work with me."

Aziz's face brightened immediately even with the mere mention of the conditional 'if'.

"Anything, Ani-moshai, anything."

"I ask for discipline and complete obedience. You have to let yourself be moulded like I wish."

"You will never have a chance for complaint, Dada."

Melting slightly, Aniruddh said he did not want a chance for regret. He couldn't understand it, but he felt some nexus with this boy. He saw in him a reflection of himself at the beginning of his own career; clean, fresh, pure as his mother's chant.

"Remember, I don't forgive twice."

"Ji, Ani-moshai."

The singer made to touch his mentor's feet but Aniruddh stopped him midway.

"You have called me a father. So, come here, embrace me like a son."

Aziz's smile lit up the room. Nandini exhaled a sigh of relief. Aniruddh thumped Aziz re-assuringly.

Aziz said simply, "Shukriya."

Such was Aniruddh's spontaniety that he looked at Nandini, the quarrel forgotten, and said "We have a situation in our film where we can use this."

"What?" enquired Nandini, sunflowers in her smile.

"A song starting with the word 'shukriya. I'm going to work on it right away."

Together Aniruddh and Aziz Masood went on to create some immortal songs, Aziz's distinctive tremolo the perfect foil to Aniruddh's composition. The vibration in his voice went a long way, further than Aniruddh's career, way past Aniruddh's decline, across the international shores of acclaim, an Indian voice surfacing on a stage in New York for the very first time. The gentleman singer, as Aziz came to be called, the man with the golden pathos in his voice, attracted devotees at the altar of his mellow and magnificent chords. As the years progressed and many new voices echoed in the music world, singers would sit in front of radio and cassette-players to imitate his style of rendering ghazals as once he himself had followed Saigal. Memories, old melodies and the moon came to be associated with his velvet tones. And he had Aniruddh to thank for this. For without that marvelous tremolo, he would have been just another flat voice, lost in the hoi polloi.

But one had to wonder whether the basis of all this was a conjugal spat, and if the urge to pacify and please, to lop off the thorns of a prickly cactus, to straighten the marital bedspread of the Ganguly household, was not lurking beneath the stratum of this particular development. Unquestionably, by whatever tremulous twist of fate, Aziz Masood had been slated for renown.

Zamaane ka dastur hai yeh purana
Banakar mitaana, mitaakar banaana

FREELANCE STYLE

I don't wish to re-employ Shamim as the director of the new film," stated Aniruddh with unusual firmness.

"Why?" asked Nandini, more out of curiosity than objection.

"He may know his stuff technically, but there's no artistry in his shot-taking. He just converts a script onto celluloid. Anyone can do that."

"But he's my brother," protested Nandini, though not with maddening intensity.

"That is not the criterion of a good director."

"I didn't mean that. I suppose he will be hurt."

"That's too bad. Emotions are okay on the screen; but behind the scene you require talent as well as considerations of business."

"So whom do you have in mind?" asked his wife, with total adamantine lack.

"Prannath."

"Prannath? But he knows nothing about direction."

"He's a writer. He can conceptualise, visualise. He and I work well in tandem, and he has some good ideas about soft-focus shots that I'm eager to try out. Besides, I've asked him to rewrite the story around a blind singer. I'm keen to work on an experiment on Indian symphonies which I can incorporate into the film."

"What kind of symphonies?"

Aniruddh felt pleased at Nandini's interest in his work, a happy change. It had been long since they'd shared anything, including a bed.

"Symphonies like there are in Western classical music. You know, Concertos, whole orchestrated pieces based on a common theme. Like the kinds written by Bach and Beethoven. We have our ragas, but they're basic. They've not been used to expand themselves around a subject."

"Why, that's a terrific idea, Ani." Nandini forgot Shamim's peremptory dismissal in Ani's excitement.

The actor Shekhar, a family friend, was chosen for hero, primarily because his fees were not too high. A pert new actress called Nimmi who had been introduced the previous year in BARSAAT, a highly successful film of Raj Kapoor's, was selected as heroine.

The next few days everything evolved in concentric circles around the symphony idea. The innovation of using ragas to centre around a conceptualized theme appealed to the broadcasting bigwigs in All India Radio, and Aniruddh was summoned to Delhi to participate in a conference for upgrading India's voice in the air.

The first person his eyes set upon on entering the broadcasting office was the genteel poet Narendra Sharma, whom he had not met since his housewarming over five years ago. Aniruddh immediately recalled their earlier meetings in the modest verandah of his Shivaji Park apartment, when friends used to gather and share literary discussions and radical thoughts. He had missed that confluence of intellectual minds, and confessed so to the paan-chewing poet.

"Arre mitra, you have moved into the commercial aspect of films, that is production. Now you are running against everyone instead of flowing with them."

"You are so right. That is a part of my life I have banished into neglect. How I used to look forward to those philosophical exchanges."

"We can once again have those get-togethers, but you must take out the time for such things."

"Then we shall revive our meetings with a regular session which will meet say, every Sunday and you, my friend shall give these meetings a name. So, are you coming to the party at Hyderabad House this evening?"

"Nahin bhai, this party-varty is for flamboyant people like you, not for simple folk like me. Your brother-in-law Prannoy and I have decided to make an early night of it."

Aniruddh entered the after-seminar party hesitantly, wondering if he would know anyone else besides the people who had been present at the meeting to organise All India Radio's Vadya Vrinda or National Orchestra and propose a plan for the National Programme.

Sparkling crystal glasses with refracting lights glistened against the red sashes of the waiters. Coloured bulbs nestled brightly in the laps of potted plants. The crème-de-la-crème floated gracefully and a dull murmur of voices bubbled in the social cauldron. Ani lifted a glass of whisky off a passing tray, eavesdropping on a high-society conversation volubly deploring the absence of white faces in the Delhi social scene.

The Minister for Information and Broadcasting, Mr. Keskar, making a brief appearance in the midst of his busy schedule, accosted Aniruddh personally. Film songs, he averred, were carrying themselves to a point of vulgarity and thereby self-imposing an imminent ban. Something had to be done, or the solitary voice of broadcasting would be closed to the film industry.

Across the room he espied Uday Shankar, whose film KALPANA had been greatly lauded. Ani had heard rumours that his dance Academy in Almorah was closing down due to paucity of funds. Somewhere in the milieu a huge diamond blazed in a nostril making him aware of the presence of Akhtaribai Faizabadi, or Begum Akhtar, as she was referred to nowadays in a more celebrated concert avatar. He started to cross the room to greet Uday. Halfway across, his progress was interrupted by a light tap on his arm. He swirled, spilling a bit of the whisky on his shirtfront. His eyes locked magnetically into two very dark ones flecked with midnight mystery. "So we meet again."

He didn't recognize this graceful woman in her Tanchoi sari with a jamaawar shawl draped casually across her shoulders. Her smile quite outshone the flicker of the huge solitaires at her earlobes. “I’m awfully sorry I didn’t....”

“Hai hai! And I thought I had made such an impression not easy to forget, kyon ji?” Her sensuous mouth bunched into a pout.

‘Kyon ji’ ..... Surely it couldn’t be... the face was fuller, the figure more plump, but the sensuous smile, the graceful movements of those dancer’s fingers, ah, those fingers, they had played such symphonies on his organ!

“Yes, now I think some recollection comes, kyon ji?”

“Ramola! I see you have not lost your capacity for mind reading. Is it really you? After all these years?”

“The very same, ji. I am sure you are wondering what I am doing here in this very posh gathering, hai na?”

“Well, how *are* you connected with this shindig?”

“Rama Ahuja has risen from a poor dancer to a high position.”

‘Rama Ahuja?”

“My real name. Who would want to see the dance of someone called by such a common name? Ramola was more..showbusiness-like? But for the woman who now runs one of the best dance academies in the capital, who organises the annual Krishna Leela, hai, Ramola is too, what shall I say, flowery? So I am back to Rama. Ramaji sounds more dignified, kyon ji?”

“And how, my dear *Ramaji,”* said Aniruddh, smiling into her eyes, “ did this progress come about? Perhaps by travelling in the first-class compartment of the Indian railways or maybe flying Tata Airlines?”

“I told you, ji, you never know who you may meet in the first-class compartment of a train? So there I am, travelling with one Dewan Purshottamdas Ahuja, of recent widower-hood. He was as much in need of consolation as I was of security. Also ji, he had a nine-year-old daughter to raise all by himself. We cried on each other’s shoulders. Now he has a mother for his daughter Damayanti, and I have the respectability I always wanted.”

"And of course the money. And the standing in society."

"Very definitely. That is why I am standing here too, in this high-class party. "

Just then the famous dance exponent cupped his palm on Ani's elbow.

"Ani-moshai. Just the man I wanted to meet."

"Uday, what an unusual co-incidence. I was actually coming across to meet you when this charming lady intercepted me."

"So. You have met the famous Rama Ahuja. The patroness of the arts. How is the sugar baron, by the way?"

"As 'sweet' as ever," she tittered, amused at her own humour. Ani raised his eyebrows, but said nothing.

"Ani-moshai, my brother Sachin was keen for you to score the music for one of his forthcoming ballets."

"I am rather busy, but a ballet? Sounds interesting. I'm always ready to try something new."

"Then perhaps Sachinji will set a whatyousay, precedent and I will follow, kyon ji? Now I can most certainly afford your charges," she tittered with a hint of conspiracy. Uday moved on, promising to arrange a subsequent meeting in Bombay.

"Sugar baron? What was that all about?"

"That is my husbandji. Come, I will introduce you. Then maybe next time you come, you may stay at our kothi in Model Town."

He followed her trail as she wove through the bunches of people and made her way towards an island of four rather influential-looking men who seemed, with insular intensity, to be debating some new commercial policy.

"Darling, I want you to meet, please, the famous Aniruddh Ganguly."

The man who turned around to meet his handshake was big and broad, almost dwarfing him in comparison. Well-combed salt and pepper hair gave him an air of suavity, and behind his thick glasses his eyes beamed with intelligence. Ani had been expecting an obese Seth with adipose chins and a corpulent paunch. But this soft-spoken, pleasant man with his refined air and sincere offer of hospitality was unexpectedly a delight to meet. He, of course, expressed ignorance over Ani' s songs confessing that he rarely got time to see films. But he was familiar with the Quit India song that had made Ani famous. Aniruddh correctly estimated that this was a man involved in his business with a studious passion. So it was quite a surprise to see him attend dotingly on Rama's conversation, bestowing upon her with noticeable regularity looks of a profound, if unexpected, tenderness. No fool like an old fool, thought Ani, with philosophic delight.

When Ahuja excused himself to get his wife a drink, Aniruddh regarded Ramola-Rama with overt admiration. "You know, you're quite a woman! He's quite besotted, anyone can see that."

"He has his uses," quoth the lady, drawing Aniruddh into an arc of accomplicity.

Ahuja returned with a glass of dangerous-looking liquid that could have been a variety of hemlock or scarlet-purple squid spit.

"Whatever is that you're drinking?"

"It's something called kaanji, made from fermented black carrots, and like everything which looks dangerous, is quite delicious. When you come to stay with us, we shall treat you to specialties of Delhi you have never heard about, ji" said Rama, skating on innuendo.

"I shall look forward to that," replied Ani with matching significance.

He admired her guts. The guts of a woman who knew exactly what she wanted and had chased it with calculated effort and single-minded determination. She made no pretence of being devoted to a husband to whom she obviously returned value for money in full measure. 'Is haath de, is haath le,' had been her motto after all.

Duniya, ye duniya, Toofan Mail
Iss ke paiyye zor se chalte
Aur apna rasta tay karte

SAHITYA SARITA was successfully inaugurated the very first Sunday after Aniruddh's return, before his enthusiasm waned or some commercial entanglement ensnared him with its headaches. It was a reservoir of intellectual waters in which sprouted, pink and ponderous, the lotus blossoms of prose and poetry. Membership was permitted on the strict basis of weekly creativity, and each person who joined had to recite compulsorily something he had composed or written in the previous seven days. A chapter on the Ramayan or Mahabharat was read alternately, followed by discussions and debates. Film topics were eschewed as a matter of rule; only subjects that would elevate, instruct or enrich were permitted. Occasionally, a revered visitor from out of town, like Faiz Ahmed Faiz, would attend.

Meetings were concluded with tea and an impressive spread of Bengali sweets. It was a close and envied circle. Friends and fellow-thinkers re-gathered with renewed interest, relieved to have Aniruddh back within their fold. He himself regarded it as a desperate attempt to regulate the wandering philosophy of his mind. Mahesh Kaul, Phani Majumdar, C.L.Kavish, Abbas and poets like Narendra and Pradip were part of this select and august group. Aniruddh missed his friend Imtiaz Ali at such gatherings. Imtiaz finally had accomplished his dream; his studio complex was established on that hilly tract in Bandra. But he had broken the vow of always and ever working together, the tartaric acid of their soured relations, when he had signed the younger Naushad.

No point now in repenting. There were other friends and other avenues.

Aur bhi dukh hain zamaane mein mohabbat ke siva

NEW SOUNDS

Aniruddh drove fast towards Bombay Lab, which wasn't far from his home. He was late. But feverish Mannu had cried with red-faced gusto at Dr. Bose's whilst being given his vaccinations. Having handed him over to his possessive but efficient nanny Nirupa, Aniruddh hastened to where his musicians and Latika were waiting.

To his dismay, he found the doors to the recording theatre closed. The red light signaling an ongoing recording was like a bloodshot eye. Jasbir Singh was pacing outside. Latika, in accordance with her newly acquired fame, had not yet arrived.

"But we were booked for the 2 o'clock shift. It's now past three. Who's recording in there?"

"Your ex-assistant, Chaitanya."

Aniruddh waited in respect for a fellow composer, but with mounting impatience. At long last the red light was extinguished. Eagerly, Ani pushed open the door. Spotting him, Chaitanya, carried his tall frame in his guru's direction. The song just recorded, a peppy, samba beat accompanied by Spanish guitars and cymbal clashes and set to some nonsense lyrics, was being played back for a final approval.

Aniruddh seemed appalled at what he thought was a breach of pure Indian-music ethics. At this rate, the threatened ban on the broadcast of film songs was inevitable.

"Arre bhai Chaitanya, what is this snazzy number? Are you trying to change the sound of Indian music?"

"Kya karen, Ani-moshai. One has to move with the times. And this is a comic cabaret situation where a Westernised tempo is more appropriate."

"Then I hope it is not popular, for if it becomes a trend you will put all of us orthodox musicians out of business. Who is the singer, by the way? Surely not Geeta?"

"You don't remember? It is the same girl you sent to me two years ago, Ani-moshai. As a matter-of-fact this is the second song she has sung for me. Anyway, it was not for the main cast so I didn't have to take a prominent singer."

Ani couldn't recollect her, so Chaitanya had her summoned before the senior composer.

The girl who emerged from the recording booth was strikingly pretty. She was tall, with skin the colour of rabri. Her tilted eyes transported you to the Naga hillslopes, and above them, darkly penciled brows rose frantically towards her temples. Large, luscious lips quivered beneath a smallish nose. Aniruddh looked further southwards. She had grown breasts!

Embarrassed by his direct scrutiny, Minoti shrouded her shoulders with her pallu, covering those tempting orbs with khadi modesty. A familiar bucolic figure materialised from nowhere, claiming paternity to Minoti's blossoming youth.

"Myself Vikramaditya Mehra. Namaste, Ani-moshai. You remember me?" he asked ingratiatingly.

"Yesyes," replied Ani, his eyes still on the alluring girl in front of him, restless to taste the sweetnes of this ripening fruit. Sahitya Sarita had opened his mind's eye, but not clouded his lascivious vision. "Jasbir, take down their address. I will certainly consider giving her a song to sing."

"So now she is ready for you, Ani-moshai?" exclaimed Vikramaditya Mehra, with some excitement at the promotion of his daughter into the big league.

The double-entendre struck Chaitanya with its saucy implications. He had been considering making an advance on the girl himself; but if Dada had a fancy for her, well, then gurus first. He smiled to himself as he walked out, noticing how swiftly Aniruddh, ever the professional, turned the girl away like the page of a book and reverted briskly to work.

The recording finished at nine. He reached home to find Nandini not yet returned from the studio, where on weekdays she was perenially ensconced. On Sundays she disappeared to the racecourse, her favourite haunt ever since she had won a huge amount betting on Motilal's horse. He felt a frisson of annoyance that she had not given her son's illness precedence above her work on the sets.

He had intended her interest only to be a diversion for his digressions. But the production unit now seemed her sole obsession. Her attention hovered greatly around her artists. Rather he should call them stars, for they appeared more concerned about their star demands nowadays than their acting. More than their lines, they concentrated on figures and numbers.

The post-war scenario was dismal. The monumental studios were closing down; new government policies and raw stock controls decimating the once mighty titans by a gluttonous requirement of funds. In their visionary place, upstarts and carpetbaggers were magnet-drawn towards this industry more for its glamour than its art. The spotlight was shifting; major footage being taken up, in more ways than one, by these stars of individual shine. Amongst them, like a bright and beautiful planet, Nandini lolled, orbited by the ubiquitous Sarang.When they poured over dialogue sheets or daily schedules, Ani noticed with considerable irk that Sarang managed to sidle his heavy Punjabi shoulder perilously close to Nandini's beautifully-rounded one.

He was perplexed by how the man had appeared out of an anonymity and gained so much importance. Nobody knew where he came from or even where he lived, except perhaps for Shamim and the production manager. He was ever-present, never requiring to be summoned, his antecedents lost in a literary mist. All they knew about him was that he had authored a book on the Partition dedicated to an even more mysterious 'Z'.

He stared out from the balcony at the sporadic traffic moving some distance away on the main road, an erratic procession of lights like horizontal shooting stars. He marvelled at the quirks of a destiny that had made him choose his residence on the very road on which Dadasaheb Phalke, the man who spearheaded this great industry, had lived and dreamed. He stuck a cigarette in his ivory holder, putting a flame to it with a click of his gold Cartier lighter. He seldom smoked, unlike Nandini, who in the company of Saro and her race course friend, Shantu, had begun to frequently patronise the reed as a symbol of feminine emancipation. Funny, how Nandini in her guilelessness had mistaken Shantu for a royal personage. The only royalty with whom Shantu was connected was an uncle of the Maharajah of Gwalior, whose mistress she happened to be. Despite the façade of French chiffons and once-royal navratnas, something brittle from her inner spaces managed to float to the top, eminent in her reptilian smile. She was as brash and obvious as the thrust of her pointed breasts. He liked strong women, not forceful women. Strength, as in his mother, was beautiful. Aniruddh much preferred women like the colourful Ramola, who, despite her forthrightness, still retained her quintessential femininity.

Thinking feminine reminded him of Minoti, of her fragile face and innocence, the way she had lowered her gaze and draped her sari around her full and fragrant body. She was a complete antithesis to Nandini, for example. God, why was he thinking of Minoti? She was but a child, half his age! The danger signal was that he was not thinking of her frivolously. To him these women came and went, like night and day. They were a sequence of events, not an essence of thought.

With sombre introspection, he realised that he had begun to think about another woman because he and Nandini were drifting apart. They lived in the same world, but in different dimensions.

He knew he had to save this marital ship from floundering on the rocks of their careers, to salvage the treasures that had once been aboard that ship from disappearing into some Bermuda triangle.

They needed quality time together. They would go away on a holiday, perhaps when Pradeep was home for his summer vacations.

Dead bodies were only fit for cremations.

Mussourie was pacifying after the dry, blistering winds of the northern plains that had chased them all the way to Dehradun. The stinging heat of Delhi had made the younger children cantankerous. Pradeep, bronzed and athletic with regular physical training at school, looked dashing at thirteen, and rode with equestrian aplomb as though to the saddle born. Nandita, dullish and with an indefinite haircut ran after sudden flowers in the wayside hedges, and Mannu, like a heavy penguin waddling along the pebbly paths on chubby legs, had to be restrained by nanny Nirupa from detailed inspection of worms and such-like creatures that he discovered in his wobbly meandering.

The tableau of the hill station de-froze and slid into motion by mid-morning. The winter-lonely paths and sylvan glades were suddenly populous with strollers, birdwatchers, and the social set of the neighbouring cities. The Mall was coloured with ladies in elegant slacks and imported sweaters. They promenaded with calculated steps and peered gracefully down hillsides, looking as cool as the lemonades they sipped. Escorted by men brandishing brass-knobbed canes and military moustaches, they made composed pictures against the majestic conifers.

Aniruddh was not at all surprised to come across Ramola and Purshottam in this milieu. Ramola sighed at Nandini's classic beauty, those luminous eyes and enviable cheekbones, the elegant nose and iridescent complexion. Nandini sensed the other woman's irrepressible rusticity, a brutal down-to-earthiness that shone brighter than the emerald pendant at her throat. In the past year, Ramola had given birth to a daughter, and it was perhaps the comprehensive warmth of recent maternity that made her twiddle Mannu's cheeks with appreciative delight.

"Such a chweet roly-poly baba, hain na?"

Baba was not at all pleased at this liberty. He manifested his displeasure in an obstreperous howl. Ramola thought it judicious to make some rightful noises and carry on.

Up ahead they met up with Saro and her three daughters, the last being born just before her separation from Kumarsen. A fate-al, fetal accident. The eldest Malini, eyes full of intense mystique, was already quite a classic beauty and her height made her appear more than her fourteen years. Saro had announced a film with her as heroine in a home producton. The middle girl Nilima, her name a re-arranged version of her sister's, looked as if only chains could arrest her fidgetiness. The youngest, Charu's, expression was so solemn that she could have been at a wake than at a hill resort. Saro had come to remove Nilima from school and admit her into a convent in Panchgani.

"Although I have a cottage here, Panchgani will be easier to visit. You should think of putting Nandita there, too. Being with other girls might help to transform her tomboy tendencies into feminine graces."

"If you find the convent suitable, let me know," replied Nandini. "I'm out at the studio a lot, and Mithimaa, whose asthma is worsening with age, is too old to restrain this one."

They walked further, reminiscing about schooldays.

At night, Upamanyu began to cough; a staccato dry sound that came straight from his guts and kept everyone awake. By morning it was much worse. He spluttered and choked with a heavy wracking till his face grew red and tears poured from his eyes.

Nandini blamed it on an evil eye.

"Must be that Ramola-friend of yours. Tweaking his cheeks like that. Otherwise how can a perfectly healthy child develop such a demoniac cough overnight?"

"Oh come on Babesie, don't talk like some uneducated woman. It must be the change of weather. You know, from the heat of Delhi to the cooler here. Just give him some ginger-juice and honey and he'll be fine."

But no amount of ginger-honey solution or crushed tulsi leaf administrations improved the child's condition. The local pediatrician declared it as whooping cough.

"But he was vaccinated," protested Aniruddh. "I took him myself."

"I know. But sometimes these vaccinations are bogus. Happens," he said with clinical brevity.

With the family history of weak lungs, it was prudent to curtail the holiday and return home.

Well, so much for family togetherness. He had tried. But the diaspora of their interests now made each of their worlds rotate on a different axis.

That first night he slept apart, and in the private darkness Minoti's invading Assamese eyes scrambled and unscrambled various meanings in his dreams. After his sincere efforts, so unfortunately aborted, he felt not a flicker of guilt to let their illegal forms mingle with the shadows under his eyelids.

TRAGIC TALES

The next day spurred a sequence of domestic events. Shubir announced that he was marrying Pratibha, his Juliet of the backdoor balcony. Pratibha's father was a Maharashtrian violinist in Anirudh's orchestra. For many months Shubir and Pratibha had carried on their romance, she in her balcony and he in his, their conversation floating on the perfumed air of the few feet that separated them. They wished for a simple, if imminent ceremony, and would remove immediately to a two-roomed apartment that was only four buildings down the road to continue their near but separate lives. Aniruddh protested that there was enough space in this large house.

"Let them go, Ani. They are newly-weds and want their privacy. They have a right to live their lives the way *they* want to," said Nandini pragmatically.

Nandini's vocal support was interpreted by Aniruddh as a machination to dispense with his side of the family. It caused a wound that slowly but surely, began to fester.

The day after the newly-weds departed, Rehmatbi took to her bed with a virulent attack of asthma. She wheezed and sneezed and writhed with breathlessness, her blocked lungs strained and battered. Considerably weakened, she clung tenaciously to her life, aided by drips and pricks. But at past seventy, age was an enemy to her recovery. Finally, when Dr. Bose announced the audibility of the death rattle, her relatives were summoned.

With a final, fatal rasp, Rehmatbi died. Her lungs, spent and spiritless, took on an eternal stillness.

In this house of mourning, there was no place for Minoti.

Aniruddh now wanted his mother to come and claim her rightful position as head of the house. But when, after a long stay in the home of a son-in-law, Konkona elected to move in with Shubir, unwrapping her idols in the roomy kitchen, it made an eloquent statement that the daughter of a Brahmin musician was more qualified to sit in the presence of her thakurs than the defiling daughter of a Muslim wet-nurse.

It drove Aniruddh's resentment deeper.

Is dil ki haalat kya kahiye,
jo shad bhi hai nashaad bhi hai

GOING FOR A SONG

Nandita fiddled with the knobs of the new radiogram, trying to tune in to Radio Ceylon. Ever since Mr. Keskar had put his threat of banning film songs into effect, the radio station had cottoned on to the advantage of broadcasting this popular brand of music. With undiminshed zeal, practically everyone in India now listened to an alien music station.

Aniruddh observed his daughter's natural affinity for rhythm, the way she swung her hips to the music with the ease and grace of a dancer.The unit members called her 'Billi-ki-aankh-waali' a fitting sobriquet. Now fondly he watched as she danced, twirling her hands to signify a lotus. He would miss her when she went off to Panchgani along with Nilima and Charu to boarding school next year.

He continued to brush the baize-green cover of How Green is my Valley, lamenting the fate of the invaluable classics he had gathered with care. Their flyspecked pages, encrusted with dead roaches and munched on by silverfish, smelt of an embalmed death. On Nirupa's departure to her native Mangalore, the house had been handed over to the care of the servants supervised by a new Nanny on the scene. Her name was Mary, and the children had begun to call her Mary-Ma, which soon began to sound like Meri Ma.

His heart was invaded by sadness at the thought of this house he had so enthusiastically built, in which echoed a forlorn emptiness. This Taj Mahal, below which lay buried a dead love, its residents in separate graves.

The strains of a rumba-samba number formed a background score to his thoughts, strutting onto his purist tendencies like an aberration. The tune rankled with familiarity, the words some non-lyrical listing of sticks and eggs. It was thanks to such numbers the ban had been enforced, thought Aniruddh with a grimace. Then he realised where he'd heard it.

At Chaitanya's recording.

Recollection of an ingenuous hill-girl skipped into his mind. He immediately rang up Jasbir to contact her for a tentative sitting.

She entered the room dressed in a simple white and red sari. A black bindi, like an eclipsed moon, stood out sharply against her fair forehead. Her sensuous eyes were lowered. The neat lines of her chiselled features, her smallish nose, her full cheeks and tremulous lips, made her appear as if she had just stepped out of a 'pat' painting.

Like a dramatic afterstatement, her father followed.

"Come here, child," Aniruddh emphasised deliberately on the *child.* "Sit here, in front of the harmonium."

She hesitated, and looked at her father for instruction.

"Go on, beti, take the great man's blessings. He is like a father to you. He will guide you."

A silken feather stroked his toes. His delight was jarred by Vikramaditya's allusion to his paternal image.

Once his fingers contacted the harmonium, he was at once the professional, the guru, quick to spot a false note, his criticism stretched, his taskmaster tactics demanding. Why did she drop off her last note so abruptly, as if over a precipice? Why did she pronounce her 'r' like an 'l'? His harshness scratched her musical softness, as if he was stroking her with a blunt knife, bloodless but painful.

"But Chaitanyasaab never criticised me like this, moshai."

Her protest coloured his rage.

"First and foremost, I am not Chaitanya and this is not criticism but correction. If you are too stupid to differentiate, pack up and go home. I want no composition of mine to be ruined by some feminine fuss."

Tears filmed Minoti's woeful doe-ful eyes. She sniffled, flambé-ing his anger.

"Yourself Vikramaditya Mehra, I want a singer here, not a snivelling brat. Does she want to sing or flow a great flood?"

"No, no sirji. She will obey. Minoo, Listen to the guru, ma."

Chastised, the girl blinked away her tears and continued, this time without a mistake.

In an unobtrusive corner, Vikramaditya sat like a benign German shepherd. He had no doubt that under Ani-moshai's expert tutelage, his daughter would take her place up there in the firmament with Noorjehan, Latika, Geeta Roy and others of such ilk.

The violinists were rehearsing in earnest when Aniruddh entered the recording-room at Famous, as his favourite Bombay Lab. was booked by a talented new composer named Madan Mohan who had made his appearance on the music scene just that year. Their violins tucked pertly under their chins, they played the interlude from their notes on the upright stands in front of them. Albuquerque the cellist had a concentrated frown and Marina the pianist, in a flowered skirt, raised sand-dune flourishes over her keys.

"Where is the female singer?" he asked authoritatively. "I don't hear her rehearsing along with the musicians."

"She is in the singer's booth, Ani-moshai," his tabla-player Ramakant informed him.

He pushed open the door of the soundproof compartment. Beyond the dangling mikes he saw a woman seated on the rexin sofa. Had it not been for her omnipresent father he would never have recognised her. She was clad in hip-hugging tights and a cream and black striped jersey. A broad black belt spanned her not too thin waist, and gold hoops like acrobats' rings, dangled from her ears. Her lips were slashed with scarlet. Rouge, in two large red spots, sat heavily on her cheeks. Her ponytail swished like a cow flicking off flies. A plump and rounded hip protruded unilaterally making a swaggering statement. A Colaba Causeway streetwalker had replaced the 'pat' painting.

"What do you think you're doing dressed like that, Miss Fancy Pants?"

The girl gazed at him in stupefaction. Vikramaditya Mehra, her mouthpiece as usual, answered.

"But this, Ani-moshai, is the latest fashion! Now she is properly in the line of films, she must dress glamorously, no?" "No." said Aniruddh curtly. "At least not for me."

"Pardon, Dada?"

"Make up your mind, Mehra, if you want her to be an actress or a singer. How is she going to breathe in those tight clothes? Are you aware that the microphone will record every inhalation of hers? She's supposed to be singing a folk song here, not dancing the fandango. It's an Indian melody, not Chaitanya's Latin-American boat-song. How do you expect to get the feel of the lyrics and the tune in clothes like these? Vikramaditya Mehra, take yourself and your daughter off to wherever it is you stay and get her back here dressed in a simple sari."

"But Dada, I stay at Dadar Station! It will take us at least two hours to go and come back by bus! How.."

Impatiently dipping into his wallet, Aniruddh removed a hundred-rupee note and handed it to the gaping bulldog. "Grab a taxi. Keep it waiting and get your butt back inside of an hour. We don't want to waste the producer's money and the musicians' time. They will be rehearsal-perfect by the time you return, so we will compensate by not making too many mistakes. Is that understood?"

The man nodded, and father and daughter were out in thirty seconds, marvelling at the maestro's sense of perfection. Wah! Wah! muttered Mehra to himself all the way back home. They returned, with Minoti this time attired in a plain Shantipuri sari. Better re-attired than retired, had been Mehra's practical thought.

Aniruddh stared sharply at her, but said nothing. Yet the expression in his eyes was eloquent enough. The song was recorded in two takes. Aniruddh summoned Mehra after pack-up had been ordered.

"Since you stay at Dadar, you can ride home with me." He pronounced it like an order.

They drove in silence, Ani behind the wheel. Minoti sat directly behind. Once their eyes crossed in the rear-view mirror, shocking both with a lurking communication. Aniruddh frowned, his forehead surrendering to furrows, and Minoti turned her frightened-doe eyes away, embarrassed, but not unaffected.

At night she curled up into a foetus, protecting herself from herself. She thought about this unusual man with the tremendous talent and the legendary fame. He was short, dark, unhandsome, but charisma emanated from him like a tidal wave. She had loved the way he had ordered her about. As if she were his property. As if she were his, simply.

She wrapped her admiration around her like a blanket. Snug, she slept.

Tere nainon ne chori kiya, mora chotasa jiya, pardesiya

DEVDAS, PARO AND CHANDRAMUKHI

On his return home, Aniruddh peeped into Nandini's room. As usual, it looked forlorn and undisturbed. He phoned the studio. She was inside the soundstage. She couldn't be reached. Pack-up was at least an hour away.

He thought of inviting a friend over for a drink, then decided against it. He really didn't feel like company tonight.

Changing into his tehmat, he peeped in on the children. They were sound asleep. The sight of Mary standing over them in the night-light, gazing at them with infinite tenderness, touched him. With her fiercely oiled hair and her granny's glasses she looked like a benevolent fairy godmother.

He lay pensively on the bed, hands clasped behind his head. The fan above him whirred and wheezed with great effort. Like a myriad leeches, particles of dust clung to its blades. On his cupboard drawer Nandita had scrawled the alphabet with chalk. He tried to erase all thought from his mind so there would be place for sleep.

But his legs shook to some subconscious tune and his errant mind meandered towards Minoti. His spontaneous outburst today appalled him by its irrationality. What difference did it make what his singers wore? Mehra had just been bullied into doing as he commanded because of Ani's awesome authority and his own ambition. But Ani admitted he had been offended by the glamourisation of her simplicity.

She was less than half his age. Too young to understand the reactions her voluptuous body aroused. This quaint result of the coupling of a Punjabi mushtanda and a delicate nightingale from Assam, was a child-woman. One, who when her bonds were free, would surge into the heavens like a lark, and sing as sweetly. She had her father's heavy frame and her mother's timorousness, but that Bengali essence had come from her early life in Calcutta, where her father had worked as a bit player in New Theatres. She must have been barely an infant when he had been struggling to establish himself there. It felt strangely pleasant to think that almost two decades ago, they had lifted their eyes to the same light and mingled in the same shadows. Perhaps they may have crossed on some street, where, his mind full of Suchitra, he had not seen her.

When Nandini peeped into his room at night he seemed to be sleeping like a baby, wearing his tehmat and an expression of peace. She wondered if she was within the space of whatever dream he was in right now. Quite unlikely, she mused with a rueful smile. All the dreams they had now were for other people. Left for them were domestic nightmares like running a house, bringing up children who had measles and mumps. Trying to keep Mary from being partial to Mannu, to prevent Nandita from tearing around like a tomboy in those petticoats their Pakistani distributor's wife, Shirin Murad, embroidered for her during her nights of insomnia. To maintain the expenditures of this house with its thieving and shirking servants who had once quavered under Mithima's jaundiced eye.

She took off her clothes and dumped them in a heap in a corner. She was exhausted, but to good effect. They had canned a couple of good shots today.

Unfortunately, Aniruddh could not do for Minoti what he had been able to do for Rajan or for Aziz Masood. True, she was gifted with a lovely voice, but its recorded version sadly lacked soul. Her voice quality was better than Latika's, but it did not have Latika's feeling and maturity at which the senior singer had worked so assiduously. One song, and then another, with ditto results. He was losing his touch, and not just the Midas quality.

Yet he could not shake off his fascination for her. The only alternative to his restless desire was to close his eyes to her supposedly inviolate child-likeness and have a fling-thing with her. Once he had stormed the citadel of her innocence, his lust fed and fulfilled, he could shrug her off forever. She might be maidenly, but she was an adult twenty. If he didn't do it, someone else would. Maybe Chaitanya. He had seen the rusty lust in his eyes, which could be interpreted by any average, garden-variety fellow-rake.

He was aware of her uncited fascination. His task was made easier by the faint trace of reverence in her eyes, food for any idol, particularly an idle idol. A look that he had not seen for some time now.

It all began with a frothy flirtatiousness. Those intentional touches, those wet intense looks. A pointed significance in his questions. The pronounced suggestiveness in her responses. Little assignations. Big assignations. And they were treading the path of an exciting, if forbidden, romance.

There was a new sun on the horizon, fading somewhat the glow of the old-timers. A composer-duo called Shivendra-Krishan had a runaway hit with their very first film. They were young and pulsating with talent. Their music had a fresh effect, cool and gambolling like a monsoon cataract. They combined Aniruddh's melody with Naushad's classicism, Sajjad's finesse and Ghulam Haider's pulsating rhythm. They had an ally in the new and improved recording techniques that made music lose its brassy shrillness. First Latika, then Rajan latched on to their success. The public turned like sunflowers towards this new sun.

For the first time Aniruddh's throne trembled. The wave that he had crested was slithering. Soon it would crash into a thousand soapy bubbles in its spent force. He started to writhe in the throes of insecurity, to feel the kind of frustration Mastermoshai at Kalamahal must have experienced at being upstaged by an eighteen-year old. He became conscious of the searing knowledge that his position, even as a pioneer of this industry, was not permanent. The vinegary quality of public fickleness replaced the sweetness of success.

In his unshared frustration, he turned towards Minoti's ample lap for consolation. He clung to the comfort of her plump arms. He imagined himself half in love with her, seeking in this undefined romance an excitement missing in his art.

With Nandini, he was like an actor in a shadow play. His motions were well rehearsed and his words spoken as if by some prompter in the wings. But with Minoti, his inner dead self pulsated and came alive. He experienced a shedding of skin, a rejuvenation. They sailed on the common sea of music, their barge the intrinsic relationship that binds the creator and its creation. Whatever he felt for Minoti, and he had not paused to analyse his nebulous feelings, he knew with unhappy certainty that his marriage to Nandini was over. They had drifted apart on rafts of their own manufacture.

And then returned Bela the vamp, waiting in the wings for her cue.

When Bela entered Aniruddh's rehearsal room and caught him with his hand inside Minoti's blouse, she immediately enrolled herself as accomplice. Randily she thought that if the singer's nipples were a dark pink, then he had literally been caught red-handed.

"I can understand Dada, I can understand," she said quickly, before Ani could offer an explanation, winded as he was by her unexpected appearance. He was quite certain he had locked the door. "Bou-di is out so much, naturally you will require some companionship..hee hee. So this is the sweet Minoti..pretty, pretty." Minoti's discomfiture at being caught so with a married man was mitigated at the thought of her providing solace to a talented and famous man whose wife had a short supply of appreciation. The lady who had made an embarrassing entry had redeemed herself by this dramatic corroboration of her own doubts.

With not surprising promptness, Bela offered her services as conspirator to this clandestine romance. She would ostensibly leave with Ani on some errand, extricate Minoti from her father's supervision, or super-vision, by climbing up the two stories of their building to establish herself as friend taking Minoti out for shopping or a film. For aid rendered, she was quite happy to be paid with a cinema ticket for time-pass entertainment, whilst the two lovebirds ran off to faraway Powai Lake or Aarey Milk Colony for a little intimate smooching.

It was *her* insidious brainwave to throw Prannath and Nandini together. Prannath's obvious attraction for Nandini might find some reciprocation if Aniruddh's indifferences became too potent. Even if it didn't, it would be a convenient platform of accusation should the need present itself. Aniruddh's earlier dalliances had not required any planning; they were all one-day stands and he had plenty of opportunity to fit them conveniently into his daily routine. But this was an *affair,* and with work a little slow, he needed plausible excuses to be missing. So he would summon Sarang for a dialogue session or a story sitting, and make off at the last minute leaving him and Nandini together. While they perused scripts and puzzled at Ani's brusque disappearances, he would coo with his lady love at some obscure, lonely spot.

Aniruddh contemplated a tentative alliance between Nandini and Prannath as a convenient possibility. After all, he was quite good-looking and had a charmimg way with words. Both were lethal attributes to sweep a woman off her feet.

In the fish market at Parel, Nandini moved from stall to stall, inspecting prawns and lobsters for their freshness. It was a rare Sunday off, and she planned to cook a fish curry.

From their slithery platforms, fishmongers called out to her in strident tones to inspect their ware. She tucked up her sari, and was looking a silver-scaled pomfret seriously in the eye when a voice drawled raspily in her ear.

It was her brother Suleiman, who had been dismissed when caught shamelessly stealing her jewellery just a few days after his mother's death.

"What Mehru? The Queen steps out amongst the commoners? Or are the servants cheating again with the bazaar accounts?"

In slow motion, Nandini turned around to face her brother, the unashamed Suleiman looking his customary crude self. With teeth stained bidi-ochre, face bleary, hair ruffled and coat crumpled, the only bright thing about him was the sardonic gleam in his eye.

At first she made to turn away, but eventually could not resist the desire to talk to him. Blood was blood, after all, however tainted.

"I'm impressed that you have money at all to buy fish for your illegitimate family. Where did you get it? Hocking Kulsumbai's jewellery this time?"

"Arre-re. Same as ever, eh Mehru? Blazing eye and scorching tongue. If I were you, I would reserve some of that anger for your husband. The tales you hear about him! Hanky-panky with some fresh young thing these days. Looks as if he's tired of you. Better to have stuck with us. After all, family is family."
"*He's* my family now, understand, dear brother? So take your malicious tales someplace else?"

"You can taunt me all you want, Mehru, but look out for yourself. Many times when I walk past the Dadar Station Road I see the red Desoto parked in a bylane. One woman gets out, and another gets in. Then the woman who gets out crosses the road to Broadway Cinema, buys a ticket and goes into the theatre all by herself. You know who that woman is? It's that witch Bela Bose. Something stinks here, Mehru, as much as that fish in your hands."

Nandini flung the pomfret away as if it had come alive and bitten her.

"So you follow women about now, at your age?"

"Since I couldn't follow the car, it was the next best thing to do. Just looking out for your interest, sister."

His diabolical cackle resounded in her ears like sniper fire. She was getting a headache, trying to dismiss his words. With the taste of bad fish in her mouth, she rushed back to the security of her home.

But the seeds of suspicion had been sown in the deep furrows of her mind.

It was true that she and Ani were drifting apart. Maybe he was having an affair, aided and abetted by Bela, who she was convinced was right in the epicentre where she always liked to be. Who was this other woman?

Troubled, she tried to recall when last Ani had made love to her. She could not. That's how long it had been.

Nandini's concentration seemed to have gone for a walk. Her mind wandered in hazy lanes looking for a red Desoto. A young girl with a blanked-out face moved about in her vision. Bela flew around on a broom, her long hair flying in thready trails around her snarling face. The inorganic wails of children tormented her with their innocence. The acid of corrosive insinuations ate into her mind. Music, strident and off-tune, swam against diatonic currents, ending up as screeches. She was mad with suspense. She decided that the only way to put her mind at rest was to find out the truth.

They were shooting at Shree Sound, and Prannath watched with concern her uncharacteristic slackness. She was visibly disturbed, and like a contagion, her lack of attention was spreading to most areas of work. In the lunch break he took the liberty of asking her if something was wrong.

"Is it that obvious?"

"Glaring as an arc lamp."

"I don't know, Pran. What is bothering me? And should it even do so? Is there anything of substance in these mists?"

"Well, if you need advice or an objective view, I'm there. You only have to ask"

"Thanks. Maybe I will."

At ten past three she called home. Runu informed her that Ani and Bela had gone out together. The smell of the pomfret psychically invaded her senses. If what Suleiman had said was true, it was too late to catch them now. Bela never missed any part of a movie; ads, trailers or The Films Division documentary.

By four she could stand it no longer. At five-thirty she announced pack-up, to everyone's professional amazement.

"You can't wrap up a shift that normally ends at 7 an hour and-half earlier!" was Prannath's initial protest. "You'll lose money!" "Don't I know that? But I'm the producer, and it's my money" replied Nandini crossly.

"Okay, you're the boss," he relented, knowing her state of disturbance.

On an impulse she asked Prannath if he would accompany her on a mission.

"If it's to resolve what you're troubled about, consider me in."

"But please Pran, no questions."

'Okay baba, no questions."

Not that Nandini was afraid to go alone. What she really needed was a bolstering to make her do something which went completely against her grain. This kind of espionage felt practically immoral, a voyereustic peep into someone's trust.

They drove onto the main Vincent Road, and around the Dadar Tram Terminus. To his surprise she navigated the T.T. Circle and turned the bonnet of her green Hillman towards the mill area instead of towards her home. Noticing her violin-string tautness he refrained from asking her where they were headed. At A to Z, the tapestry store short of Broadway Cinema, she braked abruptly to a halt. He spoke for the first time, making an attempt at lightness.

"If you're hoping I'll help you choose curtains, don't. My taste is putrid. Was this what you were so tense about, for God's sake?"

She didn't answer, only glanced at her watch. Her dial showed six-twenty.

"Oh sorry. I didn't realise I'd asked a question."

The matinee at the Broadway was getting over. The film was an Abbas production called RAAHI. People began to come through the exit. At first a trickle, it soon became a surge. She strained to spot Bela in the exiting crowd. When dispersal sieved the crowd, it left one single person standing conspicuously in a flaming red sari near a cigarette stall. A flaring postbox, a fire engine tender.

When the Broadway entrance sucked in the crowd for the next show, she still stood, a cat-like smile on her face. A passerby stopped in front of her and asked her something. She gestured to the Housefull Board. How could she stand this way on the road with a complete lack of dignity, thought Nandini? Her hands tightened on the wheel, ribbing her delicate fingers.

Prannath, following her line of vision, noticed Bela and said, "Hey, isn't that Be..." when the wine-coloured Desoto slid past like a galleon. Nandini clutched Prannath's arm. The car halted before Bela's glaring presence, and with that strange smile still pasted on her lips, she made to open the back door. But not before Nandini had seen the long hair spilling down the back of the front passenger. It was like a screening of Suleiman's verbal script.

As the car moved away from the kerb, she revved her starter. Just opposite the cinema was the turning into the Station Road. The Desoto firmly in sight, Nandini was about to cross the opening in the centre of the road which the Desoto had just passed, when a tram rattled onto the edge of her windscreen and she braked.

Dividing the road was the central tram line.

By the time the tram, like a giant red whale, swam out of sight, the red Desoto had disappeared. It could have been swallowed up by any one of the labyranthine lanes that crisscrossed the Station Road. Distraught, Nandini made a U-turn towards home.

Prannath, astute and observant, could make a good guess at the purpose of this sequence of events. But the atmosphere in the car was like a loose electrical connection, even a casual comment would have caused a short-circuit.

They reached her home.

"If you'd dropped me at the Tram terminus, I would have caught a bus to Shivaji Park from the stop opposite Valia's. Now I'll have to walk back to the Circle."

"Is that where you stay? Shivaji Park?" she said, without looking at him.

"Right behind the Scottish Orphanage."

"What is that?"

"It's an extremely good school for rich people's children run by a Scottish couple called the Ramsays. The fees are really high."

"Does that make your rent higher?"

"Now I know why you said 'No questions.' You reserved the right to ask them for yourself."

She made a feeble attempt at a smile.

"You know Prannath Sarang, from next month I'm going to raise your salary. And perhaps with my next film I shall announce you as a partner in Jubilee Pictures."

"May all employers be as gracious as you. Distributing generosity when their heart is breaking."

He placed his hand over hers and pressed it lightly.

For the first time she turned her head and through the filter of unshed tears, looked at him kindly.

You're a good friend, Pran."

"And you're a good woman. Don't let anything make you forget that." He stepped out.

He was smiling all the way home. A partnership? It was just past the middle of the century. By the seventh decade, he had targeted a villa in the suburbs, perhaps a studio of his own, and at least half a dozen cars in the driveway.

He was prepared to wait. If he played his cards right, maybe Nandini would just be the bonus with all this.

Nandini's expression quite resembled that of Kaali, a mix of wrath and complacence. Aniruddh and Bela were taken aback to see her sitting on the sofa, so unexpectedly. Usually her time of return was around eight o'clock and it was only just past seven. Their fidgety guilt contrasted restlessly with her superior control, as she turned the pages of the newspaper. She smiled as she saw them, and beckoned Mary to take the children to their room.

"Ah the vagrants! Runu has been waiting for you in his room a long time. You really shouldn't go off with his wife and leave him alone for so long. I'll have tea sent to the guest room." She stressed deliberately on the *guest.* "You must be tired driving around all day. I see you've not taken the chauffeur again today."

A retort almost framed itself on Ani's lips, but then he preferred not to spoil his present good mood by getting into an argument. Like a soft-footed cat, Bela made to follow him out of the room, but Nandini caught her arm.

"Come Bela, sit by me. We hardly get a chance to talk. You must think I'm a poor hostess."

"Oh no, Bou-di, I'm not a guest here, it is my second home."

"Really? Then I hope you will protect it."

"What are you meaning, Bou-di? Is there any danger?" she asked, apprehension resonating in her tone.

"Never mind all that. Tell me, how was the film?"

"The film? What film?"

"The one you saw at Broadway this afternoon. And where did you dump my poor husband whilst you watched it? I heard you had left the house together."

"I didn't watch any film." Bela's voice quivered, pronged on alarm.

"Is that so? Then why were you standing outside the exit? I was about to stop and offer you a ride home but then Ani arrived to pick you up, so I presumed you would come with him anyway."

"Oh...that." Bela wondered how much Nandini had seen and what she could invent convincingly.

"Yes my dear, *that.*"

"That..oh yes, I had gone to book tickets for tomorrow whilst Dada went to pick up Utpalda from his house at Parel. There was no parking space, no."

"You are sure you did not come out of the exit?"

Bela looked away. "Hein, Bou-di. I am absolutely certain."

"I didn't know that Utpalda has started to wear his hair long. Is it some new kind of fashion or he just hasn't had time to go to the barber?"

A high-density silence gripped the room for a minute.

"Guests must respect their hospitality, is that not so, Bela? I am sure a smart woman like you will not have difficulty getting my drift."

Her eyes fixed on Bela with steely sharpness. "Of course, of course. Now Bou-di, I really do want to go the..."

"Bathroom? Understandable. Run along, dear."

Bela sprang from the room as if Chandalika's lion itself were in pursuit. She had not compared Nandini to Kali in vain. In her rush she tripped over the Mecanno toy house that Nandita had been labouring over when they arrived, sending it flying. It crashed against the radiogram and fell back in pieces.

Outside, the day was darkening.

She had to gain some mileage out of this situation. In the bathroom she doused her eyes with water, and with moist eyelashes made fast and steadfastly to their room.

"This is too much, shothi baba. Bou-di has really been rude. I for one can make no sense of what she has been saying. Something about my not being a good guest. Now all I wanted to do was to help you Dada, for I know how she neglects you, and I thought, if my services can make you happy, what harm is there? We will not stay here another day." She covered her face with her hands, feigning tears.

Befuddled, Runu asked her in what way had she violated their hostess' hospitality.

With loud wails and protestations, Bela spilled the whole affair of Aniruddh and Minoti, much to Ani's embarrassment. But then Runu could afford to be faithful; he didn't have young girls throwing themselves at him all the time.

"Ani, what is all this?" asked Runu gravely, at the end of Bela's lamentations.

'Well, bondhu, I think I have at last found the love of my life. Someone who understands me; someone soft and gentle and.. submissive."

"But Ani, it was Bou-di's strength and independence you admired! What has caused this change in your preferences?"

"Once, yes. But it was a mistake. I expected her to be polished steel, not rusty iron."

"And you want to punish Bou-di for *your* mistake? That is hardly fair. She is courageous and a very admirable woman. And if she has said anything to Bela, surely she is justified." "What has courage to do with happiness?" intervened Bela furiously. "Courage is okay if you are a soldier, not a wife."

Bela, thought Runu, could hardly consider herself as role model for the ideal wife. "Nevertheless she is right in ticking you off, and you have to endure her taunts, if that is what you consider them." "Runu's right, Bela. For my sake you will have to bear with them."

"If you insist. But my time will come, just you wait and see."

"So, you intend to continue with this ..this alliance with Minoti?"

"I must. She is the air that I breathe. She is the song that I sing. I look for excuses to be with her even to the point of giving her songs when she is not a successful singer. What can I do, alas? She is both my pain and my panacea." "But how long will you carry on?" asked Runu, who thought Ani was bewitched rather than beholden.

"I don't know. I haven't really thought about the outcome."

"For one who hardly looked at women, you really have changed, bondhu. What happened to the man who could not speak of his feelings to Suchitra?"

"That was another time and space. Things change. *People* change."

"But it is hardly fair to deceive Bou-di in this manner, all for the sake of a woman half your age. Bou-di is an honest and fearless woman."

"Aahaha! It is okay for her to neglect her husband. Dada should suffer? Hein?"

"Whatever it is, it is between husband and wife. It is not our part to interfere."

"Not even if it makes me happy?"

"You are my closest friend, Ani. I will do anything for you. If it will make you happy, I will collaborate with you as well. But I will not condone it."

Bela scowled at Runu. He was not a true friend if his principles were above his friend's happiness.

Runu unlocked his eyes from her glare-stare. He was habitually a man of few words and this communication had been eloquent enough for him. Bela was foolish and stubborn and incredibly short-sighted. If he tried to proffer his own point of view in contradiction to hers, she would retaliate by throwing a good old-fashioned tantrum. As for himself, he would cloister behind the adage, One-fold silence, a hundred-fold peace.

Runu and Bela left. With their departure, the house careened into some semblance of normalcy.

Tod diya dil mera, tu ne arrey bewafa, mujhko mere pyar ka khoob ye badla diya

It was time to mend fences with skilful carepentry. A forewarned Nandini was a forearmed Nandini. Perhaps a four-armed Nandini. Mussoorie had got jammed by an inconvenient cough. But Panchgani stood like an invitation. Nandita was to be taken to the convent for admission, and Aniruddh made up his mind to accompany Nandini there.

Minoti was distraught. Aniruddh had promised her that with Nandini gone, they would spend whole days together. Perhaps nights.

Aniruddh traced her trembling lips with his finger. "I know, my darling. But the climate is not right just now. Relax. We will have our time together."

"But you promised!" wailed Minoti, childishly enchanting.

"I know. But I am not breaking promises, merely putting them off to another time. Patience, my love.'

Children are easy to appease with the temptation of gifts.

OUTDOOR LOCATIONS

The base of Tableland clasped the convent with its red gabled roof. The flat head of the plateau had been pounded by a hundred dancing steps for at least a score of films. From the courtyard below, children in uniform glanced up at the plateau with its rocky walls, and frequently espied the outline of a crane or the silver glitter of a solar reflector.

The convent occcupied three sides of a rectangle, and its open side faced the sports ground stretching like a giant palm with clumps of Jain-mauve morning-glory like gangrenous nails at its edge. Convent-broken girls stared condescendingly at the new entrant as she stepped into the hallow precincts, a protective parent on each side. In the parlour, Priyanandini was greeted by a nun, angular shoulder blades discernible under her starched white habit. A chaste rosary gripped her waist. With twinkling eyes she read the name against 'Mother' on the admission form.

"Priyanandini Ganguly. My dear, the name is different, but those eyes, those dimples; would your maiden name, by any chancse, be Mehrunissa Karamali?"

Nandini's reputed dimples concaved cutely.

"That is so, but Sister, how could you know?"

"Of course, dearie, you would not recognise me now. But then I was not a nun when I taught you literature at a school in Dadar."
"Miss Thelma D'lima?" exclaimed Nandini in sheer astonishment. "This is so incredible!"

"Gracious, girl, the ways of the Lord are strange. Imagine, I shall be teaching two generations. Do you know that Sarojini's two daughters are here too?"

"Yes Miss, I mean, Sister, it was she who recommended the school to me."

Till now, Aniruddh had been occupying a backseat, but Sister Bartholomew courteously included him in the fold of her address.

"Ah Mr. Ganguly, I must tell you that your wife was our star student."

"You won't be disappointed in my daughter either. She's been getting excellent results in the nursery she attended in Bombay."

"My my, it will be a pleasure, then, to take her under my wing. Come my girl, say goodbye to your Mummy and Daddy."

The girl looked soulfully at her parents. She could not understand why she had been brought to this strange building so far away from home. Away from Mannu, from her Bayko set, from the radiogram with its chrome dragonhead arm, away from the sole turqouise chip which took her hours to spot in the yellow and brown mosaic of her room. Away from Mary-Ma, in whose copious lap full of coconut oil smells, there was safety.

They had sheduled an outdoor shoot at Mahableshwar to coincide with the trip. From the convent they drove straight down to the main Panchgani crossing, where Mrs. Massey rented rooms behind her café, and where they were to rendezvous with the rest of the crew.

Bright and early the next morning, Aniruddh suggested a drive. Nandini in her excitement at this unexpected manouvre, jumbled her answer.

"Okay. You take out the sari, and I'll wear my gaadi. I mean..."

"Yeah Babesie, I know what you mean. Just hurry up, okay?"

Imagining they would be headed towards Mahableshwar, where they could hire one of Mr. Irani's boats and row out on the lake,

Nandini was surprised to see the Hillman turn in the direction of Bombay.

"But we're going backwards. There's no point driving along the ghats. You'll have to concentrate on the narrow hill-hugging road." "Patience was never your strong suit. Why don't you just wait and see, hmm?"

The colour of new flower-pots flowed down the hillsides and coated the roads. Against their russet backdrop, the pines were a startling green. Down the slopes spilled small villages with half-pucca houses and white temples flying orange pennants. Women with fireloads on their heads walked sensuously along the road. Nandini drew the fresh air deep into her lungs. Her hair flew in trails, making a net about her face.

Then there were buildings, more solid structures. They had reached Poona.

The car parked itself at the gates of Pradeep's school.

"But this is Pradeep's school!" stated a startled Nandini.

"That's exactly what I thought. So shall we get our son out for the weekend, and spend it in Panchgani? Just you, me, Nandi and Paddy?"

Nandini felt warm and melting at the centre of her body. She almost began to recognise Ani again.

Back in Panchgani, Nandita screamed at the thrill of seeing her beloved brother, shocking the nuns and amusing her fellow-students. They spent the night at Mahableshwar. Sunday morning brought pony rides and fresh, ripe strawberries. In the lazy afternoon they boated. Slowly they edged into the centre of the lake, curving away from the rest of the world till they were on a Ganguly planet. Shadows of trees and hills floated on the water and trembled at the dip of an oar. Indolent ducks strutted by, lake landlords offended by this trespass. Nandita lay down and looked up at the roof of the sky. This is how she had always wanted them to be; her mother and father and brothers doing things together like other families. Mannu was missed, but then it was better he was in Bombay, or he might have fallen off a pony or into the middle of the lake.

When she was returned on Sunday evening, she clung to her Pradeep-da ruefully. Her hero ruffled her hair with elder-brotherly affection.

"Nandita Ganguly, Class One, when you learn to write proper letters, will you write your first one to me?"

"Promise Dada. Cross my heart.."

"….and hope to die." continued her mother.

Dada, with his combined representation of mother and father, would perhaps be the only one to have time to read her letters.

From the womb of the morning came the sound-track van like a giant blue ant. Trailing it was the studio stationwagon driven by John, its wooden side panels spotted with sand, a rally contender. The wine-coloured Desoto followed bearing Prannath, the dialogue-director, the make-up man and the art-director. Into the silence of the central square they slid, rattling and revving, scattering the grey and apple-green pigeons, summoning sleepy locals to their fairy-tale book windows. Next day the stars would follow, and rustle up more excitement in this hamlet in the hills.

"Ah, Prannath, faithful Prannath. Here he is, the circus ring-master. Babesie, you'll have lots to discuss with him, so why don't I go and leave Paddy in Poona, then come back? I'll take John along."

Fully charged, she was looking forward to the ten-day second honeymoon with Ani as much as she was to resumption of work after the weekend.

The Desoto left after breakfast and became a speck, a pommegranate seed in the hillside 'paan.'

In the evening it was back. Without Ani.

Nandini's soundless query was answered by John's reedy answer.

"Saab took the four o'clock train to Bombay from Poona. He said he has taken permission to bring Baba for the next weekend and that I should go and fetch him on Friday afternoon."

Nandini, stunned, had nothing to say to this postman of unwelcome news. Her hopes had just been scythed, her feelings acidic at this new betrayal. Ani had promised to spend all two weeks of the schedule with her. He had no work on hand to run back to. She had welcomed this suggestion of a trip to essay a darning on what their respective careers had frayed. Had he not, then, been sincere about his portion of effort, a flippancy that had attached to it a thousand questions? Worse, had he used his son as an excuse to make his escape?

She had first to deal with the awesome fact of his stealthy departure before she anatomised his reasons. She had to summon all her skills as an actress to put up a nonchalant front before her cast and crew, so that they would not perceive the cracks in her heart.

She was not going to call him for explanations. Let him squirm waiting for reprimands and reprisals. Besides, he might just call her at night at the hotel in Mahableshwar with an explanation.

But she waited in vain.

That night.

And the next.

And the next.

Fewer retakes and a co-operative sun helped them get ahead of schedule. Thursday afternoon pack-up was announced on request of the leading lady, Kamini Kaushal. Nandini's accounts of the convent had encouraged her to enrol her daughters Kumkum and Kavita that very afternoon. With Nargis planning to send her nieces Rehana, droopy and beautiful, Zahida, frisky and fair, and tomboyish Shahida to the school next year, and Geeta Bali having an enrollable sister as well, it would be a cosy film-children sorority in St. Joseph's.

In the afternoon, Nandini slept. She woke with a terrible loneliness. Devoid of activity, she plummeted to a low depression. Not a gradual seepage this, but a sudden attack affecting every nerve.

She rushed out for fresh air.

On the low parapet wall of the hotel she sat, gazing out at the twilight lake in general. It was a night for romance, and she was all alone. A tissue veil of moonlit-spangled mist covered the rippling mercury of the lake. Aubergine shadows that patched the shoulders of the hills were darkening. On the sloping ground beneath her feet, electronic blips of fireflies moved on the dark monitors of bushes. Mosquitoes played an orchestra in bass. A single waxy leaf glowed maroonly in the dark.

She sat for a long while, luxuriating in Wordsworthian solitude. With doomed eyes, she surveyed her marriage and its certain impending collapse. They might continue to live together, but without togetherness. For where was there to go? They had come so far, side by side at first, then gradually moving away towards the edges of the road. The kaleidoscope had shuffled beautifully in the beginning, showing patterns of irridescent fantasy. Marriage to her had been like flying a kite; a little pull, a little slack. But other kites were stringing along now. And success, with its glass-sharpened string, might just strangle their kite till it crashed on the horizon. They had achieved name and wealth and all that they had aspired for; but lost so much in the bargain.

The years were coming apart.

Babesie. Bebasie. Just a shuffle of letters.

Ye sham ki tanhaaiyan, aise mein tera gham

From his window, Prannath watched her silhouetted in sadness, etched sorrowfully against the quarter moon. He noticed her bent back, and wanted to reach out and comfort her. From the day he had set eyes on her at her housewarming, and, somehow he always seemed to think of that house as hers, full of her quintessence, he had been attracted to her. But she had only Aniruddh in those green spheres. He could not understand Aniruddh's travails away from the straight and narrow. Why was man not monogamous by nature?

Here he was himself, leaning towards Nandini. It was his desperate hope, for her sake, that only he had heard Aniruddh' promise of return.

He knew he should utilise these unexpected hours to catch up with his novel that was delaying on account of this ambitious venture into direction. But of their own volition, his footsteps spilled towards her. Behind her he stood, a Napoleonesque figure glowing phosphorescently. He could reach out now and touch her shoulder, but was afraid to scatter the moment's other-worldliness. The two of them seemed encased in a square and transported to the sky, transcendentally. He could hear the sound of her breath, like the music of the spheres.

"It *is* an intense moment, isn't it? I was afraid to crack the bone china silence with some crass word of sympathy."

Nandini knew it was Prannath. Only a writer would speak like that. Again they had been circled together in geometric mystique. Communication, not necessarily in words, was what she wanted now.

"Yes," she said simply, the word a sigh.

He loped over the parapet, dangling his feet towards the hills. For a while they sat in silence. The evening mists had lifted and in the clear, crisp night, the lake shone like an opal, the moon on its mercury face.

"The coming of night always makes me pensive."

She was so vulnerable right now. A gossamer touch, perhaps a light brush of the lips...but by rushing things, he might fling them both over the precipice. And he hadn't climbed all the way to the top to fall down on the other side.

"I'm just tired. Nandita going to boarding, the shooting.."

And your husband slithering away like a scorpion with a sting in its tail, he said to himself.

Her fussy formality suggested she wasn't ready to accept anything more than friendship right now. "Look, you know the courtyard of my friendship will always be open."

She turned towards him and a significance crossed their vision. Embarrassed, she turned away, too morose to analyse what it could mean. He pressed her hand in an almost avuncular manner, shedding shades of overture.

"Well, thoughts are one's closest companions," he murmured. "I leave you to yours, if unshared they must be."

His door was open. It was for her to take the step in.

He smiled at her as he rose, almost with tenderness, she thought. When last have I seen tenderness, she wondered? Love is so beautiful, unattached. Why does marriage steal something from romance irreplaceably? A miscellanea of memories rushed in to fill the hollow inside. Sadness rose from her eyes and stained the air, echoing in the hills and reflecting in the mirror of the lake. Frangipani scent hailed down on her like shattered stars.

Inside, she tried to seal the earthquake crevices.

Yahan badla wafa ka bewafaai ke siva kya hai

The car that had left to pick up Pradeep from Poona did not return. Night fell, but the red Desoto did not arrive.

Nandini had wanted no communication with Ani till she came face-to-face with him, for actions could not be condoned nor reactions resolved over long-distance wires. Yet she had no option but to call him in case, by some weird miscommunication, the car had gone to Bombay instead. The trunk-call was answered by Mary, who informed her that Saab had gone out early the previous day and not yet returned. But this was hardly the time to sort out where Anirudh had gone frolicking for two whole days.

All night she sat on a lonely chair in the verandah, a solitary naked bulb overhead and the wind for company. A potted croton kept vigil with her.

By early light she knocked on Prannath's door.

"The car didn't come back with Pradeep last night. Which means either they're stranded somewhere, or they've had an accident. I'm taking the station wagon to go search for them. Will you handle the shooting?"

"I'll come with you. Hold on while I change."

"Don't worry, I'll be alright."

"I know, Nandini, you are quite capable of handling this on your own. But so far work has been satisfactory, and we're actually ahead of schedule. Look, I see a cloud up there. If the light isn't good we may not be able to start shooting early enough."

"Pran, you're always the one advising me about losing money. Some of yours will be lost, too. Are you forgetting you're a partner in the concern now?"

"Which means I have a stake in the decisions, too. And I say we delay the shoot. If being concerned means being silly, then, okay, I'm stupid. Besides, what sort of a friend would I be if I reneged on my commitment of friendship a day after making it?"

She didn't protest further. She could use his support. His concern felt warm, like placing your hands around a mug of hot tea in winter.

They left the leafy avenues of the hill station behind, moving slowly on the hill-hugging road. Nandini peered down the narrow gorges and the pocket valleys, her relief spilling in long sighs when she did not espy the conspicuous car lying in a crashed heap at the bottom. The road, but for a casual truck that heaved past, was singularly empty. Near the base of the rust and ochre ghat, a dramatic flame-of-the-forest leaned out of the hillside like a ray of hope. Then they were in the plains, and driving faster along the straight tongue of road in a landscape as clear and open as a child's face.

Thirty miles out of Panchgani, they saw it. Its crimson boot showed up on the opposite side of the road, a bloodied bottom with number plate clearly discernible. It stood weirdly still, desolate and incongruous in its hinterland of brush and bramble, like a mechanical carcass of some defunct animal. Its chassis was smashed, the left window splintered and door caved in. The raked trunk of a tamarind tree and the scraped paint on the left side told their pseudonym tale.

There was no one around to offer cause, comment or report of consequence.

They were alone almost, in the world, with a damaged vehicle and their anxiety.

Nandini's complacence cracked. "Omigod! Omigod! Let him be alright. Ya Allah, let my son be alright, please. Please!" The poet Narendra Sharma's horoscope prediction of Pradeep being accident-prone shook her with its horrendous implications.

Her hands clasped each other tightly for support. A tremble like oncoming malaria shook her body.

Prannath clutched both her arms as if to bind her together.

"Don't panic, Nandini. We don't know anything yet. Let's go find the nearest police station. Someone will have reported the accident."

He held her trembling hand tightly in his grip.

There was nobody in the tiny chowki except a constable. He was putting down the phone as they entered.

"BMC 3050? Arre, what coincidence! Just now I am on the phone to Bombay R.T.O. who is informing me that car is belonging to famous music-director Aniruddh Ganguly. I have told them to locate his number and inforram him. But how you are interested in case?"

"Fuck the case. Tell me first, how are the passengers?" screamed Prannath.

"They are okay, but how you are connected?"

"WHERE are THEY?"

"Well, driver is having some injuries and boy is unconscious. Late last night some lorry is bringing them to local hospital. But how you are…arre, you are some relatives or what? Perhaps you are getting me the autograph?"

Nandini found her voice. She yanked the constable by his collar.

"Damn you and your bloody autograph! Where are the injured? Take us there at once!"

"Okay okay, but why you are shouting baba. First, who are you? Are you related to injured persons?"

"I am the boy's mother. I am…"

"Arre, you are Priyanandini, no?" asked the constable, eyes sprinkling with stardust. "I have seen your PREM.." Pran grabbed him in midsentence and propelled him towards the car. Words asphyxiated in the constable's throat. He was quiet with the awe of the big station wagon and the authoritative manner of the lady whom he now placed as the famous actress of a decade ago. Just wait till he told his wife about this! Aziz Masood she was crazy about, and here he was sitting side by side with the wife of the man who had made him famous. Any further conversation was aborted by the tension that pointed over his head like a Democles' sword, hanging by a thread that could snap with a word.

The hospital had been converted from a British army barracks. The constable rapped orders, all authority.

"Hey you, ward boy. Where is last night's accident case? Tell Dr. Kotnis police is here."

Nandini looked down at her son's face, already growing into handsomeness. His green, oh so green eyes were closed. He was unconscious, with a bandage on his head, but thank Allah he was alive. His breathing was slow, but sure. Relief filled her eyes. She heard very clearly all that Dr. Kotnis had to say.

"We had to stitch a cut on his forehead, just above the eye as you see. Hopefully his optic nerves have not been damaged. But we have no equipment here to test if there has been any internal bleeding. If he does not recover consciousness within twenty-four hours, then you will have to take him to Poona."

"Oh, there was driver with him," the constable reminded. Nandini in her panic had all but forgotten John.

"Poor man, he was so incoherent with shock that all he could babble was save Baba, save Baba.," informed the doctor. "But I have found out that car belongs to famous music-director Aniruddh Ganguly. Now I will get autograph for my wife." interrupted the constable with inconsiderate glee.

"Jagdish Raj," said Dr. Kotnis. "Why don't you go back to the police station and write out the report, F.I.R, whatever."

"Yes," retorted Prannath, silent so far, "or I will punch an autograph on your jaw."

"Okay baba, why you are getting so angry? I will go make panchnama. Pleased to meet you"

"He has some bruises, and probably a fracture which only an X-Ray will show up."

John was distracted with guilt and apology.

"Jesu promise, it was not my fault, Bai. Baba wanted to drive and when I told him no, he got angry and began leaning out of the car. Trying to pull him back, my hand slipped on the wheel, Bai, and car went out of control. Thank Mother Mary I was slow, otherwise…".

"Don't worry, John. Everything will be all right. If you know some prayers, say them now. Have faith in Jesus."

She wished she could feel some of the courage she was talking about.

The minutes ticked slowly, like the glucose dripping drop by drop into his arm. With acute concentration Nandini watched it. Drip. Drip. The bottle moving gently as each drip rocked it. An intermittent nurse fluttered the curtain, checked on the bottle. Drip. Drip. Drip. Prannath went in search of food. Returned with some vada-pao and half a dozen bananas, over-ripe. She ate not because she wanted to, but because she needed the strength. The bandage on her son's temple became a focal point. At times it appeared to come alive, whitely thick, obstructing his dormant vision, strangling his eye. Drip, drip. Bottle changed. An injection into his sleeping arm. John's grey hairs around the curtain, bodyless and strained.

From time to time she felt Prannath's presence, hovering, nebulously comfortable.

Tea came, brought by the sole nurse on duty. A viscous, creamy brew with a net of scum on top, over-sweetened and reeking of cardomom. She drank it, because it was something to do. She could feel Prannath's palm around the column of her neck, stroking it with compassion. Shadows from the corridor began to penetrate the room. The day was dripping out.

Prannath moved out to the verandah with its corrugated tin roof. Beyond the compound fencing he could hear the lowing of cattle meeting the oncoming darkness. Far away to the highway could be heard the lumbering of a truck. He dug into his pocket for his cigarette pack. He really had to hand it to Nandini. Any other woman in her place would have collapsed with the worry and the strain.

"PRAN!"

The cigarette fell out of his hand at the shrill summons. He ran back into the room.

"Look, his eyelids are moving! He's coming awake, Pran! He's coming awake! Allah ka shukra hai!"

Pradeep's hand stirred, and a dry moan came from somewhere in his subconscious.

"I'll send John to call the doctor," said Prannath, sharing her relief.

She smiled at him. " How on earth would I have managed without you?" "You would have done pretty well. I'm just a prop, a supporting actor."

"Don't be ridiculous. You don't know how I value you."

"Do you? How much?" he asked, his voice laced with a tone almost lustful.

She hugged him in answer. He felt so comfortable, like a familiar overcoat. His arms around her tightened noticeably, but she did not care whether it was correct or not. It was this moment that mattered, and Pran was there in it. Not the vagrant, migrant Aniruddh, probably chasing some floozie in a Bombay recording centre. Being infamous at Famous.

When he put his lips tentatively on hers, she did not move her lips away. She needed the physical contact, she needed to be held and soothed. For the first time her eyes moistened. Then her steel was ripped with the force of a single tear, and she clung to his body, drawing his strength, sucking in his warmth with every sob. He held her quietly whilst she cried, stroking her hair with infinite tenderness, calling her name.

If Minoti had wanted proof of Aniruddh's love, she was presented it by his return. He could have sworn to it before judge and jury, but this was the affidavit she wanted.

"Come with me. Some place away from the rest of the world," he whispered into the fragrance of her hair.

Minoti could think of nothing more appealing. After all, he had abandoned his family to come all the way back to her arms.

For the first time, she was to spend a night with him. Reflections of morality, the synopsis of right and wrong troubled her not. She was the Radha entranced by the music of his flute; he was the Krishna with the endearing manner, and their love was divine. Matheran was Gokul and Brindaban.

On Monkey Point he taught her a Baul song. On the emerald paths they strolled, hand in hand, stepping over miniscule mauve flowers that sighed and crushed under their feet. They lent their voices to the wind, the heat of their passion to the cool January breezes. They had but two days, stolen from the accounts of the world, purloined from a smouldering existence. They embraced in the out-of-season glades with the junipers for witness. She shivered in her thin shawl but the look in his eyes was enough to put a fire in her heart.

Between the sheets she smelt of champas. Unlike Nandini who had sprung to her sexuality, Minoti requested guidance. Her breasts were golden melons. Her plump hip flared as he stroked it. He fine-tuned her with a maestro's expertise. He was Ravi Shankar with his sitar, Bismillah Khan with his shehnai, sublimated and rejoiceful.

She opened under him like a delicate mogra. Together, the creator and the protégé sang a beautiful duet. By the end of the last overture he knew that he wanted her in his life, submissive, so excruciatingly child-like, with the innocence and charm to convert a demon. Reciprocally, all she wanted was to be a rose in the shade of his tree.

They were like two ballet dancers dancing on the stage in an empty auditorium, merely for their own pleasure; a Nuruyev and Anna Pavlova pirouetting on the octaves of their own unexplored feelings, prancing and twirling to the striations of a notation that none but they could hear, moving in the sheer delight of their own private epithalamium.

Like two peacocks they danced in the rain in a whirl of emerald green and flourescent blue.

But then the rain stopped.

The two days and their stolen honeymoon were over. It was time to go home and face the rest of the world.

Tu mera chand, main teri chandni, hoooo
Nahin dil ka lagana koi dillagi

In the light behind her eyes, Nandini saw the relationship with Pran in opaque. The moralities of right and wrong were not weighed in the scales of conduct. There had been a single transgression born out of stress. She leaned back on the rounded top of the backseat in the Hillman as it drove her towards her home and the questions that awaited her there. It had actually felt good to be wooed in the past three days by Pran's poetic phrases. It had stroked her femininity. She had needed this attention, this pampering, absent too long from her life. They had succumbed to one day of strain, but since that day it had been relaxation to stroll along the muddy paths, his hand touching hers, shoulders nudging, silences companionable. What had happened between them was as yet unspoken, untagged by whys and hows and wherefores. Nandini never let matters go beyond sitting up late at night, perhaps on the parapet with the cold lake breeze on their faces, when the glowworms came to light. She wondered whether his warm Punjabi blood had a problem with that and whether he stole satisfaction behind the curtains of his lonely room. Right now she was content with his closeness, and the discovery that light physical contact with a male was not necessarily immoral.

As they neared Bombay, thoughts of Ani floated back like seaweed. He had not even been concerned about his son, for as sure as her annoyance, Constable Jagdish Raj would have informed him about it.

Little did she know that his indifference had been a calculated manouvre to push her towards Pran's support. As they coasted into Kurla and the outskirts, she was unsullied by guilt. His caring was a salve for the wounds that Ani had inflicted on her faith.

If he had the Helens and God-knows-who else, let him not be smug about the fact that there was no one else for her. And even if there were not, she was strong enough alone.

A sitting was in progress as she walked into her home, stiff after the long drive. The silken tones of Aziz Masood swirled down the stairwell and climbed up again with her. Ani's face, as she put hers around the hall door to announce her arrival, lit up surprisingly. She walked briskly to her room, not wishing to disturb the rehearsal. She had promised Pran she would not lose her control in front of anyone, but the promise did not pertain to privacy. When Ani strolled in ten minutes later, she thrust upon him her vituperative ire, a stream of accusations thumped squarely on his chest.

Aniruddh interrupted by pinning down her flailing hands that were slicing the air with gesticulations.

"Babesie will you shut up and listen to me for a change?"

"What lies will you now offer in explanation? It's bad enough you trick me into disappearing. But it's pretty worse that you don't care about your son, that you couldn't care less whether he lived or died."

"Now wait a minute, I seem to have lost you here. What are you talking about?"

"Don't put on an act as if you didn't know about the accident!"

"Accident? What accident? Have you been in an…God, Babesie, you're not hurt are you?"

"It's not me. It's Pradeep. You used him Ani, you used him as a pretext, and look at the result! It's true what they say about the sins of the father visiting the children. The poor boy suffered because of your manipulations."

"Hold on, what happened to Pradeep? Honestly, I know nothing about all this. I've been booking calls to you every night, but none materialised. When there was no news from your end I presumed everything was okay."

"You mean the police didn't notify you? After all it was your car that crashed."

"I have absolutely no idea, believe me. Is he alright?"

Truth was known to be stranger than fiction. Nandini's cyclone went into abatement.

"He's okay. I dropped him back to school on the way home. Your car has been left in a garage in Poona. That still doesn't explain why you did the disappearing trick."

"Because, my dear, I wanted to surprise you. Before we left, Mary requested leave to go to Goa for her niece's wedding. She invited us too, as a formality I guess. But I surprised her by saying we'll come. So I quietly came back to Bombay to make the arrangements. I thought a second honeymoon in Goa was better than a working holiday in Panchgani. If I'd told you, I'd have spoiled the surprise.

We leave in four days by steamer. Mannu will stay meanwhile with Shamim and Sumangala. So, what do you have to say to that, my dear wife?"

Dazed, dazzled, dumbstruck, Nandini said nothing.

"Speechless, aren't you? Go on, lie down, soak it in."

Nandini lay on the bed, drained. Gradually relief came in, gently, like spring. Young, green leaves materialised on the bare branches of her spirit.

Perhaps Goa would do for them what Mussourie or Panchgani had not.

"Wives have to be kept happy, and more important, unsuspecting," he explained to Minoti's long face. "So don't be upset that I'm going off with her for a week. Didn't we have a glorious two days by ourselves whilst she was away? Look, you have to give a little, to get a little. Now give us a smile, darling, darling Minoti."

Goa was the kiss of the winter angel, the warmth of a December fire-place. Goa was the magic of the sea captured in the heart of a seashell, in the song of the wind. Goa was the tap-dance of the spirit; frolicsome, unfettered, free.

Rising late in an unfamiliar hotel room in Panjim, they breakfasted on date pancakes and coconut water. Then they shopped, and after a siesta took the ferry launch and then a taxi and sped past young rice fields towards Kuxem to participate in the nuptial festivities. By the glow of an evening fire they danced the Mexican Shuffle to the tune of Konkani songs that Aniruddh adapted for a film being made on the liberation of Goa. They fed on spicy vindaloos and coconut-based fish curries accompanied by large amounts of kaju feni and Portugese wines, and at night they returned to their room and made frantic love in a replay of the first years of their marriage.

In the peculiarly horny atmosphere of a hotel room Aniruddh's virility seemed to resurface. But Nandini was sensitive enough to realise that there was a lacuna in their nearness. Something seemed to lie between them on the sheets; a presence, almost a disinclination. It was lovemaking, not loving. For Aniruddh it was a pure performance of the body. Nandini noticed the difference in the way that Aniruddh held her. The entire copybook exercise was like some deliberate effort.

She did not wish to soar with unreliable hopes; she was content to glide just above the surface; to accept what was given, to hyphenate her expectations. Even this was better than the emptiness that had existed between them.

With Marie Francis properly wed and dispensed to her in-laws in the neighbouring village, they left Goa behind with its glorious sands and its Portugese palms and its white-edged blue seas, and returned with rejuvenation to Bombay.

Nandini hoped that the holiday was a harbinger of better times to come. They would have to learn to walk together again, even if it wasn't hand in hand.

The stocky, balding man sat on the edge of his seat, intimidated by the opulence surrounding him. The crystal winked and the shining marble floors beamed. The Naga masks looked down at him with condescension.

He picked his nose out of boredom. The servants had informed him that the lady of the house was due back any minute. Otherwise he had many important things to do. Only his wife had insisted. If he got her what she wanted perhaps she might spare the radio and not fall on it each time an Aziz Masood song was broadcast.

Suddenly the lady in whose anticipation he had spent these awkward moments walked in regally. She halted and demanded to know who he was. The cook ran in from the kitchen to explain that it was the police.

"The police?" she asked quizzically. "Have you come about the jewellery theft or the accident? Both matters have been taken care of."

The oily-haired man beamed creamy teeth at her. "Arre madam, you have not recognised me? I am Jagdishraj Pednekar." He twirled his moustaches with some pride.

"Pedne..oh the hawaldar from the accident case. Your wife is a great fan of Aziz Masood."

"Arre wah, what a wonderful memory you have, madam!"

"How could I forget? So, what is the problem?"

"Nahin, madam, nothing official. I have come to collect the autographed photograph that Ganguly Saab promised me."

"Ganguly Saab promised? When did *you* meet him?"

"I have not met him as yet. But I have talked to him on the trunkcall when I told him about the accident. I knew you would have spoken to him, but still I thought, what haarm if I too ring up and inforram him? So after you left I phoned, and was surprised to know he was not having any information about the accident at all. He asked about his baba and I told him you and some gentleman had taken him to Panchgani after his discharge and he said Good, Good. Thank you very much. But I said, plain thanks will not do saheb, I am wanting the autograph of Aziz Masood for my wife, and he said Good, Good you can have his photograph also. So here I am."

"You spoke to him directly?"

"Absolutely madam, he confirmed I was speaking to Aniruddh Ganguly."

"Well, Mr. Pednekar, Ganguly Saab is busy in a recording, but if you leave me your postal address, I will personally send you an autographed photograph."

"Yes, yes, yes" he replied, his initial enthusiasm dampened somewhat by the sudden starch in her muslin. Her body grew rigid, her voice dry and the frost in her eyes sent a cold wind through his body. Perturbed by the chill in her manner, he wondered at her reaction. What the hell, all he had asked for was one fucking autograph.

The slab of ice flung on her by Pednekar's announcement had benumbed her awhile. But before the oncomimg heat of her palpitating wrath, it soon melted away. Her eyes flared, her lips clenched and her fists balled into sweaty spheres.

She spilled herself on the bed. With tremendous control, she becalmed herself so she could think with some modicum of reason instead of lashing out at him with the rant that was her wont. Was this affair, for now it was obvious that he must be involved in something desperately clandestine, weighty enough to warrant such manipulative scheming? To perpetuate this farce of a second honeymoon, so that she would look the other way? He had known all about the accident; yet he had pretended ignorance. Instead he had scuttled her along on this trip, this mockery of togetherness. Worse, he had been unconcerned about his own son. He had rewarded her faith not with undying affection, but with lying affectation.

Her anger was levelled more at her own gullibility than his deception. He had played her for a fool and she had helped him along, aiding and abetting his two-facedness with her optimism. Suleiman's ear-fillers of Aniruddh's pecadilloes now loomed into black and leaden truth. So he had fallen prey to the temptations of this industry where beautiful women, ambitious women, traded pleasure for a role or two. Aniruddh, human and vulnerable, seeking supports for his sagging career, had succumbed. But then, had she not herself had a little thing with Pran, even if it were under emotional stress? The end was the same, never mind the means. To carry fifteen years of marriage upon one's shoulder can sometimes be a burden and one is tempted to lay it aside for a while and indulge in a diversion. How many times, then, was she going to play out the drama of accusations, recriminations and bitterness? He will spray me with more lies, convince me with some wisp of logic or trick me with some further manipulation. A straying man will only be more encouraged by attempts to withhold him. Would it not be more restful to just gift him these flings so he could come back to her more chastened, more propelled by his guilt to do things like this surprise visit to Goa? Come back to her...*that* was the operative phrase. The Helens and the Bindus and the Padmas would distract him for a while. They would take some part of his *time,* but not his *life.* He would return to her eventually, for she had the legal license. She was his wife; Mrs. Aniruddh Ganguly, the mother of his children. Perhaps if she pretended not to notice, ceased to protest, he would lose that taste for forbidden fruit. Perhaps it would, in the long run, add some zip to their sagging association. When he was older and saddened by his own lack of charm, his faded fame, the absence of sycophants, the lack of admirers, he would turn towards her in appreciation, requesting the companionship of old age.

Why am I thinking like this, she wondered suddenly. Justifying his actions because he is a man and losing my own esteem as a woman? What lopsided logic was permitting him promiscuity at the cost of her own chasteness? Why should there be a separate set of rules for men and women? If he had fans, so did she. If he had problems at work, so did she. The equations and justifications were the same. Besides, if he had enjoyed so many rumoured flings, was she not permitted one transgression? Was she to play suffering wife, tormented grass widow, whilst he frolicked in the splendours of the field chasing after butterflies?

Men liked to seduce themselves into the delusion that they were smart. Women, being smarter, indulged them.

She picked up the phone and dialled Pran at the studio.

In feminine wisdom, she said nothing to Ani, reserving her knowledge for some further occasion.

Her relationship with Pran was little more than a flirtation and a little less than the real thing. There were no concrete lines, no commitment. People fell in love; she had fallen into a convenience. It reminded her once more of her feminine essence, a fragrance she had taken for granted like the scent of the jasmine on her rooftop. It was pleasant to once again celebrate the consciousness of being a beautiful woman. But not once did she besmirch the sanctity of her home. Within the parameters of that domain, he was no more than a lean-to.

The proximity generated by their work in the office eliminated the requirements of secret rendezvous since they spent most of the day together. She was still bound to Aniruddh by strings of an ambiguous morality and a bond which could colour at any time with a single gesture of a love she hoped desperately was not dead, but dormant.

Dil jalta hai toh jalne de, Ansoo na baha, fariyaad na kar

DHOOL KA PHOOL

The morning of the first day of the last schedule of their under-production film, Nandini was overcome with nausea. The realisation that she had not had her periods since her return from Goa indicated her condition was no minor indigestion. She shuddered at the repercussions of a pregnancy at this inopportune time, with emotions in a tangle and her marriage in so tenuous a state. Her film, BAHU was almost complete, which meant that again Aniruddh would be faced with the rigors of post-production. Proffessional problems notwithstanding, how would he react to news of another baby? Would it draw their separate selves together into a combined closeness, or would the unborn child complicate a situation already shimmering with unspoken implications?

It was time to tell Aniruddh. She was in her third month, and in a few days the baby within would take on a life.

He lay in a straight line, turned away from her, even in sleep. Luminosity from the street gaslight broke the darkness outside. A Christian neighbour's Christmas lantern, shone in a distant building like a symbol of peace.

For a second Nandini hesitated, loth to wake him up. Gently she lay beside him, sleek, lean body perfectly aligned with his. He mumbled and stirred as she nuzzled his neck. She flung her leg over his like in the earlier times when he used to call her 'his bolster.' He moaned, and, subconsciously, shot his hand out to grip, with unusual precision, her buttock. Slowly he began to stroke, half-asleep, half-roused. Mini is losing her plumpness, he ruminated in his semi-sleeping state. Slowly he turned, muttering her name into his sheet. He gripped Nandini's shoulder. He moved towards her.

Her breath smelled of ilaichi and paan.

This was not Minoti. He was being seduced by some apsara from Supari-land, the one who lived in the areca palm beyond his drawing room window. His eyes shot open.

"Oh, it's you."

"Who were you expecting, Marlene Dietrich?" asked Nandini, seductively skimming her fingertips over his bare chest.

He slapped her playfully on the rump, thinking about the super-blooper he had been about to make.

"Silly. I meant, it really is you. I wasn't dreaming."

She wasn't Mini. She was still his wife. He had conjugal rights, and she had made him horny.

"Ani, there's something special I want to tell you." "Can't it wait till the morning, or after.." he asked, nibbling her ear wetly.

"No Ani, I have to tell you now."

Damn women, he thought. Tantalise you with their breasts but then first want to feed you mother's milk.

Get it over with woman! "Hmmm, so tell me. Briefly, mind." He licked the cream of her breasts.

"Ani, we're going to have a baby. The cute wails of an infant in this house again."

Cute wails!

And soiled nappies. Vaccinations. School admissions. Inconveniences. Damn the fertile woman. What complications had she convoluted now? A baby? When he was in so deep with Mini? It couldn't have been more badly-timed. He catapulted out of his supine position. Suddenly, he was wide-awake.

Her eyebrows knit themselves, purl by purl, into a frown.

"You're not happy?"

"It's not a question of happiness. Look at the bloody timing. The film is nearing completion. I have to leave for the United States next month with the film industry delegation to Hollywood. Then to Moscow for discussions on an Indo-Soviet production. I'm struggling to maintain my career, which is fast being overtaken by younger men. Work isn't coming easily, expenses are mounting. The childrens' boarding school education is costing me a damn packet, this huge house takes a fortune to maintain. The servants. The cars. Babesie, we just can't afford a baby now, for God's sake."

He held his head in his hands.

So, he wasn't exactly overjoyed, thought Nandini.

She turned away, not wanting to give him the advantage of seeing her cry.

"If only your mother was alive now. As a midwife, she could have advised you how to drop the child."

The sentence fell into the silence with a resounding thud.

She turned to face him, features carved in granite. Her voice seemed to come from a distance.

"Don't even *think* that."

Like a formless figure in a nightmare, she rose and made for the door.

"Where do you think you're going? I haven't finished yet."

"But I have, Ani. This was never a discussion in the first place."

"Just listen to..."

"No, you're right. I have no sense of timing or planning. That's why I let the Goa air and the kaju feni go to my head."

On her bed she lay shocked and still, staring at the ceiling. Murder your own flesh and blood? A child that even now might be assuming a life? How finally, with this vile thought, had he closed the door between them?

She stroked her stomach lightly, soothing the baby, talking to it. Don't worry, my child. I will shower on you the love of both parents because that is what you deserve. This night, the night of April 24th,

1952, this is my solemn vow to you, my unborn child, rejected by a man who fathered you in a reckless night of moonlit abandon.

And she opened up her belly to the universe, to receive into it the energy and strength that binds woman to the cosmos in the act of birth, an event that is as much a mystery as it is a miracle.

It had been raining incessantly for three days, clogging the drains of the gully and converting it into a swirling stream. Everyone was indoors, huddled against the grey onslaught, whiling time in games like carrom and cards. The dank and dreary monotone of its pattern echoed hollowly within Nandini. Before Aniruddh had left for America with the Indian film delegation, the arctic connections between them had excluded communication regarding arrangements, travel, itinerary, even money. Never really expecting him to send a postcard saying 'Wish you were here', she had still hoped for some message with other members' messages. Probably some Hollywood starlet, enamoured by his dusky complexion and Oriental charm, must be warming his evenings, if just for the experience.

What was to become of them now?

Her perturbation, her insecurity, made her turn more and more towards Pran for support. She wondered about him and his phlegmatism regarding her pregnancy. It didn't seem to upset him as she expected it might. Since Aniruddh had gone they had not even spent an evening together. That was the worst time of day, coming home to a house that was toneless and empty, lacking the pampering that a pregnant woman felt it her privilege to receive. But he was always in a hurry to leave. Whenever she quizzed him about getting married, seeing he was in his mid-thirties, he always parried her questions by saying he couldn't yet afford to support a family in Bombay.

The phone rang, scattering her thoughts with its shrillness. It was Ashok Roy, husband of Nirupa Roy, the current reigning queen of the mythologicals.

"Namaste, Madam."

A twinge of apprehension shook her out of her depression.

"Namaste, Ashokji. I hope everything is well."

"Oh yes, yes. The delegation returns tonight, and I thought with the rain and all, would you like someone to take you to the airport?"

They were coming back, and she knew nothing about it.

"No, Ashokji, I shall manage. I have a live-in driver. What time does the flight get in exactly?"

"Actually 01.20 hrs. Are you sure it will be okay?"

"Absolutely. Thank you for asking."

So, he had not bothered to even let her know about his return. But he himself had often said that the film industry was a world of appearances. She was still his wife, if in image only. And like a good spouse, she was going to the airport to receive her darling husband coming home after a longish trip. The world would view them as a happily married couple, despite hidden girlfriends.

Throngs hovered beyond the security gate as news of the stars' return flew around the city, and the late hour was no deterrent to the film-crazy crowd that hung about to get one glimpse of their darling Dev Anand, reputedly part of the team. As she made her way through the horde of pushing people to the arrival lounge at Kalina Airport, she was surprised to espy Minoti Mehra, minus her overbearing dad. What was the girl doing here, alone, way past midnight? Curiously, instead of meeting her gaze, the girl made to turn away. Then her companion, sultry singer Gayatri Ghosh, came into view alongside her and Nandini presumed they were together, probably come to receive someone else. The flight's arrival was being announced on the loudspeakers and, shrugging Minoti's presence away, she turned towards the customs exit.

Aniruddh's expression on seeing her was, surprisingly, one of irritation.

"Why did you come to the airport at this time of night? I could have come home with someone else, or taken a taxi," he said, darting his eyes over her shoulders as if seeking out someone in the crowd.

"Were you expecting someone else?" Suspicion cooled her welcome. "Don't be daft. I'm just trying to spot the customs officer who was to help me get my stuff cleared."

"Then why the surprise, or even the annoyance? I am your wife, you know, and it's perfectly natural for me to come and pick you up at the airport."

"Really Babesie, must you misconstrue everything I say? You know perfectly well I was referring to your condition. Five months pregnant and gallivanting at ungodly hours!"

"What? And miss all this fanfare? Besides, the clock has nothing to do with my condition. I'm absolutely fine. I thought you would be happy. After all, you're always piling me with surprises like the Goa trip, why can't I reciprocate? At least try and play the loving husband for the cameras."

Once in the refuge of the car, she pressed him for reasons of not intimating her about his arrival. Aniruddh grasped his head in his hands. "For God's sake Babesie, I'm tired. I've just come back after a long flight and am in no mood for an argument. Neither do I have the stamina to deal with your sarcasm. Do you mind if we go home and sleep and continue this in the morning?"

"Look who's talking about arguments! The man who started it all. All right, we shall fight in the morning because it's more civilised to. Althought I feel like fighting right now, for all this overwhelming reaction to my kind and considerate act. It's like wanting to crap now, but postponing it for the morning because that's the normal time to do it."

"What is wrong with you? Just hear yourself. Such unladylike language!"

"Oh, so now we're slotting words. There's a part of the English language reserved for men only. And what's with this censorship by the way? Please, let me wake you up in case you're still slumbering in the Victorian age."

"Yeah! Wake me like a bloody nightmare."

She flicked her silk pallu with the profiles of Mughal kings and empresses in his face, leaving him to his unpacking and his bad temper. She was all dehydrated inside, too withered for tears.

Where had all tenderness gone, or rather, to whom had it been transferred?

Badli teri nazar toh nazaare badal gaye
Woh chandni, woh chand sitare badal gaye

Three weeks after Aniruddh's return, BAHU was released at the Majestic. Three months later an organisation in Dehra Dun adjudged it the best film with a social content, of that year. The hero and heroine picked up trophies for best acting. A seven-months pregnant Nandini took her crew to receive the awards at a specially arranged function. Saro decided to go along for the trip so she could dash up to Mussourie and have a look at her cottage.

The young girl confidences between the friends had continued into more mature and realistic exchanges. Nandini managed a free and fruitful evening to seek out and reveal her pain and problems to her childhood friend. Saro hesitantly confessed she had known about Ani's philandering for some time but refrained from telling Mehru for fear of hurting her.

"So it is true. Why, for God's sake, are wives always the last to know?"

"Because marriage is also like the movies. It's all about maintaing an image. That's why Abhi and I have decided never to marry. This way we can have an eternal romance and not destroy our relationship with untruths and explanations and accountability. Mehru, you trusted him so much, I didn't want to disillusion you. But see, how he fucked your faith!"

Nandini could see an added advantage to not having a husband. You didn't have to sugarcoat your frustration with delicate words.

"So, now I know. Tell me, because nothing will surprise me now, if you know the identity of his latest girlfriend? She seems to have made deeper inroads than the others."

Unsure of how Mehru would receive this information, Saro hesitated. To be upstaged by a woman half her age was not the kind of fate any woman accepted with equanimity.

"We..ll. The grapevine has it that it's, fasten your seat belts,... ..Minoti Mehra. They're always holed up in a rehearsal room at Famous, alone amongst silent cellos and mute pianos." "What? That little baby with the simpering looks, who blushes and beams constantly? What can she possibly have to interest him? Besides, her domineering father's stuck to her like chewing gum."

"The baby's growing up, and moves around more freely now."

But of course it all made sense. Suleiman's hint at a young singer, Minoti's presence at the airport that night, explaining why Aniruddh was livid at her arrival.

"She's become great friends with the singer Gayatri Ghosh, who's her regular chaperone."

The midnight escort. She had just remembered Minoti stayed somewhere near Dadar Station. It all fit in...perfectly.

"But why, why, Saro? What's wrong with me? Am I not as good-looking, intelligent or talented? It just doesn't make sense, why a man should jeopardise all that he's struggled to build up, just for one pretty face that would give him at the most visual pleasure, that too, temporarily?"

"As I see it Mehru, there's no fool like an old fool. He's going through some mid-life crisis, and definitely a professional setback of sorts. She, on her part, pines and frets and doses him with looks of adoration, propping up his sagging career with the music that has lessened in his life. You, Mehru, let's face it, don't know Sa from Pa."

"Naturally, I would feel distinctly foolish complimenting him on his looks when he doesn't exactly resemble Clark Gable."

" Sometimes a lie or two can be quite beneficial. But Mehru, you're not a hypocrite. And then, you didn't let success turn your head. *You* would expect an adult to sort out his problems by himself, but maybe he can't handle it emotionally, despite his intellectualism. See, the two aspects of his character, the true traditional one, and the one formed by his success, are in some sort of conflict within him. Unfortunately, the latter is winning. Secondly, you're still a successful filmmaker and he's going swiftly downhill. In the dark landscape of his failure he cannot see for himself. Minoti's luminous eyes, full of hero-worship, lead him on."

Gracefully she twirled her glass in which the whisky danced, and puffed practically at her cigarette. Mehru looked admiringly at her friend and envied her her self-confidence. Perhaps it came from being her own master. Or mistress. Oh what a hateful word in its other connotation!

"That little baby-faced trickster! That..that….husband-stealer, that home-breaker. I treated her like a daughter! For that matter, so did he, I think. She looked so innocent, full of sunshine and sweetness! That.." "It's okay to swear, Mehru. The situation demands it. Just be yourself, express what you're feeling. It's healthy. Here. Have a drink. A strong whisky will help the anger dissolve."

"I'm not supposed to be drinking alcohol in my condition. And I'm going to kill that ..bitch!" She felt decidely better after saying that.

"Come on, one drink won't do any harm. It'll make you sleep better."

It did. But in the morning the obnoxious picture of Minoti Mehra swam up again like bile, bringing with it disillusion and a tremendous irony.

Ek bewafa se pyar kiya, use nazar ko char kiya
Hai re maine ye kya kiya, ye kya kiya

Week-long, the solution to this incongruous triangle eluded her. Her morale dipped earthwards like the roots of the banyan tree.

The morning his fuss seemed magnified, Nandini sensed something was happening The smell of fish was as potent as if she were standing on the Danda beach around the drying Bombay Ducks.

"My, my we are getting extra dandy today," she couldn't resist saying, as Aniruddh sprayed an America-bought cologne over himself. "Who's the singer for today's recording,.. Minoti Mehra?" The moment it was out she regretted her lack of caution, but Aniruddh seemed too involved in fidgeting inside his cupboard for a handkerchief to notice the pointedness in her remark.

He hesitated for a moment, fixing her with a lizard look, before replying. "Gayatri Ghosh. Anyway, of what interest is it to you?"

She shrugged her shoulders as though it hardly mattered. But that split second of hesitation had triggered off a suspicion.

An hour after he had left for Mehboob Studios, she rang up and asked for the recording room. "Whose recording is it?" she enquired of the voice on the extension. "Ani-Moshai." "And the singer?" "Minoti Mehra. Who do you want to speak to, madam?"

She dropped the receiver as if it were a snake that had just hissed into her ear. The thought of them together ensconced intimately in the privacy of the singer's cabin, the proximity of their bodies, the probabilities of their touch, fuelled her fury.

Her car sped past the buildings of Hindu Colony, past the Plaza and Citylight cinemas. Mahim Creek zoomed past, a picture postcard of sun and sails. Unmindful of the stress to her protruding stomach, she angrily changed gears, her mood cannibalistic. She raced in the direction of Hill Road. Even if something untoward were to result with her rush and rage, what point in having the baby when all else was lost?

The musicians were surprised at her entry. Dada's wife, especially in this pregnant state, rarely attended a recording that was not for her home production. Jasbir, rehearsing his musicians, looked discomfited. Ani-moshai was inside with Minoti, but so was the lyricist, Pyaaremohan Dehlvi, Dada's close friend. Hopefully no hanky-panky was taking place.

"Where is my husband?" she asked with a calm that astonished her. The word 'husband' had a legal and therefore, moral affect on the arranger.

"Inside, Bhabhiji. Rehearsing the singer." His voice was subdued. In anticipation of some drama, the musicians paused in their collective playing, watching the feisty Mrs. Aniruddh Ganguly stride with profound purpose into the soundproof room.

When the door was pushed open, the three people within froze in their respective positions at sight of the intruder. Nandini stood, framed by the door, her marvellous nostrils flaring like a thoroughbred before a race.

Minoti became absolutely still within the crook of Aniruddh's arm, as if turned to stone by the wicked wave of a witch's wand. She appeared to be locked inside his half-embrace, her blush darkening into a hot flame of guilt. Pyaare's semi-uttered laugh hissed like a Primus stove being extinguished. Aniruddh, culprit in the act, went blank for a second. There was something so obscene about this nefarious tableau that nausea swilled inside Nandini, ascending with the taste of ashes.

The lyricist was obviously in on this cute association, endorsing it with the lewd humour he had been about to display before her entrance. *How many more knew*?

Pyaare spoke first, his voice a whisper. "Bhabhiji."

"Which one are you referring to?" she asked tersely, her tone like spoilt milk. Humiliation rose like a tidal wave in slow motion. Like Krishna's Sudarshan Chakra, her hand moved in the air and struck Minoti's fair, plump cheek.

"You little tramp," she screamed, enraged, deranged, not caring who heard. "You may fool him with your false innocence and your baby pout, but I see right through your schemes and that of your conniving father. You have no compunctions about promoting your career by sleeping with a married man. That too, when his wife is expecting his baby."

Minoti shrank away from Aniruddh and turned her face against the wall, not only with shame, but also with distaste at Nandini's very obvious pregnancy, symbol of her legitimacy. Damning evidence of what she considered Aniruddh's two-facedness, not only in impregnating his wife whilst simultaneously swearing his undying love to her, but furthermore concealing from her the fact. At the airport Nandini had not shown at all, and she had no idea of how to deal with this absolutely stunning revelation.

Aniruddh's eyes blazed, thawing him into action. How dare she come here and make such a spectacle for everyone to laugh at? Bearing upon her like a pirate ship in full sail, the flag of his husband status flying like a skull and crossbones, he gripped her shoulders and yelled.

"What kind of behaviour is this?"

She yanked his hand off her body.

"No better than yours." He had the grace to look disconcerted. "Couldn't you find anyone nearer your age besides this frivolous little baby-face to have a fling with?"

"You shut your mouth, Babesie, or I'll open mine to say a thing or two about you and that curly-haired Pran of yours." Now it was his turn to get slapped, hard and tight.

Breathless fom this unpleasant confrontation, she strode out, her expression a revelation of the sordid story.

Some of the musicians began to put away their notation pages.

Minoti finally found her voice. "You..you.. never said anything about the baby, Moshai?"

"Dammit, doesn't a man have the right to sleep with his wife? It's perfectly legal! Don't *you* start now for God's sake."

The mention of legality highlighted the situation for Minoti, making her shamefully conscious of her lack of it. A sob escaped her quivering lips.

The image of the slap playing again and again in his mind like a repeated film clip, Aniruddh stormed out of the cabin, leaving Pyaare to put his arm comfortingly around Minoti's fulsome shoulder, a little lecherous action he had wanted to perform for some time. She wept into what she thought was his brotherly arm.

In the orchestra section, the man with the saxophone blew into his instrument notes of a dramatic content, signalling a grand finale. The sound rang out absurdly in the hush, like a clown's crying voice.

Eyes brimming, head swimming, Minoti dashed home and locked herself in her room, responding to neither her parents' nor her beloved younger brother Raju's pleas to open the door. Her body was heavy with an immense sorrow. Finally, her shock expended, she started to think with the maturity that Fate had newly thrust upon her.

In the morning, head clear, eyes stoic with acceptance, she told her father she was ready to marry her mother's cousin twice removed, who for the past two years had been pestering them with a proposal. Vikramaditya sighed and patted her hand. He was not going to analyse what had brought about this dramatic change in circumstances; just inhale the relief of recovering his daughter from the clutches of that wretch Ganguly. Now hopefully she would get married, breed him grandchildren, and leave Aniruddh Ganguly to his wife and his family.

Befitting her off-screen role as tragedienne, Minoti released a heavy-weight sigh. Her life was imitating art, for this was how it happened in the movies; a glorious saga of love and sacrifice.

Chodh gaye baalam, mujhe hai akela chodh gaye

Aniruddh's music was invaded by his interloping thoughts,which would not be dispelled by the sound from his harmonium. The one or two producers he had left were getting impatient at his distraught performance. Understanding was not an item on anyone's list anymore. You delivered, or nobody bothered about you. Besides, his music did not guarantee silver jubilees anymore. He had to cut down his price.

Living in the same house with Nandini was sapping his professionalism and his inspiration. For Nandini would pick up Mannu and disappear and return late at night. He presumed she hung out with that rosy-cheeked sister of her's. The dichotomy in his mind between the wonder Minoti brought him and keeping his home ship on an even keel, tore at his insides. Till last week he had had a wife and a mistress. Now, there was neither. One side was non-communication, and on the other a stony silence.

It was Ramakant who informed him that Minoti had got engaged to some royal chap from Lakhimpur, a princely Eastern state. Ramakant assured him he had read it in Screen, in black and white.

It wasn't possible, thought Aniruddh, not after her sweet surrender in Matheran. She couldn't just traipse away to the Khasi hills! Admittedly she would make a pretty picture on the green slopes with the goddamned birds and clouds in the background. But why would she want to waste that magnificent voice on the sheep? And what about her career? Would she spend her husband's royal rupees in flying back to Bombay for recordings? And was he supposed to stand up on a dais and utter a congratulatory speech and present her with a bouquet on behalf of the Cine Music Director's Association?

If there was any vestige of truth in this, then she had acted on the rebound, and he was responsible for what was definitely the ruining of her life. He rang her to confirm the news, but she hung up at the sound of his voice. Damn! Damn, damn, damn! It was him, now that was being fucked from both sides.

Humein maar chala ye khayali-e-gham,
Na idhar ke rahe na udhar ke rahe

Why didn't it surprise Nandini to see Bela perched upon her trunks, sitting in the lobby as if it were a railway platform? To climb the stairs heavily in your ninth month of pregnancy and have an unpleasant sight thrust upon your vision was enough to start you off on morning sickness all over again.

"Ah Bou-di, at last you have come. Where have you been? I phoned the studio and they told me you don't come in so often now."

To think for a moment that Nandini was going to present Bela with a blow-by-blow account of her movements was stretching optimism too far.

"Bela, we were not expecting you. If you had written you were coming I would have ordered the Navy Band and a red carpet." The sarcasm flowed off her like rain off a Duckback raincoat.

"So sweet, Bou-di. But I thought I should come anyway, since you'll be needing someone to take care of the house whilst you are in hospital. Ever since Dada wrote about the pregnancy, my mind has only been occupied by how I must be here to help you."

How conveniently had the woman forgotten the ignominous conditions of her departure? Obviously, her backbone was made of rubber.

"Honestly Bela, you needn't have bothered. My friend Shireen Murad is here from Karachi. Besides, you know that Mannu has a perfectly good nanny in Mary-Ma who is also an efficient housekeeper. And my hospitalisation will only take a couple of days. So if you had bothered to check before you came, then I would have saved you the trouble of travelling."

So it was that insomniac Shireen, wife of their Pakistani distributor, who had spread her lugguage in the guest room, thought Bela, already rattled by the reflection that the machine maniac Mrs.

Murad would be pedalling away furiously at the Singer wheels all night.

"Well, if I am useless, then I can just take another train back to Bina." And earn Aniruddh's permanent compassion, thought Nandini, glancing at this real-life Kuldip Kaur with some distaste. Grow a couple of horns and a tail, Bela, and you'll be a natural for Mephistopheles.

"Don't be silly. Now that you're here anyway, you might as well stay. But you'll have to adjust in the room on the terrace."

"But can't I sleep in the children's room? After all only Mannu sleeps there now."

"No, the new ayah for the baby, as well as Mary occupy that room. Surely you will not like to sleep in the same room as the servants." Banished to the barsati. With mattresses for company. And cockroaches and bugs. But what choice was there, debated Bela.

Bela had not come to offer any assistance, Nandini knew, but to blow the bugle at the battle. She would pitch her tent on Aniruddh's side, put on the full regalia of her warpaint and dance a victory dance with each round won. Some people just could not see anyone else happy, especially when they were not so themselves. In such a situation, it was gratifying to have Shireen as an ally on her side of the camp.

Kis tarah bhoolega dil, unka khayal aaya hua,
Ja nahin sakta kabhi, sheeshe mein baal aaya hua

Aniruddh was restless with dismay. But gradually, he was trying to come to terms with the situation, the way Mini had with her newly-developed wisdom. He was pushing oars towards Nandini, attempting a truce which could see them through the baby's birth without acrimony. Perhaps Mini's staunch decision was best for all of them. Her sacrifice seemed to elevate her in his estimation. Yet, though Nandini had relented slightly, the atmosphere between them was still inimical. He now understood that his desire for Nandini, already an established star when he was a relative newcomer, had stemmed from her glamorous image. On the other side of the arc lights, she had appeared as distant, regal and as unapproachable as the Snow Queen, and he had been obsessed by the thought of possessing her. Her unexpected response had spurred him further. But success had given him power which was a stronger aphrodisiac than any other. So their ties had begun to loosen. Power for her had had a different effect. It had converted her feminine traits into masculine competence. The woman whose veneer was brash and brittle, who blew smoke rings and shuffled papers in a briefcase, who consulted race books with knowledgeable panache, was to him an unrecognisable stranger.

Ironically, thoughts of his marriage made him miss Mini. He missed her docile nature, her child-likenes, her broad smile, her faith which she had handed him wrapped in tissue paper.

If only he had met a woman like Mini, not necessarily her, for she would have been barely four when he was a marrigeable twenty, but someone like her, who would have been more the type of woman he could have taken home to mother instead of a woman who had taken mother away from him!

If only they had remained young and innocent in their minds, not been spoiled by success, not drifted apart chasing different careers.

If only. How many times, in hindsight, does man tag his actions with labels of 'if onlys,' the two words that are constantly thrown in his face by a sneering Destiny? And Destiny…who in hell could fight that son-of-a-bitch and win?

Tu kaunsi badly mein mere chand hai, aaja

"The contractions are fifteen minutes apart. We have to take Nandini to the hospital right away." Shireen shook Aniruddh awake.

The nursing home was only ten minutes away, right opposite their office at the Shree Sound Studios. Which was good, because the water bag burst on the way. As dawn spread its sheet over the face of night, a bonny son was born to them. Crinkly, red-in-the-face with the effort of coming into the world, miniature fists closed, eyes slumberously shut with the peace and undisturbed rest of the womb. Fair as the dawn that heralded him. Wrapped in the mists of his previous life.

Bela, presented with the fait accompli somewhere around mid-morning, was piqued at having been conveniently overlooked atop in the barsaati. She had been suspended there since morning, her presence forgotten like a star of yesteryear.

She and Aniruddh entered the hospital simultaneously with Prannath in the evening visiting hours. On the way, much to her dismay, Aniruddh had informed her, in solemn and simplistic tones, that he and Minoti had split.

"Oh such a chweet gora gora baba, fairest of them all" she cooed, as the baby was brought in for his evening feed. The child moved from lap to lap, and Bela placed him gingerly in Prannath's arms. He held the child expertly, as if he were well-versed in rocking babies to sleep.

It was then that Bela was struck by an idea so diabolic that even Satan would have been shame-faced at the thought.

The next morning, Bela walked the two hundred yards from the hospital to Minoti's apartment. Minoti herself opened the door, aghast to find Bela most unexpectedly on her doorstep.

"Minoti, Minoti, Minoti! How pleasant to see you after so many days? And where are your respected parents?"

"They have gone to the temple next door. They will be back in a while." "Then it is good we are alone to talk undisturbed. I believe congratulations are to be offered. A prince and all? Baba, aren't we lucky?"

A smile as dull as an early moonrise rose on the sky of Minoti's face.

"My mother has royal connections. They were unhappy when she ran away to marry a small-time actor; it is a good occasion now to mend fences."

"And hearts? Who will mend hearts? Poor Dada's heart? Which you have relentlessly broken by this cruel decision? Really, Min-Mini, this I did not expect of you!"

"Some things are not meant to be. Why talk about them at all?" Minoti bowed her head in resignation.

"Why not talk? Why become an ostrich and bury your head in the sand? Do you feel nothing, nothing at all? Oh, by the way, Boudi gave birth to a boy yesterday." She delivered this piece of news as though it were incidental, an inconvenient aside in the main drama. Minoti looked wounded.

"Precisely. How could he play with my feelings, Didi? Running off with me to Matheran when his wife was expecting his child!"

"There you go. Not knowing the truth, blaming an innocent man for no fault of his own."

"Ki bolchen aapni? It was not a fault to play with me and impregnate his wife at the same time? How do you think I felt when she appeared before me, heavy with his child?" "But who told you it is *his* child?"

"What??!"

"Who told you it was his child? It is the progeny of that devil Sarang, that man with the sweet, sweet words and a compliment for everybody."

"You do not mean what you say, Didi."

"But I do. I have just seen the baby, and it is Sarang's spitting image. Fair and curly-haired. Sarang, with whom she has been blackening her face lately. Oh, that woman has made Dada's life so miserable; one man after another. Have you never wondered how Dada composes those sad songs? They are the voice of his heart.

Then he found you. Pure as the driven snow, innocent and so lovely. With a voice like an angel. A lotus in the marshland of his marriage. You brought happiness back to his life, you made him breathe again, gave him a reason to live."

Minoti stared at Bela with incredulity.

"It is true, Minoo, don't you know they sleep in separate bedrooms?" Minoti shook her head from side to side in stupefecation.

"Can you imagine what a man must feel to see his wife's illegitimate son in the arms of her lover? Right in front of his eyes, flaunting their romance and its horrible nateeja? How it must tear him to pieces, seeing this and keeping quiet for the sake of the world."

She shook her head with gravity,

"That scoundrel Prannath holding the baby. Ooh Ma, how their profiles matched. And the baby, it stopped crying the moment it was put into Prannath's lap. What more proof of paternity can you have?"

She shook her head, eyes dilated to dramatise the sordidness of the affair.

Minoti's mouth opened, her jaws dropping like a loose latch.

Of course, why should a man seek happiness outside unless it did not exist within the marriage itself? It all made sense. A fine, creative man like Moshai with his stoic qualities; what an insensitive blow she must have dealt him with her rejection, which, conversely, she had considered was the right and proper thing to do. Watching the expressions on Minoti's face, judging their content correctly, Bela's soliloqy continued, cajoling unabated.

"Do you think I would have helped you if it had not been good for Dada? Now more than ever he needs your support. Call him, before his wife comes home. Haven't you noticed his music is suffering? He trained you, made you what you are; you have to reciprocate now. It is not fair, baba, it is just not fair."

The actress in her released a tiny sob.

"Don't let the thought of his marriage restrain you. It is a mere farce. And even Radha was not married to Krishna."

After Bela had left, Minoti sat in solemn pensiveness. Her mind was still rocking with Bela's revelations. If anything sanctified her relationship with Aniruddh, it was Bela's parting allusion to Radha and Krishna. Something about the divine comparison gave their relationship sanctity and acceptability.

At night when her parents were asleep, she dialled his number. 6-0-7-0-5.

Aniruddh, speechless with disbelief, heard the sweetness of Minoti's voice which he had been deprived of for the past two months. Was it an illusion, a wish-fulfillment, a mid-summer night's dream?

"What happened? Your prince turned into a frog?

"No, he is still very much good-looking and fair." "And by comparison, I certainly am not."

"That's not what I was saying, moshai."

"What exactly was it then?"

"I was saying.... I.. I know what you must be feeling." "If you did, my Mini dear, you would not have made this insane decision. When will you realise we are made for each other? Tomaar shur, aamar geet?"

"I am thinking....perhaps I may not marry the prince after all." "A wise decision. You would look foolish dressed in diamonds, gazing out the window waiting for him to return from shikaar." Mini's mind was a pendulum.

"I really don't know what to do. I only know that it is you I love, but I see in this only unhappiness."

Aniruddh felt suddenly lighter. "I've waited to hear you say this. Mini, my Mini, if you really mean it, we can work something out." "But what moshai? Can we fight against the world, against society, against disapproval?"

"We'll fight it out, as long as we are together. Now go to sleep, lovely child-woman. I, too, am looking forward to my dreams tonight."

She blushed.

"And Mini…"he added, elation now beginning to grow assuredly within him.

"What?"

"You say the most stereotyped things."

Now whatever did stereotype mean, she wondered.

KULDEEP KAUR KI KHICHDI

"So, did Mini call last night?" asked Bela over the cornflakes.

Aniruddh's spoon went into freeze half-way to his mouth, considering it was only yesterday he had apprised her about their break-up.

"What are you, Bela, clairvoyant or something?"

Bela's Kuldeep Kaur smile spread like the jam on her toast.

"But naturally, it has all been my own engineering feat." "What do you mean?"

"See Dada, what are good friends for? If I am not to help you in your time of distress as I did when things were funky-dory then…" "you mean hunky-dory."

"Yes yes, same thing. I went to see her yesterday and had a pep talk with her_woman-to-woman you know."

"And how did this woman-to-woman manouvre suceed where all my persuasions had failed? Really, Bela, you amaze me with your talents."

"Manouvre nahin, Dada. Manufacture. All I did was tell one itsie-bitsie lie, one chota-mota untruth."

"What convoluted schemes play hide-and-seek in your devious mind, shothi!"

"But this Dada, is a masterpiece. Hold your breath." Aniruddh quaked with anxiety.

"I told her… I told her..that… the baby was not yours, but Prannath's."

"WHAT?" Aniruddh's cornflakes choked him.

Bela, full of her own ingenuity, continued as if Aniruddh's reaction did not matter at all.

"It was so simple, Dada. You could actually notice the swing of her sympathy towards you. The poor, cuckolded husband, suffering silently at his wife's lymphoma.."

"Nymphomania, Bela. Of all the grievious prevarications! And it was hardly fair to presume that I would willingly deny my own flesh and blood. Besides, Nandini's not been at all what you described her as. This time you have really extended your limits."

"But Dada," persuaded Bela, unprepared for this disapproval instead of the pat on the back she had been expecting. "It's not in your heart you have to think this. Only to win Mini back. I have set the scene. Now it is for you to carry forward this charade into Act One, Scene Two."

"This is not only unthinkable, it is highly unethical. It is also absolutely untrue. We were together in Goa. I cannot deny my own child for selfish reasons."

"How can you be so sure, Dada? Was she not in Panchgani with that Sarang the week before your Goa trip? How do you know what went on there? How can you be absolutely, absolutely sure that the child is really yours? See how fair the baby is? He has Sarang's Kashmiri colour."

"By God, Bela, you may have a point there. It never occurred to me earlier. You're right, you know. My other children are wheatish, in fact Mannu could almost be described as dark."

Doubt became a flashing neon sign. On, off. On, off.

"But no, Nandini herelf is so fair. I don't know, Bela."

"Think of Minoti, Dada, think of Minoti. Nandini will only be her own woman. She has eroded your Bengali-ness, which Minoti will enhance. Let Runu come and this Shireen woman go. Then we will be four against Bou-di. We will instate Minoti as your wife."

Aniruddh was shaken by the morning's developments. Things had moved too fast and too complicatedly for him to be able to think straight. There was some twisted logic in Bela's case. True, Minoti had given him her youth, her faith, the tenderness of her young love.

But Nandini, she too, had given him much. Yet, could he conceive a future without Minoti's sweet presence in his life?

His dichotomy was resolved, however, when Minoti broke her engagement to the prince, much to her father's chagrin and her family's disgrace. It was, in his opinion, a sacrifice requiring recompense.

Meanwhile, Bela continued her ministrations on Minoti's psyche, stoking her fires and stroking her desires. She purred into her receptive ears promises and persuasions that made Minoti's weak, young heart flutter. She served up to Minoti's inexperienced palate the savouries of Nandini's romantic alliances with actors and directors. Minoti's waking hours were occupied with daydreams in Gevacolour.

Bela further exploited Nandini's temporary weakness of confinement. She interfered with the daily running of the house, contradicted Mary-Ma's orders, created confusions and syphoned a little household expenditure in the bargain. She wasted no opportunity in ridiculing Prannath on his visits, launching little rockets of innuendo off her barbed tongue. She pumped Aniruddh's ego with saccharine though illusionary mentions of the return of his reign in the musical world with Minoti as his natural consort. Aniruddh, swayed by her continuous persuasions, regarded his dislodgement as a temporary inconvenience. The grand scheme of Nandini's isolation had been put into place.

Nandini had never felt so alone. Baima was away to Karachi celebrating the advent of her first grandson. Work, her method of escape, was at a standstill. Even though BAHU and HUMNASHEEN had done well commercially and artistically, she had no intentions of resuming production till the state of flux at home was resolved. Prannath looked dejected at this fussy idleness, and vanished for a few days without explanation. Nandini noted with some dismay that his odes to her famed beauty began to diminish in frequency and style. Most of the staff began to leave, though a few defiantly loyal ones remained, like Dilawar, her production manager and John, her driver. Her accountant Rangeela, who co-incidentally lived in the same building as Utpalda, was showing signs of restlessness. Utpalda himself was hardly seen these days. All the old faithfuls were departing one by one.

She waited anxiously for the Xmas holidays when her children would arrive from boarding school. Unfortunately, when they did, they brought in their wake Runu and his recalcitrant offspring, now in various stages of their tantrummy teens. They came, like little ambassadors of destruction, flinging themselves like poison ivy around the house. Still vulnerable with post-natal trepidations, Nandini felt tentacles of animosity fluttering around her. She was suffocated with the foetid air of hostility.

In the absence of a formal christening which was necessarily a mutual decision of the parents, Konkona, oblivious of the dubious connotations of its birth, called the baby Khokha. He was divine and docile, crying in dulcet tones as if apologising for disturbing those present. He had a constantly beatific expression, astonishing for a child born into such a tempestuous environment. Arsenal was being piled up on all sides, but the baby gurgled and belched and slept with a beautiful and innocent sleep, imbibing his mother's milk and colicking with predictable precision.

His parents played with him at separate times. When Nandini escaped for short intervals to the office, Aniruddh, in case of possible paternity, laid him on his outstretched legs and massaged him with mustard oil, singing to him during the marination, delicate rhymes of his lost childhood. He would then cross the baby's arms and legs in exercise, and hum softly in his ears hoping that breathing in tunefulness would endow the child with a musical mind. But the baby gurgled on one note, watched over tenderly by his sister Nandita, who considered him the cutest baby in the whole wide world. When Nandini returned home, she would retire into her room with her children, whilst Aniruddh timed his departure with her arrival and left for some tryst or ostensible rehearsal. She had long since stopped bothering about his movements, too exhausted to emphasise rights of accountability. Right now her baby demanded attention, and she focused on him with a severe and singular devotion. Like a lioness with her cubs, she showered her children with a ferocious love, gathering them protectively into her bedroom where they seemed to create their own world of togetherness. Feeling safe and united within that fierce fold, they developed a concrete loyalty to this matriarchal figure to the exclusion of the man who went in and out with a maddening frequency, and shared nothing with them except an occasional tense meal.

With uncertainty living along like an unwelcome guest, and the spectre of upheaval looming ahead, Nandini became a virtual prisoner in her own home, confined to her quarters and surrounded on all sides by unfriendly influences.

Her hopes shrank, unsanforised.

Till the day Mary-Ma, despatched to Shubir's on some casual errand, returned in a great state of agitation and sharpened the hazy images with a drastic confirmation.

"Kiten sangun Bai, kitan sangun tuka," she wrung her voice, collapsing into native Konkani as she always did in moments of crisis. Wavy-haired and eagle-eyed, the fiery warhorse maintained a redoubtable loyalty and a possessive devotion to her wards. "Jesu re Jesu, may my eyes have been torn out before they could have seen this sight. May my vision have been blighted before I saw what I saw!"

"Calm yourself, Mary," pacified Nandini, although her heart was swelling with a terrible dread. "What happened?"

"Arre Bai, that obnoxious woman was there, all dressed up like a nayi-naveli dulhan. Kiten sangun! She has hypnotised the old woman with her innocent ways and her shy-shy glances. I caught them there, she and Saheb, like one married couple. She was touching the budhiya's feet, and the old woman was doling out aashirwaad like prasad. What is to become of us now, Bai, where will we go if he throws us out and invites her in? What will these small-small fatherless children do? That 'daayan' will eat up our hansta-khelta house. Oh, an evil eye has befallen our prosperity! And that no-good woman, that Bela Bose, she is behind it all."

Nandini, imagining her austere mother-in-law's face crinkling with beneficence, felt awfully vanquished. Her customary courage, like a false friend, seemed to desert her when she needed it most.

"What can I do, Mary, what can I do?" her tortured soul cried. "I thought that woman was out of his life after I had humiliated her. But she seems to have re-appeared, clinging like'deemak.'. And you are right about Bela, she is looking nowadays like a silky and well-fed cat. But let her take one false step, and down the stairs she goes, and out of this house forever."

Bela was indeed behind it all; right this moment literally behind the door, shamelesly eavesdropping on their conversation. Throw me down the stairs indeed! We'll see who gets thrown down the stairs, madam. Smugly she reflected that this had been one of her smartest moves, having Aniruddh introduce Minoti to Konkona as a second wife. She was elated with the success of her latest brainwave. Konkona, wiry, weathered and wise, must have clasped Minoti to her bosom in a last desperate hope. Her Mohammadan daughter-in-law was barely tolerated for the sake of domestic peace. Bela had illuminated this fact to Dada with her diabolical perception. Around Konkona's wizened figure they would rally once more, centering her in their familial bindings like ribbons around a Maypole, and once that sophisticated witch was out, they would return to their quintessential existence. Once more the house would be aromatic with mustard oil and resound with Rabindra Sangeet. It would be like the old days back in Calcutta, and they would be one large family again.

One large homogenous, happy, Hindu family.

Chota-sa ghar hoga, baadlon ke chaaon mein, asha deewani man mein bansuri bajaye

"*Ai, koi hai*?" bellowed Aniruddh, exercising his proprietorship. "*Kahan mar gaye sab*?"

"Ji Huzoor," answered Mahbub the khansama, coming out of the kitchen quarters. He was maintained as additional cook along with the sooty-faced Babu, and between them they cooked dishes both Bengali and Mughlai to please the palate of their respective employers.

"*Dekho*, I want some snacks made for a picnic. Here's a tin of Kraft cheese for sandwiches and a box of chicken patties. Serve these warm, understand. And chill some bottles of beer in the fridge. Remember, beer is served in tall glasses, so don't embarrass me by bringing it up in small squat ones."

"Up, Saab?"

"Upstairs, you duffer, on the terrace. Not in heaven. Today's guests are special, *samjhe*? Tell Mary to have a durrie and some gao-takias laid out upstairs."

The servants rallied together, helping each other to accommodate this suddenly thrust programme into the tranquil routine they had allowed themselves to slip into. Guests were not so frequent now, except for the Sunday conclave of poets and radicals who also appeared to have been attacked by the tedium of a gathering that was gradually losing its zing as the frenzy of Independence, the devastation of Partition, the dynamics of film-making found themselves replaced by a superficial commercialism. Values, ethics, patriotism, respect were shifting perspectives. Life was turning on rollers.

"Who are these guests coming in the middle of the day?" grumbled Mary. Saab had just fussily peeped in to remind her that there was also a cardboard carton of bitter-chocolate pastries in the fridge. As if she hadn't noticed. A picnic on the terrace? In the middle of the day, in the middle of the house? Why couldn't they just go to Aarey Milk Colony?

"He didn't say," replied Mahbub. His wiry grey hairs bristled as he bent over the counter, cutting onions. "They must be special.

I haven't seen Saheb pay so much attention before. Perhaps it is because his Sa-re-ga-ma-pa is less these days. At least he seems in a good mood today; as if we haven't noticed that he and Bai don't exchange a word and both go around with faces like overloaded clotheslines. Anyway, what is their fight to us? So long as we get our pay in time and there is food in our stomachs, why should it matter?"

"Yes, but my heart grieves for Bai. Her baby only four months, and that she-devil Bose Memsaab, chie, I don't like to call her that, she doesn't deserve any respect. No signs of going, although it is way past Christmas and New Year. Surely the holidays must be finishing. Even Nandita Baby has to go in two days."

"They are leaving, too. I heard BoseBabu tell Saheb he has procured the train tickets."

"Thank Mother Mary."

"Here, you cut the bread, I'll butter the sandwiches."

The bell jangled. Mary went to open the door.

She would gladly have jabbed the tip of the knife she was holding into the cottony paunch of the figure who stood outside the collapsible grill. Her eyes glowered like coals with disparagement at the visitor. How had this little upstart dared to place her foot upon these stairs, or had the gall of stepping into this house whose sanctity she would demolish the moment she put one toe-painted foot beyond the threshold?

The two women stood facing each other like two captains of opposite armies waiting for the bugle to blow. One was a tremendous force, the other acutely aware of her weak status. The older woman stood in her fluffed sari like some insurmountable object, her expression stating eloquently that she would have to be reckoned with before the other could venture one step further.

Before any word could be spoken, however, Bela sallied forth upon these stormy waters like a gay, streamer-bedecked launch, pushing aside Mary and her pointed knife, and exuded warm words of hospitality, thumping and bumping like a hammer on ice, to crack the tableau.

"Welcome, Mini, welcome. For the first time in your proper status."

The girl stepped in.

Mary came out of shock with the incensed observation that Madam Bela was welcoming this unwanted person as if this was her blessed father's residence. Bela pushed her away with an expression of disgust.

"Move, Mary. Have you no manners, obstructing a guest, brandishing a knife at her? Go inside and do your work. Honestly, Mini, the servants in this house have no discipline. What to tell you."

Mary stared at Bela's departing buttocks as if she would have gleefully plunged the tip of the knife right in the centre of their dividing line. What audacity, referring to her as a servant! She was a member of this family, a surrogate mother to the children. It was she who lullabied them to sleep, who poured parrafin oil into their anuses so that their ablutions were smooth and their intestines clear of worms, she who cleaned the wax from their ears. Did Madam Bela do that? No, she wiggled her fat bottom and kowtowed to actors, and dipped low whilst serving them savouries so they could see her drooping cleavage. She roamed in luxury cars and stuffed her trunks with stolen goods and never once, not even once, paused to tell the children a story. I hope the jute bristles of the durrie poke her ass like needles. Both she and that sourfaced, limpid-eyed, expressionless, characterless Minoti. Maaze Jesu, have mercy. Poor, ignorant Bai. Not knowing how she was being stabbed in the back by those that lived off her bounty. Ungrateful wretches, making holes in the plates in which they ate.

Against the terrace wall Aniruddh leaned, looking over the ledge where the champa had flowered and where the spilt fragrance of the raat-ki-rani still lingered. The majestic mango tree beside the garage had overgrown the building and splayed its branches over the parapet. It was only January, yet it was surprisingly heavy with raw fruit and blossom. Through the web of its old-limbed branches, plump green mangoes dangled like emerald pendants. At least the rhetoric of stones swishing through the tree indicated they were as precious to the children of the block. The mango tree symbolised his love for Minoti, which had also overgrown the house. Like the tree, too, it had unobtrusively grown upon his heart, till it now thudded with the weight of it. This was such a perfect location to await her; this Perfumed Garden, to eventually declare to one and all the value of their relationship. He found no need to keep it concealed any longer and demean it by this cloak-and-dagger business.

She rose out of multi-coloured glass, almond eyes luminous.

She was a symphony in black and white, large black bindi like an eclipsed sun on the brilliant sky of her forehead, dark heavy tresses gathered blackly around her gazelle neck. Their eyes met in a moment of significance, mitigating for Minoti the abrasive eye encounter of the maid Mary.

The storage room in the corner, erstwhile habitation of disgruntled Bela, protested silently in one corner of the terrace. In the shadow of its eave they sat. Escorted by Bela's encouraging arm, Minoti coiled herself gracefully on the durrie. Prelimnary tension began to peter away with time, and soon they were spreading out in ease. Minoti glowed, soft and warm like a bedside lamp. She began to consume cheese sandwiches with all the elan of a person accustomed to eating imported foodstuff all her life. Relaxing on the mat, her jutting hip forming a neat and rounded curve, she could not but be contrasted with Nandini's classic angular lines

The raucous blaring of an impatient horn splintered the porcelain peace. The repercussions of Nandini's unexpected arrival occurred to everyone present. Laughter trickled, and anxiety flowed like a thin stream of water into the grooves of the atmosphere.

Bou-di." announced Bela unnecessarily, with some trepidation.

"She told me she was going to be away all day for some story session. She had even instructed the cook to send lunch to the studio. That is why I arranged this, Dada. How was I to know she would change her mind?"

Aniruddh darted a look of re-assurance to Minoti who resembled a frightened doe. Minoti had given him back his roots and his heritage. Nandini had taken away his pride and self-esteem by overtaking him in matters of proffession and style. Minoti, therefore, by this simple equation, had earned the right to be protected. "Never mind. It must be that spy of hers, Mary. Anyway, this had to happen some time. Better suddenly without warning, than to crease our brows with protracted preparation. Relax, Runu," he calmed his friend, whose forehead had ribbed into a washboard of worry. Runu, pushed along by everyone's persuasion, had never been comfortable with this deceit and manipulation. "I'll handle it. Sooner or later, this had to be faced. But now we know of her approach, I certainly will not allow her to slap Mini like last time."

Frantic angry steps dashed up the stairs, thunderous in the silence. And then she was upon them with a kind of Tantric force, Kaali's fire flashing from her magnificent eyes, her face eloquent with multiple expressions of hurt, disgust, anger and frustration.

The scene that confronted her became immobilised, like when a whirring projector stops and freezes film on screen. The facing figures stared at her with the sharpness of scythes, and the collective defiance in their Brutus eyes made her feel she had been stabbed in several places all at once.

"Aniruddh!" she screamed, and her voice contained all the bitterness of the past few months. "Have you lost all sense of honour that you bring your mistress into my house? Openly, shamelessly, in front of the servants and these small children? Are you going to make her leave now, or shall I ask the servants to throw her out like yesterday's garbage?"

Her words smouldered and seared onto Aniruddh's consciousness. But before he could think of a fitting reply, with amazing sang-froid, Bela spoke.

"It's you who should leave, Bou-di, and not she." Her voice was edged with icicles.

"You keep out of it, you Judas-bitch. I am talking to my husband."

"No, let her speak, Babesie." He called her that still, the name adhering to his tongue with the adhesive of long years. "She is only expressing my own sentiments. If you have any self-respect, you will leave. Can't you see you are an outsider, you don't fit in here anymore."

"I am your wife, Ani."

"You used the wrong tense. You were. So, take your belongings and leave gracefully."

"Where will I go? This is my home."

"I don't know. Anywhere. To the office, to the studio where you practise your production, or whatever else sordid thing you do there."

"Yes, you get out, you hear," shouted Bela, encouraged and enthused by Aniruddh's stand. "You are a discarded wife. So leave, leave, leave, get out!"

Their words exploded in her ears like firecrackers, and their faces caricaturised into images seen through a concave lens; sometimes Bela's face loomed larger than her body and approached her like a threatening monster, then receded and merged with Minoti's and presented itself like a two-headed beast. Aniruddh's face shrank and seemed to scurry away from his body like a lizard; Runu's was as impassive and empty as one of his blank blackboards.

Their outbursts assaulted her senses like a swarm of attacking crows. Bela advanced on Nandini like a motor-car that would run her down, and began poking and prodding her towards the stairs. Her hands on Nandini's body made Nandini feel unclean and indecent, like being stroked by an immoral leper, and her cant of

Leave, Leave echoed in the hollow valleys of her mind and throbbed in her eyes. Minoti stood hyperventilating in her spot, face ashen and expression lunatic. Nandini, was flung down the steps, clutching onto the bannisters, rolling down till she landed with a loud thud at the bottom. She screamed as her back hit the landing, a cry like one tortured in hell, more with the indignity than the pain. In a dead faint she lay, solidified into wood, her hair spread like a fan beneath her neck, her legs blue-ing with bruises. Dark blobs like rotting water chestnuts began to appear on her arms. The shocked faces of the servants encircled her inert form.

Dazed and frightened, Nandita rushed to the roof, terror spreading like a dark stain on her face.

"Baba, come soon. Mummy's dead! Mummy's dead!" Aniruddh stared at the hysterical child for one uncomprehending moment, then lashed his strong fingers across her face. The girl shrank with shock.

"Didn't I tell you not to disturb me, you silly child? Now go down at once."

"Her mother's too tough to die so easily," interpolated Bela with an eloquent smirk.

Nandita tore down the stairs and squatted by her mother's side. Her child's eyes were choking with fear. She clasped her little arms around her mother's neck, moving her hair away with tender hands. Placing her head close to her mother's cheek, she began to cry.

No one pulled her away. For what seemed a lifetime she sat there, keeping vigil, her traumatic sobs pulsating through her thin body, her fingers holding on tighter and tighter as if she would never let her mother go. Till Mary came and prised her away.

"Mummy's dead," she moaned into Mary-Ma's wrinkled neck, as the older woman clasped her protectively. "Jesus Christ has taken her."

"No, baby, no. She has only fainted. Sahiba re Sahiba, what is to become of these poor children?"

Mera sundar sapna beet gaya,
Main pyar mein sab kuch haar gayi
Bedard zamana jeet gaya

TRAGEDY QUEEN

The woman laboured up the steep stairs one at a time, balancing her five-month baby on one hip and a suitcase in the other. Whoever had christened this grim, grey building, tucked away in an obscure Mahim bylane as Sunshine Mansion, must surely have been the world's greatest optimist. Breathing hard, she reached the top floor.

"Arre Bai," exclaimed Sumangala, lifting her head from the fish she was cleaning, as Nandini walked through the open door. "Why didn't you shout from down? I would have come and helped you. Here, give me the baby," she said, wiping her hands on a wet towel.

The baby beamed at his aunt, astoundingly pacific despite being bumped and bounced up three flights of stairs. Nandini plonked on the sofa to catch her breath and was stung by a broken spring. It was amazing how Sumangala had transformed her Brahmin self to adapt to her husband's non-vegetarian requirements. She cooked meat and poultry like a proper bawarchi. It's always us, she mused, always us women who change and twist and turn ourselves to suit our husbands. In the bargain we lose our true shape.

Sumangala looked enquiringly at Nandini. It was rarely that either of her sisters-in-law visited.

Nandini answered her silent question with a single succinct sentence.

"I've left home."

Sumangala gaped at Nandini, her buckteeth startlingly prominent in her astonished face

"Why?"

"Don't be dumb, Mangala. Obviously because I can't live there anymore."

"But what caused this sudden decision? Though it's not a secret that things haven't been so smooth between you and Aniruddhbhai for some time now."

Briefly and with incredible control, Nandini recited the incident of the terrace picnic.

"He actually brought her into the house?" Sumangala exclaimed in disbelief. The two women, for people so dissimilar, were surprisingly close.

"That is not all. She now has my mother-in-law's blessings!"

"That budhiya is senile to endorse such a thing!"

"Who will explain this to her?"

"What to say, Bai, it's not only her. It's that wicked Bela's planning. She is jealous of your looks and your success, not to mention wealth. Some people can't tolerate seeing others happy when they are not happy themselves. But Bhaisaab, what has become of his brains to prefer that silly girl with her pretty-doll looks to a woman of guts like you?"

"That girl has cast a spell on him. When he comes out of it, he will find everything gone-his money, his name, and his woman. Then he will come crying home to me."

"But what will you do now, Bai? Have you thought about the future? About the children and the effect this will have on them? I mean, you are welcome to live here, but a well-known woman like you in this locality__so many mouths, so many stories."

"That is why I have left, so that people should know I cast him off, instead of the other way around. As for the children, my self-respect is too damaged to allow me to think at all."

"Will you go back to acting to support your son, if the other children stay with him? What about Jubilee Pictures?"

"Perhaps I'll start a new company without that man." She couldn't yet bring herself to abuse him. "I have all my jewellery here. There's enough there to finance a dozen films. Or perhaps I'll run off and marry Prannath Sarang,"

Sumangala was struck by deja-vu.

"No Bai, you can't marry Prannath Sarang."

"Why not? He's quite mad about me, writes me love poems and all."

"No Bai, I don't mean that. You can't marry him, even if you wanted to, or *he* did, which I'm sure he doesn't."

"Oh, if you're worried about his being a couple of years younger, that doesn't make a difference to *me*."

"Sarang can't marry you, Bai."

Nandini glared at Sumangala in indignation. What was all this negativity? She didn't know half of it, stuck here on the third floor of a building that was nearing collapse.

"How can you be so sure?" she asked warily, tensing herself to hear the unexpected.

"Prannath Sarang is already married!"

"What? Rubbish! Pran's never mentioned a wife even once. And that's something a man can often let slip by mistake. No one's even *seen* a wife, leave alone heard of her. Hai Mangala, a wife is not a ten rupee note you can tuck away inside your blouse!"

"Lots of heroes have wives nobody's heard of or seen. That Abhijeet for instance."

That was true.

"Abhijeet does have a wife stashed away conveniently in Delhi. So do one or two other heroes. But Pran! I've often asked him about marriage and he's always said he couldn't afford a family."

"In Bombay, maybe. But pickled in Jammu, he has an absolutely legal spouse."

"How do you know all this, when I don't?"

"Don't ask me. Chikna hai. Believe me or not Bai, he has used you, too. Now he has made his place in the industry, see how he will throw you away like a fly from milk."

"That's not true. Prannath is a good human being. He has been close to me in my time of need. How can you make such accusatory remarks about someone you don't know? And what do you mean, *too?*"

"It is not my position to judge. I just say if a man is involving himself in lafdas and not telling the truth, then something is not right. You are married too, so it might not have made a difference to you. But to others, more innocent ones…you see, it becomes a habit to lie because the man is a practised hypocrite."

"What others are you talking about? Do you know something I don't?"

"No." Sumangala's lips clamped, taking on the stony appearance of the Sphinx.

"You're an awful liar, Sumangala. Tell me. I insist on knowing."

"No, no. Here, give me the baby, he's gone to sleep."

Nandini caught her arm. "Meri kasam hai, you have to reveal what you know."

"Honestly.. maybe your brother should tell you. I'll wake him up."

"Shamim is home, and sleeping at this hour? Hadn't he begun working with some friend of his from Prabhat?"

Sumangala shrugged her shoulders and closed her face.

What point in telling her that Shamim spent most nights out, and that the woman ironically lived just behind Nandini's own house in Hindu Colony?

Shamim emerged from the bedroom, rubbing his eyes sleepily. "Arre Mehru? How come you are at the house of this poor relation today?"

What she asked him brought him wide awake.

"He kept it a closely guarded secret. How else can he phasao women with such ease unless he poses as one single aashiq? He has pretty prose. And you, my dear, had a pretty shoulder he used to climb upon."

"But the production people used to go to his home. Surely someone would have seen her?"

"Look, sister. He is always so affable and so available. How could he function so freely if he were burdened with looking after a family? And even if the unit members knew, they were not going to whisper it into your ear, especially after rumours of your intimacy began doing the studio rounds. After all, you are the boss. Besides, you never asked."

"Naturally, he said he could not support a family whenever I asked him about his marriage, so I presumed....'

"See, he's very chaalu. He never really said in direct terms that he was *not* maried. His family generally stays in some ancestral haveli in Jammu with his father and stepmother, and comes to Bombay for the holidays. Now, I believe he has brought them here permanently, ever since he bought the room he used to rent as well as the room next door. So, he can conveniently stay in one room and still maintain his single image."

" I'm having some trouble accepting this. To think he could easily have brought her to the house whenever she was in town. What was there to hide?"

"And be embarrassed to death? A dehati in the midst of all those sophisticated and glamorous film people? Who might slurp tea from a saucer and say 'Hai Rabba' if she saw you women smoke? A poet and writer, take an unlettered woman from the village, with salwar naada hanging, into the circle of people like *you*? Besides, his kind of men will use other women as playthings, but their own women they keep strictly behind the curtain."

Nandini's countenance flushed with a controlled anger. Only she was not sure who to direct it at.

"This is not just a spiteful fabrication because Ani ousted you as director."

"See, I knew you would think I was talking out of khunas. Mujhe kya hai, believe it or not. But remember, what was he but a struggling journalist before you picked him up and made him a director and a producer? "

"It's actually so believable…if it weren't so unbelievable. I should be confused, but it all makes too much sense," Nandini babbled. "Men in Northern India marry early; why should he have been an exception? Then.. he always discouraged my going to his house…"

"…in case the neighbours opened their mouths. Even I wouldn't have known had it not been for the Zeba affair."

"Zeba?" asked a mystified Nandini.

"She is very much in the eye of the storm. You remember the day Saajanbhai died? That was the day he saw her, and as she claimed, fell in love with her. Zeba so innocent and pretty, and he the expert romancer, wooing her with shairi-wairi. Poor girl didn't stand a chance. Then, meetings on the sets, love-notes being passed. Baap re baap, what chedha-chedhi went on under the black hood of the camera!"

Nandini gasped. Yet, through the waves of shock, hazy images floated out like scrambled newspaper print, then crystallised into headlines. "Yeah, come to think of it, she was always there during story sessions or hanging around the sets. And I thought it was her interest in films, or her attachment to me! Allah, what a rogue he was to have ruined a young girl's innocence."

"Allah jaane, maybe he really cared. He did dedicate his book to her. In the end she did the very same thing. Landed up at our house with her clothes and jewellery, insisting I take her to his house. Okay, I said. If you really love him and he wants to honourably marry you, it's fine. I am sure Kulsumbai will understand eventually and not mind this Hindu-Muslim thing. So, I took her to his home, and what do we find? There is this woman pressing his legs and calling him 'suniye jee.' He is very much shaadi-shudha. Poor Zeba was heartbroken and went home and accepted the first proposal that came for her. Said he had left her in a Sahara wasteland with the cacti of harsh memories. See how he even inflicted his poetry on her."

"So that explains why she married a sober banker! But why have you kept this such a secret all this time?"

"Because she made us promise. However, under these circumstances, I am sure she will not mind my telling you." Nandini pursed her lips. Shock at Shamim's revelations was an anaesthetic against pain. That would come later, when the shock wore off and left her crushed under a double betrayal.

There was no regret that Prannath was married. The regret was that he had been dishonest, and dishonesty was as alien to her as it was to God.

"He used you, Mehru. He has no sympathy for your problems more than lip-service. All he cares about is himself and his own progress."

Users and weaklings. Traitors and tormentors. The men in her life had marauded her values and raped her virtue, but they were not going to dance on her corpse.

She made a decision. She would not leave her house. She would stick on steadfastly to what was her own and the legacy of her children. The rats could desert if they wanted. But first she would beard the lion in his den. If a fox could be referred to as that, even metaphorically. So many animals. It was beginning to sound like a zoo.

Sumangala said softly,"Chhota mounh badi baat, Bai, but both of you are at fault."

"That's right." admitted Nandini gracefully. "But my mistake was in trying to be more than a mere housewife. Still, it is not such an unforgivable or irremediable fault." "Then, why should you leave your house and make yourself and your children homeless? Let him leave if he must. Imagine, the wife he kept on a bed of flowers, he throws down the stairs because now he wants not her, but somebody else. Men are like that only.

Still, it is a cruel world for a woman who has neither husband nor home. She becomes a trophy for other men to gain. At least in your own house you will be queen, even if you are kingless." "You are absolutely right, Sumangala. I acted with despair and emotional vulnerability. I'm going back, but first, I have to do something. I have to see this Pran thing for myself. He's not at the studio, so perhaps he will be at home." "Yes" interjected Shamim.

"So shall we present the good writer with an award-winning script that might have come straight from his own pen?"

"Why not?"

"Mangala, take care of the baby, please. He doesn't trouble. Anyway, we'll be back soon. Just a swift and short execution."

Shamim looked forward keenly to the next sequence of events, to see that pompous and polite smile ripped off Sarang's lips. And not only to see that smooth son-of-a-bitch receive some choice words from Mehru's spirited tongue, but to see *her* expression when she set eyes on his chubby, chubby sons! This would be a priceless tamasha indeed.

She was incredulous, but not so incensed as she had expected to be. Perhaps Aniruddh's treachery had set a precedent, and it didn't surprise or hurt as before. Driving her sleek Hillman with practised ease, Nandini tried to figure out, not Prannath, but Sumangala. Was she realistic, mature beyond her youthful years, or just fey? With an uncanny grasp of reality, she had held up to her the mirror of the situation so that it could be seen more clearly than through the soft focus lens of her confusion.

But how could she understand it so well? *Her* husband wasn't cheating on her. Or was he? And was she humbly accepting it? In how many homes was the same story being enacted?

They drove into a tiny lane where the car needed expert manouvreing. Bedraggled boys playing cricket with wooden stumps had to uproot their wickets to let her park. The stairs went up a dingy hallway littered with refuse to a second-floor door where they stopped abruptly. It had a black name plaque hanging from one nail with the painted legend: P.N.Aawara. The takhallus was now astonishingly apt.

The woman who opened the door was carved from mahagony. Her expressionless face was half draped with a phulkari dupatta, and below its edge a sindoori bindu peeped. Her eyes wore a lost-in-the-city glaze, as though she were still searching for her misplaced saanjha choolah in Gurdaspur. A blousy magenta kurta covered with large yellow flowers and a generous dusting of wheatflour at the midriff covered her matronly form, and her hands had fingers of dough. Nandini's eyes travelled southwards. Two inches of naada with a maroon tassle at the end were predictably visible.

"Saarang Sahab ji? Haanji, he stays here only. Please, enter, enter," she exclaimed in gravelly Punjabi, no doubt considering that such big people visiting their humble abode required no credentials for entry. "Main kya ji," she said to a closed door, "some people are here to see you." She tittered and said with wifely warmth, "He's always taking long in the bath. Please sit." She placed a cane'mooda' in the centre of the room.

"Please excuse, I will wash my hands. It was time for his roti, you know. Moment he is out of his bath, he wants food." More snippets of domestic familiarity.

Nandini surveyed the area. Two lumpy mattresses covered with crumpled sheets, took up most of the floor space. A pair of plump boys played animatedly with a broken toy airplane. One of them grinned up at her and announced with inflated pomp, that Papaji was going to take them to see the real thing, pata hai? In one corner of the mattress an infant dozed with his lips clamped tightly on a pacifier, oblivious to the tragi-comedy on which the curtains were about to rise.

"My three sons," explained The Wife, with oblique reference to her fertility. "Vadda is playing cricket downstairs." So, one of the ruffians with the broken bat was also his, thought Shamim. In the past two years his family had increased by one. The virile bastard!

Nandini had been prepared for a wife, but the sight and mention of his progeny was too much for her to digest. Anger began to bubble in her eyes. The Wife was so confounded by it, that she scampered like a rabbit behind a flowered curtain on the pretext of making tea. Nandini was tempted to stomp out of the room, but the idea of seeing Pran's face as he came out of the bathroom and saw her sitting centrally in his home was so alluring, that she held her position determinedly. Then, like some horror movie sequence, the bathroom door creaked on a broken hinge, and the villain emerged, tying his pyjama strings. At sight of the unexpected figure staring at him, the pyjamas dipped but were timely retrieved.

"Nandini! Why have you come here? You should have sent for me," rolled the words off his contorted face.

"Why are you speaking in whispers, Pran?"

Prannath darted a furtive glance in the direction of the flowered curtain.

"You should have warned me you were coming." His voice dropped a further decibel, conspiratorially.

"Why, darling? So you could hide her conveniently in the next room along with the three, oh sorry, four healthy heirs to your literary fortune? "

"SShhh. She'll hear you."

"She? Oh, don't you take the name of your wives, like they don't take yours?"

Prannath looked as if scales were about to erupt on his body. In a cringing tone he argued,"I would have told you if you'd asked. You only kept saying 'Why don't you marry?" and I replied 'I can't'."

"But you always maintained you could not support a family."

"That was also true. I meant 'in Bombay.' I must have forgotten to mention that. In any case you never directly asked 'Are you married?"

"Oh, so you're pinning it on her now?" piped Shamim.

Just then the lady under discussion re-appeared balancing two cups of milky tea and a saucer of flaky biscuits. She smiled with benign hospitality, as though instead of orange pekoe she was offering them divine vardaan. She disappeared behind the curtain again.

Nandini posed with the cup of tea, Shamim watching her with some consternation. Was she actuually going to sit here gracefully and partake of the friendly beverage? Her expression certainly looked relishing, as though she was feasting eyes upon some rare Chinese flavour. She took a sip. Prannath relaxed, feeling the situation diffused.

With admirable daintiness, Nandini then picked up her cup and poured the hot beverage gracefully and directly over Prannath's curly head.

Stung by the hot fluid, the fancy-faced director yelled. The woman came dashing out from behind the curtain, her face hot with concern and alarm.

"Nandini! Have you gone mad?"screamed the äffected poet.

"No, my dear, just come to my senses."

She crushed the flaky biscuits and garnished his face with the crumbs. "That is for Zeba, whose innocence you murdered. Come on Shamim, I think this talented writer can write his own script from here. I'm certain he'll figure out a convincing scenario for his beloved wife and mother of four. By the way, don't bother to introduce us. I'm sure her name is Premvati or Karmaanwali or whatever."

"It's Dhanwanti, actually."

After the guests had departed, the plain-looking woman with the sawed-off expressions picked up the cups and retired behind the curtain, leaving her swaami to reconcile to his situation. Calmly she whipped some detergent and proceeded to rinse the chipped crockery in the sienna-stained sink. The outburst of the tempestuous woman made not a ripple on her placidity. These dramas she had long since learned to ignore. She was aware of his romantic interludes, but she understood with a cool wisdom born from generations of adjusting and happy women, that he needed these beautiful inspirations to add verve and poetry to his writing. How could she, simple and unlettered, inexperienced in the ways of the word, influence or inspire him? But he was doing it for them, for their future. He was a good husband and a devoted father.

What had this latest one erroneously called her? Mother of four? She stroked her stomach lightly. Nobody knew as yet, but it was mother of five already. She had understood the words 'literary fortune. The pot of gold was there, somewhere at the end of the rainbow, and he would bring it home as a legacy for his sons. Of that she was sure. As sure that he would get it, as she was of never asking him how he had procured it.

She glanced around at the plaster-peeling walls of their modest room, from where calendar avatars of Ram and Krishna smiled down upon her with a future promise.

Ab tere siwa kaun mera Krishna Kanhaiya

The volatile affair with Prannath was buried without benefit of epitaph. Though he continued to attend office, he sat in his cabin and she in hers. It surprised her that he would even come to the studio at all.

The problem of ousting him from the concern with minimium upheaval or scandal was solved surprisingly by Aniruddh himself.

"I'm closing down the company."

"You can't do that, I mean, just like that."

"I very much can. Prannath is a partner only by verbal understanding. The staff doesn't come under any union. What's to stop me?"

But this should be half my decision, too. We started this company together.

"Maybe, but it's mostly I who finance it. The company is idle, and a running establishment has recurring expenses which are going out of *my* pocket."

She had presumed everything they had was 'ours'.

"Give us time. Artists can't produce like factories. The day Pran comes up with a worthwhile script, we'll start work."

"By that time I'll go bankrupt, paying the office staff and the maintenance. It's a year since any work was done."

"Admittedly my films won't go down in cinematic history, but the last three in particular have been box-office hits. Profits are meant to tide over exactly such times. Besides, there were my own earnings as an actress."

"Of coure there were," he said with a snigger, "a meagre 500 rupees monthly; a fortune for those times, but a pittance twenty years later. Besides, most of that money went into constructing this house and a chunk of joint funds pays for the servants and the cars and the children's fancy boarding school education and the tea-bill your idle staff logs up at the studio. So, prepare to shake hands and make your farewell speeches."

He wrapped it up so fast that he had obviously set the plan in motion long before consulting her.

Time now hung heavily for Nandini, and tensely for Aniruddh waiting with some impatience for his obdurate wife to pack her belongings and leave. Contradicting her humiliation, she clung tenaciously to the house whereas Aniruddh spent most of his time away and came home with expectations of seeing her gone.

With resilient ignorance, the children played hide and seek behind the great teak doors and the servants functioned with morbid uncertainty. Their jobs, her sanity and everyone's future teetered on a tightrope.

Karun kya aas niraas bhayi, karun kya aas niraas bhayi

Suspense turned into dread as months passed without amend in the situation. A stalemate lingered as each rotated on his own axis, and the universe began to mean different things to them. No music lurked in the sepulchral silence that existed as communication closed its doors. But hope continued to quiver, as the baby Amitav began to crawl and cut teeth, that some day he would get over his infatuation. But not even when the intrepid Konkona passed away in her sleep, did Aniruddh seek any solace from Nandini. On the contrary, the cause of the severance between mother and son, and the subequent deprivation of her maternal company, now began to vitiate the situation.

After the rituals were over, Aniruddh confronted her with packed bags.

"I'm going."

"Where?" she asked with economic enquiry, in the shorthand speech that now symbolized their communication.

"For good. I'm not coming back." The unexpectedness of the announcement left her speechless.

"I'll send you my forwarding address. Right now, I will be staying at Pyaare Mohan Dehlvi's till I find a place of my own."

This is your place, she wanted to say, but words seemed to have become traitors. Finally, one struggled out of the wicket gate. "Why?"

"Because we can't stay together anymore. It's torture for us both, we're so unlike."

Marriages were made in heaven and broken in hell.

"Dissimilar people do manage to live together," she remarked with practical wisdom, "if I can stay on even after you threw me down the stairs, why can't you? It's merely a case of adjustment."

"Who can adjust with an unfaithful woman?"

"And an unfaithful man? Is everything excusable for him, because of the masculine gender? Let's face it Ani, we've both been unfaithful to each other. Why don't we just call it quits? My affair was merely instigated by your indifference. We're adults, we can resolve this through mutual effort. Most marriages have problems. One doesn't just pack them in a bag and walk away. We have four children between us. Think of the upheaval this will cause in their young lives."

She was astonished to find an uncharacteristic pleading creep into her voice. There was an unusual firmness in his as he answered.

"No, Babesie, we have only three children. I am certain that Amitav is not mine. That's the cruellest cut... that you should stoop to this level." Nandini felt her ears on fire. Often she had noticed Aniruddh look queerly at Amitav, but that *this* had been the basis of his observations was absolutely astounding!

"Do you really think I'm this low? Do you really know me so little that having the gall to bear another man's child, I would lack the guts to admit it? How can you accuse me, when your own infidelities have been proven without a measure of doubt?"

"That's the whole point; I cannot live with the *suspense* of never really knowing. After all, he is so fair, unlike any of our other children."

"And it never occurred to you that one of our children could take after *my* side of the family? Haven't you noticed that Amitav looks exactly like Esabha's daughter Sabira? No you haven't. You're too involved in tracing some weird resemblance to Sarang, for your own convenience. Besides, it's fine for you to sleep around because you are a *man*. For a woman, it's unpardonable. And, by the way, I'm talking generalities."

Aniruddh could not look directly into the eyes of her argument.

Nandini was motivated now by the conviction of her own faultlessness. "Ani, stop making a fool of yourself over that young girl. People are laughing at you. Give yourself some time to get over it." "Your opinions, or those of the rest of the world, cannot change mine. I have made up my mind."

'And how do you propose I look after the children singlehandedly?" "I don't know. Maybe we'll set up a trust fund or something. We'll discuss it when we meet at the lawyer's to settle the terms of the divorce."

He couldn't have shocked her more if he had flung acid on her face. The word struck her like a jagged stone. Not even once had she imagined that their situation would lead to this desperate consequence. Deluded wife, deceived wife, deprived wife could still be handled; but divorced wife had the ominous knell of finality.

"Don't Ani, please don't do this. We've been together for almost twenty years. Struggled and fought and grown side by side. Doesn't that count for anything? Does this home, these children mean nothing at all to you?"

She hated herself for begging, but she would go down on her knees if she had to. She did. But his feet turned and walked away from the sphere of her vision. Nandini was left staring unbelievingly at the empty space that a moment earlier had been filled with his entity.

She needed air. Hyperventilating, she scrambled down the stairs. With a furious thrust of gears, she headed the Hillman on the road to Juhu, towards the fresh spaces of the beach. Her heart was thudding like a piledriver. Had he actually ended everything, destroyed in one drastic moment what they had taken a lifetime to build? In his single-minded selfishness, in his inexplicable obsession for an insignificant woman, had he actually turned his back upon the children she had borne him with so much pain and pleasure, without even a goodbye embrace? And what of love? Where had it gone? Had it been eroded by power, effaced by fame, erased by indifference, and withered by carelessness?

She searched the sea for answers. But there was no response from that infinity, only a foamy silence.

She drew her arms around her as her body shivered. Dismay and desperation outlined her carved features and the salt of the sea mixed with the salt of her tears, stinging doubly. The sun bled with her pain. Raw and red, it dipped itself into the Arabian Sea, seeking absolution. Nandini stood motionless, stark and solitary as an exclamation mark. The waters before her were gray as her life;

the scarlet shame of the scuttling sun the open raw wound of her discarding. Behind her, her footprints were scars on the gravelly sand.

As darkness fell, the wind whispered in her ears: You are alone. You are alone. You are alone. The tide came in with twilight fury and smashed waves in frothy bits over her feet.

After a war begins the process of salvaging. One has to step over the dead bodies on the battlefield and proceed with saving those that are left, the surviving wounded.

She checked her bank accounts. The ledgers showed no balances. He had cleaned out every penny of their joint earnings. She was left with two hundred and sixty-three rupees in her purse, and most of her jewellery, fortuitously removed from the joint locker in her mad dash from the house and not replaced since. What he could not take with him were the two houses; immovable assets fortunately in her name.

He had left her life in shambles, her self-respect in tatters, and the children's future in jeopardy. She would now become and remain forever, if she didn't remarry, a question mark in society.

But he would not have everything. She had grovelled in front of him, and he had been unmoved. Now *he* could grovel all he liked. She was never going to give him the divorce he wanted. Minoti would ever remain a concubine, a mistress, a kept woman. *She* would be the question mark in society, devoid of status.

Nandini would always remain the legal Mrs. Aniruddh Ganguly. The only way Minoti could ever become that .... was over her dead body.

Duniya mein hum aaye hain toh jeena hi padega
Jeevan hai agar zehar toh peena hi padega

THIS IS NOT THE END; IT IS THE BEGINNING

Other titles by Bluejay

Distress to De-Stress: a practical guide to stress free living
Dr Sujatha Sharma, Dr Avdesh Sharma and Dr Ruchi Varma

Magic Mantras to a Pain-Free Back (with 60 b/w pictures)
Dr Yatish Agarwal and Dr A P Singh

Pursuit of Happiness: made easy
Rajendra Tandon

Mastering English from Day One
Kavita Kumar

Mahatma Gandhi: the Man and his Philisophy

Winning Personality: the magic key to success
F Oss

Brain Building for Achievement
Herbert N Casson

Cheiro's: language of the Hand

Indian Palmistry
J B Dale

How to Start a Business & Ignite your life:
A simple guide to combining business wisdom *with* passion
Ernesto Sirolli

Why You Can't Lose Weight:
A guide to solving your weight-loss puzzle
Dr Pamela Wartain Smith

Do This Get Rich!:
Twelve things you can do now to gain financial freedom
Jim Britt

Natural Birth Control: made simple
Barbara Kass-Annese

Manage your Manager: dos and don'ts @ work
Kriti